DON'T
LOOK
NOW

Also by Linda Lael Miller

Banner O'Brien
Corbin's Fancy
Memory's Embrace
My Darling Melissa
Angelfire
Desire and Destiny
Fletcher's Woman
Lauralee
Moonfire
Wanton Angel
Willow
Princess Annie
The Legacy
Taming Charlotte
Yankee Wife
Daniel's Bride
Lily and the Major
Emma and the Outlaw
Caroline and the Raider
Pirates
Knights
My Outlaw
The Vow
Two Brothers

Springwater
Springwater Seasons series:
    Rachel
    Savannah
    Miranda
    Jessica
A Springwater Christmas
One Wish
The Women of Primrose
Creek series:
    Bridget
    Christy
    Skye
    Megan
Courting Susannah
Springwater Wedding
My Lady Beloved
    (writing as Lael St.
James)
My Lady Wayward
    (writing as Lael St.
James)
Last Chance Café
High Country Bride

DON'T
LOOK
NOW

Linda Lael Miller

DOUBLEDAY LARGE PRINT HOME LIBRARY EDITION

ATRIA BOOKS

New York London Toronto Sydney Singapore

This Large Print Edition, prepared especially for
Doubleday Large Print Home Library, contains
the complete, unabridged text of the original
Publisher's Edition.

ATRIA B O O K S
1230 Avenue of the Americas
New York, NY 10020

Copyright © 2003 by Linda Lael Miller

ISBN: 0-7394-3851-4

ATRIA B O O K S is a trademark of Simon & Schuster,
Inc.

Manufactured in the United States of America

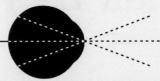

This Large Print Book carries the
Seal of Approval of N.A.V.H.

For my critique group,
the Goddesses of Denny's,
Allison Davidson,
Deborah Wellborn,
Dar Tomlinson,
and
Susan Yarina,
with love and gratitude.

Chapter One

CAVE CREEK, ARIZONA

I didn't kill Harvey Kredd; somebody beat me to it. That night at the Horny Toad, a week after his untimely and gruesome death, my brain fried by an afternoon in the courtroom, where I was hammered by an assistant D.A., I was ready to dig the boss up and empty my trusty .38 into his chest, just in case there was so much as a flutter of life left in him.

Stopping by the Toad for beer and burgers wasn't my idea; all I wanted to do was go home, put up my feet, and knock back a couple of glasses of Chablis. I ended up there because my car was in the shop and my friend Loretta, having picked me up at the courthouse, was behind the wheel and therefore in control of my immediate destiny. I guess she figured neither of us was in any condition to cook; she'd worn herself out taking back-to-back yoga and Pilates classes while I'd argued, and lost, one of the half-dozen crappy cases I'd inherited after Harvey took a bullet between the eyes and ended up facedown in a bowl of yakisoba, breathing noodles. Since his death, everybody in the firm had been scrambling to take up the slack, and we were all stressed out.

Now, I was tired and stressed out, and not just because of Harvey's recent demise and its many and varied ramifications. A year before, I'd defended a guy named Ned Lench on charges of drunken driving and negligent homicide, and won an acquittal on the proverbial technicality. I'd lost a lot in the process—most notably, my quasi-relationship with Detective Anthony Sonterra, who had busted his very fine butt for eight months to nail Lench in the first place. To make matters infinitely worse, a few days prior to Harvey's murder, Lench, tanked up on coke and booze and God knows what else, had crashed his pickup truck into a minivan at the corner of Scottsdale Road and Chaparral, killing himself in the process. Thanks to him—and partly to me—three others were dead besides, two of them children.

Reporters had been dogging me ever since, clamoring for comments. I guess they wanted to know how I managed to face myself in the mirror every morning, and the answer to that was simple: I was careful not to look too closely.

So far, I'd kept my face out of the papers, but my name was all over the place.

Clare Westbrook, attorney at law, tireless champion of scumbags everywhere.

Loretta was in one of her save-the-world-starting-with-Clare moods that night, determined to see me through the latest crisis, or *drag* me through, if necessary. And she'd feed me in the process, or die trying.

"Clare," she'd said, during the ride up Highway 51 in her Lexus, "you're running on the nutritional dregs, and I'll bet there isn't squat to eat at your place, so we're having dinner out."

One of the most exasperating things about Loretta—besides her seemingly bottomless bank account and the fact that she's drop-dead gorgeous—was that she was nearly always right. What with all the drama in my life of late, I hadn't had a chance to hit the grocery store. My thirteen-year-old-niece, Emma, and I had been living on stuff from the freezer and donations from Mrs. Kravinsky, our neighbor. Tonight, Emma was doing homework at a friend's house. Since Mrs. K spent every Wednesday afternoon hunched over a collection of bingo cards at one of the casinos, I couldn't count on finding one of her strange but nourishing casseroles waiting on my doormat, and the last entrée in the freezer was sprouting ice-fur.

The Horny Toad's parking lot was particularly crowded, which is most likely why I didn't spot a certain SUV in time to save myself a major dose of aggravation. As Loretta and I went in to give our names to the hostess, we passed a lot of cheerful tourist types gathered at the picnic tables, waiting for inside seating. The Toad is a popular hangout for both tourists and locals, especially in late September, when the snowbird season begins in earnest.

Loretta vanished as soon as we'd been told it would be at least thirty minutes, making her way to the back room, where a country band was playing. No doubt she was hoping to snag a cardboard carton of free pretzels.

I sank into a chair at the video-game table near the front door and waited, keeping an eye out for media types. The narrow space between where I was sitting and the bar was packed with an elbow-to-elbow crowd of winter visitors, obsessive golfers, and up-scale types with swanky homes hidden away in the rocks and behind the gates of walled communities sporting names like Estancia, Whisper Rock, and Troon.

I sighed and cupped my chin in one hand, resting my elbow on Pac-Man, staring glumly down at my own shadowy reflection in the dark glass, with its intermittent sparks of light—little universes, dying and being born, endlessly.

I thought of Harvey.

I could hardly believe he was dead, though I'd definitely fantasized along those lines a time or two in the five years of our professional association, especially after the Lench case, and when he dumped the worst rich-brat felony cases on my desk. At Kredd and Associates, we weren't expected to fight the good fight and abide quietly by the court's decision, we were mandated to *win.* No excuse would suffice if the verdict was "guilty"; Harvey took every defeat personally, whether he'd argued the case or not, and there was always hell to pay back at the office when the dust settled.

A hand on my shoulder brought me back from my wanderings. I figured it was Loretta, returning at last with the pretzels, so I got a wicked shock when Tony Sonterra lowered his hot self into the chair opposite mine. If I'd had a list of everybody I did *not* want to see at that moment, Sonterra would have been near the top, right up there with the aforementioned reporters, my first college boyfriend, and Harvey's ghost.

He let his dark gaze slide over my best suit; Sonterra may be a pain, but he is also seriously fine to look at: thirty-five, half Irish and half Hispanic, his hair almost black, his eyes brown. He's six feet tall, with the kind of build that belongs in a Bowflex commercial, and that slow Latin smile of his ought to be registered somewhere. My coloring is similar to his, and I'm five-nine. I found myself speculating that if he and I were to have children . . .

Well, I rounded up and corralled *that* stray thought quickly enough. Although we'd had

some steamy sex in our brief and tempes-
tuous time as an item, before the Lench
case, these days Sonterra and I were about
as compatible as Pakistan and India. I was
still a little hung up on him—I'd hardly dated
since our breakup—and though our paths
crossed occasionally in the halls of justice, I
usually made a point of staying clear.

Mrs. Kravinsky flitted into my mind just
then, like an absentee fairy godmother—my
thinking really *was* scattered—but she
served to distract me from memories of
Sonterra and myself in the throes of sweaty,
mind-blowing passion, so I was grateful.
Mrs. K was seventy-four years old, a dear
friend who lived in the condo across from
mine, looked after Emma when the need
arose, and spent a significant share of her
time lighting pink candles in a brave but altogether pitiful effort to conjure up an affair
to remember for yours truly. If Sonterra was
the result, the Cosmos definitely had a
sense of humor.

I sensed Loretta hovering somewhere in
the mob behind me, giving us room to hang
ourselves. Loretta is as much of a romantic
as Mrs. Kravinsky, though her matchmaking
efforts are subtler. Why bother with candles,

moon phases, and rhyming chants when it's so easy to steer two people together in a crowded restaurant and then conveniently vanish?

"What do you want?" I asked. With Sonterra, it pays to be direct. He's smart as hell, but he's a man and, by virtue of the testosterone factor, somewhat obtuse.

"We don't have time to cover the subject of what I want," Sonterra answered, a little wearily. He carried a folded newspaper under one arm and smiled again, showing those great teeth of his. "You get a real job yet?"

I ignored the remark, hoping he'd go away, knowing all the while that I couldn't get that lucky.

"Too bad about Kredd taking a bullet in the frontal lobe," he said.

I wanted to tell Sonterra that I thought he was a rude and insensitive bastard, but I refrained. One of us had to show some decorum; there was, after all, such a thing as respect for the dead, even when the corpse in question was Harvey Kredd's.

"*Hello*, Clare," Sonterra said pointedly. The silent treatment never worked with him. "Or should I call you 'Counselor,' since our relationship is strictly professional these days?"

"What 'relationship' would that be?" I snapped, wishing Loretta would put in an appearance already. She knew the whole sad story of my thing for Sonterra—or most of it, anyway. Even if she hadn't set me up, she'd abandoned me. Some friend. "We didn't relate, Sonterra. We had sex."

His dark eyes glowed. Maybe "smoldered" would be a better word. "Oh, yeah," he agreed, in a sort of rough-edged purr. "We definitely did."

A scene flashed into my mind; the two of us lying under an overturned rowboat during a visit to his lake cabin up north, while a summer rainstorm pocked the earth. Sonterra, touching me in places that had since frozen over. I felt light-headed all of the sudden, and a warm, spreading sensation settled between my pelvic bones.

I promptly put the reaction down to a combination of malnutrition and the emotional rigors of the last ten days or so. When you grow up the way I did, denial is second nature.

"Go away," I said, without much hope that he would oblige.

"Not a chance," Sonterra replied, and a muscle tightened in his jaw. He set the still-folded newspaper on the game table with a slight whack.

I braced myself, refused to look at Sonterra *or* the newspaper. "Harvey's funeral was nice," I said, aware that the remark was inane, but desperate to dodge what I knew was coming. Sonterra and a slew of his cop friends had been present for the services, wearing dark suits and looking suitably grim. I suspected they'd only wanted to make sure Harvey was in the box.

Super Cop offered no comment; he took a sip from his beer, and I found myself looking at him after all, watching his throat as he swallowed. He set the chilled bottle down with a thump, leaving a frosty ring on the glass tabletop; his eyes narrowed, and a muscle flexed in his jaw. I knew that look well enough, since Sonterra and I have a history; denial no longer served. This was no casual encounter—he was after something, and I concluded that it must be big, if he was willing to speak to me in even a halfway civil tone. Following the Lench trial, which was held in the judge's chambers, Sonterra had trailed me back to the offices of Kredd and Associates, in Scottsdale, breathing fire. There, in my cubicle, we'd had the kind of no-going-back yelling match that can be broken up only with a fire hose.

Sonterra had never forgiven me for unraveling a righteous bust. The way I saw it, I was just doing my job, which is not always pleasant.

Feeling cornered, the Toad's cheerful atmosphere notwithstanding, I tried to establish a psychic link with Loretta. *Get over here, damn it. I'm in way over my head, and going down for the third time.*

Nothing. According to Emma, who was terminally pubescent, I don't have a psychic bone in my body. Furthermore, she maintained, I'm so practical, so "lawyerly," that I probably don't even *have* a right brain.

"You didn't cry at Krudd's funeral," Sonterra observed, when I failed to pick up the conversational ball. It was a little joke with the cops, mispronouncing Harvey's last name. To say there was no rapport between the Scottsdale Police Department and my employer would be elegant understatement, and the Phoenix contingent hadn't been wild about him, either, nor had the sheriff's office. The lawmen spent their time rounding up bad guys, and Harvey had devoted his very successful career to springing them in grand style—at a price, of course. Zero down and a few dollars a month, for the rest of their arguably natural lives, for the 1-800 crowd, which was probably the most lucrative, due to the sheer volume of idiots out there, and serious up-front bucks for the well-to-do.

"Neither did you," I retorted acidly, wishing I had a beer, too. It would have served two purposes—cooling my dry throat and giving me something to hide behind.

Sonterra's eyes darkened, but there was a spark of humor lurking in them as he sat back in the short chair and looked me over again. The newspaper lay between us like a bomb, explosive enough to turn our insides to soup when it went off.

"What are you doing here, Sonterra?" I demanded when he didn't answer.

"I just stopped in to have a beer with some of the guys," he said.

The liar.

"You followed me."

"You flatter yourself, Counselor. Cave Creek is a small town. We ended up at the same watering hole, that's all."

"Whatever," I said, just to bug Sonterra. He hated dismissive tones.

He didn't bite, but simply splayed the fingers of one hand in an idle acknowledgment of our surroundings. What the hell was he up to? "Place like this"—he scanned the bar—"good food, good beer—I figured you had to be celebrating."

"Celebrating?" God knew, I was no champion of Harvey Kredd's good name—after all, he didn't exactly have one—but *still*. The man had been gunned down on his own property, for heaven's sake. He'd left behind a busy, complex law practice, a smart and sexy wife, two exes, and three greedy offspring who would probably spend the next decade wrangling over his estate. "Listen, *Detective* Sonterra, Harvey might not have been your favorite person, but he *was* a human being. He was murdered, in the prime of his life, and at least a *pretense* of concern would seem appropriate."

Sonterra appeared to shrug off everything I'd said, the way he usually did, sticking with his own agenda. I should have guessed what it was sooner than I did, but I was worn out, and not as quick on the uptake as I might have been otherwise.

"I understand you and Krudd—Kredd—had words a few days before the murder. Loud words. In public."

So I was a suspect? Perfect. I sighed and gave the room another quick visual sweep, searching for Loretta. She was as elusive as a desert mirage.

I bit the bullet and met Sonterra's gaze head-on. "Yes," I said, stiffening my spine and jutting out my chin a little. "Harvey and I 'had words,' and they were indeed public." I paused, gathering my waning forces. Remembering the confrontation with my boss, which had taken place, not in the relative privacy of the firm, but in one of Harvey's favorite restaurants, in the middle of the day. "This ought to make you really happy, Sonterra. CNN wanted to do a special report, after Lench wiped out that woman and her kids, and Harvey thought I ought to take the heat, even though he dumped the case on me in the first place. I refused, Harvey got angry, and I fought back. It got ugly."

"But he didn't fire you?"

Harvey, fire me? Not in a million years. Harvey and I had had a contract; he'd paid my way through law school, as well as pro-viding a stipend for my living expenses dur-ing those three years, and I was virtually indentured to the firm as a result. I had never told Sonterra any of this, partly be-cause it was none of his damn business and *mostly* because I knew he'd see it as one more instance of Clare selling her soul to the devil.

"No," I said moderately. "He didn't fire me. I'm a good lawyer." Yet again, I looked for Loretta, but there was no sign of her big hair and tasteful black ensemble. I was get-ting really irritated with her, and really hun-gry, even though Sonterra made me nervous as hell. Unfortunately, nothing much ruins my appetite; I've been losing and gaining the same ten pounds ever since high school.

Sonterra unfolded the newspaper, tapped the headline with one forefinger. "Yeah," he said dryly. "You're a good lawyer. Which makes this all that much harder to stom-ach."

I tried not to look, but my gaze went straight to the headline and the sobering photo beneath.

"CHRONIC OFFENDER KILLS SELF, OTHERS, IN FIERY CRASH." The picture showed the twisted, blackened remains of the minivan, which contained the bodies of Janice Murdock and her children, Ethan, four, and Abigail, two. Lench's truck lay on its side, also burned.

I closed my eyes against the images that had been haunting me since I first learned what had happened, but it didn't help. And Sonterra didn't need to say a word: if I hadn't fought so hard to free Lench on that earlier rap, those people would still be alive.

"Put it away," I said.

Sonterra complied. I like to think he might have been a little ashamed of himself, but I doubt it.

"Tell me what you know about Kredd's murder," he said, after a few moments of anything but respectful silence.

"Just the basics," I said, mildly surprised to find that I could breathe, let alone speak coherently. "Janet Baylin called that Monday morning, early, to tell me Harvey was dead. I heard the rest of the details when I got to the office at nine." And gory details they were, too.

Poor Harvey. He'd worked late on Sunday

night, in the converted guesthouse behind his sprawling mansion in nearby Paradise Valley, dining at his desk, as he'd made a habit of doing. He'd been a driven man, with a seemingly endless supply of energy, a workaholic's workaholic.

He'd been found by his wife, Betsy, late that night, facedown in food and blood, with a tidy little bullet hole between his eyes and a nasty exit wound at the back of his head.

"Am I a suspect?" I asked bluntly, when Sonterra had mulled my answer over for a while, "or is this just garden-variety police harassment?" I was a bit sensitive where the cops were concerned, I admit. It went with the kind of work I did, though I had a few personal misgivings about them, too. Shades of my troubled youth.

"You probably had a motive," Sonterra said, dead serious.

"So did half the population of Metro-Phoenix," I responded.

Tony gave a gruff chuckle at that and lifted his half-empty beer bottle in an off-hand toast of agreement.

"Any leads?" I asked, figuring it was my turn to steer for a while. "Real ones, I mean?"

"Yeah," Sonterra said, and that bleak smile appeared again, though briefly. "There's a comprehensive list—all we have to do is start at *A* in the phone book and work our way down to *Z*." He leaned in a little, lowered his voice. "You seeing anybody?"

I couldn't believe his nerve. "Yeah. My love life is a torrid whirl, one steamy interlude after another."

He drew back, as if to dodge a blow. "I've got some advice for you, Counselor," he said, after a few moments of potent silence. "Get your hormone levels checked." Trust Sonterra to think my problem was a lack of estrogen. If he'd had his way, I would have quit my job, moved in with him, and spent the rest of my days barefoot and pregnant.

"And I've got some advice for you," I retorted. "Be all you can be, Sonterra. Join the circus."

That familiar muscle bunched in his jaw.

"Westbrook, table for two," the hostess called, from the midst of chaos.

I practically turned Pac-Man on his ear, getting to my feet, casting about for any sign of my best friend. There she was, with her blond helmet of hair, lush figure, and elegant gold jewelry, holding court at the far end of the bar like Mae West in a thirties musical. She waggled her fingers at me, smiling a little, and I tossed her a look hot enough to scorch the grass off an acre of ground.

Sonterra stood, too, beer bottle in hand. He cleared his throat. "You'll be in your office tomorrow?" he asked, with surprising moderation.

I nodded. Harvey had left me a fresh batch of cases that nobody else wanted, before checking out, and I wasn't due in court until Wednesday afternoon.

"Westbrook!" the hostess called a second time, over the noise. She was waxing impatient, and little wonder, with all those customers jostling for seats.

"Here," I called back, making my way past Tony, beckoning curtly to Loretta.

Sonterra caught my elbow in a loose grip, and, without warning, a lot of complex sensations surged up out of the past, washing over me in waves. I pulled free, maybe a second or two later than I would have liked. "I have to go."

"I'll see you in the morning," he said. "Around eleven. This is important, Clare."

"Then maybe you shouldn't have wasted time torturing me with that newspaper," I replied, and walked away.

I didn't look back.

Chapter Two

Loretta and I connected at the doorway leading into the first dining room. The Horny Toad has patio seating as well as a second inside eating area, and we ended up in the latter, sharing one of the rustic wooden booths.

"Did you know he was going to be here?" I demanded, the minute we'd been given our paper menus and put in preliminary orders for ice tea.

Loretta opened her blue eyes wide, trying to look guileless. She and I go way back to college days at the University of Arizona; while I pounded the books in the prelaw program, she majored in keeping her options open. She eventually married a multimillionaire cowboy-type by the name of Kip Matthews, who owned homes in Aspen and Scottsdale, besides a good-sized working ranch outside of Tucson. That was how she happened to be in Cave Creek in my hour of

need, ready, willing, and able to interfere
with my life; Kip and some partners were
slapping up a shopping mall off Highway
101, and, having redecorated the Scottsdale place and bought out all her favorite
designers, Loretta was left with time on her
hands.

"Did I know *who* was going to be here?"
she asked innocently, interlacing her be-
diamonded fingers on the tabletop.

I picked up my menu and gave it a snap,
pretending to study the selections, even
though I'd already made up my mind. I was
having a cheeseburger and fries, carbs and
fat grams be damned. After all, I'd had a hell
of a day, a hell of a *week,* and I needed sus-
tenance. "Oh, knock it off, Loretta," I grum-
bled. "I know you saw Tony and me
together."

She smiled, studied her flawless mani-
cure. She called the color "Bitch Pink" and,
just then, I thought it was fitting. Loretta
made a predatory sound in her throat, half
growl, half purr. "No red-blooded woman
could have missed him," she said. "Lord, he
looks good in Levi's."

Some shrewd observer I was, I thought. I
hadn't even noticed what Sonterra was

wearing. I'd been too busy keeping my force field in place, so he couldn't get to me.

Like *that* ever worked.

"If you say so," I said, laying down the menu with a sigh and rubbing my temples with the fingertips of both hands.

The ice tea arrived, and Loretta sat stirring hers with a straw after the waitress had taken our food orders and left again. "I think you have a thing for him, even now," she said.

I took a long sip of my tea, wishing I could trade it for a double martini or a Singapore sling. I had Emma to deal with when I got home, however, and that required a clear head, like nearly everything else in my life. My niece, due back from her friend's house at nine, had been fairly uncommunicative lately, and I needed to collar her and get some answers.

I sighed as a waitress passed our table with a tray full of cocktails. I guessed I would have to save the sweet oblivion of down-and-dirty drinking for some future, and less complicated, incarnation. "I do *not* have a thing for him," I said stiffly. Not unless I counted the skimpy orange Jockey shorts I found under the seat of my car a month or so after we broke up, I thought wickedly, and I wasn't giving those back. Let him wonder where he'd left them, the bastard.

"Hey," Loretta said quietly, "this is me you're talking to. Your old college roomy and fellow Nipples veteran."

I had to smile, albeit grimly, at the reference to the bawdy nightclub where both Loretta and I had waited tables, back in our undergraduate days, wearing shorts and tight T-shirts with naked breasts screen-printed on the front. The place was a hell-hole, and the customers, like the boss, Freddie Loren, were mostly jerks, but the tips were good, and that was why I'd stayed on until I got my bachelor's degree. By my senior year, my sister, Tracy, had vanished and Emma was living with me, and the arrangement looked permanent.

"You know the story, Loretta," I reminded her. "Tony and I had an affair. No love, just sex. Then the real world exerted itself, and that was the end of it." If there'd ever been a chance of our getting back together, the Lench-Murdock crash had fixed that for good.

"You're still hooked on Tony Sonterra," Loretta insisted quietly.

I refused to answer, and for a while, we just sat there, in the midst of merry confusion.

When the food came, I busied myself cutting the hamburger into four tidy pieces and lining up my french fries. Loretta dined on taco salad, holding her knife and fork European style, as if we were dining at the Ritz in Paris, instead of the Horny Toad in Cave Creek.

"I can't believe he's dead," I said, chewing. I couldn't believe that O.J. had gotten off, either, or that I had only two more payments to make on my car. The scope of my incredulity seemed wide indeed.

"Who?" Loretta asked, dipping her fork delicately into a little bowl of dressing before spearing a morsel from her plate.

I just looked at her, glaring a little. Granted, she and Harvey were barely acquainted, and she'd attended the memorial service only because I needed moral support, but she had to know whom I was talking about.

"Oh," Loretta said, with a little wave of her fork, "you mean Harvey."

I sighed, and bit into the second quarter of my hamburger.

"So maybe this means you can get another job, or go into practice for yourself," Loretta speculated, fork in hand. "Did you think of that?"

I graduated with honors and passed the bar exam on the first try; of *course* I'd thought of it. It's not as if I'm stupid. "Shhh," I hissed, barely suppressing an urge to look and see if Detective Sonterra was lurking somewhere nearby, taking in all the nuances of our conversation. "If anybody hears you, they'll think I killed him."

I couldn't help imagining myself tried and convicted of Harvey Kredd's murder, awaiting sentencing in the Maricopa County Jail and boasting my very own ugly orange jumpsuit. But no, a stint on one of Sheriff Joe's famous road gangs, which, being nothing if not progressive, now included women, would provide fashion relief. They wear stripes.

So much for Emma's theory that I was born without a right brain.

"Well, of *course* you didn't," Loretta said.

I pushed away my plate, a good thirty fat grams short of the finish line, and leaned forward, lowering my voice. "Since I didn't have the distinct pleasure of doing Harvey in myself," I said darkly, "I hesitate to take the credit."

Loretta chuckled and shook her head. "Did *everybody* hate that poor man?"

"I think his dog liked him," I replied, though I wasn't ready to state the fact unequivocally. His dewy bride, Betsy, must have found him tolerable, too; after all, she'd lived with him for the best part of six months. Harvey's first wife, Madge, had hung in there for thirty-seven years, dutifully entertaining clients, decorating a succession of houses, and putting on weight. The second Mrs. Kredd, a Sweet Young Thing named Tiffany, hit the road on day two of the honeymoon, taking her jewelry and Harvey's new Jaguar with her. Must have been some wedding night.

"That's kind of sad, don't you think? That his best friend really was his dog, I mean?"

I considered the question. One of my last memories of Harvey was of him standing in front of my desk, slapping down the arrest report on a kid named Trevor Trent. Trevor had crashed his prominent father's Porsche through the front window of a restaurant in

Scottsdale, injuring four people in the process, after a waitress refused to doctor the credit card receipt for his meal and hand over the difference in cash. Apparently, the old allowance hadn't quite stretched through the week.

I'd looked the documents over with thinly disguised contempt, still smarting from the set-to about the CNN special. Why not let the little shit take the consequences of his actions for once in his life? Who knows, it might turn him around, make a decent human being out of him. I'd said as much to Harvey.

Harvey's right temple had begun to throb visibly as I spoke, and he'd leaned halfway across my desk to make his coffee-scented point. "Get the charges dropped," he'd ordered.

I hadn't been ready to back off. "But—"

"Just get it done," he'd snapped. "Bribe somebody. Boink the judge. I don't care what you have to do, just so *the charges are dropped*."

I blinked myself back to the present moment and the Horny Toad. There was more laughter, more clinking of glasses, and I was feeling a little sick. Sonterra was still around somewhere; I felt the heat.

"What is it?" Loretta prompted. Sometimes I wish she weren't so damn perceptive. For all my education and Harvey's expert tutelage in the finer aspects of bullshit, I've never been able to put much over on her.

I glanced over at the long table in the middle of the dining room, where a number of my esteemed colleagues were again hoisting glasses, Harvey's name floating amidst their laughter. I remembered seeing several of them at the funeral and shrugged, unable to verbalize what I was thinking, even though it was crystal-clear in my mind. When I died—and naturally I hoped that wouldn't be for a long, long time—I wanted people to be sorry that I'd passed away. I hoped they might mourn a little, and remember me fondly, not gather somewhere to rejoice in the fact that I was finally out of their hair.

The waitress brought the bill. Loretta and I split it and left a tip, then made our way out of the restaurant. Loretta's car was parked in the gravel lot, and we climbed in.

It was a short drive to my condo complex,

a series of two-story stucco town houses with private garages and patios. Every light in the place was on when we pulled in, and that made me smile. Emma was a brave soul, independent to a fault, but she didn't like the dark any more than I did. I wondered if it was genetic.

"Want to come in for a glass of wine?" I asked, standing by the passenger door, when Loretta didn't get out of the car.

Loretta shook her head. "I'd better get home. Kip's flying to D.C. in the morning for an investors' meeting, and I've hardly seen him this past week."

Secretly, I was relieved that she'd turned down my invitation, even though Loretta is one of my favorite people. I needed to check in with Emma, take a long hot bath, and tumble into my bed.

Tomorrow, and my next encounter with Detective Sonterra, would come around all too soon.

Chapter Three

The TV was blaring in the empty living room, and tuned to CNN. I caught a glimpse of Danny Murdock, sole remaining member of the family Ned Lench had wiped out. He was ordinary-looking, Murdock was, and he seemed too slight to carry such a burden of grief.

I practically tripped over my own feet, getting to the *off* switch.

My niece appeared at the top of the stairway, a slender creature in mid-morph: part gangly, knobby-kneed gamine; part rebel, with spiky blond hair and fake piercings all over her body. There was enough metal in her ears alone to pick up electronic signals from the next galaxy.

I found the energy to smile at her. "You're home early," I said, consulting my watch. It wasn't quite eight o'clock; I'd given her permission to stay at her friend Cammie's until nine.

"Mrs. Phillips dropped me off on her way to the supermarket a couple of hours ago," Emma said. "I checked in with Mrs. Kravinsky when I got back. She won seventy-five dollars at bingo." She paused, studying me. "You look really bad, Clare. Are you okay?"

"I'm fine," I said, with an effort. "Are you hungry?" Silly question. Mrs. Kravinsky didn't confine her magic to love spells and prosperity rituals. She was a wizard in the kitchen, too. Her steady culinary overflow was one of the reasons I'd graduated from a size eight to a ten.

Emma grinned, and in that moment, it seemed I'd simply imagined the things that had concerned me about her lately. "Stuffed," she said. "Mrs. K's been cooking ever since she got home from the casino. She left a slice of quiche in the fridge in case you forgot to eat."

I chuckled and ruffled her hair with one hand, a gesture I could get away with in private. In public—at the mall, say—the very same move would have brought on a storm of sullen angst.

I kicked off my black pumps, took a half-filled bottle of Chablis from the refrigerator, after admiring the cellophane-covered quiche, and poured myself a glassful. The Mexican tile floor felt cool and smooth beneath my feet. "Get any homework done?"

"All of it," Emma said. "Can we get a dog?"

I wandered toward my office, housed in the downstairs bedroom, and glanced inside without flipping on the lights. The little red button on my telephone–fax–answering machine was blinking rapidly. Sometimes—often, in fact—I wish high-speed communication had never been developed. I might get five minutes of peace that way.

"A dog?" I asked, distracted, and sipped. I was often a beat or two behind Emma. Perilous, during the teenage years.

"You know," she teased, "those furry things with four legs and bad breath?"

I crossed the office, unable to resist, and pressed the *play* button. "Emma, this is a rented condo," I said reasonably. We'd moved there six months before, from a smaller place in one of the less desirable sections of Phoenix; the place still felt like a palace to me, and I was very conscious of the rules. "You know dogs aren't allowed."

Before she could respond, Betsy Kredd's

voice rose from the machine to fill the small, darkened room, a sniffly, raw sound that made me wonder yet again if wife number three really married Harvey for his money, like most people thought, or if she'd actually loved him a little. "Clare? I need to talk to you. Will you call me tonight? Please?"

Resigned, I reached for the receiver. And then the second message kicked in. "Hi, Clare. This is Tony Sonterra. Just a reminder that I'll be stopping by the firm to talk to you tomorrow, around eleven or so. It's important, so don't try to dodge me." A quick glance in Emma's direction left me more than a little worried; the triumphant smile on her face spelled trouble. She'd always liked Tony and was no doubt planning our wedding, ever the hopeful romantic.

The last message caught me off guard, and hit me harder than the startling news of Harvey's untimely death had. "Ms. Westbrook? My name is Mike Fletcher. I'm James Arren's parole officer. We need to discuss his release date and a few other details. Please call me as soon as you can." He followed up with a number, which I didn't bother to write down, since it might as well have been branded into my brain, and hung up.

Emma, hovering in the doorway until a moment before, whirled and went pounding up the stairs. I heard the door of her room slam.

I pulled back my desk chair and sank into it. James Arren, Emma's natural father, who had done a six-year hitch in an Arizona prison for armed robbery, was about to be paroled. Of course I'd known that—there had been a little counter clicking away in the back of my mind since the day he was sentenced and Emma was turned over to me—but outside the perimeters of my career, in personal territory, I'm a master of avoidance.

I drew a deep breath, let it out slowly, and stepped back into my lawyer-skin. *One crisis at a time, Clare,* I thought. *Pace yourself.*

I switched on the lamp, opened my Day-Timer, and methodically made a note of Tony Sonterra's planned visit in the morning, then picked up the cordless receiver again and dialed the Kredd residence.

Betsy answered with a breathless hello, as if she'd been waiting by the phone.

I frowned, concerned. "Hello, Betsy," I

said. "It's Clare. Is everything all right?" A gavel banged in my head, and my own private judge thundered, *Dumb question, Counselor. Her husband is dead, remember? How can anything be 'all right'?*

Betsy sniffled bravely. She was a gorgeous, leggy blonde, thin as a model, a type that seems to be indigenous to the moneyed areas of Scottsdale, Paradise Valley, Carefree, and Cave Creek, but I liked her anyway. In addition to those spectacular looks, she had a degree in political science. "It's Bernice," she said, and then sobbed.

"Bernice?" I echoed, confused, and then remembered, which didn't help much. We were talking about Harvey's dog? "Has something happened to her?"

"She's so depressed," Betsy said.

I closed my eyes, rubbed my temple. "I suppose that's natural," I ventured. I was at a loss to console Betsy herself; how was I supposed to help the dog? "When some time has passed—"

"I can't bear it," Betsy broke in. "Every time a door opens or closes, that poor little creature runs to meet Harvey, all excited and eager, and—and of course—he isn't there—"

The picture Betsy painted was indeed a sad one, but I wasn't sure what she thought I could do about the problem.

She wasted no time filling me in.

"Bernice has always adored your Emma. Would you—could you—take her?"

I flashed back to Emma's earlier request—*Can we get a dog?*—and guessed that she and Betsy had already *had* this conversation. I had been set up, big-time.

"I don't know, Betsy," I began cautiously. "I'm renting this place, and there are rules about pets—"

"Bernice is just a little terrier," Betsy argued, rallying on a swell of conviction. "Cats and small dogs are fine."

It occurred to me that Harvey's widow knew whereof she spoke; the complex I lived in was one of the Kredds' numerous tax shelters. Technically, I was dealing with my landlady.

The lawyer in me wanted to make a counteroffer—"Okay, it's a deal, all you have to do is let me out of my contract with Harvey, so I can get a new job and hold my head up in the legal community"—but it would have been crass to broach such a subject before the man was cold in his grave. I'd give it another week.

"All right," I heard myself say. "We'll try it, Betsy. But if the dog isn't happy here—"

"Not 'the dog,' " Betsy said, with a little snap in her tone. "Her *name* is Bernice."

"Bernice," I repeated. I leaned over and banged my forehead against the blotter a couple of times, though not hard enough for Betsy to hear. I didn't want to hurt myself, or spill what was left of my wine.

"Good," Betsy replied. "I'll have someone bring her right over."

Before I could attempt to reason with the woman—surely tomorrow would be soon enough—she'd hung up. I took a final gulp of Chablis, then dialed the number Mike Fletcher had left, and got his pager. He called back before I had a chance to get out of my chair.

"Clare Westbrook," I said, in a businesslike tone. *Next disaster, please.*

"Mike Fletcher," responded the caller.

"I got your message," I said. "They're letting James Arren out of jail." I might have framed the statement like an accusation, I don't know. I wasn't rational where that son of a bitch was concerned. I was certain he'd killed my sister, and it appeared that he'd gotten away with it.

"Yes," Fletcher said, with a sigh. "I didn't like leaving news like that on your answering machine, but I didn't really have a choice."

I was wasting my breath, but I couldn't help saying it. Not that anybody had ever listened, not the press, not the police. "They're letting a murderer go. Turning him loose to kill again."

Another sigh. "Ms. Westbrook, I'm aware of your belief that Mr. Arren was responsible for his wife's death, but there simply is no proof of that. As far as I know, no body was ever found."

I didn't dare speak. As far as the powers-that-be were concerned, no body usually meant there hadn't been a killing in the first place. The official view was that Tracy had simply ditched the daughter she'd adored, then barely seven years old, and skipped out without a word. The Tucson cops believed she'd run off with a boyfriend, and never looked back—to them, my sister had been little more than a statistic, a bad girl reaping what she'd sown.

"According to the file," Fletcher said, with

careful ease, "a judge ruled that Mrs. Arren was most likely a runaway."

I couldn't help remembering the day I'd visited Arren in jail, right after he was convicted of the convenience-store heist, and asked him to sign papers allowing me to adopt Emma, who had already been staying with me for several months by then. He'd sneered at me and refused, saying he wanted a chance to prove himself as a daddy when he'd served his time, especially since Emma no longer had a mother. The look on his face had been as good as a confession, as far as I was concerned, and if there hadn't been a heavy glass panel between us, I probably would have strangled him on the spot.

He'd written Emma faithfully during his incarceration, long letters she chose not to share with me. On the advice of our joint therapist, I didn't hassle her about it, though I lay awake nights sometimes, wondering what kind of twisted misconceptions he was planting in her mind.

"Tracy Arren," I said, measuring out the words syllable by syllable, "is dead. She was murdered."

Another sigh from Fletcher's end of the

line; then he went into the familiar bureaucratic song and dance. "Mr. Arren has been a model prisoner," he said. "While behind bars, he completed a computer science course, and he has a job lined up in Phoenix. The reports say he has maintained contact with his daughter."

My stomach did a flip, and I clasped the bridge of my nose between my thumb and forefinger. "And?" I prompted, knowing what was coming.

"Mr. Arren wishes to see his child."

It's strange how a simple statement can buckle a person's knees, both literally and figuratively, even when it comes as no real surprise. "I have legal custody," I heard myself say.

Fletcher cleared his throat. "Yes," he said, with exaggerated patience. Maybe, like Sonterra, he didn't like lawyers. "Mr. Arren is not contesting that." There was an unspoken "not yet" in his voice. "He is entitled to supervised visits with his daughter, however, and he chooses to exercise that privilege."

For a moment, I actually thought I would have to drag the wastebasket out from under the desk and throw up in it. Working for Harvey these past two years, I'd gotten a lot of practice at controlling nausea, however, and a few deep breaths brought me around. "When?" I croaked.

"Are you asking when Mr. Arren is scheduled for release?" Fletcher inquired, still sounding terse. "Or when would the visits begin?"

"Both," I murmured.

"He gets out tomorrow. A social worker will contact you about establishing appropriate contact between Mr. Arren and the child."

"Tomorrow?" I couldn't believe it. I'd been assured of a lot more notice than that—which only went to show what official promises were worth.

"I'm sorry," Fletcher said.

"Why didn't somebody call me? I was supposed to be notified!"

Fletcher cleared his throat. "There was an error. Paperwork."

Afraid of saying something that might come back to bite me in the caboose later, I took the high road and slammed down the phone. The Chablis surged into the back of my throat, burning like acid. James Arren was a hardened felon, and Emma was an impressionable thirteen-year-old, with all the attendant vulnerabilities. Exactly what kind of "contact" was "appropriate" in a case like that?

The doorbell jolted me out of my fugue state, sending a rush of adrenaline through my bloodstream. Half expecting to find James standing on my threshold, benefiting from some further bureaucratic snafu, I was dizzy with relief when I actually opened the door.

Harvey Kredd's bereaved Yorkie had arrived.

Chapter Four

James Arren loomed at the foot of my bed and, worse, he had Emma in a choke hold. His face, acne-scarred and hardened by years of bitterness, was contorted with rage, and I thought I caught the nickel-blue glint of a pistol in his left hand. A scream of fury, protest, and stark, primitive fear burbled up from somewhere deep in my middle, and burned like acid as it passed my throat. I leaped out of bed, still entangled in the covers and flailing to get free, my body cold with sweat. Forget "flight," I was in *fight* mode, pure and simple.

I crouched, grappled with the lock on the gun safe that was affixed to my bed frame, desperate to retrieve its contents.

"Clare!" The voice seemed out of context, as if it came from some parallel universe.

Consciousness slammed into me with the impact of a battering ram.

"Clare?"

I trembled, blinked. And finally woke up.

I was kneeling on the floor, and Emma stood in the doorway of my room, the hall light glowing behind her, Harvey's little dog tucked protectively into the curve of one arm. She flipped the switch, and the lamps on either side of my bed came on. I saw her look furtively into each corner before taking a step toward me. "Are you okay?"

Her voice was small, a poignant reminder that my niece was still a child, for all her thirteen years, her fake piercings and tattoo aspirations, her intermittent Attitude.

I wiped damp palms on my thighs, tried hard to smile, and levered myself up onto the edge of the mattress, not trusting my knees to support me, even now, when I knew I was back in the real world, knew James wasn't really in the room, ready to cut off Emma's air supply.

"Bad dream," I said. Understatement is a habit I picked up in childhood, when teachers, school nurses, and social workers asked me how things were going at home.

Emma looked truly sympathetic; of course, she'd had more than her share of nightmares along the rocky path to adulthood—how could she help it? She'd spent the first half of her young life flailing on the fringes of the storm that was my sister's violent, and eventually fatal, marriage. "I get those, too, sometimes," she confessed, probably thinking that this would come as a revelation to me.

Her blue eyes were wide, enormous, and her gaze strayed to the gun safe beneath the bed, installed primarily for her protection. The Yorkie whimpered sympathetically and strained to lick Emma's chin. "Do you want Bernice and me to sleep in here with you?"

Although I'd said nothing about my telephone conversation with Mike Fletcher, regarding Arren's impending release from prison, it was obvious Emma had correctly deduced that we had a problem. She'd fled the office after hearing the original message; possibly she'd listened on her extension after she got to her room. I patted the bedspread, inviting my niece to sit beside me. "You can stay if you want to," I said gently, remembering only too well how it was to be a kid, feeling scared and vulnerable in the dark, with all its special dangers, "though I think you'd rest better in your own bed. In the meantime, though, we need to talk."

My niece sat down, Bernice small as a toy in her arms. Most Yorkies have long coats, but this one boasted a puppy cut instead, though she was getting scruffy. Harvey had not been one to fuss with little niceties like pet grooming; indeed, it still puzzled me that he'd owned a dog at all. He'd been one of the most self-absorbed people I'd ever encountered, probably a family trait, given that I hadn't heard from his cousin, my father, once since he'd turned his back on my damaged mother, a few months after my conception. "He's finally getting out of jail, huh? My dad, I mean?" Emma said, her tone indefinably odd. Plainly, she already knew the answer, and the look in her eyes, at once hopeful and scared, told me she was deeply conflicted about it.

I put an arm around Emma. She was a teenager, God help us both, but she seemed so much younger, so much smaller, that night.

"Yes," I said. "Tomorrow."

She stiffened almost imperceptibly and looked away.

"And he wants to see me." Despondent

resignation, and something else. Something I groped for, in my dazed and disjointed brain, but couldn't quite reach.

I nodded, blinking back tears of frustration and residual fear, and gave her a fierce squeeze. "Talk to me, Emma. What's going on with you? You haven't been yourself lately." *Little wonder,* I thought. Since the Lench crash and Harvey's murder, our lives had taken on a frog-in-a-blender element that made it hard to think straight.

Emma's thin shoulders moved in a shrug, but she still wouldn't meet my eyes. "Nothing," she said.

"I don't believe you," I replied calmly. "And I'm not going to give up until you level with me, kiddo. I don't care how long it takes."

She searched my face. "Will I be going to live with him?"

Ah, I thought. *So that's it.*

I swallowed hard. I wanted to say no, unequivocally *no, you will never, not ever, live under James Arren's roof, I'll die first,* but of course I couldn't do that, knowing the mysterious ways of the legal system as well as I did. The fact was that a bleeding-heart judge might well see fit to award custody of a child to a dangerous ex-convict, out of concern for the vicious scumbag's *rights*; trust me, stranger things happen every day of the week in the courtrooms of America.

"What has he been telling you? In those letters, I mean?"

Defiance flickered in Emma's eyes, and vanished just as quickly. "Nothing," she said again. That word was a stock response with her, especially when she wanted to stonewall me. "You didn't answer my question, Clare. Am I going to live with my father?"

I drew a deep breath, let it out slowly. "Not if there's anything I can do to prevent it," I replied, when I could trust myself to get the words out with some degree of equanimity.

She leaned against my side. Child and dog gazed forlornly up into my face, looking for miracles. I sorely wished I could come up with one. "Maybe he's changed," Emma said. "He's got an education now. He studied computers."

I added James Arren's education to my list of grudges against the system. Murder someone, rob a convenience store at gunpoint, and the taxpayer foots the bill for a sheepskin. Honest citizens, on the other hand, have to scramble for tuition and books. "Does that seem likely to you?" I asked, willing my heart rate to slow down. "That he's changed, I mean?"

Emma mulled that over for a few moments, and I felt another shiver of concern. "Maybe we could just take off," she suggested, after a brief and troubling silence, during which she studiously avoided my gaze. "You and me and Bernice. We could go someplace where he'd never find us. Start over, with new names and everything."

"Running away won't solve anything," I said quietly, though I'd given the concept of a desperate, headlong rush for elsewhere some intense consideration myself. "Besides, you'd miss your friends and Mrs. K. And what would I do without Loretta?" I smiled, somewhat wanly, I imagine, and resisted a maternal urge to ruffle Emma's cap of fair hair. "Come on. Let's go downstairs and brew some herbal tea. Maybe that will help us get back to sleep."

"Are we going to talk about my dad?" Again, that strange mixture of wariness and optimism.

"I don't give a rat's behind about your dad," I replied. "It's you I care about. And, like I said, I'm not going to leave you alone until you open up, whether that's tonight, tomorrow, next week, or when you're seventy-two."

Emma hesitated for a moment, then smiled a little and shook her head, as if marveling at my gall, and then followed me downstairs and into the kitchen.

I was just taking our cups out of the microwave when the phone rang. I peered out the window and saw Mrs. K across the way, looking out *her* window, with a telephone receiver to her ear. I nodded to her and took the call. "Hello, Mrs. K," I said.

"Is everything all right over there?" my friend asked. "When I saw your lights go on, I got worried. Do you know what time it is?"

I smiled as I set steaming cups of Emma's and my favorite tea, Raspberry Schmazz-berry, on the table and glanced at the digital clock on the stove. Three-twenty-seven A.M. "We're fine," I said. "Just a little case of group insomnia." I would tell her what little I knew about James's release later, when I could talk freely and express my misgivings without Emma overhearing. "What about you? Are you okay?" By her own admission, Mrs. K was usually tucked up in bed by eight-thirty, watching prerecorded episodes of *Unsolved Mysteries*, and sound asleep by ten.

"I'm fine, dear," Mrs. K said. "I've been working a prosperity spell for my friend Evelyn. She was married to a famous singer years ago—you'd die if I said who it is—and he's never given her a cent, if you can believe it. She managed to get along on her own for a long time, but now her health is breaking down and she's just about destitute." She paused for breath. "Well, let me tell you, I got so charged up after she called and told me what happened that the air was fairly crackling. Now I have to wait for the energy to die down in here so I can sleep."

"I see," I said sagely. Once, I would have scoffed, in the privacy of my own thoughts, but since then, I'd become a believer, albeit a reluctant one. Three months back, when my health insurance had reached the end of its yearly allotment for Emma's and my counseling, I'd found myself strapped for cash. Short of hitting Loretta up for a loan, which my pride wouldn't allow, I was out of options. Ever sympathetic, Mrs. K had spun one of her spells to remedy the problem, and sure enough, I'd started to win like crazy at Monopoly. I was up to my eyeballs in funny money. A few magical refinements on Mrs. K's part, however, and, *voilà*, in an apparent burst of guilt over the Dickensian salary he paid me, Harvey had coughed up an unexpected bonus—just enough to pay for more sessions with the shrink.

I thought of the encounter with Sonterra, at the Horny Toad. "Mrs. K—you haven't been lighting any pink candles for me lately, have you?"

Her answer should have been reassuring, but somehow it wasn't. "I can honestly say that I haven't," she said.

"See that you don't," I advised, but kindly, because I knew she meant well.

After that, we agreed that everyone was all right, all around, and ended the call.

Emma sipped her tea, holding the cup with both hands, while Bernice perched in her lap, barely able to see over the edge of the table. My niece's changeable eyes, haunted by night-worries and private quandaries only moments before, were suddenly alight with mischief. She knew something about Mrs. K's spell casting that I didn't, that was clear.

I shook a finger at her, trying to look and

sound stern. The dog growled, as if prepared to defend her new mistress from all comers, beginning with me. "Out with it, Emma," I said.

She favored me with an ingenuous smile. "Mrs. K isn't lighting pink candles," she said. "Not for you, anyhow."

I waited, arms folded.

Emma giggled. "She's using red ones. They're a lot stronger than pink."

"Oh, Lord," I murmured. I was no expert on candle magic, but I understood the basics—pink symbolized romance, green meant money, and red stood for grand passion, among other things. Evidently, Mrs. K had decided to forget hearts and flowers and bring out the big guns. She wanted me hooked up with a man, any man.

Even if that man was Sonterra.

I almost called my neighbor the witch back, right then, and insisted that she cease and desist, but it was late, and her kitchen light was off.

Later, with the benefit of hindsight, I would wish that I'd gone straight over there, with a bucket in each hand, and doused the whole place so thoroughly that no candle would ever burn within those walls again.

Upstairs, when I was sure Emma was settled in her room, I closed my door, knelt beside the bed, and slowly, carefully, removed my .38 from the gun safe. Then I checked to make sure the thing was loaded—six brand-new hollow-points, present and accounted for—and stashed it in the back of the drawer in my bedside table.

A Girl Scout is always prepared.

Chapter Five

I was at something less than my best when Sonterra put in an appearance at the Scottsdale offices of Kredd and Associates, promptly at eleven-thirty the next morning. My desk stacked with files, my computer choked with e-mails, many of them urgent, and the waiting room jammed with the usual crowd of alleged miscreants, some genuinely innocent, others hoping to avoid personal responsibility in ten easy payments.

Sonterra lounged in my doorway, clad in a good suit and sporting a slanted grin. He cocked a thumb toward the front of the large suite of offices. "Business is booming," he said. "Krudd must be thrilled, wherever he is."

I narrowed my eyes. "Thank you," I said, "for those sensitive and gracious words."

"Anytime," he said. Then he stepped into my cubicle and closed the door, the grin having left his mouth to gleam in his dark eyes. The image of Mrs. K lighting her red candles crossed my mind, but in the bright light of day, it seemed silly to be concerned.

"I'm swamped here," I said. "I believe you *said* this was important."

Sonterra turned serious on me, always a scary proposition. He helped himself to the extra chair, without asking, and sat down. "Kredd's home office was ransacked," he said. "The night of the murder, I mean. There were personnel files and all kinds of documents scattered from hell to breakfast. Our people did some gathering and sorting, and there was a folder for everybody in the firm. Everybody but you, that is."

He waited while the implications of that sunk in.

"Harvey's killer took *my* personnel file?" Oddly, even while facing the prospect of my own demise, I reflected that it was in character for my late boss to keep duplicate folders at home; he probably had another set of financial records, too. One for the IRS, a more accurate one for his eyes only.

"Unless it's here somewhere. We checked his car and the main house, with Mrs. Kredd's permission, of course."

I felt that now-familiar little pitch in the pit

of my stomach, a danger signal. For once, it had nothing to do with Sonterra's proximity. "I'll check with Heather." I reached for the intercom button on my phone. My tone was businesslike as I put the question to the receptionist, but my gut was churning. I guess I knew even then that the extra file would be nowhere to be found.

Heather disclaimed any knowledge of an extra dossier, and produced my regular employee jacket. Sonterra and I made a quick but thorough search of Harvey's office, the inner sanctum, and came up dry.

"Not good," Sonterra said when we'd finished plundering the boss's desk and credenza and returned to my cubicle.

I was acutely aware of two things: One, that Harvey's killer had not only access to a lot of my personal information, but a reason to *want* said information, and two, that I was alone in a small space with my sexual nemesis. I like to think it was the fear, and not a lack of morality, that made me want Sonterra to tear my clothes off, then and there.

"Think, Clare," Tony prompted, jarring me out of the steamy fantasy I'd taken refuge in. "Who could be that pissed off at Kredd *and* at you?"

I sighed. "Clients get irate when the verdict doesn't go their way," I said, "and then there's the opposing faction. They usually don't appreciate getting run through the judicial wringer." I shrugged. "Lawyers make enemies."

Sonterra gave me a look. "You can say that again," he replied tersely. "Listen, I'm going to get some people in here to go through the client records and try to pick out the live wires. If necessary, I'll get a court order. In the meantime, Clare, you'd better be more than careful. And if you remember anything that might help us identify this yo-yo, I want you to call me immediately. Day or night, doesn't matter."

I felt a shiver trip down my spine. "You really think—?"

"It's a possibility that somebody out there wants to kill you," Sonterra said. He seldom minced words. "Watch your back."

I nodded, inwardly stricken, outwardly as stubborn as ever.

"You still have that little thirty-eight?" Sonterra had helped me buy that pistol, in the old days, and taught me to clean and fire it, too. He'd also installed the gun safe and threatened Emma with mayhem if she ever touched the thing.

"Yes," I said. My throat felt thick and a little raw. I couldn't help remembering the vivid dream I'd had about James Arren.

"Keep it handy," Sonterra counseled, "and keep it loaded."

I made a halfhearted salute, and he scrawled his cell phone number on a scrap of paper, said good-bye, and left.

Heather happened by, moments after he'd gone, ostensibly taking lunch orders, but mainly angling for news.

I told her the police would be coming in to go through the files, but gave up nothing more than that. The subject of food arose, and since Heather had her pen and notepad at the ready, I put in an order for tuna on wheat, with low-fat mayo, and a diet cola.

I might have been terrified, but there was nothing wrong with my appetite.

The meal was delivered within twenty minutes, and I actually managed to finish most of it before the phone rang again. Janet Baylin, the firm's unofficial second in command, was on the other end of the line. Her office was next to Harvey's and though she wasn't a partner—he didn't believe in raising mere associates to his own level, no matter how valuable they were to the firm—she had elbowroom, a décor of sorts, and a view of Scottsdale Road. Since I didn't even have a window, I was impressed by these amenities.

"Meeting," she announced, in her shorthand way. In the office, Janet always talked like a telegram, no wasted words. In the courtroom, she waxed eloquent, Perry Mason in panty hose.

"Now?" I asked, which, in retrospect, was a stupid question. Ms. Baylin made a science of living in the moment; *now* was her favorite word.

She huffed out a sigh. "If it wouldn't be too much trouble," she said.

"Right," I replied, gazing ruefully at the mountains of work on my desk.

"Five minutes," Janet said. "Conference room." The line went dead.

I ran into Heather in the hall, and she waggled her perfectly sculpted blond eyebrows at me. "That cop—Detective Sonterra?—is seriously cute," she said, sotto voce. "Isn't he the one you used to date?"

Date was too polite a term for what went

on between Sonterra and me, but of course I wasn't about to confide that to Heather. Especially not in a busy hallway lined with doors as thin as my own. I pretended I hadn't heard and slogged dutifully toward the conference room.

Marisa Mancito, fellow peon, came out of her office as I passed, arms loaded with files, and Flip Talmadge was waiting by the water-cooler. The other three junior "associates," Jack Reeves, Mary Ellen Steadman, and Darren Bryant, brownnosers all, were already seated around the big table in Harvey's war room, each one sporting a black armband. Without the boss, the place seemed larger, the ventilation better; Harvey'd had a way of sucking the oxygen out of a room and taking up more than his share of space.

Janet had installed herself in Harvey's place; no surprise there. She'd been the first lawyer he'd hired, back when his private practice had expanded enough to justify calling the outfit a firm. She was a plain, busty woman, with sharp features and a seemingly inexhaustible collection of cheap suits, but there was no question of her legal acumen. When it came to litigation, she was a shark, as ruthless, in her own singular way, as Harvey had been.

The chairs on either side of hers were taken, of course; Flip and Marisa and I claimed the leftovers.

Janet bestowed her imperial stare on the newcomers, one by one. Letting us know who was in charge, now that Harvey had gone on to his just reward—as if there'd been any question.

"As you have no doubt deduced," Janet began, when she was sure she had our undivided, if not adoring, attention, "Mrs. Kredd and I have agreed that Mr. Kredd would want us to carry on as normally as possible."

Janet and Harvey had been on a first-name basis, of course. They'd played golf together and taken numerous joint business trips as well. No doubt referring to him formally was a polite concession to his being, well, *dead*.

Marisa clutched her stack of files to her bosom, the way she might hold a feverish baby, instead of laying them on the table. Though she'd never confided as much, I suspected that Marisa, like me, was slave labor. She was a single mother, in her mid-thirties, with a couple of small children, and her car was an eyesore; getting through college, let alone law school, must have required superhuman effort, even if Harvey *had* underwritten her tuition, books, and modest living expenses, as he'd done for me. "Mr. Kredd wanted these cases reassigned," Marisa said, as if she expected an argument. In a room full of lawyers, too. Go figure.

Janet eyed her coldly. "We'll get to that." Ms. Baylin pretty much disliked everybody, especially if they were female. Once, having had a few too many drinks at a company function, she'd accused me of trading on my looks to curry favor with Harvey, among others, and things had been bristly between us ever since.

Marisa subsided.

The dragon consulted the legal pad lying on the table before her, squinting through her trifocals at the tiny hand-printed words inscribed there. "Talmadge," she said, as if beginning a drumroll. Out of the corner of my eye, I saw Flip wince slightly. "You'll take the Johnson, Schemmicker, and Walker cases. Heather will leave the files on your desk."

Flip turned his pencil end over end on the top page of his legal pad, nodded, and wisely offered no comment. We all knew that Harvey had bequeathed worse cases than the ones Janet had just mentioned; Flip, being the newest and, let's face it, the least competent, had gotten off easy.

The other cases were parceled out, and the attending lawyers dismissed. All of the sudden, Janet and I were alone in the conference room.

Uh-oh.

"Westbrook," Janet proceeded. I sat up a little straighter. Our gazes connected, and she consulted her notes again, though I knew she could have recited them verbatim. She was renowned for her photographic memory and, if she hadn't been the poster woman for hormone replacement therapy, I would have wanted to be just like her when I grew up.

"I understand the police intend to come into this office and go through the files," she said, with no inflection at all.

I held her gaze. "That's right," I said. I was damned if I'd explain that Sonterra, and maybe some other people on the force as well, thought I was in danger of meeting the same fate Harvey had.

"Do you realize how disruptive that will be?"

I suppressed a sigh. "Detective Sonterra said he would get a court order, if need be. I didn't see any point in arguing."

She inspected me for a long moment, as though I were a new and mutant species of cockroach. "Well, then," she said, after trying, and failing, to glare me into squirming. "Back to the business at hand. You already have Trevor Trent. You'll take Mrs. Hildebrande, as well." She narrowed her gaze, and her nostrils flared. "And the Justin Netherton case."

I sat up a little straighter. "I thought you were handling Dr. Netherton's defense," I said, alarmed and trying hard to hide the fact.

Janet's smile was acidic. She looked me over. "It seems Dr. Netherton caught a glimpse of you, Ms. Westbrook, during one of his recent visits to the firm, and asked that his case be assigned to you."

"I don't understand—"

"Of course you understand," Janet said

sweetly. "You knew exactly what you were doing, setting the stage—"

I felt heat surge into my face. "Now, just a minute—"

She smiled again. "You'll never win this one, though. Dr. Netherton is sure to regret his choice, in good time, but that will be his problem, won't it? His problem, Ms. Westbrook, and yours."

"I didn't ask for this case and I don't want it."

"Dr. Netherton put up a seven-figure retainer, Ms. Westbrook," Janet said. "Therefore, it doesn't matter what you want."

I swallowed hard, managed to hold my tongue. I couldn't afford to lose this job, much as I would have liked to tell Janet Baylin to roll up the Netherton file and shove it where the sun didn't shine.

"Now," she went on, with a little note of triumph ringing in her voice, "about Trevor. You'll need to get that one out of the way quickly, so you can concentrate on more important things."

Trevor Trent was the mega-brat who'd crashed his car into the front of a restaurant a couple of weeks before, and I'd had time to get used to the idea of defending him, so that was no big deal. How unfortunate if such a promising young man went to jail come fall, instead of some Ivy League school. And Mrs. Hildebrande was a scion of society with a penchant for periodic sprees of shoplifting; her mortified son and daughter-in-law always made prompt restitution, and when she got as far as the courthouse, the judges invariably let her off with a lecture and a fine. In fact, many local merchants simply skipped the arrest phase altogether and called Harvey for a check, which was promptly remitted, then double-billed to the younger Hildebrandes. Her defense would be the proverbial piece of cake.

Justin Netherton was a whole other matter, and not just because of the Janet dynamic. Netherton practiced in Tucson, my old stomping grounds, and I was acquainted with his reputation if not with the good doctor himself. Several of the other waitresses at Nipples had gone to him for breast enhancement surgery, one with disastrous results, and his detractors were legion. Now, I was expected to convince a judge and jury that he was not incompetent, not criminal, but merely misguided?

Janet was probably right: landing this one in the win-column would be tough.

"Good luck," she said insincerely, rising from her chair.

I sat alone in the conference room for five minutes after she'd gone, trying, with limited success, to compose myself.

Flip Talmadge was idling in the hall when I came out.

"I heard she gave you the Netherton case," he said.

"Were you listening at the door?" I shot back, impatient. Someone might be trying to kill me. James Arren was a free man, as of this very day, and now I'd managed to land a case I didn't want and to infuriate the acting-boss, all in one fell swoop. I did *not* need crap from Talmadge on top of everything else.

"Our Leader is seriously pissed," he confided, as if I hadn't noticed. "She spent weeks getting the Netherton case ready for trial, and then, *pfffft,* she's out and you're in. You should have heard her and Harvey battling that one out." He paused, and I tried to make my way around him, but he blocked me, speculating, "Maybe you knew the doctor in Tucson?" He gave my breasts a measuring glance, probably wondering if they were real, and I would have loved to backhand him then and there, even though I am really not the violent type.

Well, not usually.

I stared him down "Stay out of my face, Talmadge," I said. "I don't have time for office gossip."

He smiled and waggled his eyebrows, but he did step aside. "And a lovely face it is, too."

As I stalked down the hall to my office, I wondered, not for the first time, how so many idiots manage to get through law school.

At four-thirty, I surfaced from the depths of a pile of paperwork to call home, and Emma answered on the second ring. I could hear Bernice yelping cheerfully in the background. I tried not to think about James Arren being on the loose, not to mention Harvey's killer; I wanted to caution Emma to be careful, draw the shades, keep the doors locked, but infecting her with my paranoia would have served no purpose.

Besides, she'd had all the safety lectures.

"Hi, babe," I said, keeping my voice light. "How's my favorite niece?"

Emma was getting a little old for that joke, but she still played along, probably for my sake. She was that kind of kid—to spare my feelings, she'd pretended to believe in Santa until she was nine, when the whole charade got to be too much and she finally folded and broke the news to me that the whole Kris Kringle thing just didn't fly with her anymore. "I'm your *only* niece," she said.

In my memory, I heard another voice, Tracy's. *You're my favorite sister,* she used to say to me when we were kids, temporarily at Mom's, between foster homes, well before our grandmother's always uncertain health improved enough for her to take us in. *I'm your* only *sister*, I'd reply, right on cue.

"Everything okay at home?" I asked. *Did your father call?*

"Yeah," Emma answered, as though it were an ordinary day. "Everything's fine. Mrs. K took me to Albertson's a little while ago. Bernice needed food—she doesn't like that yucky stuff Mrs. Kredd sent over."

"Did you do your homework?"

Emma sighed, long-suffering. "Yes," she took the pains to say, drawing out the word.

"Good," I answered crisply. "I'll review it when I get home."

"Which will be when?" my niece asked, rather casually.

"Soon," I said, feeling guilty. There were times when I wished I could be a stay-at-home aunt, but the impulse always passed if I took a few slow, deep breaths. When that didn't work, I stood on my head in the corner of the womens rest room to get some blood to my brain. "While you were getting kibbles, did you buy a snack for yourself?" I was mindful of the still-dire grocery situation at our house.

"I'm okay. I had a grilled cheese sandwich after school."

"Great," I said. "I'll be home by six or so. I need to stop by the supermarket on the way. Hold down the fort, don't watch any cable TV, and don't answer the door unless you know exactly who's there."

Another sigh. Except for the part about the supermarket, it was the same speech I always made. "Right," she said, with a verbal eye-roll.

"One more thing," I said, sensing she was about to hang up.

"What?"

"I love you, kiddo."

"Cool," Emma replied. "See you." With that, the line went dead.

Smiling a little, I turned to my computer and started wading through e-mails, deleting jokes and cutesy forwards as I went. It's not that I don't have a sense of humor, and I guess there's a place for the sentimental crap otherwise intelligent people like to scatter from one end of cyberspace to the other, but that place isn't on my hard drive, damn it. I'm trying to work, here.

Heather peeked in just as I was logging off. The messages I intended to answer, all job-related, were chuffing their way out of the printer.

"Justin Netherton is here to see you," she said, and ducked a little, as if expecting me to throw something. "I'm sorry, Clare. He was on Ms. Baylin's schedule, and I forgot to switch him over to yours."

She might as well have goosed me with a cattle prod. "Damn," I muttered, and congratulated myself on my restraint. I know a few worse words.

Heather looked truly regretful, but implacable, too.

"Can you reschedule?" I was desperate.

"I don't think he'd go along with that," Heather said, checking her watch. She was taking paralegal courses at night, starting at six sharp, and it was already five-fifteen. "I'll try, but he drove all the way from Tucson, so he won't be too happy if you blow him off now."

I felt a headache bounce through my head, temple-to-temple, like a Ping-Pong ball. "All right," I said. "Send him in, but do me one favor before you go. Call Emma and tell her I'll be home closer to seven."

Heather nodded and went out.

Dr. Netherton was tall, slender, and silver-haired. His clothes were tailor-made, his shoes Italian, and he boasted a tan that would have made George Hamilton seem downright anemic by comparison. He adjusted his gold cuff links as he surveyed my office, which was such a far cry from Harvey's, and Janet's, too, that it wasn't even a whimper.

No leather couches here. No oil paintings, no well-stocked wet bar, no oversized flat-screen TV discreetly hidden behind massive carved mahogany doors.

For a moment, I cherished the fatuous hope that Netherton would turn up his nose and leave. Go back to Janet, or get himself another lawyer entirely, one with a real office instead of a hole in the wall.

No such luck.

His gaze went straight to my breasts, and I put it down to a professional interest. I was trying to be philosophical about the whole thing, even if I did grit my teeth a little. My jaw was starting to ache from biting back hasty words.

"Hello," he said, and I wasn't sure if he was greeting me or my anatomy.

"Your reputation precedes you, Dr. Netherton," I said, after offering a responding hello.

He beamed.

Just like a man to think I'd meant the statement as a compliment.

Chapter Six

Okay, so maybe I wasn't cut out to be a defense attorney. I'd been contemplating a career change anyway. I wouldn't have minded being a storm trooper, for instance, or a hanging judge.

As Dr. Netherton sat down gingerly in the chair facing my desk, I was doing some high-speed thinking on a variety of levels: first and foremost, it bothered me that Emma was essentially home alone. Suppose James tried to see her while I wasn't around? And what about Harvey's killer? It wasn't out of the realm of possibility that he or she might be watching us.

On a more mundane note—my mind always operates in at least half a dozen dimensions at once—I was wondering what I could whip up for supper that was quick, cheap, and at least passably nutritious. And there was yet another track: Why did they let letches like Justin Netherton prescribe drugs and handle scalpels?

I suppressed an urge to inquire about Sylvie Wyand, who had worked at Nipples with Loretta and me. At Freddie Loren's urging—he'd also loaned her the money to pay Netherton's fee—Sylvie had had her breasts "enhanced," and for her it had been the beginning of a nightmare. According to Loretta, who kept in touch with some of the old crowd via e-mail, she'd suffered horribly with silicone leaks and infections and unremitting pain, and was finally hospitalized several months after the operation, following a complete physical and emotional breakdown. Her then-boyfriend, a guy named Rock—unquestionably a *Jerry Springer* reject, though she'd been crazy about him—had promptly ditched her, without so much as a fare-thee-well. The word on the cyber grapevine was that he had a new woman in his life now, one with better implants.

I glanced at my watch. My jitters about Emma's safety, and my own, hadn't subsided, but obsessing was not an option. I needed to keep my mind on my work, distasteful as it seemed at the moment.

Netherton raised silvery eyebrows, the bushy kind that make me want to take a Weed Eater to them, and crossed his legs at the knees. Clearly he'd noticed my lapse; his tone was curt. "Am I taking up too much of your time, Ms.—?"

"Westbrook," I answered, and forced a civil smile, though of course he already knew who I was, since he'd gone to the trouble of requesting my services. "Clare Westbrook."

He beamed, apparently appeased, and bestowed his beneficence. "I'll call you Clare, then."

His assumption that I *wanted* him to use my first name nettled me, but there wasn't much I could do about it. If I told him to address me as "Ms. Westbrook," he would probably complain to Janet, who would in turn make my life as miserable as possible. I fumbled for his file and opened it. Why had I ever studied law? I asked myself, and not for the first time. I'd probably be happier if I'd gone to cosmetology school instead, and at least I'd have a pair of scissors in my hand much of the time, for purposes of self-defense.

Netherton cleared his throat impatiently.

I looked up. Smiles gone, his *and* mine.

"You haven't even *read my file*?" he burst out. "Are you aware, Ms. Westbrook, that my career and reputation are at stake here?"

I sighed inwardly and refrained from reminding him that my taking over the case from Janet had been *his* idea, not mine. "Dr. Netherton," I replied in a quiet and, I hoped, even tone of voice, "your case is certainly important to this firm." *If not to me.* "However, as you probably know, Mr. Kredd died recently, and things are in a state of upheaval around here. I assure you, it's temporary." I paused for a judicious breath. "I was assigned to represent you just this afternoon, and I haven't had a chance to go over the facts of the case."

Netherton folded his arms, flushed a little, probably from annoyance, rather than any sort of remorse. " 'The facts of the case' are that I'm innocent of these ridiculous charges." He paused. "I heard about Kredd," he added, somewhat grudgingly. "Too bad."

I was relieved that Netherton didn't pretend to mourn Harvey's death; he didn't give a damn, and I knew it. The good doctor was worried about saving his own ass; from what I knew of him, little else mattered.

"If you'll just let me skim through the file for a few moments," I said, in measured tones, "I'll be able to discuss the matter more intelligently."

He cleared his throat again, looked skeptical, and sat back in his chair. He kept his mouth shut, though, which I suppose was the most I could hope for, under the circumstances.

I truly wanted to prove myself wrong about Netherton as I scanned his arrest report, the written statement he'd given prior to his release, and a few cryptic notes in Harvey's handwriting, but alas, nothing I found there served to change my initial opinion. The state was alleging that Dr. Netherton had been criminally negligent in four separate cases, though Sylvie's name was not mentioned on the claimants list. Three of the women had been permanently disfigured, and one had actually died. In addition to the state charges, Netherton faced a round in civil court and a lawsuit filed by his insurance company. Without some fancy footwork on my part, he'd be lucky to come out of this with a nickel in his pocket, let alone to stay out of prison.

Because of his "standing in the community," Harvey's term, not mine, Netherton had been released on his own recognizance a few hours after his arrest. The state of Arizona had scheduled his criminal trial in ninety days.

I let out a long breath and closed the folder.

"Can you handle the job or not?" Dr. Netherton demanded, glowering. His supposed fascination with my appearance must have been diminishing by the moment. Or maybe I just didn't look all that good that day.

I wanted to sigh, but I didn't. "Yes," I said. The sad truth was, with some hard work and a measure of luck, for which I was overdue, I probably could keep him out of jail, even if I failed to save his stock portfolio and medical license. The question was, would I be able to live with myself if I did any one of those things, let alone all of them? "I'll require some time to prepare a solid defense, however. Obviously, these are serious charges."

"How long do you need?" Netherton snapped, tugging at his cuffs.

"A week, perhaps two," I replied, with no inflection whatsoever. My brain, meanwhile, was groping for a way out. Refuse to accept the case? If only to spite me, Janet would see that my contract with Harvey was enforced; I would be sued, and immediately liable for a very large sum of money. Pack up Emma and the dog and flee the country? Another bad idea, though not without its singular appeal. Running away from trouble went against everything I believed in, everything I wanted *Emma* to believe in. Ask for a payment plan, at interest rates a loan shark would be ashamed to set, and buy my way out of the agreement to work a full seven years? That amounted to exchanging one trap for another. I would probably end up working at the prosecutor's office, at an equally underwhelming salary, and though that would definitely provide job satisfaction, factoring in the debt to the Kredd estate, financial ruin was sure to follow.

"*A week or two?*" Netherton looked apoplectic. "I paid a seven-figure retainer— do you see *that* noted anywhere in my record, Ms. Westbrook?"

It was some consolation, I thought, that he hadn't called me Clare. My stomach sort of folded in on itself. I looked at the file again, and sure enough, there was a yellow receipt copy, bearing Harvey's own signature, verifying that a cool million had indeed changed hands. I felt an odd brush of sorrow, seeing the boss's name scrawled there so confidently; for a moment, I almost missed him a little, faults and all. There must have been *some* good in him, somewhere. After all, he'd loved his dog.

Thinking of Harvey made me think of his killer, and so ended my brief respite from fear.

"Yes, Doctor," I said moderately, "I'm aware that you have a substantial amount of money invested in your defense. And I assure you, we will provide the best possible representation. In order to do that, though, I will need a week to prepare, at the minimum. Two would be ideal."

"One week," Netherton crooned, leaning forward in his chair. "That's what I'm giving you. *One week*. After that, my retainer will be refunded, with interest, and I will engage another firm. Do you understand me?"

I wanted to point out that, since English

was my first language, I had managed to divine his meaning without any particular strain, but of course I didn't dare.

Did I understand him? Only too well. I'm something of an authority on sleazeballs; no matter what their social position, I can usually spot them.

"Yes," I said, that being the only response that came immediately to mind. I wondered how I would possibly get anything else done during the coming week, and still map out a decent defense. "I'll be ready."

Talk about whistling a happy tune.

We spent another hour going over all the reasons why Dr. Netherton believed himself to have been not only maligned, but singled out as the subject for a harassment campaign by the plaintiffs, their families, and the state of Arizona—the human capacity for self-deception is an amazing thing—and then, much to my relief, he left.

I waited fifteen minutes before locking up my files and heading for the back staircase. I didn't want to run into the doc in the underground parking garage; I'd be seeing more than enough of him during the next three months as it was. Besides, it had been a long day, I was quietly terrified, and I couldn't keep up the dedicated-attorney front another minute.

I climbed into my practical blue Saturn, which had been delivered to my house that morning by the repair people, engaged the locks, and started the ignition. Half an hour later, I was in Carefree, the small town next door to Cave Creek, wheeling a grocery cart through Albertson's.

Maybe it was the ordinary nature of the task that lulled me into a false sense of security. It was dark when I left the store, and as I went toward my car, feeling virtuous for having made comparatively rational food choices, I spotted someone sitting behind the wheel.

My heart seized with all the ferocity of a leg cramp, and I froze, staring, too startled to reach for my cell phone or even turn around and hustle back into the store. I looked around; there were a few cars in the parking lot, but I couldn't see another human being.

I took a step closer, peering through the window on the driver's side.

The intruder was a woman, sitting rigidly, hands on the wheel, staring straight ahead. I ran my tongue over my lips, which were suddenly dry, though my heart had mobilized itself again, racing.

Don't be a ninny, Clare, I thought. *This is just some confused person who's gotten into the wrong car by mistake.*

Fat chance, answered the left side of my brain.

Still holding on to the handle of the shopping cart with one hand, I rapped on the window with the other and said, "Excuse me?"

Nothing. The woman didn't even turn her head.

I leaned down, reaching for the door handle at the same time.

"Hello?"

No response. I opened the door and the woman immediately toppled toward me, but before I could let go of the shopping cart and use both hands to catch her, she fell, her head striking the pavement with a sound like the thump of knuckles against a melon. She was young, wearing shabby jeans and a skimpy T-shirt.

She was also dead.

Chapter Seven

A blossom of crimson covered the center of the girl's forehead.

I screamed, and the cart rolled away, crashing hard into a neighboring car. My purse clunked to the ground, and I knelt, grasping the girl's wrist, searching in vain for a pulse. A man approached, from the periphery of my vision, and fresh terror surged through me. I groped for my purse, and the cell phone inside it.

"Jesus!" the man cried, seeing the body. "What's going on here?"

Somehow, I focused on the supermarket logo on his polo shirt. He was a store employee, not a mad killer. I began to rock slightly on my knees, and the random thought crossed my mind that my panty hose were history. "Call the police," I said. "Please—just call the police."

By the time the first cruiser screeched into the parking lot, a crowd had gathered—

a man in golf shorts was taking digital video of the scene—while I leaned against one of the lampposts, arms folded, knees like jelly. A kindly older woman had tried to persuade me to wait in her Buick, but for some reason I needed to stand.

Sonterra arrived within fifteen minutes of the uniforms, which was not exactly seren- dipity, since I'd called him on my cell phone while the store manager and I were waiting for the first wave of cops. I had answered a few questions immediately—no, I hadn't heard anything, and yes, I would have no- ticed a gunshot; no, I hadn't seen anyone; no, I didn't shoot her myself—but procedure is to wait for the detectives and let them do the serious grilling. Enter Sonterra.

"Holy shit," he said, after a good look at the body. He beckoned one of the uniforms over. "Do we have an ID?" he asked, and someone handed him the victim's wallet. His partner, Eddie Columbia, was with him; it was Eddie who noticed I was shivering and draped his suit coat over my shoulders.

"You okay, Clare?" he asked.

I nodded, though of course I *wasn't* okay. I'd just found a fresh corpse in the driver's seat of my car, after all.

Sonterra conversed with the other cops for a while, had a word with the EMTs and the people from the M.E.'s office, then sauntered over to where I stood, still trembling inside Eddie's coat.

"Who was she?" I heard someone ask in my voice. I felt oddly disembodied, as though I were floating somewhere slightly behind and to the left of myself.

"Her name was Denise Robbins," Sonterra said, glancing back at the dead girl, who was being zipped into a body bag for transport to the morgue, where further indignities awaited. "Seventeen. According to her sheet, she was a part-time prostitute and a shoplifter. Did you know her, Clare?"

I shook my head. "I've never seen her before."

Sonterra took a light but firm hold on my elbow and squired me over to his SUV. I climbed into the passenger seat, and he started the engine and turned on the heat, then came around to lean against the frame of my door.

"Was anybody following you?"

"I didn't see anyone," I said, and another violent shudder coursed through me. It was probably seventy degrees out, but I felt as though I'd never be warm again.

"You realize, of course, that the perp probably thought she was you."

I swallowed hard, managed a nod. Denise Robbins hadn't resembled me in any significant way, but it was dark and she'd been in my car, and that had apparently been enough to earn her a bullet. I pictured her bloody forehead; she'd taken the same kind of hit Harvey had.

I sat rigid, remembering my niece, and started to scramble out of Sonterra's rig. "Emma—she's home alone—"

Sonterra put a hand to my shoulder and stopped me. "I sent a car over there first thing," he said quietly. "She'll be all right until you get home."

That was when I broke down. I guess it was the magnitude of my relief, coupled with the shock of another murder.

Sonterra reached past me, took a travel-size package of tissue from the glove compartment, and shoved it into my lap. I plucked, blew, plucked again, and dried my eyes.

"What the hell is happening?" I whispered. "What was that girl doing in my car, anyway?"

"She might have been trying to steal it," Sonterra answered, watching me with those dark, inscrutable eyes, "but since there's no evidence that anybody tampered with the ignition, my guess would be that she was either looking for some stray cash or just goofing off. Maybe she was high—we'll know more after the autopsy."

I cringed at the attendant images. "You'll have to impound the car," I said, musing aloud.

Sonterra nodded. "Sorry about that," he said quietly, and looked around as they loaded the body bag into the back of an ambulance. The uniforms were writing up reports, canvassing for witnesses, dispersing the gawking bystanders. "The interior's a mess," he went on. "You wouldn't want to drive it the way it is."

I shuddered again. "No," I agreed.

A policeman came toward us, pushing my shopping cart. "These things belong to you, ma'am?" he asked, after a nod to Sonterra.

I nodded.

"I'm afraid there was some damage to another vehicle," he said. He was young, slightly overweight, and very earnest. "If you'll give me your insurance card, I'll take care of the report."

I fumbled for my purse, found my wallet, pulled out the card. Sonterra relayed it to the officer, then unloaded my groceries into the back of his SUV.

"I'd like to go home," I said when he'd finished.

"Should be okay," he replied. He went back to confer with the other cops, collected my insurance card, and returned. The process probably took less than ten minutes, but it seemed like an hour to me.

Neither Sonterra nor I spoke during the short drive to my condo. There was a squad car parked in the driveway, just as Sonterra had promised, and I saw Emma peer through the front window before rushing out to meet us. Mrs. K and two uniformed police officers followed.

"I was scared," Emma told me, her tone accusing. "I thought you were dead, and they"—she cocked a thumb at the cops— "just didn't want to tell me."

"I'm obviously not dead," I said gently. I sensed that Emma wanted to hurl herself into my arms—God knows, I could have used a hug myself—but she held herself apart, and stiff.

"What happened?" It wasn't a question; it was a demand. Emma had already lost her mother; losing me would mean she was alone in the world—except for James Arren, of course.

I put an arm around her. "Come inside," I said. "I'll tell you all about it."

Sonterra proceeded to unload the groceries, and the two policemen went to help, but Mrs. K hovered, a mother hen with a caftan and hard hair.

"I made a tuna casserole," my neighbor said. "It's in your oven, on low heat."

"Thanks." I managed a shaky smile. "For everything."

Mrs. K nodded. "Call if you need me," she instructed. "No matter what time it is."

I promised that I would, and she retreated into her own condo as Emma and I went into ours.

Sonterra came in through the door to the garage, set the supermarket bags on the kitchen table, and began putting things away. The two cops he'd sent to watch over Emma, apparently dismissed, did not reappear.

I sat on the couch, and Emma huddled beside me, though a little apart. Bernice bounded into her lap and sat there, looking from one of us to the other.

"Tell me what happened," Emma insisted when I hesitated.

I raised my eyes, and my gaze locked with Sonterra's through the doorway to the kitchen. He gave a slight nod.

I related the story for at least the third time since discovering the body, and Emma listened with wide eyes, clasping the dog to her chest.

"Oh, my God," Emma said, when I'd finished the gruesome tale. "Clare, somebody wants to kill you! They thought that woman was you—"

I took her hand, squeezed it. "Maybe," I said.

" 'Maybe,' nothing," Emma ranted. "Do you think it was my dad? I mean, he would know what you look like up close, but it's so dark—"

A glance at Sonterra revealed just what I'd expected: he was listening shamelessly.

I sighed. "I suppose it could have been him," I admitted, after a little thought, "but the shooting had certain . . . similarities to

Harvey's murder. And James was still in prison when that happened."

Emma erupted off the couch, started pacing up and down next to the coffee table. The little dog went along for the ride.

"If it wasn't him, who was it?" she raved.

"Honey, we don't know," I said. I indicated Sonterra with a motion of my head. "The police will find this person and arrest them."

"Like you believe that!" Emma blurted. When I was a kid, the police were regular visitors at my mother's house, but they never did anything but write reports, issue warnings, and drive away, leaving Tracy and me stranded at Dysfunction Junction. I hadn't seen much in the intervening years to change my mind, and as a result I had very litle confidence in the boys in blue; an opinion, I realized belatedly, that I needn't have shared with my very impressionable young niece.

Naturally, my antipathy toward cops, carefully moderated though it was, had always been a sore spot between Sonterra and me.

"We have to trust them," I said.

Sonterra rolled his eyes, and Emma glared at me.

"What do you want me to do, Emma?" I asked, waxing impatient and, to my surprise, hungry. The scent of Mrs. K's tuna casserole was enticing. "We have to go on living. I can't move us into an underground bunker."

Apparently dissatisfied with my answer, Emma turned and ran up the stairs, banging her bedroom door shut behind her.

I sat there on the couch for a few moments, numb, and then got up, walked into the kitchen, shouldering my way past Sonterra, and washed my hands. That done, I picked up a couple of pot holders and pulled the casserole out of the oven.

Sonterra didn't wait for an invitation; he took three plates from the cupboard and set the table.

I looked at the third plate. "Emma won't be joining us," I said.

"Yeah," Sonterra countered, "she will. She just needed to slam something."

Sure enough, by the time we sat down to eat, my niece had returned, her expression at once sullen and chagrined, Bernice in tow. She took a generous portion of the tuna-noodle concoction, feeding the occasional morsel to the dog, who waited patiently at her feet. She and Sonterra chatted as if it were an ordinary night, but Emma barely looked at me, and Sonterra made no discernible effort to include me in the conversation. Just as well, I figured, since the things going around in my head just then had no place at the dinner table.

After the meal, the team effort between Emma and Sonterra continued. He cleared the table; she loaded the dishwasher. I just sat there, staring at the wall, trying to figure out who wanted me dead.

Not counting James, who hated me because I'd testified against him after the convenience store robbery, there were probably only a couple of hundred.

Emma excused herself, once the dishwasher was running, and vanished, and Sonterra brewed a pot of coffee. I didn't even ask if it was decaf; I didn't expect to sleep that night anyway.

"Why did Emma ask if you thought her dad was the one who tried to kill you tonight?" Sonterra asked. I should have known he hadn't stayed to hold my hand.

He knew very little about my past, considering how intimate we'd once been, and I sorted through my befuddled brain, going over things I didn't mind telling him, and things I figured were my business and no one else's, and trying to decide which were which.

"James Arren, my ex-brother-in-law, killed my sister," I said. "Since there was no love lost between him and me, and since my testimony was at least partly the reason he got six years at Yuma, I guess it was natural for Emma to wonder if he'd tried to do me in."

Sonterra frowned. It was his processing frown, slightly different from the disapproving one, or the one that means you're-full-of-crap. "He's out of jail, I take it?"

A sigh. "Since yesterday."

"Have you heard from him?"

I shook my head. The coffeemaker chortled, and since Sonterra had done the honors by making the stuff in the first place, I got out of my chair and poured us each a cup. He took his black—funny how you remember things like that—while I used a couple of packets of sweetener.

"It probably wasn't him," Sonterra concluded. "As you pointed out to Emma, the

M.O. was similar to Harvey Kredd's murder, and unless this Arren character was on work release or something, he didn't have the opportunity." He paused, sipped his coffee, studied my face. Sonterra was big on nuance; it comes in handy in his profession. "Why didn't you tell me your sister was murdered?" he asked presently. "And why did he only get six years?"

"We weren't exactly into baring our souls, you and I," I pointed out moderately. I might have given the words more of an edge, but I was still pretty shaken up. It isn't every day a person stumbles across a dead woman, after all. "And the six years was for armed robbery, not murder. The cops never believed that Tracy was murdered. They thought she skipped out."

Sonterra raised his eyebrows, drank some more coffee. Cops must have that stuff running in their veins, instead of blood; I'd seen him put away a couple of pots all by himself, then sleep like a baby. Of course, there had been a couple of hours of sweaty sex in between, and I'd slept pretty well myself. "There must have been a reason the police thought she took to her heels," he ventured. He was on delicate ground, and he knew it. Like I said, Sonterra was good with nuances.

"Yeah," I said, with quiet bitterness. "Tracy was a little like Denise Robbins, when she was younger, except for the prostitution part. She had some run-ins with the cops, did some drugs. But she turned around when she had Emma—she was a completely different person. The law disregarded that part of the story, though. To them, once a bad girl, always a bad girl. They went through the motions, then let the whole thing fall through the cracks."

"No body was found," Sonterra surmised.

I was defensive. "That doesn't mean she's not dead."

He shook his head. "No, it doesn't," he said. "But you're a lawyer, Clare. You know how hard it is to make a murder case without a body."

"So they just gave up!"

For a moment, I thought he was going to take my hand, but he evidently thought better of the idea. I wasn't sure how I felt about that, relieved, or disappointed. "Tell me more about it," he said.

I reviewed the facts in my mind, and related them. Tracy had been divorced from

James Arren for some six months at the time of her disappearance, working at Nipples with Loretta and Sylvie and me.

Emma was seven years old at the time, and one rainy day, Tracy had left Emma with me, after picking her up from school, saying only that she had something really important to take care of, promising to be back before my shift started at the club, speeding away in her ancient station wagon.

I'd never seen my sister again.

For a time, I couldn't track James down, either, and I believed, very briefly, that the two of them had gone off together on impulse, with some crazy idea of starting over. But when a week had passed and Tracy still didn't come back for Emma, or even call to see how she was, I filed a missing-person report. In a matter of days, James turned up again, flush with money, drinking a lot, bragging to his buddies at Nipples that he was a free man now. I'd tried to talk to him after his pals staggered out of the bar, and while he was saying nothing about Tracy, not to me, anyway, he did flash some cash and invite me to sleep with him.

I declined, of course, and none too politely. But I kept bugging him about Tracy, and he kept drinking, and he mentioned the robbery. Maybe he was trying to impress me.

I played it cool until he left, then called the cops. They took the drunken confession seriously, and later found enough evidence to make it stick, but my suspicions about Tracy's disappearance didn't seem to resonate with them. James had been arrested and put on trial, and there was still no sign of my sister.

A couple of months went by, and by then, the cops had written me off as an irritating hysteric. In desperation, I arranged to visit James in jail, which took some nerve on my part, given our history. I probably wouldn't have gotten in if I hadn't brought him cigarette money.

He glared at me through the Plexiglas for a while, trying to wilt me, I guess, but I kept asking. Finally, he said he didn't know where "the bitch" went, and didn't care. His eyes told me something different, however— there was a glint of triumph there, evil on a scale I had never seen before, even when I was very small, and Mom was bringing home guys whose pictures were probably pinned to the bulletin board at the post office.

I'd kept my cool, somehow, and asked him to sign papers releasing Emma to my permanent custody. He'd smirked and flatly refused. He loved his daughter, he'd said.

I'd barely been able to eat or sleep for a week after that little encounter.

Eventually, the courts granted me provisional custody of Emma. I continued to insist that Tracy had been murdered. The police thought differently. Now it had been nearly seven years since she disappeared, and I was no closer to knowing what had happened to her than I had been in the beginning.

Sonterra took all this in as I spoke, weighing and measuring, keeping his own counsel. "I'll have Arren checked out," he said when I finally finished, and pulled out his cell phone.

I listened while he made the calls.

"I'm not leaving," he said after hanging up.

All the appropriate alarms went off in my head, but when it came to Sonterra, my normal good judgment had a tendency to lapse. I'm only human; I wanted him close to me, for that night at least, wanted what I knew he could give me.

"What about Emma?" I asked.

"We'll be quiet," he said.

Right, I thought. I felt a charge in my midsection. "Okay," I said. I didn't dare meet his eyes.

Emma was asleep by ten o'clock, no doubt as emotionally exhausted as I was, and Sonterra and I were in my room by eleven, staring at each other from either side of the bed.

"This is dumb," I said.

"Take off your clothes," he replied.

It seemed like a good idea at the time, so I did it. Sonterra didn't even pretend not to watch; his dark eyes burned laser-hot and made my flesh sizzle wherever his gaze landed, which was everywhere. Once I was naked, he took off his jacket, unbuckled his shoulder holster and set it aside, tugged his T-shirt up over his head, unsnapped his jeans.

"Bad idea," I said, addressing myself as much as him.

He took my hand, led me into the small master bath, started the shower running. We lathered each other, between frantic, can't-get-enough kisses, and then Sonterra began working his personal magic. He rinsed the soap from my body and used the hand sprayer to good effect, getting me thoroughly worked up while he nibbled at my lower lip, my ear, the side of my neck, and, finally, my breasts, one and then the other.

My fingers entangled in his hair, I held him close, and when he began kissing his way down my body, I sank against the shower stall with a combination whimper and groan.

You're going to hate yourself in the morning, warned the little lawyer in my head.

Ah, answered another part of me, the red-hot lover, raised in the wrong part of Tucson, *but right now, at this moment, I'm riding high.*

"Riding" was the operative word, as it turned out. Sonterra knelt, bracing me against the wall of the shower, positioning one of my legs over his right shoulder, and one over his left. When he moved in to take what he wanted, I gave a strangled cry and my thighs tightened compulsively around him.

He cut me zero slack; he wanted to drive

me out of my mind, and he knew just how to go about it. He teased and suckled, and it wasn't long before I was caught up in the throes of an orgasm so elemental that every cell in my body seemed to resonate with it.

A lot of men would have stopped then, satisfied themselves, but Sonterra wasn't through with me. He kept right on doing what he was doing, and before I'd recovered from the first climax, I was well on my way to another one. And then another.

Only when I sagged against him, bones melted, totally spent, did he show any mercy at all, untangling my legs from around his head, lifting me into his arms, carrying me no farther than the fluffy rug on the bathroom floor. There, he laid me down and had me as thoroughly, as completely, as I'd ever been had. Our bodies, wet and slick from the shower, clashed over and over, and if he hadn't put a gentle hand over my mouth when I reached the final, highest pinnacle, the whole neighborhood would have known exactly what we were up to.

During the next couple of hours, we did sweet battle in our own singular fashion, and it was bliss. I was outside myself, transported, swamped in fevered sensations that separated me from the terrifying, as well as the ordinary, aspects of my life.

Early the next morning, I awakened in my bed, alone. Sonterra had gone back to crime fighting. I lay there for a while, gathering all the scattered pieces of my mind and spirit, reassembling my psyche, and gradually coming to terms with cold reality.

Interlude or no interlude, things hadn't really changed between Sonterra and me. We had no common ground upon which to build anything lasting. With us, it was all about sex and, as good as we were together, that wouldn't be enough.

Chapter Eight

Sonterra had left the keys to his SUV on the kitchen counter, next to the coffeemaker, along with a note. *"No smoking, drinking, and/or stray corpses, please. I'll call you later. S."*

"He likes you," Emma said, admiring Sonterra's fancy ride from the living room window. If she'd figured out that he'd spent most of the night in my bed, she gave no outward indication of it, and I wasn't inclined to ask.

"Hmmm," I said. I hadn't even had coffee, and I was already hedging. Damn, but I'm good.

My niece turned to face me. "Why can't you trust him, Clare?"

I cleared my throat. Looked away; made myself look back. "It's complicated," I said. "Tony is a good man—brave, thrifty, honest, loyal, and true. All that. But our jobs and our philosophies put us at odds in ways you can't begin to understand."

"Bull," Emma said, jutting out her chin, looking and sounding so much like Tracy that, for a moment, she took my breath away. She leaned to scoop Bernice, who was scrabbling at the leg of her jeans, up into her arms. "I understand a lot more than you think."

I was afraid of that, but I wasn't fool enough to say so. "Let's have some breakfast and get going," I said. "I'll drop you off at school." Emma normally rode the bus, but with all that had been going on lately, I could hardly bring myself to let her out of my sight. I had already recruited Mrs. K to pick her up.

"Coward," she said. "You don't play fair. You want me to open up, talk to you about everything that's on my mind, but you hold out on me, Clare. You hold out on everybody."

Thirteen, I reminded myself silently, is a difficult age.

"Get ready for school," I said, and went back upstairs to shower.

I put on a brave face, along with my makeup and the requisite lawyer suit, and after dropping Emma at school and watching until she was safely inside, I headed for the offices of Kredd and Associates. All the while, my niece's accusation was going around and around in my head.

Was she right? Was I an emotional coward?

I hadn't reached a conclusion by the time I arrived at the office, parked Sonterra's rig in the underground lot, and took the elevator to the third floor.

I nodded at Heather as I passed the reception desk, trying not to notice the avid curiosity in her face, dropped my briefcase and purse off in my cubicle, and headed for the coffeemaker.

A box of designer doughnuts lay in wait when I walked into the employee lounge. I was wearing half a pound of concealer under each eye, and trying to project the image of a normal person, the kind who doesn't find bodies in supermarket parking lots and then spend half the night making love with the wrong man.

I managed to ignore the doughnuts as I helped myself to a mug of stout brew, but they were definitely calling to me, and I could almost taste their sweet glaze. Not wanting that extra ten pounds to become twenty, I opted for a quick getaway, nearly dousing Janet with my coffee when I turned around.

She was automatically annoyed, being Janet, but managed one of those smiles that look as though they might have been scraped into her face with the blunt end of a nail. "Good morning, Ms. Westbrook," she trilled. "Are we late this morning?"

I took note of the royal "we" and glanced at the clock on the wall above one of the cheap, uncomfortable sofas specifically chosen to discourage lounging around on company time.

Janet was shoehorned into a navy blue suit, just right for a court appearance, and her eyes were even smaller and beadier than usual. "I'm not sure what your schedule is, Janet," I said sweetly, and with a blinding smile, cultivated back in my Nipples days, when I wanted to keep certain customers in line but still score a decent tip when they paid their check, "but I'm not due to arrive for another twenty minutes. That makes me early, not late."

A small crease appeared between her eyebrows, which needed plucking, but she recovered quickly, favoring me with another rigid smile. She inspected my good tweed pants outfit, bought at one of Nordstrom's half-yearly sales with my second or third paycheck from Kredd and Associates. "Do you have a case scheduled for today?" she asked, leaving me to wonder whether she found my apparel suitable or not. In the final analysis, I didn't give a damn what she thought. I was pretty cavalier, I guess, for somebody with my limited financial options, but there it is. Discretion probably *is* the better part of valor, but I've never managed to integrate the concept beyond the most superficial level. Maybe it's my lower-middle-class background.

"Show time isn't until two o'clock," I answered pleasantly, and in my own sweet time. "The client is Trevor Trent. Between now and then, I have a lot of research and thinking to do."

Heather had followed me into the lounge, and she was watching me with a sort of gruesome fascination. "You found a body in your car last night," she said, sounding awed. "It was on the ten o'clock news."

I closed my eyes for an instant, mentally squared my shoulders. "Yes," I said.

Janet was staring at me in shock. Apparently, like me, she had neither tuned in to the broadcast nor opened the morning newspaper. "What—?"

A small crowd had gathered, all but encircling me. I began to feel claustrophobic. I explained what had happened the night before, as simply and briefly as I could.

"Good God," Janet said when I'd finished. "This person—whoever it is—must have thought—"

"That Denise Robbins was me," I said, with a rueful nod.

"The woman sustained a head wound? Like Harvey did?"

I nodded again. "Same M.O.," I admitted.

"This is terrible," Janet fretted, and her eyes lost focus, a clear sign that she was thinking. I was just beginning to believe I might have misjudged her when she went on. "I'm not sure you should be here. If someone is after you, then the rest of us are in danger just because you're around." *And thanks so much for your caring and concern.*

"I suppose that's true," I said evenly.

Janet was still reflective. "Perhaps you should work from home for a while."

"Fine by me," I replied. I might have been talking to a post; my colleague was still staring through me, her gaze fixed, and I doubt she heard a word I said.

"A great deal depends on your handling of the Netherton case, of course," Ms. Baylin mused on, "and it was important to Harvey that the Trevor Trent situation be handled with the utmost care and finesse. Trevor's father is—was—a good friend to him."

I felt heat rise in my cheeks. I might have been a *touch* defensive, and it bothered me that most of the staff got to listen in while Janet decided whether it was safe to have me around or not. My own well-being didn't seem to be an issue.

"I'll do my best," I said. *And my best is pretty damn good.*

Both of Janet's eyeballs were pointed in the same direction again. "Until further notice, Ms. Westbrook, I think you should keep a low profile. Stay out of the office as much as possible."

"No problem," I said, and started for the door.

"I want a full report," Janet called after me, with a mild grudge in her voice. "Win or lose. Leave it on my voice mail if you can't reach me directly."

I might have saluted if I'd been facing her—I admit it, I'm something of a smart-ass—but fortunately I'd already turned my back, and gotten as far as the door. "No problem," I replied cheerfully. No problem, that is, unless I didn't get poor little Trevor off the hook for ramming a restaurant with his father's car. In that event, Trevor would have a *big* problem, and so would I.

I returned to my cubicle and was gathering files and computer disks when the receptionist put through the call I'd been braced for ever since my conversation with Mike Fletcher, and dreading.

"He says his name is James Arren."

Chapter Nine

I pushed the blinking button on my phone. "Hello, James," I said, using my best courtroom voice.

"Clare," James said, making a smarmy caress of the word. "You've really come up in the world, girl. From Nipples to a high-toned Scottsdale law firm. That's quite a jump. Tell me, do you wear that silk-screened T-shirt and those little shorts when you go to court? The sight of you in that outfit would sway any red-blooded judge."

I closed my eyes and, by calling upon every sensible instinct I possessed, held my temper and my tongue.

James chuckled at my silence. "I'm an upstanding citizen now," he said. "I've got a job—not as fancy as yours, but good—and I'm engaged, too. Monica's a librarian, with a nice little house out in Chandler. I'll be moving in right after the wedding."

I braced myself. Waited.

"My lawyer figures I can get custody of Emma without much trouble, now that I'm doing so well. What do you think of that, Clare?"

"You know what I think," I said quietly. "And how the devil did you get hooked up with a librarian?"

He laughed, though I certainly hadn't meant the question as a joke. "The Internet is a wonderful thing. I 'met' Monica in a chat room, and we hit it off. Started writing each other, and e-mailing, and before we knew it, we were in love."

I felt sick, but it had nothing to do with James's impending nuptials. I'd gotten snagged way back on the word "custody." I dropped into my chair, grateful that my former brother-in-law couldn't see my face. "Before the cartoon birds appear, chirping a happy melody, let me just say that your Monica must need deep therapy if she's picking up prisoners in chat rooms. Does she know you murdered your last wife?"

"Now, now," James scolded, in an oily tone that made me want to find him and rip his lips off, "don't be like that. You should be *happy* for me, Clare. After all, Monica and I are going to be able to provide a real home for Emma."

"Emma *has* a real home," I said. "And I'll die before I turn her over to you."

"Let's hope it doesn't come to that," James said benignly.

"Is that a threat?"

"Wouldn't it be convenient for you if it was?" he countered. "You could just call your cop boyfriend, make a complaint, and get me sent back to the slammer. I'm not stupid enough to give you that kind of ammunition." He paused, while I mused on the fact that he knew about Sonterra; obviously, Emma had told him, in her letters. When he went on, his voice had taken on a hard edge. "I want to see my daughter. It would be best if you didn't get in my way."

I concentrated on my breathing, determined to stay calm. "You can *count* on my getting in your way," I answered. "At every turn."

"Then I guess we've got a fight on our hands."

"Guess so," I replied.

"About my reunion with Emma," James said. "Monica and I were thinking tomorrow night. Dinner and a movie, just the three of us. What time shall I pick her up?"

My right temple began to throb; I rubbed it with my fingertips. "I still have legal custody of Emma," I pointed out, hoping I sounded reasonable. I certainly didn't *feel* that way. "And you're not entitled to unsupervised visits. Which means, if Emma goes, so do I."

James let out a long and expressive sigh. "What do you think we're going to do, Clare? Take Emma and disappear?"

"It wouldn't be the first time someone disappeared on your watch, would it?" I countered. "That's the deal, James. Take it or leave it."

"You're very confident."

"You're just figuring that out?"

Another sigh. "All right. We'll meet at the restaurant, and go on to the movie. I'll get back to you with times and places."

"I can hardly wait."

"I didn't kill her, Clare." He actually sounded sincere. No great trick; he'd been a con man before he went into prison. Six years in the joint would have given him time to polish his bullshitting skills.

"Right," I said. My hand was trembling as

I hung up the phone, and for a while, I just sat there in my chair, light-headed and weak with anger, frustration, and grief.

I managed to drive Sonterra's SUV all the way back to my place without finding a body, though. I guess that was progress.

Chapter Ten

I was still reeling over the telephone conversation with James four hours later, when I stepped into a courtroom in downtown Phoenix, a nervous, perfectly groomed Trevor Trent close on my heels. He was just nineteen and blessed—or cursed—with the kind of good looks that would fit in well on Cape Cod, or up at Kennebunkport.

"You seem a little distracted," he fussed, in a petulant undertone, when we took our places at the defense table. The previous session had just ended, and Jeffrey Wade, from the D.A.'s office, was slipping a fat file into his briefcase, looking very pleased with himself. A crew-cut man in orange jail garb was being led away by bailiffs.

Another one off the streets. Was I wrong to want to punch the air with my fist when it wasn't even my triumph?

"Well, I'm *not* distracted," I told the accused, in a brisk tone. "Sit down, Trevor, and do not speak again unless you are spoken to—*capisce*?"

He fell into his assigned chair with a disgusted sigh.

"Hi, Clare," Jeffrey said. Trevor might have been invisible, for all the notice my colleague gave him. "Sorry to hear about Harvey."

I'll bet you were, I thought, but without rancor, since the man was at least going through the motions, and out loud I said, "Thanks." Harvey had been the bane of the prosecution's existence, of course. While the D.A. and his people, being normal human beings, with a few inevitable exceptions, probably hadn't erupted in cheers and huzzahs at the news of my employer's demise, there had to be *some* joy in Mudville, if only because a thorn had been pulled from their collective sides.

Jeff, a regular sort in his early thirties, finally slanted a glance at Trevor, who was staring off into space and fiddling with his tasteful silk tie. His devoted parents were looking on anxiously from the front row of spectator seats. "Good luck," Jeff said, making a point of addressing the sentiment to me alone.

A moment later, I realized his words had been slightly more than polite chitchat. Pete Alexander, the D.A.'s top gun, had just entered the courtroom. He nodded to Jeff when they passed in the aisle, and gave me a sparse smile as he swung his briefcase onto the surface of the other table.

"Ms. Westbrook," he said, with cordial dispatch. I had been acknowledged, then mentally filed away under "no problem."

Shit, I thought, already framing the excuses I'd make to Janet for losing the Trent case. Alexander, fifty-ish, handsome in a quietly cynical, pipe-and-elbow-patches sort of way, was one of the biggest fishes in the judiciary pond, and he had a reputation for eating minnows like me in two bites. "Mr. Alexander," I responded, feigning unshakable confidence.

I suspect he saw through my act.

To my surprise, he approached. He looked Trevor over, plainly found him wanting, and met my eyes. "If you ever want a real job, Ms. Westbrook," he said, "call me."

I couldn't very well say that I would have walked through fire to work for the D.A., especially with my client sitting right there, looking at some serious time. I couldn't even risk a smile. So I just lifted my chin and held Alexander's gaze.

After that little exchange, things moved with the jostling speed of an army tank stuck in fourth gear and headed for the edge of a cliff. Trevor, the judge, the six-person jury, and the spectators melded into a blur roiling at the periphery of my vision.

Alexander made his case, listing the injuries Trevor had caused and giving facts and figures on the damages to the restaurant, and I made mine, without so much as a tremor in my voice or a quiver in my hands, trotting out an expensive expert or two, arguing that Trevor was a bright and patently misunderstood young man, and should be given a second chance. Obviously, making Trevor look like a solid citizen with a promising future in, say, Congress, was a challenge, but I rose to it, and I think I made a credible case, even if it *was* mostly sheep-dip.

The jury was out for twenty-five minutes, something of a record for brevity in superior court, and their verdict was "guilty."

Trevor promptly began to hyperventilate, once the word came down, and his mother and father rushed from their seats behind us to clutch him to their bosoms, patting and bemoaning. I hated the desperate sorrow I saw in their faces; like most parents, they'd believed in their son, and cherished great dreams for him. If this conviction stuck—there would, of course, be as many appeals as necessary to win an acquittal—Trevor's life, from their viewpoint at least, was essentially over. He would do time.

Did they allow ex-cons to join country clubs?

I asked that bail be set, and my request was granted, though the sum was astronomical. I led the way out of the courtroom, hoping to serve as a barrier between the Trent family and the reporters waiting outside, silently planning the speech I would make to Janet when I got back to Sonterra's car and ferreted out my cell phone.

Trevor Trent, Sr., took my shoulder in a hard grip and wrenched me around to face him. His refined features were contorted with cold fury. "You are incompetent, Ms. Westbrook," he snarled, "and if my son goes to jail, I will personally see that you pay for it!"

I opened my mouth, closed it again.

People streamed past us on all sides, and I felt dizzy.

I watched, numb, as the Trents scrambled into a limousine waiting at the curb and sped off, and when I turned around, Tony Sonterra was standing right there in my face, so close I could smell his cologne. Aramis. My favorite.

"Hello, Counselor," he said. "Fancy meeting you here."

Fancy that. I was driving his SUV. Maybe he'd planted a homing device in the damn thing. "What do you want?"

He grinned, unruffled. "My car?" he suggested, with a slight lilt in his voice. Lord, but the sight of him made my heartbeat skitter. It was pure Latin magic, that smile of his, with a dash of Irish mischief to up the wattage. For a moment, I forgot about Harvey's death, Emma's and my dinner date with James Arren, Trevor Trent's conviction, and the unavoidable call to Janet. But just for a moment.

Sonterra wasted no time in spoiling the effect of my little brain vacation. "Why don't you just give it up?" he asked, having deduced, evidently, that I'd just lost an important case. Trust Sonterra to rub it in. "Find a decent job. Put that fancy degree of yours to good use and go to bat for the good guys for once?"

We'd had this conversation before, to no discernible advantage whatsoever. I glowered at him, but it was mostly bravado. I'd had a long day, and it was about to get longer. "Since you obviously missed the first day of Criminal Justice 101," I said, "let me bring you up to speed, Detective. In this country, *everyone* has a right to the best available legal representation, and they're innocent until proven guilty."

Sonterra squinted at me, though the grin, now quizzical, was still in place. "Lighten up, Clare," he said. "I was just kidding."

I let out a long sigh. "It was a bloodbath in there," I confided. A TV-news crew had set up on the sidewalk nearby, and the bad news was going out over the airwaves even as we spoke. In another five minutes, my cell phone would ring, Janet would tell me I was fired, and I'd be left with no way to pay off the debt I owed Harvey's estate. I even pictured Emma and me in rags, selling pencils over by the dog track on Washington Street, which would have been an improvement over her going to live with James and Monica, the disturbed librarian.

"I gathered that," he replied, with gentle humor. "The Trents looked ready to chew their way through a chain-link fence, and Alexander was swaggering when he came down the steps." He curved a finger under my chin. "Come on, Counselor," he chided, "cheer up. Or did *you* miss the first day of law school, where some professor probably broke the news that, hey, you win some, you lose some."

"Duly noted," I said, a little stiffly.

"How about I drop you at your place?" he said.

There were things inside me that were still thrumming from Sonterra's *last* visit to my place. On the other hand, I needed a ride, since my car was still in police custody.

When it comes to Sonterra, I have the personal resolve of a jellyfish on my best day, and losing a case only made it worse. Besides, I wanted to tell him about the phone call from James and find out what he'd learned about Harvey's case, and Denise Robbins's murder, if anything.

"All right," I said, and I wasn't proud of

the little thrill of anticipation I felt at the prospect of passing time with him, even without making mad, passionate love.

"Come on," he said, and put an arm loosely around my waist.

I let him squire me to the SUV, where I gave up the keys. After opening the passenger door for me, he got behind the wheel.

While he was pulling out of the lot, I fished my cell phone out of my purse and dialed Janet's number. Best get it over with.

"You're not going to like this," I said, avoiding Sonterra's gaze, when her voice mail picked up. "We lost the first round." I disconnected, then called Emma at home. I let out my breath when I heard her voice.

My niece sounded distracted, but she was where she belonged, and unharmed, and for the moment, nothing else mattered. I said good-bye, hung up, and stared straight ahead. The traffic blurred into a congested gob.

"Okay, Clare," Sonterra said, when I didn't speak right away. "What's up?"

"I've got a problem."

"Besides the dead body in your car and

getting stomped in the courtroom this afternoon, I presume?"

I bit my upper lip. I was so glib in court, but with Sonterra, my language skills too often failed me. "James Arren called me today."

"Your sister's ex-husband?"

"My sister's murderer," I clarified.

"And?"

"He wants to see Emma." Good thing I wasn't driving; the rush hour tangle was something else, even for Phoenix.

"You knew that was coming," he reminded me.

"Yeah," I said, and let out an audible breath. "But now he's talking custody. He's got a responsible job, for once in his life, and he's getting married. To a librarian with a house. They want Emma."

"He's a felon, Clare. No judge in his or her right mind would let him have custody of a child."

"Apparently," I said, "you and I haven't been dealing with the same judges. It happens all the time."

"What if *you* got married?"

"Don't go there," I said. And for some reason, Emma's voice rang in my head. *Coward.*

I could tell that Sonterra was disgruntled, even without looking at him. Which I was careful not to do. We made our way toward the 101 North in silence for a few minutes; then he had to open his mouth.

"Would that be so terrible?" he asked. "Being married, I mean?"

I suppressed a sigh. "There is one catch. I'd need a husband."

More silence.

Again, Sonterra to the rescue. "A lot of my friends are married," he said. "Some of them even like it."

I laughed, and it felt good, after the day I'd had. "Now, there's a ringing endorsement," I replied. Then I did what came naturally; I changed the subject. "What's going on with the Kredd case?"

In a sidelong glance, I saw Sonterra's broad shoulders slouch a little. I had memories of those shoulders, a rush of them, all better left alone.

"Not much," he admitted.

"Denise Robbins?"

"Zilch," Sonterra said. "The M.E. said she

was definitely high, but that's about all we know. The crime scene techs came up dry on fingerprints and trace evidence. Ballistics is still working on whether or not the bullet came from the same gun that killed Harvey."

"I'm not surprised," I said, referring to the lack of progress on the case, as we swung up the on-ramp and joined the flow of northbound traffic.

"These things take time, Clare," Sonterra replied. To his credit, he didn't sound defensive.

"Yes," I agreed. "But the question is, how much time do we have?"

Sonterra didn't answer.

Emma was in my office when we reached the condo, sitting in front of the computer. At first, I thought she was absorbed in some game or kid-friendly web site, but when she turned in the swivel chair, I saw that her face was white. Bernice, hunkered in her lap, whimpered.

"What is it?" I asked, my words getting tangled with Sonterra's similar ones.

"Look," she said, indicating the screen.

I stepped closer, my heartbeat already racing, and Sonterra was right with me.

"Jesus," Sonterra murmured.

There, in glorious color, was Tracy, sprawled on the ground, arms and legs askew, her flesh gray-blue. Underneath, in bold letters, was a caption.

"YOU'RE NEXT."

Chapter Eleven

Sonterra touched my arm, then homed in on the computer. Emma wafted out of the chair, like a wraith, glancing in my direction once, guiltily, I thought, and then stepping aside so Sonterra could get to the keyboard. He peered at the screen, apparently analyzing every grim detail, then printed out the picture.

"What—?" I made one false start, only to add another. "How—?"

"I was checking my e-mail, that's all," Emma said.

"This picture was sent to your screen name?" I asked. I might have sounded calm and cool, but I had to perch on the edge of the desk, since I didn't think my legs would hold up. I could barely look away from the monitor, even though the image tore me apart.

Emma allowed me to draw her to my side and hold her loosely in the curve of one arm.

If the sight of my murdered sister was agony to me, what must it be doing to Emma? She hung her head, buried her face in Bernice's silky fur.

"The little flag came up on the mailbox," she said. "I thought—" She paused, still refusing to meet my gaze. "I don't know what I thought—I was just curious, that's all. So I opened it."

"Can you trace it?" I asked Sonterra.

"I'm trying," he said. "In the meantime, I'll forward it to the lab and get them working on it." He glanced back at Emma, over one shoulder. "If there's something else you want to tell us, kid, now would be the time."

Emma's spine curved; she seemed to be trying to fuse with the dog. I felt her go tense against my side, and when she started to talk, the words poured out. "Okay, I was in a chat room with my dad. We were talking about going to dinner and the movies on Friday night. He's getting married." She tilted her head slightly to steal a look at my face. "He's changed," she added stubbornly.

"He's a killer," I said.

"Clare," Sonterra warned.

"I don't see what one thing has to do with

the other," Emma lamented. "I wasn't doing anything wrong. Dad and I have been writing back and forth for a long time. You knew that, Clare."

I felt my lips tighten, and made a conscious effort to relax, unbend a little. "Chat rooms weren't part of the deal," I reminded her. "The letters were bad enough, in my opinion, but at least Dr. Dennis was monitoring those." Emma's and my therapist had reviewed each one, and if she'd found anything amiss, the good doctor hadn't troubled herself to inform me of the fact. I planned to put in a call to her as soon as I got the chance. "You did show them all to her, didn't you?"

Emma looked as though I'd slapped her. "You think I'm really sneaky!"

"I think you're thirteen," I came back.

"Library in Chandler," Sonterra said.

I blinked, momentarily confused. "I beg your pardon?"

"That's where the e-mail originated," he explained patiently. "From a branch of the public library, in Chandler. I just got an instant message from the lab."

"Monica," I said.

"Who?" Sonterra asked.

"James's *fiancée*. Her name is Monica, and she's a librarian in Chandler."

"She wouldn't send something like that!" Emma cried, pulling away from me.

"Wouldn't she?" I countered, and got another warning glare from Sonterra.

Emma burst into tears and fled, pounding up the stairs, slamming her door.

"Well," said Sonterra, "you handled that well."

"Shut up," I answered.

He sighed a saintly sigh, got to his feet, and laid his hands on my shoulders. "I'll check out Marian the Librarian," he said gently. "You try to chill out a little. You can't afford to be rattled right now, Clare—you've got to stay on the alert every second. Whoever sent the snapshot of your sister wasn't just blowing smoke. As far as I'm concerned, that picture is as good as a murder confession. It's also a very real threat."

I put one hand over my mouth, struggled to recover my composure, and nodded. "You believe me, then?" I dared to ask, when I could speak. "About what happened to Tracy, I mean?"

He glanced back at the computer screen,

now mercifully empty, though the file was still lurking in the wiring somewhere, like a demon ready to leap out and consume both Emma and me. "I believe you," he confirmed quietly. "And for the record, Clare, it was never a matter of *dis*believing. It's my job to look at all the angles."

I nodded again. "Thanks," I said.

"Lock the door behind me," he said, planting a light kiss on my forehead, then glancing up at the ceiling. "And take it easy on Emma. She's dealing with a lot right now, but she's a smart kid. She'll come out of this okay."

I didn't make a comment, but simply bit my lower lip.

Sonterra gave my shoulders one last squeeze and stepped around me to leave. I stood still, listening, and flinched slightly when I heard the front door close. Moments later, I made my way through the living room and engaged the locks.

It seemed a futile effort to me, at that particular point in time. My gaze strayed in the direction of the office, where the computer brooded.

There were so many ways for evil to creep in. What good would locking a door do?

Chapter Twelve

Work has always been my drug of choice. When other people are overwhelmed, they drink, spend money, or just crawl into bed and pull the covers over their heads. I find a project, push up my sleeves, and dig in.

That's what I did after Sonterra left, and since it was obvious that Emma wasn't planning to come out of her self-imposed exile anytime soon.

The police delivered my car after I'd eaten a solitary supper at my desk. I thanked them, inspected the interior for residual gore, and was relieved to find none. I guessed Sonterra had pulled some strings to get me back on wheels, and was grateful enough that I could almost forgive him for not calling me back with a report on the librarian.

It was after ten o'clock, and I was engaged in compiling my plan of attack for the Netherton case, when I discovered that I was missing a computer disk I particularly needed. I must have left it on my desk at work.

I debated for a while, going back and forth between giving up for the night and seeing the job through to the bitter end, then gave in to my obsession, dashed off a note of explanation to Emma, in case she woke up to find me gone, grabbed my keys, and left the condo, locking the door carefully behind me.

There were two other cars in the underground parking lot when I reached the Kredd Building and, to my dismay, I recognized one of them as Janet's, a blue Saturn, like mine. Besides our gender and our law degrees, our cars were probably the only things we had in common. The other vehicle was a gray Toyota, utterly nondescript, and apparently empty.

I parked, feeling jittery but still confident, and took the elevator up to the third floor. The suites on the lower levels were rented to an insurance agency, a naturopathic physician, and a telemarketing outfit, and all three companies had long since closed up for the night.

I felt a soft shiver move up my spine as I

got off on our floor, which was only dimly lit, and rummaged in my purse for my office keys. I'd found them and fitted the appropriate one into the lock before I realized that the door was already open. That struck me as odd, since Janet was a prudent sort by nature, not given to leaving doors unlocked, and we'd all been a lot more security conscious than usual since Harvey's murder.

I walked into the deserted waiting area.

"Janet?" I called. It was typical of her to work late.

I shrugged. Might as well get the confrontation over with and take my lumps over the Trent case, so I could concentrate on Netherton once I got back to my home office. I tried calling out again when there was no answer, and started down the corridor toward the inner offices.

Janet's door stood ajar, and her radio was playing softly, but there was no sign of her. I decided she was either in the ladies' room, or in the lounge, brewing a caffeine cocktail to sustain her while she burned the midnight oil.

I decided to find the disk I needed, then go in search of my interim boss. I pushed my cubicle door open with one foot, only half registering that the lights were on when they shouldn't have been, and stepped over the threshold.

My heart leaped into my throat when I spotted Janet seated at my desk, and I gave a gasping scream.

A good part of her chest had been blown away, and blood was everywhere, soaking her clothes, the papers she'd been working with, the walls and the carpet.

I took a step backward, out of instinct, I suppose, then remembered the gray Toyota, the only other car besides mine and Janet's, in the parking garage. That might well be the killer's car, and he or she could easily be somewhere nearby, hiding in the darkness.

A strange, deadly calm descended over me, like a mantle. I drew a shallow breath— the smell of death was strong in that confined space—reached for the phone next to Janet's elbow, then withdrew my hand in the next instant. This was a crime scene, I reminded myself, which meant I shouldn't touch anything before the police had had a chance to gather evidence.

I pressed my back to the wall beside the open door, fumbled through my purse, just as I'd done in the supermarket parking lot when I'd come across Denise Robbins's corpse in my car, and found my cell phone. My fingers shaking so badly that I had to try several times before I succeeded, I managed to dial 911.

Chapter Thirteen

The offices of Kredd and Associates swarmed with officers from both the sheriff's department and Scottsdale P.D., as well as a few reporters working the night shift. My cubicle was cordoned off with yellow tape, while people wearing rubber gloves and plastic shoe covers ducked in and out.

I'd speed-dialed Sonterra right after the 911 call.

The memory of the fear I'd felt waiting for help to arrive had turned my brain to jelly. Sonterra had spoken calmly, telling me to shut and lock the cubicle door and stay *exactly* where I was until help arrived. He stayed with me on the cell phone, talking, talking, while he and the police sped toward me.

Sonterra showed up roughly two minutes after the first cops got there. They knocked politely at the door of my office, and I let them in. I recognized one of the officers from the supermarket incident, and thought I glimpsed a *you again?* in her eyes.

I was escorted to the conference room and settled in a chair.

I heard Sonterra's voice from the hallway before I saw him. He made some comment about the body, then asked where I was.

Moments later, he crouched in front of my chair, took my ice cold hands in his. "Are you hurt?" he asked. Since I'd expected something more along the lines of "What is it with you and dead bodies?" I was relieved.

I shook my head. "I'm—I think I'm okay—"

"What the hell were you doing here in the middle of the night?" So much for tender concern.

"I came to get a disk—"

He shook his head. "I thought we agreed that you'd be careful."

"I *was* careful."

He looked unconvinced, and not particularly mollified. "Did you see anybody?"

"No," I croaked. "There was a strange car in the parking garage when I got here, though."

By then, Sonterra's partner, Eddie Columbia, had arrived. Without being asked, he got me a glass of water. My hero.

"Describe the car," Sonterra prompted when I fell into another mini-stupor. I guess I must have been in shock.

"Give her a chance to catch her breath," Eddie told him. May his children's children rise up and call him blessed.

I told them what I'd seen, between sips. Gray Toyota, no distinguishing marks, on the old side. Nope, sorry, hadn't thought to take down the license number.

Somebody came to the doorway of the conference room and spoke to Eddie, and he promptly left the room.

"What about the librarian?" I whispered to Sonterra, once we were alone. My throat felt as though it had been scalded. "Did you talk to her?"

His right temple pulsed. "Yes," he said. "At length. She's codependent as hell, but I don't see her as the type to send a digital image of a dead body to anybody, for any reason. Her background is clean."

I nodded, perhaps a bit woodenly, then sighed. "James could have killed Janet," I said.

"Not likely," Sonterra replied, throwing

cold water on my theory. "Whoever did this thought they were hitting you—same car, same office—and Arren would have known he had the wrong woman."

I put an arm across my middle, remembering the sight of Janet—sitting there, dead—and trying not to be sick.

"Clare," Sonterra said firmly, to get my attention. "Stay with me, here. What do you suppose Ms. Baylin was doing in your office?"

"She didn't like me, and she must have been seriously unhappy over the Trent verdict. She was probably looking for a reason to fire me." I put a hand to my mouth. "My God," I whispered. "She was a bitch, but she didn't deserve this."

"No," Tony agreed.

"The cops are going to blame me. It's just too coincidental, my discovering Denise Robbins, and now Janet—"

"You didn't have a motive," he pointed out. "But somebody did. Come on, Clare. Think. Who could be this pissed off?"

"Lots of people," I said.

"We're not looking for 'lots of people.' Just one. Who, Clare?"

I remembered the look of hatred on Trevor

Trent, Sr.'s face when I'd lost his son's case to Pete Alexander. The man could cheerfully have killed me, right there in the courthouse. But Denise Robbins had died before the verdict was rendered, which made him an unlikely candidate.

The Lench case popped into my mind, but I hesitated to bring it up. After all, it was an incendiary topic with Sonterra and me, and I was fresh out of fight.

"I really don't know," I said. "If you find out who sent that photo of Tracy—"

Sonterra shook his head. "I'm not convinced there's any connection. This is the same person who killed Harvey Kredd. Did your boss, or Ms. Baylin, know your sister?"

I sighed. "No," I said. "I don't think so." Hello, Square One. I rubbed my temples. "Can I go home now? Emma's alone."

The look Sonterra gave me did not exactly make for a Hallmark Moment. "Oh, that's great," he said. "That's just great." He got to his feet, went out into the hallway, and waved over a uniform. I heard him tell the officer to send a car to my address, but not to ring the doorbell. He spent some time conferring with Eddie, then came back to stand beside my chair.

"You're not going anywhere alone," he said. "I'd take you home, but I can't leave until the body's been removed and the paperwork's done. Call Loretta."

"It's so late."

"Call Loretta," Sonterra repeated.

I did, though I hated to wake her up, especially with news like this. She appeared within half an hour, wearing old jeans, scuffed boots, and a Diamondbacks T-shirt, and she still managed to give the place an air of class. Taking one look at my face, she opened her expensive hobo bag and brought out an equally expensive flask.

"You look like hell," she said, shoving the bottle at me. "Have a swig."

I was more than glad to see my friend, and the Jack Daniel's would have been welcome, too, if I hadn't been about to drive. No way was I going to leave my Saturn in the parking lot, where it just might attract another body.

"I'm sorry to put you through this," I said, waving away the booze.

Loretta and Sonterra exchanged glances. "Never mind that," she said, turning her full attention on me. "Let's get you home before something else happens. In fact, I think we ought to pick up Emma and the dog and head for my place."

I wasn't about to argue. If Loretta wanted to fuss and fetch a little, it worked for me. "I need the disk."

"The frickin' disk," Sonterra marveled.

"What disk?" Loretta wanted to know.

"Forget it," I said, a bit peevishly.

Of course, there would be more questions—a *lot* of questions—but thanks to Sonterra and Eddie Columbia, the police were willing to lay off until morning.

There had been no love lost between Janet and me, and everyone knew it. Theoretically, I could have come into the office, shot the woman, hidden the weapon and any other signs of my guilt, and then called Sonterra in a pseudo-panic.

What an irony it would be, I reflected as I got shakily to my feet and followed Loretta out of the conference room, if I had to retain counsel to defend myself. The thought gave me an even greater respect for the rights of the innocent.

Chapter Fourteen

Loretta and Kip's place is lush, but it could have been a trailer up on blocks that night, for all I would have cared. My friend ushered Emma and me to our separate guest suites; mine looked like something out of the pages of *Architectural Digest,* and Emma's was similar.

Loretta presented me with silk pajamas and a robe—Emma was already in a night-shirt, having been asleep at home—and sent me stumbling off for a restorative shower and a decent night's rest.

In a daze, I stripped, being careful not to slip on the spectacular marble floors of the bathroom, and stepped into a glass-enclosed stall the size of my condo's living room. I chose a spigot from an impressive assortment, turned on the water, and availed myself of Loretta's special herbal soap, custom-made for her.

The smells of death and fear rinsed away

easily, but the memories would be more of a challenge.

After drying off and slipping into the borrowed pajamas, I stumbled into the bedroom and collapsed.

Somewhere in the depths of the night, I woke to find Emma and Bernice curled up beside me. I smoothed my niece's hair, cried a little, and went back to sleep.

I was up early the next morning. Leaving Emma to sleep, I wandered into the kitchen and perched on one of the stools at the long, gleaming marble counter bisecting the huge room. Sunlight glinted, blue-green, off the tasteful Grecian swimming pool in the backyard.

Loretta had brewed tea and whipped up a delicate little egg concoction with a crust. I was starved, to my everlasting surprise, and made short work of the feast.

"I take it Emma's still sleeping?" my best friend ventured.

I nodded, my heart tightening as I thought of my niece. "I think she ought to stick close for a few days," I said.

"Damn straight," Loretta replied.

In that moment, I was so glad to be with her that tears came to my eyes.

She smiled. "You're going to be okay, kid," she told me, patting my hand.

I lifted my teacup in a sort of culinary salute. "I get by with a little help from my friends," I replied, and I was including Sonterra in that group, though I wouldn't have told him so.

Loretta was thoughtful. "Word of what happened at Kredd and Associates must be all over the news by now, so I figure you ought to lie low for a while. I'm suggesting we girls head down to the Tucson place for a week or so, just to catch our breaths. What do you say, Clare?"

A getaway like that sounded beyond good, but I still had work to do, and there was the upcoming dinner-and-movie gig with James.

I put my head in my hands. "I'd love to go," I said. "But I can't." I told her about Emma's upcoming visit with James and outlined all I had to do regarding the Netherton case. In addition, I wasn't sure the police would let me leave town, considering my newly discovered talent for stumbling over corpses.

"Too bad," she said, her mouth tightening a little. "It would do you good to go back to the old hometown. Might give you some perspective."

It was odd to think of Tucson as home, but both Loretta and I had been born and raised there, so I guess it qualified. We'd become friends at Nipples, and she'd met Kip at some upscale party, fallen in love, and gotten married.

I didn't answer, except to shake my head, and concentrated on finishing my tea. Before I could carry the cup to the sink, Loretta had whisked it away and shooed me back to the guest room.

There, I took two aspirin, pulled down the covers, and went back to bed.

When I woke up, hours later, the house felt quiet and empty. If Emma and Bernice were around, they were walking on tippy-toe. I pressed a button that brought a big-screen TV down out of the ceiling, found the local news channel, and fluffed up my pillows.

Poor Janet. Even in death, she'd been upstaged, rating only a couple of sound bites and on-screen shakes of the head. Most of the coverage concerned me, controversial attorney, finder of bodies. The footage had been taken on the courthouse steps, after the Trevor Trent decision, and I looked grim, efficient, and frazzled.

I was wondering if I should get a makeover when the phone jangled on the bedside table.

"Hello?" I said, rather hesitantly, expecting Loretta to pick up somewhere else in the house.

"Clare?" It was James Arren.

I sat bolt upright in bed, wondering if he was having me followed, or maybe doing the honors himself. "How did you know where to find me?"

"Thought you could hide, huh?"

I felt a chill trickle down my spine. Emma must have contacted him, given him Loretta's number. "What do you want?"

"Don't be so bristly, Clare. We have a date tonight, remember? You, me, Emma, and Monica. By the way, your fuzz boyfriend paid her a visit, asked a lot of questions. You wouldn't be trying to throw up any roadblocks, would you, Clare?"

"I'd love to," I said, "but Sonterra doesn't take orders from me."

There was a greasy smile in James's voice. "I see you're famous now. Stumbling across two murders in a couple of days.

Seems pretty convenient that you were around both times."

"Why don't you go to the D.A. with your theories," I suggested, my voice taut. "I'm sure they'd be grateful for your input."

He sighed. "About tonight," he said. "I thought we could meet at Desert Ridge at six, have dinner at Mimi's, and then take in a show. Feel free to bow out and let Emma and Monica and me have an evening to ourselves."

"You wish," I said. Desert Ridge is a shopping center, about fifteen minutes from my condo. "We'll be there at six. Are you paying, or do they still not give convicts a salary for making license plates?"

"You're a bitch," James said conversationally.

"So I've been told," I replied.

"Six o'clock," James said.

I hung up.

Half an hour later, I was showered and dressed and making a solid effort to pull my emotions together.

Emma and I sat out by Kip and Loretta's pool, the turquoise water dazzling in the midmorning sunlight, and I explained, as moderately as I could, about Janet's murder. She knew the basics, of course, but she needed to hear my version, and not just what was on TV. She listened, subdued, and was silent for a long time after I'd finished.

"That person wanted to kill you," she said, "not Ms. Baylin."

"Maybe," I agreed. "We don't know that for sure."

"Bet you think it was my dad."

"Actually," I said evenly, "I don't. As far as I know, he had no grudge against Janet. And he would never have mistaken her for me."

She relaxed a little, but immediately tensed again when I went on.

"You called your dad and told him we were here, didn't you?"

"Yes," she said.

"Why?"

Emma didn't look at me, but sat petting Bernice and staring belligerently at the pool, even though the brightness must have hurt her eyes. "I wanted to talk to him, that was all."

"About what?"

Her glance was defiant. "Stuff," she said.

"Be careful, Emma," I warned quietly. "I know you want to believe that your dad is a good guy who's had a run of bad luck, but there's more to it than that. Keep in mind that he's no Ozzie Nelson."

Emma's brow wrinkled. "Who?"

"Stop being obtuse. You know what I'm talking about."

"You hate him," she said.

"Bingo," I replied.

Emma stood. "I don't want to talk about this anymore," she said.

"That's something you'll need to get over," I answered. "As far as your father is concerned, we haven't even gotten started."

My niece flung one arm out; the other was cradling Bernice. "Do you always have to act like a lawyer? Can't you just be a normal person for five minutes?" She didn't wait for an answer, but simply stomped into the house. In a place that big, there are a lot of places to hide out, and I didn't see her again for over an hour, when she and Loretta decided to make a run to the condo for clothes and dog kibble.

At loose ends, I used Loretta's kitchen computer to log on and check my e-mail. I don't know what I was hoping to find— maybe a notice that I'd won the Publisher's Clearing House Sweepstakes, maybe an

apology from Janet's killer, who had probably been aiming for me. Who knows.

There were two messages, one from
Heather, saying she was going to have a
breakdown if people in the company didn't
quit getting themselves murdered, and one
from an unfamiliar address. I replied briefly
and, I hoped, soothingly, to Heather's note,
then opened the other file.

The message was printed in a gothic font
of some sort, the letters large and dripping,
as though partially melted.

NOW I KNOW WHAT YOU LOOK LIKE.
SO PRETTY.
TOO BAD I HAVE TO KILL YOU.

Chapter Fifteen

Monica was not at all what I expected. She wasn't the stereotypical codependent, the kind of woman you would expect to fall in love with a convicted felon; just a pleasant woman, a few pounds overweight, with good skin and a steady gaze.

James, standing beside her in the entryway at Mimi's Café, wore chinos, an inexpensive sports jacket, a shirt, and loafers. His blond hair, shaggy and a bit greasy the last time I'd seen him, was neatly trimmed, and he sported a small mustache. I might have believed Emma's implications that he'd found God, if it hadn't been for the hard glint in his eyes as he studied my face. I wondered if he'd looked at Tracy the same way, before he killed her.

Now, at the moment of reunion, he and Emma stood watching each other, a little warily, neither one knowing, it seemed, exactly what to do next. Lord knows, I was no help. I was trying to suppress the shivers dancing up and down my spine, and would rather have been practically anywhere else on earth but where he was.

Monica broke the conversational logjam by putting out a hand to me. "Hello," she said, with a sort of reserved goodwill. "I'm Monica Carson."

"Clare Westbrook," I replied, shaking her hand, and though I tried to smile, I couldn't manage more than a slight quirk at one corner of my mouth. All my alarm systems were going off, but it wasn't Monica I was afraid of.

"Hey, midget," James said to Emma, sounding shy. They engaged in a stiff hug, and Emma averted her gaze.

"Hi," she said.

James and I exchanged glances over Emma's head. Again, I felt the chill.

"Clare," he said.

"James," I responded.

To say our meal was awkward would be the understatement of the year. We picked our way through the next hour, literally and figuratively, and then set out for the movie house at the other end of the mall. The film, no doubt chosen for its G rating, was entertaining—a Disney animated feature—but I can't say I got much out of it. I sat beside Emma, rigid and fidgety, feeling as if I should grab her by the hand and run for both our lives.

Emma, for her part, was calm, if not particularly comfortable. I think she was as grateful as I was when, at last, the evening ended. She and I got into the Saturn, after I'd surreptitiously checked for intruders, dead or otherwise, and headed for Loretta's place to pick up Bernice and our things. We'd decided earlier that it was time to go home, lest we wear out our welcome.

I had a thousand questions churning in my mind, and ten times that many subliminal burrs, but I waited for Emma to speak first. It was one of the hardest things I've ever done, as reticence does not come naturally to me.

Another understatement.

"They were trying really hard," Emma said, not looking at me.

"Yes," I agreed carefully. I made a conscious effort to loosen my white-knuckle grip on the steering wheel.

"He's not the way I pictured him."

No, I thought. "How did you imagine him?"

She flashed me a self-conscious smile. "In stripes," she said. "Or maybe dressed like a biker, with leathers and all kinds of tattoos."

I chuckled, flexed my fingers. It was tough letting go of the wheel, and even tougher letting go of Emma. "Monica seemed—okay."

This time, it was Emma who laughed. "That was really hard for you to say, wasn't it?"

Why lie? "Yes," I said.

"You don't like them." She sounded less amused.

"I'm trying here, Emma. Give me a chance."

She surprised me by reaching over to pat my arm. "You did all right," she said. High praise indeed, from a thirteen-year-old.

"Thanks."

She settled back against the seat. "Next time, though, I'd like to see them alone."

"Not yet," I said, surprised to find myself near tears, with my throat tight and my sinuses threatening to clog up. "We'll have to consult the social worker first." She tossed me a look, and I hurried on. "I'm not trying to be difficult here, Emma. It's just—"

She heaved a sigh. "It's just that you think he murdered my mom."

"That's exactly what I think," I admitted.

"I'd remember if he was mean to her," she said, with a note of challenge in her voice.

"I *do* remember." I paused for a steadying breath. "He had a lousy temper."

"Can we just let this drop? Please?"

"For now," I answered, because I'm nothing if not honest, and I knew the problem was only going to escalate.

Chapter Sixteen

As if we didn't have enough problems, Harvey Kredd, Jr., descended on the firm like an enemy paratrooper the following Monday, fresh from the reading of his father's will. Whatever was in it hadn't made him happy, that was clear. He looked ready to bite something—or someone—in half.

With his artfully sun-streaked hair, mechanical tan, and floral-print shirt straining at its buttons, Junior looked like a surfer several decades past his prime, though I knew, heaven help us, that he was a lawyer. Last I'd heard he was running a storefront operation in Ventura Beach.

He elbowed his way into the center of the reception room and clapped his hands loudly. "People!" he shouted, over the inevitable hubbub. *"People!"*

I was on hand for his big entrance only because I had come in for some files, including the computer disk I'd wanted the night I found Janet's body. I'd just come out of her office, in fact, where I had been making calls to her former clients, trying to reassure them that their cases would be handled with the utmost dispatch and discretion. My former cubicle remained a no-woman's land, even though the crime scene people had long since finished their work and the mess had been cleaned up.

We all stared at Harvey, Jr., with a mixture of alarm and fascination. I knew him from barbecues at Harvey, Sr.'s—he was, after all, a very distant relative of mine—but we'd never had a real conversation.

"Listen up!" Harvey, Jr., commanded, clapping his hands again. The hound-dog pouches under his eyes suggested he'd either been mourning his recently deceased father or slugging back Bloody Marys on the milk run from California. He held up a pair of square, blunt-fingered hands, like a politician demurring in the face of frenzied admiration.

The chatter died away to a titter. Everybody, including me, was braced for a figurative massacre. Rumors about the contents of Harvey's will were zipping around the office like laser beams—apparently the estate boasted more debts than money—and just that morning there had been a call from the old man's accountant, announcing that the firm's assets had been temporarily frozen. Our forthcoming paychecks might not be so forthcoming after all.

Junior's bristly eyebrows rose as he zeroed in on the titterers, and they fell silent at last.

"I don't need to tell you that we've seen some trying times here at Kredd and Associates," he said. He was right; he didn't need to tell us. "Some of you will be laid off, regrettably. However, the firm itself will continue to operate for the foreseeable future. I'll want to meet with each one of you individually, of course, and be brought up to speed on the cases you're handling." He turned, ran his gaze over me in a way that would have earned him a beer-dousing in my Nipples days, and waggled his eyebrows. "Shall we start with you, Miss—?"

"It's *Ms.*," I said tartly, but with a dash of sweetness thrown in. "Ms. Clare Westbrook."

"Whatever," said Harvey, Jr., mercifully putting me on a back burner for the moment and turning his attention to Heather, who was standing by the watercooler. He by-passed the few men in the firm to approach her and shake her hand.

She flung a mildly desperate glance in my direction, then smiled feebly and said, "How do you do?" Heather was understandably on edge, but she was holding on.

"We'll start with you," Junior said to her, and I wondered if he knew Heather was the receptionist, not one of the attorneys. "Half an hour, my office," he finished.

Reminded of her by Junior's shorthand way of talking, I observed a moment of silence for Janet, whose name had not been mentioned.

Right away, Harvey, Jr., ensconced himself in his father's plush haven, switched the big-screen on to take in CNN Headline News, and began the systematic inquisition.

I was next to be summoned after Heather, who had apparently come out of the interview with her job intact.

It was distracting, the way Harvey, Jr., kept glancing over my shoulder while we were talking about cases—Trevor Trent, Dr. Netherton and crew—to follow the latest stock market scandal on CNN.

"Are you married, Ms. Westbrook?"

Harvey inquired, focusing first on my breasts, then on my face.

"No," I said, and barely kept myself from reminding him that not only had we met on several occasions, but his father and mine were shirttail cousins and he shouldn't be checking me out like that.

He smiled with smarmy aplomb, revealing a set of chompers that could have doubled as piano keys. Definitely capped. "I hope we can be friends, whatever happens," he said.

Don't hold your breath, I thought, but I managed a semblance of a smile. "I hope so, too," I said.

He stared at me for a long moment, waiting for God knew what, and I gave him the same level gaze I use in the courtroom whenever I catch a juror's eye.

Harvey, Jr., cleared his throat, straightened a stack of files that didn't need straightening. "I understand from past conversations with Dad that you had an agreement with him. He paid your tuition and fees and granted you a stipend for living expenses while you were in law school. Is that correct?"

My heart felt as though it might be trying

to escape my chest. I sat up a little straighter in my chair. Was he going to set me free? As one of Harvey, Sr.'s primary heirs, he surely had the option. Or did he intend to send me packing and demand payment in full? "Yes," I answered, praying he wouldn't notice the tremor in my voice. "That's right."

"Hmmmm," he said, file-straightening again. He stole another glance at the murmuring television set beside me, evidently making sure the financial world hadn't changed overmuch in the last twenty seconds, then fixed his gaze on my face again. "Your contract still has a few years to run, doesn't it?"

I wanted to bite my lower lip, shift in my chair, but I didn't move a muscle. *Don't give away a single thing.* I'd learned that much in law school, at least. Hell, I learned it on the *playground*. "Yes," I replied, cool as could be.

"Well, given the circumstances, I think it's time you were promoted. You have the best win record in the firm, after my dad and poor Ms. Baylin, of course. How soon can you make a permanent move into her old office?"

I stared at him, practically agape. So much for inscrutable courtroom faces.

He chuckled at my surprise. "I think we'll make a great team," he said.

"Am I getting a raise?" I heard myself ask. It really scared me, too. Everything was too easy all of the sudden. I was being kept on, singled out, even favored, it seemed. I wasn't sure I liked the feeling—did he perceive me as an I'll-do-anything-to-score type, one of *them*?

"An increase in salary would seem to be in order, given the level of responsibility we'll be placing on you," Harvey, Jr., said cheerfully. "I'll review the matter and get back to you as soon as I can."

I was stunned speechless.

"Of course, you'll have to take over Janet's cases. We're cutting back on staff around here, as I said earlier."

I could barely keep up with the workload I already had, but I was too taken aback by the prospects of a comfortable office and a raise to think rationally. I simply nodded.

That was when the other shoe dropped. I should have known it was going to happen, but I'd been living in the center of a whirlwind for a while, and my focus was a little off.

Junior settled back in his chair with a creak of leather, cleared his throat, and assessed me again. "I have a proposition for you, Clare," he said. I wondered if it had been an afterthought, and precisely what *kind* of proposition he was about to make.

"I'm listening," I said, biting the inside of my cheek to keep from adding something in haste that I might repent at leisure.

"You're handling the Netherton case," he said speculatively.

"Yes," I said. I'd wanted to say, *I know*, but that might have qualified as a smart-ass remark, and I couldn't afford to make any of those at the moment. Even a small raise would make a big difference in my life and in Emma's. If James sued for custody, as he well might, my position would be just that much better.

"I'm willing to release you from your contract with my father," Junior said in a ponderous tone, as though he was just then making the decision, "on one condition."

The room tilted to one side, righted itself again. I gripped the arms of my chair and waited, afraid to breathe. I pictured myself arguing cases from the other side of the aisle down at the courthouse, working my way up in the D.A.'s office, Prosecution Woman.

"Justin Netherton paid this firm a sizable amount of money toward his defense," Junior said after a torturous interval of silence, "and I don't mind telling you that we're on the edge of financial disaster, here. Win that case and you can stay on here as a junior partner or go your way, as you choose."

I opened my mouth, but nothing came out.

"Clare?" Junior said, looking concerned.

"It's a deal," I managed to say, and even though I was jubilant, I also had a feeling that I was selling my soul in a way that made indenturing myself to Harvey, Sr., look downright noble.

Imagining what Sonterra's take on the situation would be didn't help, either.

Chapter Seventeen

"He fired practically everybody," I told Loretta that night when she stopped by the condo to visit Emma and me, bringing along an elegant cold supper from the deli at AJ's, an upscale supermarket. Emma was seated in the middle of the living room floor, like a yogi, with my notebook computer in her lap, playing solitaire.

Loretta watched as I raced back and forth across the small kitchen, dumping a variety of exotic, tasty-looking salads into a hodge-podge collection of bowls, getting out plates and silverware, filling water glasses. "But not you?" she asked.

I looked away. "Not me," I said, very quietly. Then I met Loretta's gaze. "He offered to let me out of the contract," I confided. "All I have to do is win the Netherton case."

I thought Loretta's stare would burn a hole right through me. "Ah," she said.

"What do you mean, 'ah'?" I demanded, feeling defensive.

"You know damn well what I mean," Loretta shot back. "Netherton's a butcher, and you know it. How can you defend a man like that—for any reason?"

I glared at her, my force field firmly in place. "Cheap shot, Loretta," I hissed. "You can call your life your own. Am I so wrong to want to do that, too?"

"I've offered you the money to buy your way out, and you refused," Loretta said. "That stubborn pride of yours is going to be the death of you one of these days."

I gave up on the supper project, for the moment, and sank into a chair at the table, across from my friend. Places were set for the two of us, for Emma, of course, and for Mrs. Kravinsky, whom I had invited earlier.

"I have to solve my own problems. Depend on myself."

Loretta reached for her wineglass, took a sip. "Horseshit," she said flatly. "You're just afraid of being obligated."

A rap at the door signaled Mrs. K's timely arrival; she swept in through the front door when I called out, looking delightfully dramatic. Her hair was big, and Elvis-black, and she wore a green caftan made of some shimmering, never-still material. She had three white candles, the kind that come in a tall glass jar, tucked under one bangle-spangled arm.

"For protection," she said, holding up one candle.

"I'll take all the help I can get," I murmured, thinking aloud. Then, "You remember Loretta?" I said graciously, as my friend rose to greet the newcomer.

"Of course," said Mrs. K, beaming. "I gave you a tarot reading a few months ago."

Loretta smiled and nodded. By then, Emma had appeared in the kitchen doorway, laptop in hand, Bernice in attendance.

Loretta raised an eyebrow when Mrs. K turned her back to greet Emma and the dog. "Candles?" she mouthed.

"Don't knock it," I said, and all of a sudden I was back in motion, setting things on the table, tearing off paper towels to serve as dinner napkins. I wanted to believe in Mrs. K's supermarket magic more than ever, with Janet and Harvey and poor Denise Robbins all dead, and someone out there gunning for me, as well.

Supper was pleasant; for a little while, I

was able to put all my worries aside. Once we'd eaten, Mrs. K made quite a ceremony of lighting the three candles, muttering indecipherable incantations and shooing little trails of smoke into this corner and that. One by one, she placed the candles on top of the refrigerator, warning that they must be left to burn themselves out, if the spell was to work properly.

Later, when Mrs. K had thanked us for the meal and the good company and gone home to watch her taped reruns of *Unsolved Mysteries*, I carried the candles into the downstairs bathroom and set them on the floor of the shower stall, in the interest of fire safety.

"Do you really believe in that stuff?" Loretta asked, watching from the bathroom doorway.

I shrugged, straightening. "It can't hurt," I said, and stood watching the flames dance on their wicks for a few moments before turning away.

Chapter Eighteen

A couple of hours later, I was at home, peering at the grisly portrait of Tracy on my computer monitor and searching for any clues I might have missed, when the telephone rang, nearly startling me out of my skin. Emma was already in bed, worn out, and Loretta had left for home as soon as we'd finished our after-supper decaf.

"Hello," I said, wishing I'd thought to look at the caller ID panel before picking up. There were a number of people I didn't want to talk to—James Arren, for one, and Harvey, Jr., for another.

"You have to die," a man said regretfully. While I was catching my breath, I groped mentally, but I couldn't place his voice.

"Who is this?" I rasped.

"You must know I'm not going to tell you that."

I peered at the caller ID window. "UNKNOWN NAME, UNKNOWN NUMBER."

"You killed Mr. Kredd, and Janet Baylin? And the girl, Denise?"

"Yes," he replied. I was still scrambling to figure out who he was.

"You thought Janet was me?"

"It's your fault that she died. That girl, I mean."

"Talk to me. Tell me what this is all about."

"So you can figure out who I am and have me arrested? Not a chance, Ms. Westbrook. Though I have to admit, after you're dead, I'm not going to care what happens to me." He paused. "Three for three," he said. "But it's all because of you."

"What do you mean, 'three for three'?"

"Good-bye, Ms. Westbrook. Fitting word, 'good-bye,' because you're not long for this world."

"Wait—don't hang up—"

A dial tone buzzed in my ear. I immediately dialed *69, but there was no answer. The killer had probably called from a phone booth.

Three for three. I stared at the picture of Tracy's corpse and knew, at last and for sure, that Sonterra had been right. We were dealing with two separate killers, here, with wholly different grudges.

I dialed Sonterra's cell phone number.

He barked his name on the third ring.

"It's Clare," I said.

"Is everything all right?"

"I haven't stumbled across another body, if that's what you mean." I took a long breath, then told him about the phone call I'd just received. Including the fruitless *69 effort.

" 'Three for three,' " Sonterra echoed, musing. "Any idea what he was talking about?"

"Not a clue. And I didn't recognize the voice."

"So it's more like zero for zero."

I sighed. "Afraid so." I was still staring Tracy's image on at the computer monitor. My heart hurt.

"What now?"

"I was hoping *you* could tell *me* that, Sonterra."

"Here's what I can tell you, Clare. You're in a lot of danger. That guy called because he wanted you to know he was coming after you."

I thought about Mrs. K's candles and hoped they were spinning their magic.

"Any suggestions?" I asked.

"Stay behind closed doors and keep the locks engaged."

"Thanks," I said, without conviction.

"Hire a bodyguard," Sonterra threw out.

"I can't afford one, and you know it."

"Guess that leaves me. I'll work for sex."

I smiled, in spite of myself. "That's the last thing I need."

"On the contrary," Sonterra said smoothly. "You need some serious mattress action, with me."

"This isn't helping, Sonterra."

"I was just trying to distract you."

"Well, stop it and come up with something constructive."

"I'd come over, but they just pulled a floater out of one of the canals in Scottsdale. Stab wounds, hands and feet tied with duct tape. I'm going to have to hang around here for a while."

I flinched at the pictures Sonterra's words brought to mind. "Thanks for cheering me up," I said.

"Anytime, Counselor," Sonterra replied. "Check the locks and go to bed."

I said good-bye, hung up, and saved Tracy's picture to a file before shutting down the computer.

I double-checked all the locks, doors, and windows, and then climbed the stairs. I looked in on Emma, took a shower with the curtain open most of the way, so nobody could sneak up on me, à la *Psycho*, and re-tired to my room.

Before crawling into bed, I opened the drawer of my bedside stand and checked the .38.

Maybe I'd start carrying the thing in my purse.

Chapter Nineteen

Dr. Netherton was waiting in my new quarters when I arrived at work the next morning, sitting with his legs crossed and his hands folded, serene as a preacher. My nerves were jangled, but I think I managed to appear professional.

"Good morning, Ms. Westbrook," the doctor said pointedly.

"Good morning," I replied, instead of asking what he thought he was doing, barging into my office uninvited. I couldn't let myself forget for a moment that my whole future, and Emma's as well, might be riding on how I handled this guy. "Did we have an appointment?"

He bared his teeth in a grimace that might, or might not, have been meant as a smile. "We do now," he said.

I set my briefcase on Janet's—my—desktop with a little thump and dropped into the leather-upholstered swivel chair behind it, waiting with raised eyebrows and steepled fingers for the explanation I knew he was dying to give.

"I brought you the reports Ms. Baylin prepared, before her—er—unfortunate demise, along with a list of satisfied customers."

"You could have sent them by e-mail, or FedEx," I said uneasily. "It's a long drive from Tucson."

"I thought you and I could have lunch or something. Get to know each other a little better. We sort of got off on the wrong foot, it seems to me."

I didn't dare tell my client that I already knew him better than I wanted to, and lunch was out. I used a noon meeting as an excuse and added, "I'll look over the material you brought, but I think we can make an adequate case as it is." In between threats on my life, I'd been working hard on my plan for Netherton's defense.

"Mere adequacy will not suffice," he replied smoothly. "I want complete exoneration. In fact, I want apologies." His jawline tightened. "I want *restitution*."

" 'Restitution'?" I echoed, certain that I must have misheard. This did not seem like an opportune time to mention the distinct possibilities that he would lose his license entirely, rack up a prison term, or both.

"Yes," he said, glowering. "Once this is over, I intend to countersue for *liable.*"

It took all the legal-eagle poise I'd garnered watching late-night reruns of *Law & Order* to keep from laughing in his face. "Well," I said moderately, "one step at a time. First of all, we need to prepare your defense."

"*You* need to prepare my defense, Ms. Westbrook," he pointed out, plainly miffed that we weren't doing lunch, or anything else he might have had in mind. "I don't believe your new boss wants to refund my retainer and see me go elsewhere, do you?"

He had me there. My personal stake in the outcome was as big as Harvey, Jr.'s.

Just then—speak of the devil—Junior appeared in my doorway. He'd forsaken yesterday's floral shirt for an expensive suit, but the fancy threads fell just a tad short of the upgrade he'd been going for; he still looked like an ambulance chaser with a beach practice. He flashed a big-bucks smile at the doctor, and I realized then—duh—that he and Netherton had already spoken. Had lunch and "getting to know each other better" been Harvey, Jr.'s idea? I felt a flush creep up my neck.

"I won't keep you," Harvey, Jr., said cheerfully. "I can see you have work to do."

With that, he vanished into his own office, and strains of CNN began to seep through the wall separating his den from mine.

Netherton and I spent the morning mapping out strategies, some of which were pretty good, if I do say so myself. The only problem was, of course, that I would have felt better about defending the devil.

At noon, when Netherton had just left and I was collecting myself, Sonterra swaggered in. When Heather led him into the new setup, he let out a long, low whistle of exclamation.

"Hey," he said, "maybe I ought to put you back on the suspect list."

"Funny," I said, making it plain that I was not amused.

He shut the door. "I thought you'd decided to work at home," he said.

"That was temporary," I replied.

Amazingly, he didn't press the matter. Nor did he make any of the comments I'd dreaded, about my selling out to get a raise and a bigger office. "Have lunch with me," he said.

"I'm turning down lunch dates today."

"I'll take you to El Encanto," Sonterra wheedled. He knew, damn him, that I can't resist good Mexican food. In my imagination, I was already biting into a chicken enchilada. He took in the new office again. "I'll even pay, though it's obvious that you've come up in the world."

What was Harvey, Jr., going to do if I went out to lunch with Sonterra instead of his favorite client? Fire me? I should be so lucky. I retrieved my purse from the bottom drawer of the desk I still thought of as Janet's, slid the strap over my shoulder, and stood. "Make it dutch," I countered. "I wouldn't want to strain your budget." There was a touch of irony in the remark; Sonterra had more disposable cash than most cops, due to an inheritance, if I remembered correctly. He lived in a nice house, drove that shiny SUV, and maintained a weekend cabin up by Flagstaff.

We met Harvey, Jr., in the corridor. He seemed to do a lot of lurking, for somebody with a busy law firm to run.

"Leaving early, Clare?" he asked.

I flashed him a smile. "Just going out to lunch," I replied in sunny tones. "Bring you back something?"

My bravado worked, apparently, because Junior backpedaled a little then. "Oh, no," he said, patting his expanding stomach. "Watching my weight, you know."

When the elevator doors had closed behind Sonterra and me, and we were zipping down to the first floor, I scowled. "Scumbag," I said.

Sonterra looked wounded, pressing his free hand to his chest and widening his eyes.

"I was referring to Junior," I told him. Not that I hadn't used that term to describe *him* a time or two, after our breakup, but there was no point in dredging up the past.

"The guy who promoted you?" Sonterra said, with spirit. "The heartless bastard."

I let the remark pass. The elevator whisked open, and we crossed the downstairs lobby, headed for the outside parking lot. Sonterra rushed ahead to hold the door for me. "I don't suppose you've made any progress on the murders?"

"Ballistics confirmed that Robbins and Kredd were killed by the same gun," he said. "We're working on the rest of it." He held open the door of his SUV, with its fine leather seats and fancy dashboard, and waited until I got in. "The trouble is, other people keep getting whacked." The CD player came on when he started the engine, along with the air conditioner. Sultry, sexy jazz flowed from the speakers.

" 'Getting whacked'? That's a touch irreverent, don't you think?"

"Get 'reverent' in this business," Sonterra countered, "and your stomach lining erodes."

"Another pleasant lunchtime topic."

He smiled. "There's always blood-spatter patterns, if you get bored with anatomy," he said as he pulled out into traffic and headed north, toward Carefree and Cave Creek. "How are you, Counselor? You look like hell warmed over."

"Thanks," I replied, leaning forward to adjust the air-conditioning a little. It seemed hot in that car. "Being the target of a killer tends to wear on a person."

"How'd the dinner-and-movie date go with Arren and his main squeeze?"

"About like you'd expect," I answered. "We were civil to each other, for Emma's sake." I shuddered, remembering the expression I'd glimpsed in James's eyes, more than once that evening. The man hated my guts, and little wonder—he probably blamed me for every second of the six years he'd spent in the big house. "She thinks he's a candidate for Father of the Year."

"That sucks," Sonterra said.

I simply nodded. Within minutes, we were pulling into the restaurant parking lot, claiming a table, placing our orders.

It's my curse. No matter how bad things get, I can always eat.

Chapter Twenty

"How's your wife?" I asked Sonterra, maybe because I was feeling unusually vulnerable to his charms and needed to establish a little emotional distance, while we were waiting for our lunch. We were seated in the restaurant's outdoor dining area, near the duck pond, which was a rich, murky emerald green that sunny mid-September day, and our table was in the shade.

Sonterra arched an eyebrow and leaned forward a little. "Whoa, wait a minute," he said. "Where did *that* come from?"

I looked away. "Strike that from the record," I said.

"Not a chance, Counselor. And Jackie is my *ex*-wife. There's a big difference."

"I heard you went back to her for a while after we broke up."

"You heard wrong," he said, leaning in a little. "Jackie has a son by a previous marriage. His name is Ryan, and he's nine years old. His Little League team qualified for the state championships, and I went to watch him play."

"If you wanted to make me feel like a fool, you succeeded," I said, none too charitably.

Sonterra chuckled. "You are one abrasive broad, you know that? Too bad you also have legs up to here and a face that ought to be carved into a mountainside." He paused, raised his eyebrows slightly. "If you ever get tired of chasing ambulances, Westbrook, you might make a very good journalist. You're nosy enough."

"I do *not* chase ambulances!" I couldn't deny the nosy part; it would have stuck in my throat.

He shrugged. "Whatever."

"You really hate my job, don't you?"

"Yeah," he said. "I really hate it. What grates on me is that *you* don't seem to hate it. You're better than this, Clare. Why don't you walk away from that place and do something that would make things better instead of worse?"

"Here we go," I said, and flung out my hands. "What would you have me do, Sonterra? Get married, have a houseful of babies, and spend the rest of my life folding laundry and watching soap operas?"

"That was a sexist remark. There's nothing wrong with staying home, if that's what a particular woman wants to do."

I agreed, and he knew it. He was just trying to get my goat. I thought about throwing my ice tea all over him, but the waitress came with our meals, so fate must have been on his side. "If anybody's sexist around here, Sonterra," I whispered furiously, "it's you."

"I give up," he said. "There's no talking to you."

I took up my fork and prodded my enchilada a little, to let some of the fragrant steam escape, and at the first whiff, my appetite went into high gear. "You could have told me about Ryan's baseball game," I ventured.

"You weren't speaking to me then, remember? That was a lot of our problem, I think. We didn't talk, we just had sex every time we got the chance."

I couldn't refute that. I was tempted to tell him the truth about my work then, that I *did* hate it, but I was trapped. In the end, though, I was just too proud to get the words out—the bargain I'd made with Harvey made me look and feel like a fool. Besides, it was none of Sonterra's damn business.

He forked in a mouthful of Spanish rice, chewed, and swallowed, watching me, waiting for me to bat the verbal ball back over the net. It's one of the wonders of Sonterra that he can look good even when he's feeding his face. I shifted my gaze to my plate, but not before I flashed on the old days, when he and I would have left the restaurant right then, just because our gazes had connected and then locked, to go over to his place and get naked the second we'd closed the front door behind us. Not that I ever kept a record or anything like that, but it seemed to me that Sonterra and I had made love standing up more often than lying down. We rarely got as far as the nearest bed.

A wave of primitive sensation swept over me, and I flushed with the heat.

Sonterra grinned, evidently reading my mind. His knee touched mine underneath the table, and not by accident, I'm sure. "Is it the jalapeños, Counselor?" he teased. "*Something* is definitely making you hot."

"You're imagining things," I said crisply. My hand shook a little as I reached for my ice tea glass and took a restorative gulp.

"Oh, yeah," he agreed. "I'm *definitely* imagining things. I'm imagining you naked, and the way you throw your head back when you—"

He was deliberately trying to annoy me, and I didn't appreciate it. I blushed harder. "If you lured me out of the office with the idea of getting me into the sack, Sonterra," I hissed, across the metal table, "you are dangerously out of practice."

"I *knew* you were thinking about sex," he said, with quiet triumph. "The hot, wet, slow kind, I'll bet, with just the slightest risk of getting caught."

I squirmed on my chair. "Shut up, Sonterra," I warned.

He grinned. "Remember that last Fourth of July we spent together?" he drawled. "You made strawberry shortcake, but all we used, if I remember correctly, was the whipped cream."

I put down my fork, glared at him.

"All *right,*" he conceded, sounding put-upon, but his dark eyes were dancing. "I'll stop."

"Thank you," I said primly. I might have made a dramatic exit then, but unfortunately we'd driven to Cave Creek in his vehicle. My Saturn was miles away, in the underground lot at Kredd and Associates. I frowned, distracted by the thought. "Did you ever get a line on that gray Toyota I saw the night Janet was killed?"

"Stolen," Sonterra said, reaching for the salsa. "No prints, except those of the rightful owner. The perp must have worn gloves."

"Which means he's smart."

"Criminals aren't usually rocket scientists, Clare. They don't anticipate the consequences of their actions—pull a heist, go to prison. They don't see the connection. He probably learned the glove trick watching cop shows."

"What about that 'three for three' thing?"

Sonterra was chewing, and pondering. He shook his head. "Zip," he said. "But there's something about that that clicks. It'll come to me."

"Let's hope it comes to you while I'm still alive," I said.

He lifted his ice tea in a sort of salute of agreement, and we ate in silence for a while.

When the conversation started up again, we didn't talk about Tracy, the murders, the phone call, or James Arren. We spoke of ordinary things.

The sex talk had left me feeling deliciously uncomfortable, and though I wouldn't have admitted as much, I was glad. For a little while, my life didn't seem so bloody complicated—I was a woman, Sonterra was a man, and there was a definite crackle between us. Normal stuff, if ill-advised.

After we'd eaten, and Sonterra had paid the bill, despite my attempts to put up half, he took me back to Kredd and Associates, dropped me off at the entrance, and calmly went on about his business. I think he knew he'd rattled me, and he was enjoying the effects.

My knees felt a little wobbly as I stepped out of the elevator into the welcome air-conditioned quiet of the reception area. Several clients flipped through magazines, but the place was blessedly peaceful otherwise. These days, I always felt like ducking when I stepped over the threshold, and not just because there might be bullets flying around.

Chapter Twenty-one

I'd barely gotten settled in my new office when Harvey, Jr., paid me a visit. He meant it to seem impromptu, I'm sure, but I knew it wasn't.

"About that raise we discussed," he said after closing the door. I'd been getting poisonous glances from the resentful underlings, whenever I encountered either of them, since my sudden ascension from the comb of cubicles, and I wondered if somebody had planted a microphone while I was out at lunch with Sonterra. If so, it seemed incumbent upon me to make the eavesdropping worthwhile.

"Sit down," I said, crossing my legs and folding my hands. It was probably vocational suicide—as if my career wasn't terminal anyway—but I intended to set some boundaries, come hell or high water. Sonterra would have been pleased to know he'd shamed me into it.

Junior ignored the invitation to have a chair—sitting would have brought him to eye level with me, after all, and he was clearly having none of that—and leaned against the edge of my desk, bracing himself with both hands. His breath smelled of peppermint and the components of a cocktail.

"About your raise," he said, with an edge to the words.

"First, I have a question," I interjected, fearing that I'd lose my nerve if I didn't jump right in.

"Shoot," he said, trying to look receptive.

I wasn't touching that one. "Does it bother you at all that Justin Netherton is probably guilty of everything he's been charged with?"

Junior assumed a righteous expression. "Under the law, Clare, as you undoubtedly know, every citizen of this country is entitled to a fair trial, regardless of anyone's opinion, including that of their attorney."

He was right, of course. I'd just cherished the wild, brief hope that he might have a conscience, that was all.

I didn't have an answer ready, but I held

his gaze. Sometimes, pure stubbornness is all a person has to fall back on.

He lowered his bushy eyebrows and narrowed his eyes. "Are you suffering from an ethical dilemma, Ms. Westbrook?" he intoned. So much for our being on a first-name basis. "Or can I expect you to give this case your fullest attention?"

I took a steadying breath and then wimped right out. "I'll win it."

"And then?"

And then I'm out of here so fast my high heels will leave a trail of smoke, I thought. "And then I'll review my options," I said.

"Let me remind you that if this slips through your fingers, you won't *have* many options."

There's always bankruptcy, I reflected, and I was damn near desperate enough to file the necessary forms. Desperate, but not meek. A girl learns early, in the rougher sections of Tucson, that the meek aren't likely to inherit anything but broken bones and bloody noses.

"Point taken," I said, and hoped he would let the matter drop, since we weren't getting anywhere with it anyway.

He straightened his tie. "Good. If you

mess with me, Clare, you will find that I am a formidable opponent—not half so soft-hearted as my father was."

Harvey, Sr., softhearted? Please.

I smiled winningly. "You mentioned a raise?"

He showed his teeth in a triumphant grin, and I was reminded of a shark zeroing in on a much smaller fish. "Indeed I did, Clare," he said. The clouds parted, the enmity was gone. He actually beamed at me, and I found myself wanting to blink in the glare. "I'm prepared to offer you a very impressive package—a twenty percent increase in salary and a partnership."

My breath caught in my throat. The raise alone was enough to send me into shock, never mind the partnership he'd already offered. For a second, I forgot that I wasn't really cut out to be a defense attorney, and I got all hung up on the status thing. "That *is* impressive," I said. Then I frowned. "But why me? Why not one of the others?"

"Because I've looked at your win-lose record, and you've kicked extensive ass, if you'll excuse the terminology." He didn't wait to see if I'd excused anything, but rushed on, flushed with sly enthusiasm.

"Besides, what jury could resist that face, that body?"

I remembered, just in time, that I was dealing with a lawyer. Harvey Kredd, Sr.'s baby boy, at that. "I wish you'd said, 'that mind,'" I told him, holding on to the reins of my temper with all my strength. It was like trying to restrain a team of runaway horses.

"If you win the Netherton case," he said, "you can write your own ticket. In the meantime, you'll have the raise and the junior partnership, on a trial basis, if you want it."

I sank back in my chair, my pent-up breath escaping in a whoosh. Wait until Sonterra heard about my name going up on the door, even in small type. He'd probably tell me to eat dirt and die.

Junior was confidence personified. "Well?" he said.

I ran the tip of my tongue over my dry lips and immediately regretted it. Junior's leer said he'd interpreted the gesture all wrong. "Okay," I said cautiously, "but what if I lose?"

"But you *won't* lose, Clare," Junior crooned, "now, will you?"

I resisted an urge to prop my elbows on the edge of the desk and bury my face in my hands. Instead, I stared straight ahead. "It won't be an easy one to win," I reflected. "The man was criminally negligent."

"I needn't remind you that there is a great deal at stake here," Junior said quietly, but with a point to his words. "Under the terms of our special agreement with the doctor, if we don't win, we don't collect, and paying back Justin Netherton's retainer will bankrupt this firm."

I made no comment on his unholy pact with Netherton. "I'll need something in writing, of course," I said, referring to the terms of my promotion and raise. Sonterra was bound to wash his hands of me, once and for all, when he heard the latest, but I didn't figure we would have made it anyway.

"Of course," said Harvey, Jr. "I'll have the new contract on your desk by five o'clock. In the meantime, you just concentrate on Dr. Netherton's case. I'll handle the stuff Ms. Baylin left behind." He paused. "You might start by going down to Tucson—at the firm's expense, of course—to see what you can dig up on the opposition."

My stomach did a guilty little flip. By "the opposition," of course, he meant the small group of women who had rallied to press charges against Netherton, women like Sylvie Wyand, my former coworker. I thought of the private investigator's report that Netherton had taken the trouble to bring me. Not much there, although there were a few leads I might be able to follow up on. The burden of proof was on the prosecution, I told myself; my task was simply to keep them from convincing the jury, beyond the prescribed reasonable doubt, that the good doctor had screwed up.

I comforted myself with a silent reminder that that's the way the system is set up. Maybe it isn't perfect, my law school professors had repeatedly said, but better a hundred guilty defendants go free than one innocent person gets sent to jail.

Junior didn't pause to ask if I was having second thoughts; either he didn't notice that all the blood had drained from my face, or he flat out didn't give a damn. My money was on the latter.

Once he'd gone, closing the door behind him, I gave in to impulse and laid my head on my arms. When that didn't help, I took myself into my new private washroom, raised the lid on the commode, and vomited until my stomach turned inside out.

Chapter Twenty-two

"You're going to Tucson after all?" Loretta asked. She and I were seated at a table on the patio next to her pool, late that same afternoon, a large umbrella shielding us from the late-afternoon sunlight. Emma was in the water with her sidekick, Cammie Phillips, while Bernice sat on the sidelines, watching the happy frolic with curious absorption. "Is this about Tracy?"

"It's about getting out from under my contract with the Dreaded Kredds," I said. If I got half a chance, though, I intended to ask around and find out if any new information had surfaced regarding Tracy's disappearance, and I also planned to check out the contents of Gram's storage unit, so I took advantage of the opening Loretta had given me.

"By doing what?" Loretta persisted.

I folded. There is no withstanding Loretta.

"Getting Justin Netherton off the hook," I said.

Loretta stiffened and glared at me. "Does Sonterra know what you're planning?"

I bristled. "What does Sonterra have to do with the Netherton case, or with Tracy's disappearance?" I countered. "He works for the city of Scottsdale—Tucson is outside of his jurisdiction. *Way* outside."

Loretta's eyes took on a determined glint. "I'm going with you," she said.

"I can't leave Emma and Bernice with anybody else but you," I said, "not for that long." I was prepared to beg, and did so. "*Please,* Loretta. There's the James Arren thing, and whoever shot Harvey and Janet and Denise Robbins. This is the only place where Emma is truly safe." Mrs. K was a dear, but she was old, and she lived perilously close to my condo, which might well be ground zero. If the killer knew my phone number, he certainly had my address as well.

"All right, all right," Loretta said, with the utmost reluctance, "don't get your panties in a twist. Of course Emma will stay here. It's just that—well—I don't like the sound of it. You could get hurt. Are you going to tell Tony Sonterra about this?"

"No," I replied quickly, keeping my voice down. "And don't you tell him, either. He's got his hands full with the investigations he's already been assigned, and all he'd do is get on my case about taking the law into my own hands." I paused for a breath. "Don't you see, Loretta? I need to do whatever I can to put things right, and I need to do it myself, so I know it's been done." My confidence in the system was still at a low ebb; there hadn't been any justice for Tracy, and a wholesale killer was still running amok. "I'll be careful, I swear."

Loretta sighed. "You don't know *how* to be careful, Clare," she said. "You've got a mouth on you, and you don't always think before you shoot it off. And I think you're completely wrong to shut Tony out of this."

"I will be the personification of diplomacy," I said, while raising one hand as if to give an oath, letting the gibe about Sonterra pass.

Loretta gave a snort. "Right," she scoffed. I waited her out, sitting primly in my chair and smiling at her. "How long will you be gone?" she asked, in due course, looking skeptical.

"A few days," I answered bleakly.

"Okay," Loretta said, resigned. "You're taking your cell phone along, right?"

"Right," I agreed, almost dizzy with relief. I had already discussed the trip with Emma, telling her it was business—which, of course, it was—and her suitcase was in the trunk of the car, along with Bernice's gear. That's how much I trusted in Loretta's friendship. "I promise I'll stay in touch."

"Where will you be staying?" Loretta wanted to know.

"I'm not sure," I said. "I'll call you from my hotel tonight and let you know."

Loretta's thoughtful gaze rested on Emma. "Be careful," she said. "I don't have to remind you that you're really all she has—do I?"

She had James, of course. Which was worse than having nobody, as far as I was concerned.

I shook my head, then stood and leaned over to slip an arm around Loretta's shoulders. "Thanks," I said. "And don't worry."

"Impossible," Loretta said, as I walked

away to stand at the edge of the pool, watching Emma.

My niece approached, laughing with the joy of being wet. She's always loved swimming; when she was a baby, Tracy used to take her to a public wading pool, where the two of them splashed around together for hours, coated in sunscreen. "You're going now?"

I nodded, feeling a little choked up. "Be good and do your homework. I'll be back as soon as I can."

"Aren't you going to tell me not to speak to strangers?" Emma teased, squinting in the dazzling volleys of light bouncing off the water. Her friend Cammie listened, grinning, from nearby.

I wasn't nearly so worried about strangers approaching her as I was about James, and what I perceived as his increasing influence over her. I had no doubt that they were communicating via the computer, if not by telephone as well, while I was being kept carefully out of the loop. *Or* I was simply being paranoid.

"I didn't think I *needed* to tell you that," I replied.

She tried to splash me, and Bernice

began to bark with excitement and trundle back and forth beside the water. I smiled and turned away, feeling as bereft as if I'd be gone forever, instead of three or four days.

Chapter Twenty-three

The drive to Tucson takes about two and a half hours, allowing for a few stops along the way, traveling east on Highway 10. I was there before sundown, standing in the lobby of a mid-price hotel and forking over the company credit card Harvey, Jr., had given me before I left the office. Reaching my room, I dumped my bags, checked out the bathroom, and ordered a Caesar salad and ice tea by phone.

Then, while I waited for my supper to arrive, I dialed Loretta's Scottsdale number.

I got Kip. "Hey," he said cheerfully.

I couldn't help smiling. Kip has that effect on people, even lawyers. He's an even-tempered guy, smart and good-looking as well as rich. Too bad they couldn't clone him. "Hey," I replied. "Is Loretta around?"

"She took Emma and the dog to Wal-Mart," he said. "Do they allow dogs at Wal-Mart?"

A more pertinent question would have been, What would Loretta be doing at Wal-Mart? but I kept it to myself. "Guess so," I said. Then I gave him the phone and room number at my hotel and asked him to tell Loretta and Emma that I had arrived safe and sound. He agreed, and we said our good-byes and hung up.

Frankly, I was relieved that Loretta hadn't been there to grill me for fifteen minutes.

I did a little unpacking, and then the food was delivered. I signed for the charges, adding a modest tip, and the waiter took his leave, promising to return for the tray in an hour.

I washed my hands, consumed the salad, and then exchanged my suit, panty hose, and pumps for jeans, a cotton top, and sneakers. I took my purse, my keys, and my cell phone and headed for the parking lot, where I'd left the Saturn.

We'd sold my grandmother's trailer house right after she died, but I drove by there anyway, for old times' sake. It looked a little shabby now, and smaller than I remembered. The lawn was overgrown, too, but pink geraniums thrived in the plastic window boxes, and there was a swing set under the purple jacaranda tree. I slowed a little, but didn't stop; the people living there were strangers, after all.

From Gram's neighborhood, I made my way to Nipples, in a seedy part of town not far from the university.

The same giant neon breast flickered offensively against the otherwise beautiful desert sky, and I felt a twinge of reluctance as I pulled into the gravel lot and parked between a polished Harley and an old truck with a "*Vote Redneck*" bumper sticker. The pit bull tied in the back of the pickup lunged at me, snarling as if he'd like to tear out my throat, and I reached into my purse for my pepper spray, prepared to let him have it if the chain didn't hold.

Fortunately it did, and I turned away from "Brutus," making my way toward the side door, which was propped open with two cases of empty beer bottles. As an employee, I'd entered by the back way, through the kitchen, but those days were over, thank the Lord. No more boob T-shirts for me.

The building that houses Nipples used to be a speakeasy, and before that, it was an honest-to-god Old West saloon. It still has the original pocked, greasy wood floors, though they're covered in three inches of peanut shells and other less innocuous discards, and so many initials have been carved into the bar that it looks as if it's been savaged by generations of worms. The walls are pocked with bullet holes, and not all of them date from gunslinger days.

That night, the jukebox was going full blast, the booths, most of the barstools, and the pool tables were all taken, and slender creatures in short-shorts and the requisite T-shirts hustled hither and yon bearing trays full of draft beer. Dear God, I thought, was I ever that young?

The customer base was made up of cowboys, bikers, out-of-town businessmen, and gawking college boys, just as I remembered. I didn't recognize the bartender, which was a relief. I wasn't there for a reunion, after all, and running into Freddie Loren would have meant hashing over old times, times that were best forgotten.

Whistles, catcalls, and woefully unimaginative suggestions greeted me as I passed through the crush, bellied up, and ordered a draft beer. I don't drink and drive, but I felt out of place enough without asking for a diet Coke.

The bartender looked me over insolently, and I pretended not to notice. Like Loretta said, I have a mouth on me, but I'm no fool. I can hold my tongue if it's absolutely necessary. Most of the time, anyway.

"You alone, honey?" he asked. He was bullet-shaped, sporting a ragged muscle shirt, and almost as much hair billowed from his nostrils and ears as his underarms. I caught the rancid odor of B.O. from across the bar.

I ignored the question. "I'm looking for Sylvie Wyand," I said, taking a single tidy sip from my beer and then pushing it away, as if I'd found it wanting. "Is she still around?"

He peered at me, his expression recalcitrant, as though he suspected me of something shady. "Who's asking?" he countered.

I took a business card from the side pocket on my purse and held it out to him.

"Clare Westbrook," he said, after staring at the lettering for a while. "That name rings a bell."

I wasn't about to tell him I'd worked at Nipples while I was in college; like I said, this wasn't old home week. I just waited for him to scramble onboard the clue train.

He squinted at the card again. "Says here you're a lawyer," he said suspiciously.

I held my tongue. I should get some kind of award for letting that one pass. "Yes," I said.

"What do you want with Sylvie?"

"I'm a friend," I replied. I was stretching it a little. Sylvie would probably remember working with me, but we hadn't been buddies. I'd hung out with Loretta back then and, of course, with Tracy. Between school and work, I hadn't had much free time.

The bartender took the card, went to the other end of the bar, showed it to a tall, scarecrow-like woman, probably in her sixties, with lipstick leaking into the creases around her mouth. She bent forward to get a look at me, then slipped off her stool and ambled toward me. Her smile was cadaverous and, when she put out her hand, I saw a tattoo on her right forearm, a red heart with three swords stuck through it.

I felt an odd little thrill of dislike, and barely kept myself from recoiling.

For a moment, curiosity got the better of me, and I almost asked what had prompted her to literally wear a heart on her sleeve, but then, I'm a lawyer, not a shrink. I didn't have any illusions that I could help her turn her life around, or anything like that, but I felt sorry for her, even though she scared me in some weird, indefinable way, and I shook her hand.

"I'm Ellie Mitchell," she said. Her voice was the raspy scratch of a lifetime smoker. "What do you want with poor Sylvie? If you're figuring on making trouble for her, I'd advise you to get your little butt back on the road."

"We used to work together," I replied, hoping that would be enough.

She looked me over, waxing skeptical. "You worked here?"

"Once," I said, keeping my chin high and my gaze level. *Law & Order 101: never let them know you're intimidated.* "Is she around?"

"She might be."

I suppressed a sigh. "Maybe you could call her," I said. "Tell her Tracy Arren's sister, Clare, would like to see her."

The scarecrow studied me for another few moments, and once again I resisted an urge to step back. "You're Tracy's sister?"

she asked. She peered at me through the smoke and the neon-tinted gloom. "Didn't she run off someplace a few years back?"

"I believe she was murdered," I said quietly.

"Is that what this is about?"

"No," I replied, though of course if Sylvie knew anything about Tracy's death, I wanted to hear it. I wasn't going to admit that I represented Dr. Netherton if I didn't have to; I wasn't sure if I could count on the bikers, or even the cowboys, to come to my rescue if Mrs. America there took a notion to beat me to a pulp, and she might, since she was obviously very protective of Sylvie and not overly fond of lawyers. "It's personal."

"Sylvie isn't exactly feeling her best these days. She might turn you down."

"I can live with that," I answered, bluffing it out. "Just ask her, will you?"

There was another pause while the woman carried on some internal debate. Then, with a muttered curse, she turned, peanut shells crunching under her battered boots, and stomped over to the wall phone to pop in a quarter and punch seven numbers.

Within a couple of minutes, she returned, clearly as suspicious of my motives as ever, but she gave me an address, and I was out of there without so much as a backward glance. In the lot, the pit bull was still guarding that rusted-out wreck of a truck, and he practically barked himself inside out when he saw me, but now, in comparison to the woman I'd just met, he didn't seem quite so threatening. I didn't bother getting out the pepper spray.

I checked the backseat before getting into the car, though, and didn't start the engine until I'd locked the doors. Thinking back to my Nipples days, when I used to leave the bar after closing time, often alone, I shivered. I hadn't had the good sense to be scared back then, but I was older now, and hopefully wiser.

The address "Medusa" had given me was a familiar one, in a trailer park near the one where Gram had lived, and I drove there immediately, feeling nervous as hell. Sylvie had evidently agreed to see me, but that didn't mean she would be receptive, especially after I told her I represented Dr. Netherton, which, ethically, I had to do. She might have a big, nasty dog, or a big, nasty boyfriend, or both, and sic them on me.

I was glad I didn't have to do this sort of stuff often. I don't have the stomach for detective work.

Chapter Twenty-four

The big, nasty boyfriend was standing on the weathered deck of the trailer when I drove up, a hulking shape even in the thin glimmer of a bug-spattered porch light, and I figured the matching dog had to be somewhere close at hand. I took in the tow truck parked at the curb, made sure the pepper spray was on top of the other stuff in my purse, shut off the engine, and got out.

"Clare Westbrook," I said, as cheerfully as if I were there to give a sales spiel for cosmetics and a free facial, instead of pry into Sylvie Wyand's personal life. The dog put in its two cents as soon as I opened the gate, growling from the shadows. "I represent Justin Netherton."

The boyfriend spat, though whether my name or Dr. Netherton's prompted that response was anybody's guess. "Ellie said you was coming," he said, adding, for the dog's benefit, I presume, "Put a sock in it!"

Ellie, I recalled, was the unnerving woman I'd just spoken with at Nipples. I started up the walk, with its crooked flagstones and intermittent mounds of weedy grass. The dog, wherever it was, had fallen silent, though I could almost feel it breathing, and I knew it was watching me with evil, unblinking eyes.

Reaching the step leading up onto the porch, a rickety-looking arrangement of two cement blocks jammed together, I summoned up my most winning smile. I still couldn't see the guy's face, but he was three hundred pounds of high-grade mean if he was an ounce, and about as easy to warm up to as the pit bull in Nipples's parking lot.

"Now, don't you upset Sylvie," he warned, in a dangerous undertone. "She ain't feelin' too well these days." Mentally, I cataloged his outstanding features: in sore need of a shower, bad dental hygiene, overhanging belly, a leather vest with no shirt underneath.

Oh, Sylvie, I thought. *What could you possibly see in this dude?*

A female voice sounded from behind the screen door, surprisingly cheerful, given the boyfriend, the dog, and the surroundings. "Stop giving Clare the third degree and let her in, Henley. I swear, sometimes you act like you're with the FBI or something."

Henley? I would never have matched the name with the actual man. He seemed like more of a "Bubba" to me.

Henley lumbered aside, though with an uncooperative air, and I recognized Sylvie's tiny, familiar figure against the screen, a scant shadow in an aura of lamplight.

"Come in," she said, with a sort of reluctant eagerness.

I stepped past Henley, very carefully, and found myself in a time warp. Sylvie's place was reminiscent of many others that I'd seen, growing up—fake wood paneling on the walls, shag carpet on the floor, camper-sized kitchen, bookshelf divider between the kitchen and living rooms. I might have been at Gram's, except that her place had been a little fancier and a whole lot cleaner.

"You just go on now," Sylvie told Henley. "I'll be fine."

Reluctantly, Henley left, whistling shrilly to the dog as he crossed the yard. I heard the gate open and close, the roaring start-up of

an engine, the rubbery screech of somebody peeling out in a snit.

I registered all that, but my attention was
focused on Sylvie. She was even smaller
than I remembered, barely bigger than
Emma, and clad in battered jeans and an
ancient T-shirt. It wasn't her clothes or her
diminutive size that really caught my attention, though. It was her flat chest. Even before her surgery, Sylvie had been built.

"It's been a long time, Clare," she said.
She was pretty, in a faded way, with her fly-
away blond hair, guileless blue eyes, and
freckles. At a distance, she could have
passed for twelve or thirteen; up close, she
looked older than the thirty-something she
must have been.

I started to shake her hand, then hugged
her instead, momentarily stuck for something to say. I knew I would have to make a
concentrated effort not to stare at her nonexistent bosom while we talked.

"Sit down," she said, indicating the plaid
couch, which had probably come stock with
the mobile home sometime in the seventies,
when it was still spiffy. "Can I get you some
coffee or tea? Henley's on probation, so we

don't keep beer or wine or anything like that around."

"Tea would be great," I said, not wanting to think what Henley might be on probation *for*.

I hoped a hit of caffeine might give me the boost I needed. It had been a long day, and between the visit to Nipples and the confrontation with Henley and his invisible dog, I was running on fumes.

Sylvie brewed tea for both of us, and served it in souvenir mugs, mine from the Grand Canyon, hers from Harrah's, up in Laughlin. She sat in the chair across from the couch, one leg tucked under, like a teenager. She seemed pleased by my visit, if a bit wary, and I felt guilty because I hadn't just stopped in to see how she was—I had an agenda.

"You're a lawyer now," she said, swirling her tea bag around in her mug. I'd already fished mine out and set it aside on the saucer she'd provided. "I can't get over that—you were just a kid when I met you, barely old enough to serve liquor. Do you ever see Loretta?"

"Yes," I answered, smiling and sipping. "I work for Kredd and Associates, up in

Scottsdale, and I see Loretta all the time." I didn't mention that Loretta and Kip had a ranch near Tucson, since I couldn't assume they'd want to invite Sylvie and Henley over for a barbecue or something like that.

Sylvie crumpled her small nose, thinking. "Kredd? Isn't that the guy who was murdered?"

I took another drink from my tea, this one substantial, and in the few moments that elapsed, I struggled to come to terms, yet again, with the fact that Harvey had died in such a horrible, senseless way. For all his faults, he hadn't deserved that.

And now I had Janet's demise to assimilate, as well. Her memorial service had been scheduled, though Sonterra had told me the M.E. wouldn't be releasing the body in the near future, and, anyway, poor Janet was in no shape for a viewing. I intended to pay my respects, despite the fact that we hadn't been close.

"Yes," I said. "Harvey was shot in his office at home."

"Do they know who did it?"

I shook my head. "No leads so far."

"That's awful," Sylvie said.

I couldn't stand any more small talk.

"Sylvie," I said, "I'm here because I want to ask you about your breast enhancement surgery. And I don't know if you heard me tell Henley outside or not, but I need to make sure you understand that I'm Justin Netherton's lawyer."

With a little clatter, she set her tea aside on an end table, which, like the couch, was vintage seventies. Color pulsed on Sylvie's freckled cheekbones, and she bit her lower lip. It was hard not to look away from the anguish I saw in her eyes. "How could you?" she asked, in an awed whisper. "How could you defend that terrible man?"

I'm not proud of it, but I parroted what Harvey, Jr., and my professors had said. "Everybody is entitled to representation, Sylvie. Even if they're guilty." Did I really believe that? I was beginning to wonder.

She brooded on my answer for a while, then apparently shook it off. "Did you say 'breast enhancement'?" she asked bitterly, indicating her chest with a gesture of both hands. "Do these look like they've been *enhanced*?"

"What happened, Sylvie?" I put the question softly, not because she seemed edgy, which she did, but because I felt genuinely

sorry for her. Fate had obviously handed her
more than one dirty deal.

"Dr. Justin Netherton happened, that's
what," she answered. Tears filled her eyes.
"Christ, Clare, I can't tell you what it's been
like—"

"Try," I said gently, perched on the edge
of the couch, leaning forward a little. This
was no courtroom-style body-language
gambit; I was truly interested in what she
had to say, and the horror I felt was real.
Just imagining the fear, anger, and humilia-
tion she must have felt made bile surge into
the back of my throat.

"He botched the job," she said, dashing
at a tear as it escaped down her cheek.

"Tell me," I urged.

She pulled her other leg up into the chair,
sitting meditation style, gripping a knee in
either hand, the knuckles white as paste.
"You know how it was at Nipples," she confided, simmering down from fury to a sort of
helpless sorrow. " 'Tits for tips,' the boss
used to say."

I nodded. My stomach turned over again,
and a hard lump formed midway up my
esophagus. It had been suggested, during
my tour at Nipples, that I get a boob job, for

economic reasons, and I'd refused. My none-too-gracious refusal had nearly gotten me fired.

Sylvie gazed at the screen door, as if watching the bugs dive against the mesh, but I knew she wasn't really with me. She was drifting somewhere in the past, and the memories clearly hurt. Finally, she met my eyes again, and gave me a chilling little smile, out of context with what I knew she must be feeling. I began then to understand why she'd admitted me into her home; she was lonely. It was that simple.

"It was great at first," she said brightly. "I looked sensational. I brought home twice as much in tips every night, and I never had so many dates." Her face crumpled again, and she averted her gaze, just for a heartbeat. I sensed that she was setting something away on an inner shelf, in hopes that I wouldn't pick up on it. "It was afterwards that I met Henley," she said.

Score one point for Henley, I thought, but I didn't want to spoil her momentum, so I sat in silence, listening for all I was worth.

She tried for another smile, making a brave and wobbly attempt, and fell short. "Then they began to hurt—my breasts, I mean. One of them got real hard, like a baseball or something, and it slipped, down and to one side." She gestured to show me, and I grimaced before I could get control of my face.

Earlier, I'd kept my mouth shut out of consideration for her feelings; now, it was because I couldn't find words.

"I went back to see Dr. Netherton right away," she explained. "I figured he'd fix me up and that would be it. Only he wouldn't, unless I gave him another six thousand dollars. Hell, I sold my car to pay Freddie back for the *first* surgery, and I couldn't have come up with more than two or three hundred to save my life."

I waited, feeling sicker and sicker. I hated Dr. Netherton just then, and I hated Harvey, Jr., for making me represent the bastard. Most of all, I think, I hated myself for having that damn job in the first place.

Meanwhile, Sylvie went on. "I hurt all the time, and I looked—well, uneven, no matter what I stuffed in my bra. Freddie, he finally let me go. He said I was depressing the customers, moping around the way I was. So here's me, with no job, and no insurance, and one boob hard as a rock. I started running fevers, and sometimes the pain was so bad, I'd just lay on the bathroom floor for hours, too weak from puking even to make it to bed. I finally applied for help from the state, and they gave me food stamps and medical coupons, but they said reconstructive surgery wasn't covered because it was 'cosmetic.' " She paused, gnawed at her lip again. "I told them I was sick from the things, that I thought those implants were killing me, and that was the truth, but they wouldn't listen. I got even sicker, and almost died, and they finally took them out."

I closed my eyes, bracing myself, blood thrumming in my ears.

"One night, I got as stoned as I could, and I—I went into the bathroom—I was going to take them out myself, but when it came right down to it, I couldn't. I took an overdose of my pain and sleeping medications then, and I figure I would have died, if Henley hadn't stopped by to see if I wanted to go to Burger King with him. He found me, out cold, and freaked right out. He called nine-one-one, and they took me to the hospital and pumped my stomach."

Her eyes. I will never forget the look of wretched, trapped-animal desperation in

Sylvie's eyes as she sat there, remembering. "I had a couple of breakdowns after that and I've never been good for much since."

"You didn't try to sue Netherton?" I asked, my voice small.

"I didn't have the money to sue anybody!" Sylvie said, hugging herself, maybe trying to hide her chest. "I went to Legal Aid, but they've got their hands full with other stuff, like back child-support and restraining orders and things like that."

"I'm so sorry, Sylvie," I said, and I meant it, but I also knew my pity was too little, too late. She was already scarred, physically and emotionally, and from the looks of Henley and the trailer, the rest of her life wasn't in such great shape, either.

Sylvie recovered her dignity, with touching effort, and sipped delicately at her tea.

I wished I could help her, volunteer my services for free, and go after that son-of-a-bitch Netherton, but of course that was out of the question, since I was *his* lawyer. Talk about your conflict of interest. Which didn't mean I couldn't enjoy the fantasy, for a few precious seconds, of busting his balls in court.

I wouldn't have asked about Tracy, not after putting Sylvie through an emotional wringer the way I had, but she spoke up on her own.

"I hear James Arren's out," she said grimly. "He'll go right on with his life, you can bet, while Tracy rots under some pile of rocks, out there in the desert somewhere."

I set my tea mug down on the coffee table, not trusting myself to hold it without spilling. Her terminology was pretty specific. "Sylvie, do you know anything about what happened?"

She stared at me rather blankly for a couple of seconds. Her mouth moved, and then went still. "No," she said.

"I'm sure James killed my sister," I persisted, feeling the tension-bearing muscles in my neck and shoulders tighten into throbbing knots. "But I've never been able to convince the police." I paused, debating whether or not to tell Sylvie about the e-mail I'd received, the photograph of Tracy's corpse. In the end, I decided it was worth the risk of upsetting her. The sight of that photograph might spark some memory, something she'd heard or seen, some tidbit of information that would convince Pima

County to reopen Tracy's case. "Sylvie, do you have a computer?"

She looked confused and a little scared. Maybe she thought I was going to turn her on to some work-at-home scheme, or ask if she'd mind sending out a few thousand chain letters for me. "I've got an old laptop," she said. "Henley swapped some truck tires and a secondhand transmission for it."

"Are you on-line?"

She nodded. "I like to cruise the chat rooms late at night, when things are bad and I can't sleep," she said. "Why?"

"I want to show you something I received the other night. You might have some insight, see something I've missed—"

"Sure," she said, brightening. She got up, hurried down the hall, and returned in a few minutes with a prehistoric laptop. She set it on the little divider with the bookshelves, plugged it in, and waited. It took forever to get on-line, but finally, there was MSN's welcome page. Sylvie stepped aside, and I flexed my fingers, typed in my password, and brought up the e-mail.

The picture filled the screen, and even though I'd seen it many times, the impact of the thing hadn't abated; I felt as though I'd been punched in the gut.

"My God," Sylvie whispered. "Is that—is she really—she looks—*dead*?"

I nodded grimly. "Probably," I said, forcing myself to face facts. "A cop friend of mine showed it to the medical examiner, up in Maricopa County, and she thought so."

"Don't you think you should go to the sheriff or somebody?"

After showing the photo to Sonterra, I'd never considered reporting the e-mail in a more formal fashion. I'd just assumed he'd handle it. I made a mental note to check with him first chance. "They're not much help," I said.

"Tell me about it," Sylvie agreed. "Did the cops ever find out anything about what happened to Tracy?"

Bitterness flooded the lower regions of my heart. "They were convinced she'd left under her own free will."

"But a *picture*," Sylvie said. "Clare, that is so awful, and it ought to convince them. Do you have any idea who sent this thing?"

"I think it was James Arren," I confided. "You know, taunting me because he killed my sister and got away with it. But somebody in my friend's office traced the thing to a library up in Chandler. After that, the trail went cold."

Sylvie stared at the picture for a long time. Then she looked at me again, and really seemed to see me—as Justin Netherton's lawyer. The enemy.

"Leave it alone, Clare," she said. "You can't bring Tracy back."

My temples were pounding out a nauseating beat. I squeezed the bridge of my nose between a thumb and forefinger, then met her gaze. "I can't 'leave it alone,' Sylvie. This is my sister we're talking about. I won't rest until I prove James killed her and see him punished for it."

"What if you're wrong?" she asked, in a hasty whisper. "What if James didn't do it?"

Just then, the sound of a motor came through the screen door; Henley was home. I didn't get a chance to answer her.

"Get out of here," Sylvie told me. "Now. And don't ever come back!"

"Sylvie—"

"Get out," Sylvie raved, her eyes flashing as Henley and the dog came toward the house. "Get out of my house!"

I put up both hands, palms out. "All right,

I'm out of here," I said, but I fumbled for another card and shoved it at her. Sylvie crumpled it and gave it a toss.

I opened the screen door and went out. Henley and I sidestepped each other on the porch; he was holding a German shepherd, none too securely I might add, by the collar, and the look that man gave me was one of pure poison. I wondered if he'd been listening under an open window or something, it was the only thing I could think of that would account for Sylvie's about-face attitude.

Once I was safe in my car—I checked the backseat again before getting in—I locked up. As I pulled away from Sylvie's place, I was already fumbling for my cell phone.

Chapter Twenty-five

"Sonterra," Tony said, picking up on the second ring.

"It's Clare," I explained, somewhat sheepishly. I was glad he couldn't see my face; if he had, he might have known how much I had needed to hear his voice.

"Where are you?" he asked, as if he had every right to know.

"Tucson," I admitted, with an inward sigh. I braced myself for the coming storm of Latin-Irish temperament.

"So that's why you didn't answer at home," he concluded. His voice was cold, with an accusing edge. "You gave me the slip."

My tone was the verbal equivalent of a girlish simper. I admit it, I was trying to warm him up a little. "Detective Sonterra," I said, "your powers of deduction are unparalleled."

Not a shred of humor in the man's whole

body. "What are you doing in Tucson?" he demanded. "Have you lost your mind?"

"One question at a time," I said calmly. "And I'm going to overlook the fact that you have no business asking me anything like that in the first place."

"You called me, Counselor. If you don't like the way the conversation's going, hang up."

I couldn't do that. I was hanging on to the sound of his voice, though I wasn't about to admit it. "I need a favor, Sonterra," I said.

"That doesn't surprise me," he said, still cool and noncommittal, but with slightly less of an edge.

I wondered if he was at a crime scene, or worse, out on a date with another woman. I steered with one hand, held the phone with the other, glancing often at the rearview mirror. The hair on the nape of my neck seemed electrified, and my stomach was jumping. "What's happening with the e-mails I showed you? Have you learned anything new?"

"As a matter of fact, that's why I tried to call you earlier. It's going to be difficult, make that impossible, to identify the sender. I've got some people asking around,

though, but we haven't been able to prove
any connection with Arren or his girlfriend.
Just about anybody could have walked into
the library and used that computer." He
paused for one dangerous beat. "Now it's
my turn. I repeat, Counselor—what are you
doing in Tucson?"

I sighed. "I'm representing Justin Netherton exclusively, as of today. Looking for
holes in the prosecution's case, you might
say."

"Good luck," Sonterra said, without a
shred of sincerity. "I read all about Netherton on the Web. The guy stinks, and so
does your case, Clare."

The remark raised my hackles, which, in
this instance, was a relief. Being mad is better than being scared, in my book at least.
"There you go again, Sonterra, setting yourself up as a one-man judge and jury. Did it
ever occur to you that, just this one time,
you might not know what the hell you're
talking about?"

He laughed, which totally pissed me off. It
seemed, in that dark moment, that he'd
never taken me seriously. He probably
thought it was cute that I was a lawyer, but
I'd come to my senses someday, especially

if I let him back into my bed on a steady basis.

Headlights glared behind me, but Tucson is a big city, Arizona drivers are pushy, myself included, and the street was busy. By that time, I was so thoroughly into the sniping match with Sonterra, I barely noticed. "I can always count on you for nothing," I snapped.

"You sound a little shaky. What's the matter, Clare—is your conscience bothering you? Or have you even got one of those?"

I remembered the look on Sylvie's face when I told her I was representing Dr. Netherton, the man whose incompetence and greed had caused her so much pain and grief. My conscience *was* chafing a little, but I was giving out information on a need-to-know basis, and Sonterra didn't need to know.

"Maybe it's being back here," I said. "Where I grew up. Where Tracy disappeared. Where the *cops* acted like she didn't count because she had a few bad breaks and came from the wrong part of town."

He was silent for a moment. Then, "You're

not playing detective down there, are you, Counselor?"

I couldn't think of an answer. The car behind me sped up, then fell back.

"Clare?" Sonterra persisted.

I spotted my hotel in the distance and took the appropriate exit. "I'm not playing at anything," I said. "My sister is dead, and I want to know who killed her."

"That's a job for the police," he said pompously.

"Like they ever gave a damn," I replied. The car behind me turned off a block before I did, and I let out a sigh. I guessed I'd been more nervous than I realized.

"Listen to me, Clare," Sonterra said. "This is not a game. This is not TV or a movie or some stupid book. And you are not a cop or a P.I. If you ruffle the wrong feathers, you're likely to end up dead in a culvert somewhere."

I pulled into the hotel's side lot, found it full, and went around to the back. There were spaces, but it was dark. I circled to the front again, thinking I'd spring for valet parking, but the attendant was nowhere in sight, and I had to go to the bathroom, badly. I'd already decided I didn't have the

stomach for detective work; now I knew I
didn't have the bladder, either. "And you
think I should just sit back and trust the police? Don't look now, Sonterra, but so far
that's gotten me exactly nowhere!"

He let the remark regarding the compe-
tency of his profession pass, though it probably would not be for long. "That's *exactly*
what I think, Clare. The picture will force
them to reopen the case, especially with the
M.E. confirming—what she did." Sonterra, it
seemed, was actually trying to be tactful,
which is not his natural state. If he'd been
talking to just about anybody else, he would
probably have said, "According to the M.E.,
this is definitely a snapshot of a stiff."

I parked as close to the hotel as I could,
and I had the presence of mind to get my
key-card out, figuring the rear doors would
be locked for security purposes. I was still
talking to Sonterra when I left the car, juggling my purse, the car keys, and the card,
when a pair of headlights blinked on at high
beam, not twenty feet away, and rushed toward me.

I shrieked and lunged for the hotel door,
just as the assailant's vehicle struck the side

of my car, doing at least forty. The sound of it rattled my fillings.

Sonterra panicked. "Jesus, Clare—what's going on?" he shouted.

My Saturn was crunched from stem to stern, but I had no time to inspect the damage. The other car was backing up to take another run at me. I jammed the key-card into the slot, shouldered the door, and dived inside, just as whoever was after me took out a couple of shrubs and smashed into my Saturn again. The phone was lying at my feet; I kicked it over the threshold as I leaped for safety.

"Clare!" Sonterra shouted, from somewhere on the floor.

I scrabbled for the phone and peered out through the glass door, now shut and locked, breathing hard and trying to get a glimpse of my attacker or, at least, of his or her car. Nothing. Whoever it was peeled out as he or she left the lot.

I remembered Trevor Trent, playing demolition derby with the front of a restaurant, and wondered if he or his father had followed me to Tucson to extract the promised revenge.

"I'm all right," I told Sonterra, which was

not entirely true. It was a miracle I hadn't wet my pants.

"I'm coming down there," Sonterra said. "Where are you?"

The women's rest room on the ground floor was being cleaned, so I went into the men's. "I'll call you back," I told him, and disconnected as I dived into one of the stalls.

My phone was ringing again before I finished washing my hands. I'd never given Sonterra my cell number, but it had probably shown up on his caller ID. "Hello," I said, wondering if it would be safe to go outside and check out the damage to my car. *Two payments left*, I thought. *Shit.*

"Damn it, Clare," Sonterra barked, "what the *hell* is going on?"

I stepped into the hallway, pushed the elevator button, waited for the descent. I glanced back at the outside door a couple of times, half-expecting a monster face to be looming there. A memory tickled the back of my mind; Tracy, mimicking one of the characters' lines, after we'd watched *Twilight Zone: The Movie*. *"Wanna see something really scary?"*

"You were right about the detective business," I said. "It's dangerous. Somebody just tried to run me down."

"What?"

The elevator arrived, empty, and I got in, pushed the *close door* button. I wasn't up for company, innocent or otherwise. "I'm not repeating myself, Sonterra. It was hard enough to say it once. I'm going to my room now, and I'm calling the police, for all the damn good *that* will probably do, and then I'm calling my insurance company."

"I'm coming down there," he repeated, measuring out the words a syllable at a time, in case I'd missed his meaning the first time.

"No," I said firmly, though another, weaker part of me wanted him within grabbing distance. "I'll be fine."

"Right," Sonterra snapped. "Or maybe you'll be dead, instead."

"Do me a favor and check up on Trevor Trent, will you? The kid I was defending for smashing into that restaurant with his car?"

"Damn it, Clare—"

"Good-bye, Sonterra," I said as the elevator stopped on my floor and the doors opened.

"Don't you *dare* hang up on me!" Sonterra yelled.

"Don't you want me to call the police?" I knew my tone would annoy him, and it did.

He swore. I could just see him look at his watch and glower, the way he does when he feels stuck and has to spin his wheels for a while. "I can get the name of your hotel," he said presently.

That was true enough. "Okay," I said, and pressed the *end* button with my thumb. When the phone started to ring again, before I got my room unlocked and stepped inside, I turned it off.

I splashed my face with cold water before calling the local police on the land line beside the bed, and combed my hair while I was waiting. When I'd gone to them about Tracy, years before, they'd written me off as an obsessed relative. At least this time I could show them my demolished car, and the sheared-off shrubbery.

After taking a few deep breaths, I called the manager downstairs, explained what had happened, and told him the police were on their way. He was concerned for my safety, of course, but I could tell he wasn't all that thrilled at the prospect of one or more squad cars twirling their blue and red lights in front of his hotel.

Next, I called my insurance agent, in Scottsdale, and left the pertinent information on his voice mail. With luck, he would get back to me by breakfast. I would try to reach Harvey, Jr., in the morning; if my policy didn't cover a rental car, I planned to put one on the company credit card. Whoever had come after me, and Trevor seemed the most likely candidate given the M.D., had rattled me for sure, but they hadn't scared me off. I was more determined than ever to stick out this assignment.

The police were actually quite cordial. They looked at the car, measured the tread marks on the pavement, collected a few paint chips, and shook their heads over the shrubbery and the dent in the wall of the hotel. I tossed Trevor's name out there, along with Henley's, and they promised to follow up, told me to be careful, asked me to sign a report, and left. I was relieved, and I know the manager was, too.

I went back upstairs to my room, secured both locks, and propped a chair under the knob just to be sure.

The message light on my phone was blinking.

I sighed. Sonterra had found me, just as he said he would.

I sank onto the edge of the bed, lifted the receiver, pushed the proper button. "You have *one* new voice mail message," the recorded voice informed me.

I shoved a hand through my hair and waited, biting my lower lip.

"Leave it alone, bitch," the caller said, in an evil voice I didn't recognize. I was sure I wasn't dealing with the same guy who'd called me at home, threatening my life and going on about "three for three." Nor did this person sound like James, though I was convinced I was talking to him. "You keep poking around, and you'll end up as bug bait, like your sister."

I had the presence of mind to save the message, though even that effort was enormous. I couldn't move, couldn't think—I simply sat there, knowing in my heart that I'd just heard the voice of Tracy's killer, James or not, and very possibly my own.

The phone rang; I stared at it blankly, then answered, still in shock.

"Clare?" It was Sonterra.

I was numb. "Where are you?"

"Downstairs," he said. "Give me your room number. I'm coming up."

I mumbled the number, and when he knocked, I yanked open the door and threw myself into his arms.

So much for my image as a hard-ass crimefighter.

Chapter Twenty-six

Throwing a body slam on Sonterra the way I did, I felt his service revolver, tucked into its handy shoulder holster, through the light-weight denim of his jacket, and I reacted as if I'd been burned.

Sonterra looked down at my face, which must have been at less than its best, and chuckled as he eased us both into the room and closed the door. "Yes," he joked huskily, "that's a gun in my pocket, and yes, I'm glad to see you."

By then, I was backpedaling like crazy, in a vain effort to recover some of the dignity I'd lost by flying at him the moment I opened the door and saw him standing in the hall. "What are you doing here?" I demanded, a few beats and a whole lot of torso-to-torso contact too late. "Things must be pretty quiet in Scottsdale if they can spare a homicide detective—"

"Eddie's covering for me," he said, studying me with those smoldering eyes of his. There was more he wasn't saying, but I guess I wasn't ready to hear it, because I didn't press, not then, anyway. "Are you hurt, Clare?"

I plunked down on the end of one of the two queen beds in my room, sitting up straight and keeping myself as close to the edge as possible. "I'm fine," I said.

Sonterra took off his jacket and draped it over the back of the chair at the small desk. He wore a white T-shirt underneath and sported the ever-present holster, along with his service revolver. I've often wondered what it is about a man wearing a shoulder holster that turns me on, but I'm not prepared to ask anybody who might actually know. Like my therapist, for instance.

"You don't look all that good," Sonterra remarked. "You've got bags under your eyes."

"Thanks," I shot back.

"Relax, Counselor. I'm not here to jump your bones."

This news should have come as a relief, but it didn't. It was something of a disappointment, in fact, and there was, of course, no assurance that *I* wouldn't do the jumping. I did manage to chill out a bit, though. "How did you get here so fast?" I asked, hoping to normalize the atmosphere, which was just short of combustible.

He pulled back the same desk chair where he'd hung his jacket, turned it around, and sat astraddle, facing me, his arms resting across the back. I tried not to notice the corded muscles in those arms, the deep tan, the dusting of dark hair, but that would have been a tall order. As a package, Sonterra is formidable, and just about impossible to ignore.

"I drive fast," he said. "And I was already in my car when you called the first time, so I headed this way. Eddie ran a check on Trevor Trent—seems the kid was at his church youth group meeting, atoning I'm sure, while you were trying to get yourself killed tonight. There's a room full of witnesses prepared to swear to his alibi. His dad's clean, too—out of state at some seminar."

So much for that handy-dandy little theory. I drew a deep breath, released it slowly. Then I began to shake. I nodded my head toward the phone. "Listen to the message," I mumbled, unable to look at him. "It was waiting when I came back to the room, after talking to the police."

Frowning, Sonterra got up, ambled over to the nightstand between the two beds, picked up the receiver, and pushed the appropriate buttons. I watched his profile as he listened, saw his jaw clench. He saved the message, as I had done, hung up, and turned to look at me.

"Any idea who we might be dealing with, here?" he asked.

"Probably James, or maybe one of his friends. I'm not sure I'd recognize his voice if he tried to disguise it."

He sat down on the other bed, and I scooted around to face him. Our knees were touching the way they did under the table at El Encanto, when we went to lunch. "I checked out your car before I came up," he told me quietly. "You sure you're going to be all right?"

I nodded again, though it was a lie, and he knew it as well as I did. I wasn't sure of anything that night.

"Did you get through to your insurance agent?"

I tried to smile. "Sort of," I said. "It wasn't like the TV commercial, where they rush over with a check, swerving between fallen trees and downed power lines—I got his voice mail."

Sonterra's expression didn't change; he was dead serious, no goofing off. "Whoever did that meant business, Clare. They weren't just trying to shake you up. They wanted to kill you—the idea was to pin you between their bumper and the side of your car. Crunch city."

I winced. Being fresh out of smart answers, I merely nodded.

Sonterra sighed. Relented a little. He was used to grilling murder suspects, and he probably could have kept questioning me for hours. "You're exhausted," he said. "When was the last time you got any sleep?"

I was a sucker for somebody taking care of me; it was such a novelty that I couldn't resist indulging myself a little. "There's been a lot going on," I answered.

He offered no further comment on my obvious fatigue, but went to the desk instead and rummaged for the room service menu. "I'm starved," he said, and I welcomed the change of subject. He studied the offerings.

"A cheeseburger sounds good. Want something?"

I thought about it. "A BLT," I decided. "Ice tea, too."

He reached for the phone, and I ducked into the bathroom, where I ran a hot bath, stripped off my clothes, and sank to my chin. Whenever I have a hard day, or suffer some trauma, I want to soak. Go figure.

I luxuriated for a while, and when I heard Sonterra answer the door and accept delivery of our late-night supper, I got out of the tub, dried off, and put on the hotel robe I'd found in the closet earlier. A rollaway table stood between the two beds, and Sonterra sat facing me, ready to dine.

"I'd stand in honor of your entrance," he said, "but it's a little cramped in here."

I waved off the offer and squeezed in on my side. The food looked good, and I ate ravenously.

"Feel better?" Sonterra asked when he'd finished. I was still swiping French fries off his plate and dragging them through a pool of ketchup amid the wreckage of my own meal.

"I'm a new woman," I said.

He laughed. "I *guess* that's encouraging,"

he said, and toasted me with the last of his ice tea. "Though I admit to a certain weakness for the old one."

No way was I taking up *that* conversational thread. It could only lead to trouble, and I had more than enough of that already. "I can't believe you're here," I said.

"Believe it," he replied. The words rumbled from his throat.

"You can have the extra bed if you want," I ventured. Sonterra was hot, no doubt about it, but if we had sex again, I knew I'd be left with no judgment at all, and I needed to keep my wits about me if I planned on staying alive.

He regarded me with amused silence for a long time, his gaze slipping to the place where the sides of my robe met in a V, and then sighed sadly. "Fine," he agreed.

"Assuming you were planning to stay at all, I mean."

"Oh," he drawled, "I'm planning to stay, all right."

"What about your job?"

"I told you," he said, "Eddie's covering. I'll head back tomorrow—after getting you settled in another hotel, if I can't talk you into going with me."

"I can't go back until I've finished my business here," I insisted quietly.

"Check," he said, with grim acceptance.

I finally had enough of the fries, and Sonterra wheeled the cart out into the hallway while I stood between the two beds, wondering how I managed to get myself into these situations.

"You must have been a room service waiter in a past life," I said, when he came back in, closing and locking the door.

He was grinning when he turned to face me. "Actually, it was this one. How do you think I put myself through college?"

That reminded me of Nipples, where I'd earned the money to pay for my undergraduate degree, but this night's visit to my old stomping grounds was still too vivid to talk about.

"Which bed do you want?" I asked.

Sonterra sighed and shook his head. "The one you're sleeping in," he said. "But since I'm not going to get my wish, I'll take the one closest to the door. That way, I can defend your virtue, such as it is, if anybody breaks in."

I closed my eyes. Sonterra was teasing, but from my viewpoint, the possibility of an attack was too real to be funny. "Fine," I said, and I got into the other bed, pulling the covers up to my chin and lying rigid in the middle of the mattress.

Sonterra seemed to find that amusing, too; he chuckled as he unfastened his shoulder holster, and I squeezed my eyes shut. All the same, behind the red glow of my eyelids, I could clearly picture him pulling the white T-shirt off over his head and revealing that buff chest, kicking off his boots, undoing his belt buckle. Mercifully, if not quickly, the sounds of undressing finally ceased, and Sonterra flipped off the lamp. I decided it was safe to open my eyes.

"You know anybody around here, Counselor?" Sonterra asked, out of the darkness. I knew he was lying on his side, propped up on one elbow. Don't ask me *how* I knew. I just did. Where Sonterra is concerned, I've got some kind of sensory radar. "Someone you could stay with while you're scrounging for evidence to get the mad butcher acquitted?"

Kip and Loretta's ranch was a likely choice, but too far out of town for my purposes. Besides, I'd been leaning on them for favors a lot lately. "No," I said, fingers clutching the sheets as if I expected Sonterra to leap out of bed, tear the covers back, and ravage me.

A girl can always hope.

"Friends, then?" The gentleness in his voice was a dirty trick on his part; I have defenses for everything except kindness. It's connected to the caretaking thing; I'm just not very good at being fussed over, but at the same time, I crave it.

Sylvie was the only person in Tucson who could have remotely qualified as a friend, and she wasn't likely to invite me for a sleepover and girl talk. Besides, now that Trevor and his father had been eliminated from the suspect list, I wasn't entirely sure my parking lot attacker hadn't been her own sweet lovin' man, Henley. "Give it a rest, Sonterra," I said. "I'm a big girl, and I can take care of myself."

His reply surprised me a little. "You've made that pretty obvious," he said. I couldn't help remembering other times when we'd talked in the darkness, usually after sleeping off a few hours of wicked sex. "Still, there must be times when you'd like to let down your guard and be looked after." He paused. "What is it with you, Clare, that you've got to keep everybody somewhere in the middle distance?"

I had to swallow the hard lump that formed in my throat before I could answer. "There are some luxuries a girl like me can't afford," I told him crisply, "and getting too close to other people is one of them."

" 'A girl like me'? What the hell is that supposed to mean?"

"It was a figure of speech, Sonterra. Shut up and go to sleep."

He sighed, and I heard him shifting his weight around on the mattress across the twenty-four-inch no-fly zone between us. It set my ragged-edge nerves jangling again, that simple and probably innocent movement of his body.

Trust him to push for the last word. "What was it like for you, Counselor? Being a kid, I mean? Whatever happened, it really messed you up."

I couldn't have explained the tears that came to my eyes just then, and I was damn glad he couldn't see them. "Thanks for that, too, Sonterra. If I'm such a basket case, why don't you quit hanging around?"

"I've asked myself that question a time or

two," he said. "Never got a straight answer. Talk to me, Clare."

Damn him. If he got the idea to crawl into bed with me and take me into his arms, I would be completely lost. "It's a dull story," I bluffed. "You'd be bored before I got past kindergarten."

"Try me."

Chapter Twenty-seven

Like a damn fool, I started to cry. And not delicately, either; I sounded like a cow with a sinus condition.

I heard Sonterra toss back his covers and sit up. I knew what he was going to do, knew there was no stopping him. Just as I'd feared—and, okay, *hoped*—he slipped in beside me and pulled me into a loose embrace, his chin propped on top of my head.

"Screw you, Sonterra," I sobbed.

He chuckled, his breath warm in my hair, his arms strong, so strong, around me. "I get your meaning," he replied, "but that may not have been the best choice of words."

My pride was at low ebb, and I was out of ammunition. Sonterra was getting dangerously close to the real me, and that was a place no one was allowed to visit. Hell, I wasn't sure of the exact location myself.

"If you make love to me tonight," I snuffled, "I will never forgive you."

"I would never forgive *myself*," he replied. "I'm in this bed strictly as your friend, Counselor. You're in no shape for any kind of sport."

I had to laugh, even though I was still blubbering, because his use of the word "sport" sounded so, I don't know, *un-Sonterra*-like.

I needed some space, even if it was only verbal. "Tell me what it was like to be little Tony Sonterra."

I pretty much knew the details, since Sonterra had been a lot more forthcoming about his past than I had been about mine, but I liked hearing it, the way I'd liked hearing *Goodnight Moon* over and over again, when I was a little girl and Tracy was into mothering me, and reading bedtime stories every night.

"As far as I know," he said, with a grin in his voice, "nobody has ever referred to me as 'little Tony Sonterra' in my life." He shifted, making himself comfortable, making me deliciously *un*comfortable. "I grew up in Phoenix," he recited dutifully. His arms were still locked securely around me, his chin touching the crown of my head, and I gave a small, inward sigh. "One side of the family is Irish—one side, Hispanic. I have seven aunts, all Catholic—you've never seen so much lace, or so many candles, in your life, and they pretty much raised us—my brother, sister, and me—after Mom died."

"What happened to her?" I'd known his mother was dead, but couldn't recall the details, if I'd ever heard them.

"She was hit by a car one day, while she was crossing the street," Sonterra said. "Coming home from the supermarket. I was eight at the time. Joey was fourteen, and Angie was four. It was hard, but thanks to Dad and the aunts, life went on." There had been a substantial insurance settlement, I recalled. Hence Sonterra's high degree of solvency, which was fairly unusual for a cop.

"Your dad got married again." It was a statement, not a question, because I'd met his stepmother, as well as his father and aunts, at one of their chaotic family picnics. The longer I kept Sonterra talking, I reasoned, the longer I could keep the attention off my own history.

"Yeah," Tony said fondly, "about five years after Mom died. Dad stepped down and let Joey take over the family landscaping business; then he went off on one of those cruises for retirees. I think he was mainly trying to get away from all the nice church ladies the aunts kept sending his way. The best-laid plans—he met Bertie on the boat and brought her home with a ring on her finger. They've been into happily-ever-after ever since."

I'm not a lawyer for nothing. I can keep a conversation going. "Tell me about your brother and sister."

Sonterra's sigh indicated that my tactics weren't fooling him, but he was willing to play the game, at least for a while. "Joey is married to a woman named Kayla, and they have four kids, all boys, the bane of their parochial school. Angie is a widow; her husband died three years ago. She works for Social Services."

I yawned. "I'm getting really tired, Sonterra," I said.

His easy hold on me did not slacken. "Good," he replied.

I'd been telling the truth about being

sleepy, and when I closed my eyes, I zonked right out. I dreamed that Henley was chasing me in a dented red kiddie-car, pedaling like mad.

My subconscious must be a real pit.

Chapter Twenty-eight

I heard Sonterra get up in the middle of the night and hit the shower—presumably, a cold one—and when he came out of the bathroom, I pretended to be asleep. I held my breath, and he got into the other bed. As so often happened with Sonterra, I couldn't decide whether to regret this new development or rejoice over it.

He awakened me a few hours later by tossing a McDonald's bag on my stomach.

Fast-food breakfast; I'd know that aroma anywhere.

I sat up, blinking and scrabbling for the sack. Sonterra was wearing yesterday's clothes, and he needed a shave, but he looked the way the food smelled: delectable.

"It's about time you woke up, lazybones," he said.

I glanced at the digital clock on the nightstand: 7:15 A.M. Yeah, I was a regular Rip

Van Winkle. I plundered the bag, bringing out a sausage biscuit with egg and a carton of hash browns. "Where's the coffee?" I demanded. I am not at my personal best in the morning, especially when I've acted like a fool the night before.

Sonterra arched those dark brows of his, but his eyes sparkled, and a corner of his mouth tilted upward in a ghost of a grin. "There's a pot brewing on the bathroom counter," he informed me.

I'm no kitchen maven, but it seems to me that there's something wrong with brewing coffee in the bathroom, even when you're on the road, and therefore, improvising. "Great," I said, trying to be civil. After all, the man *had* ventured out into the cruel world to bring back a week's worth of scrumptious fat grams.

He chuckled and left the room, returning momentarily with the coffee.

Meanwhile, I bit into the biscuit. Bliss.

"Thanks," I said, with my mouth full.

"Your insurance agent called," he said.

I swallowed. "I didn't hear the phone ring," I told him.

"No," he replied, pulling out the desk chair and sitting down. "I don't imagine you did. You were down for the count until you smelled grub."

"What did he say?"

"It was a she. She'll be here to look at the car at eight-thirty. You're covered for a rental, and somebody will bring that by before ten."

"You're pretty efficient, Sonterra," I admitted, dabbing at my mouth with a wadded paper napkin.

He spread his hands. "That's why they pay me the big bucks," he said.

"Did you eat?"

Sonterra chuckled again. "I notice you didn't ask me that until you'd finished off the biscuit," he said. "As a matter of fact, though, I wolfed down my share on the way back."

"So now you can go back to Scottsdale and find out who killed Harvey and Janet and the Robbins woman."

He was undaunted, as usual. When it comes to broad hints, Sonterra has the sensibilities of a rhino submerged to its nostrils in a mud hole. "Right now," he said, "I'm more interested in making sure nobody kills *you*, Counselor."

In the bright light of day, the previous

night's attack seemed like a footnote instead of a major attempt on my life.

"I don't need your help," I said.

"Like hell you don't," he replied, unruffled.

I made sure the front of my hotel bathrobe was secure, then got out of bed, giving Sonterra a wide berth as I headed for the desk to check my cell phone for missed messages.

There were none.

Sonterra cleared his throat, and I tensed. I knew he was about to tell me something I wouldn't like.

"What?" I demanded, putting my hands on my hips.

"I got a call from the department on the way down here last night," he said, forcing himself to look at me. "James Arren missed a meeting with his parole officer. There's a bulletin out for him."

My knees sagged. "Emma—?"

"She's fine," he hastened to assure me. "Loretta and Kip have been advised, and they're taking appropriate measures."

Incredulous fury simmered up inside me. "Why didn't you tell me last night?"

His gaze was direct. "Because you had

just been through an attempt on your life.
You needed time."

I assimilated that. "So James *could* have
been the person who tried to run me down.
And he was probably the one who left that
message."

"It's a possibility," Sonterra agreed grimly.

I turned and went into the bathroom, hoping to recover some of my lost composure.
Deep down, I was processing everything,
but on the surface, I'd shifted to la-la level.

The mundane observation struck me that
Sonterra had been to the store, during his
morning outing; he'd bought himself a
toothbrush and paste, a packet of disposable razors, and a can of shaving foam.

Emergency grooming measures, I assured myself. If Sonterra had intended to
stay in Tucson and drive me crazy, he would
have bought at least one change of clothes,
too. He was always a neat freak.

The trivia diversion lasted just so long.

James Arren was on the loose. Knowing
that scared me more than anything.

I pushed the thought into the basement of
my brain, to simmer for a while. Next, I
started the shower, then sashayed out to
get fresh underwear, jeans, and a cotton

blouse from my suitcase, which was on a stand in the closet. Maybe if I ignored Sonterra, I reflected, he'd go away.

Fat chance.

He was stretched out on his rumpled bed when I came out of the bathroom showered and dressed, remote control in hand, flipping his way through the limited selection of channels comprising the hotel's entertainment system. He paused to take in a few sound bites of CNN, while I retrieved my cell phone, which I'd forgotten to charge, and dialed Loretta's number in Scottsdale.

My friend answered promptly.

"You've heard about James?" she asked.

No more dodging the true state of affairs. "Yes, I said. "Let me talk to Emma."

"She's okay, Clare. Kip took her to school and left one of his people there to serve as a bodyguard."

"A bodyguard?" I croaked.

"We thought it would be a good idea. Just till they round up Arren."

Out of the corner of my eye, I saw a flash of fire on the TV. "What else is going on?" I pressed.

"Clare," Loretta said, "you'd better sit down."

Sonterra was staring at me now, the TV on mute. Something was blazing away on the screen.

I plopped onto the end of my bed. "What?"

"Sylvie Wyand was murdered last night," Loretta said.

The room seemed to pitch sharply to one side, then righted itself with a sickening lurch. "That can't be—"

"Somebody torched the trailer, and she didn't get out." Loretta's voice was small. "It's been all over the news—I'm surprised you didn't know."

"Jesus," I whispered, hugging myself. My eyes were glued to the TV screen now; I gestured to Sonterra to turn up the sound.

"An acquaintance of mine died in a trailer fire last night," I told him.

He swore under his breath and cranked up the volume. The ugly details of Sylvie's death flowed into the room, as if through a sound tunnel from hell.

"Who's there with you?" Loretta asked, sounding suspicious.

"Sonterra," I answered, keeping one eye and one ear on the TV.

"You're not safe down there, even with Tony around," my friend insisted. "Get in your car and come back home, Clare."

"You're breaking up," I told Loretta, alternately shouting and whispering. "I'm going to have to ring off—"

"Don't you dare—"

I made some garbly sounds in my throat and shut the phone off. There would be hell to pay when I got back to Scottsdale, but, hey, at this point, getting home alive might be an accomplishment in and of itself. Something to celebrate.

Because I knew Emma was being looked after, I was able to stay fairly cool.

Sonterra flipped channels until he found another Tucson station running the Wyand story, and we got it in its gruesome entirety. A burned-out trailer filled the screen, and the camera panned to Henley, standing beside his wrecker, with his German shepherd slavering in the driver's seat. Tears slicked Henley's face.

"I wouldn't have left her alone if I'd known this was going to happen," he sobbed. A band across the bottom of the screen read "Live, on the scene of Tucson arson attack."

The reporter turned away from the wreck that was Henley, with a sympathetic shake of his carefully coiffed head, and spoke with the gravity of an undertaker with his work cut out for him. "Brian," he said, apparently addressing somebody back at the news desk, "this is a real tragedy. As stated earlier, evidence of arson has been found at the scene. Yesterday, this was a peaceful neighborhood. Today, a woman is dead."

I fought to keep down my breakfast. *Sylvie.*

"How well did you know this woman?" Sonterra demanded, suddenly all cop, after thumbing the *off* button on the remote.

"Her name was Sylvie Wyand," I said miserably. "I used to work with her, at Nipples."

"At where?" Never very proud of my career as the redneck equivalent of a Playboy bunny, I'd kept the details of my early employment history to myself. All Sonterra knew was that I'd waited tables in college.

"It's a bar," I told him, snatching a couple of tissues from the travel packet I kept in my purse to dab at my eyes. "I served drinks there, while I was getting my undergraduate degree at the university."

"Couldn't you have clerked at Wal-Mart or something, like a normal person?"

I glared at him. "I hardly think this is the time to discuss my old job," I said. "I visited Sylvie last night, and I'm pretty sure I was followed after I left her place. *Then* somebody tried to grind me into their grillwork. I don't believe that was a coincidence, Detective. Do you?"

He was on his feet, reaching for the phone.

I practically dived onto the thing. "What are you doing?"

"Calling the Tucson police," he said.

I flung myself backward onto the bed in abject frustration, arms wide of my body. "That's *just* what I need!" I yelled. "More cops!"

"What you need is not the point," Sonterra said, punching buttons. "A woman has been deliberately incinerated and apparently you were with her just prior to her death. Better to call them than wait for them to track you down, trust me." Someone answered on the other end. "Detective Anthony Sonterra," he told the operator. "Scottsdale P.D., Homicide. I'd like to speak to Lieutenant Browder, if he's in." He gave me a look of wide-eyed warning, effectively quelling my next lame protest. "Sure, I'll hold." He looked at his watch, grimaced slightly. Sonterra hates holding. "Arlo," he said presently, and with the heartiness of one old friend greeting another. "How've you been? Yeah?" Long, sober pause. "Actually, that's why I'm calling. I've got a potential witness here." Another pause. "Right here in Tucson."

I sat up, waving both hands in an attempt to keep Sonterra from spilling his guts to this Arlo guy. By that time, I'd realized what was going to happen: I'd spend the whole day answering questions, and I might even find myself on the suspect list, this time, for real.

Sonterra ignored me, gave Browder the name of my hotel, as well as the room number. I couldn't help thinking that the people downstairs were going to be just thrilled when the cops showed up a second time, asking for me. Harvey, Jr., would be pleased, too, once word got back to him. From his viewpoint, Clare's Tucson Adventure would definitely qualify as bad press.

Sonterra hung up, turned to me. "Let's go have a look at what's left of your car," he said.

"Piss off, Sonterra," I replied, but he led the way, and I followed.

Chapter Twenty-nine

Lieutenant Arlo Browder turned out to be a cowboy type, wearing boots, a white hat, and a crisply pressed western shirt with his beat-up jeans. In any other setting, he would have been a stand-out, but in southern Arizona, he practically blended into the landscape. He and Sonterra shook hands in the lobby of the hotel, grinning and exchanging pleasantries, while I stood by, waiting to be introduced, then interrogated again. I had no doubt that Henley would have told the cops about my visit to Sylvie the night before, just prior to her murder, but now that I'd had time to think, it seemed unlikely that they'd view me as anything but a possible witness. After all, I'd had no motive.

Lieutenant Browder took off his hat for my benefit, which made me like him right away. So did the crinkly lines shooting like sun rays from the corners of his blue eyes.

His face was tanned and craggy, his smile easy. "I'm Arlo," he said. "You must be Ms. Westbrook."

"Clare," I corrected, smiling. I had put James Arren's disappearance on an emotional back burner by then, knowing I wouldn't be able to function if I let it rule my thoughts.

"We can talk in the bar," Arlo said. The cocktail lounge was closed at that hour of the day and therefore empty, which made it the ideal place for a private conversation. The lieutenant showed a badge to the desk clerk who, after peering around him to give Sonterra and me the once-over, produced a key ring and jangled down the lower hallway to open the door.

The clerk flipped on the lights and slipped out; Arlo chose a table and drew back a chair for me. Once I was seated, he and Sonterra sat down, too, one on either side of me. Arlo took a small spiral notebook from his shirt pocket, along with a pen.

I gave him all the basic information first: my name, address, telephone numbers, place of employment, and so on.

"I understand from a Mr."—he flipped back a few pages in his notebook, though I

didn't for one moment believe he'd forgotten any detail of the case so far—"Henley
Eggleman—Ms. Wyand's boyfriend—that
you visited her at their home last night. I'd
like you to tell me about that, if you would."

As if I had a choice.

Glad of Sonterra's presence, I told Arlo
how I'd come to Tucson on law firm business, and sought Sylvie out because we'd
once worked together and I knew she'd had
an encounter with my client, Justin Netherton.

I left out a few things, like how Sylvie had
told me to get out of her house and never
come back, and my suspicion that she'd
known something about Tracy's murder.
The fact that I would never know what it
was lodged in the bottom of my stomach
like a thistle.

From there, we moved on to my account
of the car-smashing episode, and Arlo
made notes and asked questions, by turns.
I searched his face, his words, and his nuances, but I could find no indication of his
private opinion on the matter of Sylvie's
murder and my waking near-death experience; he might have been making a grocery
list.

"Let's talk about Ms. Wyand's relationship with her boyfriend," Arlo prompted, when I'd finished. "Do you know anything about that?"

I shook my head. I personally found Henley unattractive, to say the least, but that didn't make him a murder suspect. He might have been the one to bash my car, and try to kill me. He might even have been the one to leave that scary message on my hotel-room phone, though I was still sure James had been behind that. The bottom line was, Henley didn't have any more motive for bumping me off than I'd had for killing Sylvie. For him, the crime would not have been worth the inevitable time. Being on probation, Henley probably tried to watch his step.

"I hadn't seen Sylvie in years and, as far as I know, I've never met Henley before."

"You'll be in town for a few days?" Arlo asked.

I nodded, after slicing a glance at Sonterra. His face, like his friend's, revealed nothing of what he was thinking, but I knew all the same.

"Good," the lieutenant said. "I might have some more questions for you." He produced a card. "Meanwhile, if you think of anything else, or feel that you might be in any kind of danger, give me a call." He nodded to Sonterra and started to rise. "Of course I'll let you know if we get any solid leads in your case," he added.

I thanked him, pocketing his card. Later, when Sonterra had gone back up north, where he belonged, I planned to call Lieutenant Browder and quiz him about the investigation into Tracy's disappearance. If he hadn't seen the digital photo of my sister, I would show it to him and demand action.

My rental car, a white subcompact, arrived while Sonterra and Browder were saying their manly good-byes, out by Browder's huge extended-cab truck.

"What were you guys talking about just now?" I asked, after Browder drove away and Sonterra ambled over to examine the rental.

"Tracy's disappearance," Sonterra answered, without hesitation. He was peering through the passenger window and frowning, probably calculating the legroom, or lack thereof. "I asked him if he'd had a chance to look at that picture of her, and he said he had." He straightened, studied me over the roof of the little car. "Were you planning to mention any of that to the Tucson police," he asked, "or just go bungling ahead on your own?"

"I would have gotten around to it," I said. *When you were gone,* I added, in silence.

Sonterra rolled his eyes, bracing his left arm against the car roof. A warm desert breeze ruffled his dark hair, and I wondered why he'd bothered to buy a razor and foam, only to leave last night's five o'clock shadow untouched. On some level, I think he knew he was driving me crazy, and he loved it.

He gave me the look. "One of these days, Clare, that attitude of yours is going to get you into serious trouble."

"That," I said, pulling open the door on the driver's side and jingling the keys at him, "would be nothing new. Are you riding with me, Sonterra? Or are you too macho to be seen in a subcompact?"

He shook his head. "Just to prove what a modern, politically correct guy I am, I will let that little gibe pass." He pulled open his door, folded himself into the seat, and glowered at me as I took the wheel. His knees were wedged against the dashboard, which made buckling his seat belt a supreme challenge.

I enjoyed watching the struggle.

"Where are we going?" he asked, somewhat belatedly, it seemed to me, as I pulled out of the hotel parking lot.

"I want to talk to Sylvie's boyfriend. You know, Henley—the guy on the TV news."

"What, if you don't mind telling me," Sonterra droned peevishly, "does that bozo have to do with Netherton's case?"

"Nothing, as far as I know," I answered.

"Your expense accounts must be very creative," Sonterra observed. "Didn't you say the firm sent you down here to dig up dirt on Netherton's victims?"

I set my jaw, drove around behind the hotel, to the scene of my near-miss, and pulled up beside Sonterra's SUV, stopping with a barely audible screech of tires. "I know you have things to do in Scottsdale," I said evenly. "Don't let me keep you from your work, Detective."

He sighed dramatically, a good man sorely misused, but made no move to get out of the rental, maybe because he meant to stand his ground, and maybe because it would have been impossible to make a graceful exit. I wasn't entirely sure we wouldn't need a Jaws of Life to extract him.

"Well?" I prodded, when he sat there, silent and unmoving. I don't know what I wanted him to do. Stay? Leave? Shave off the sexy stubble he'd probably grown just to exhibit his excessive testosterone level and thereby irritate me? Maybe I merely wanted to rile him a little.

He studied my face, looking all serious and Latin. " 'Serve and protect,' " he drawled. "That's the motto. And that's why I'm here—to serve and protect."

"I don't need protecting," I said, heading for the parking lot exit with a spurt of speed that nearly caused Sonterra's knees to collide with his chin. I put a lilt in my voice as I watched for an opening in the passing traffic. "If you want to serve, however, I wouldn't mind a pedicure."

I expected the remark to get under Sonterra's hide, since that was what I'd intended, but instead of taking the bait, he merely leered at me and waggled his eyebrows. His temper might have been Latin, but the sparkle in his eyes was pure Irish.

"You want to play toesies, Counselor? I'm shocked."

"I didn't say—"

"Yes, you did."

I found a space and zoomed out. Some loser in a Geo honked and flipped me the bird. When I glanced at Sonterra, I saw that he'd scrunched down in the seat and squeezed his eyes shut.

Wimp.

"Where did you learn to drive, a theme park?" Sonterra rasped when I smiled at the guy in the Geo and waggled my fingers. Let him read between the lines.

I didn't rise to Sonterra's bait. Now that I had wheels again, and the latest interview with the police was over, I was feeling downright revitalized. "I have some phone calls to make," I said, "but I couldn't spend another minute in that hotel." In less than twenty-four hours, I'd already racked up some pretty traumatic memories of the place. Consider the equation: me, plus Sonterra, fully rested and alone in a room with beds. Talk about a recipe for chandelier-swinging sex.

Not that any place Harvey, Jr., put me up

would ever be fancy enough to have chandeliers.

And not that Sonterra and I had any business having sex. We'd tried *that* before, fairly recently, in fact, and where had it gotten us? Only at each other's throats.

I spotted a Denny's—the fast-food breakfast had already started to wear off—and whipped in, inspiring a few more honks from anal-retentive drivers.

"Are we getting out?" Sonterra asked, in a forbidding tone.

"I am," I responded, shutting off the engine, slipping out of the rental, and setting my purse on the seat so I could dig for my cell phone. "Feel free to wait in the car if you want. I might be a while, though."

Sonterra gave me a look that would fade paint and began the comical process of unbuckling, unfolding, and standing up. He conked his head trying to clear the doorframe and the goose egg he got did nothing to improve his surly disposition.

I consoled him with a winning smile, turned, and marched into the restaurant.

While Sonterra rubbed his head and studied the extensive menu, I put in the call I dreaded most: the one to my boss. I still hadn't charged my phone, but it was operating perfectly, more's the pity.

Heather answered, giving her canned spiel. "Kredd and Associates," she sang. "You're innocent, and we can prove it. How can we help you today?"

"It's Clare," I said, hunkering down in the vinyl seat of our booth. Sonterra was across from me, giving the menu a brisk little snap at regular intervals and refusing to meet my eyes. "Is Harvey, Jr., in?"

Heather relaxed, now that she knew I wasn't a potential client. "He's not taking calls," she said. "He's meeting with the estate lawyers. Big doings here. The other two sibs and both Harvey, Sr.'s ex-wives are in town. Word is, the late Mr. Kredd's assets, already frozen, have now been *attached,* and we're all waiting for the ax to fall."

Frankly, especially in the face of all Heather had just told me, I was relieved that Junior wasn't available. "Have any more heads rolled?"

Heather cleared her throat, which probably meant that someone was nearby, trying to get the gist of the conversation. "Only a matter of time," she chirped; then her tone returned to normal. "I've scheduled your interviews for the Netherton case. Believe me, these people are not going to be your new best friends."

I sighed. I hadn't expected a warm reception in Tucson, especially after my trial run with poor Sylvie the night before, but I like to confine my confrontations to the courtroom whenever I can, and live my private life amicably, the go-rounds with Sonterra not withstanding. I opened my notebook and tapped the end of my pen, ready to make notes.

"Okay," I said. "Names, times, and places, please."

Heather gave me the necessary information, and I got it all down. The waitress came, flirted with Sonterra, took his order for a piece of apple pie and coffee, mine for a cheeseburger and a diet cola, and left again.

"Harvey's family is in town," I said after I'd ended the conversation with Heather.

"Where's Norman Rockwell when you need him?" Sonterra replied. I'd love to look in his personnel file and see what the department says about his attitude. A sunshine boy, he ain't.

"It's going to be ugly."

Sonterra sighed. "Don't look now, Counselor," he drawled, "but where the Kredd clan is concerned, it's *always* been ugly."

"You don't know them," I challenged. "They might be perfectly nice." Why was I compelled to defend those people? If Harveys Jr. and Sr. were any indication of the family's general caliber, Sonterra was totally right. Their gene pool ought to be flushed.

"Please," he said, with a roll of his eyes.

I allowed the subject of the Kredds to drop. In the final analysis, I wasn't that interested. I looked over the list of appointments Heather had given me; two that day, three the next. I hoped there wouldn't be any more surly boyfriends and big dogs.

The food came, and Sonterra's mood improved, once he'd scarfed up some sugar and shortening. I bolted my cheeseburger; detective work made me hungry.

We finished our meals, managing to pick our way through a verbal minefield without blowing ourselves up, and went back to the car. I almost felt sorry for Sonterra, getting back into that tin can. Almost, but not quite.

If he'd minded his own business, and trotted his truly exceptional butt back to his own turf—or better yet, just stayed there in the first place—he wouldn't have been having these problems.

Chapter Thirty

Our first call was scheduled for ten-thirty, and we pulled up in front of a tidy stucco house on the outskirts of the city, right on time. Mr. and Mrs. Evan Dorsett had agreed to talk to me about their daughter, Sara Ann, who had died a few days after being operated on by Justin Netherton. Some enhancement, I thought grimly, as I forced myself up their front walk.

Sonterra rang the bell, badge ready in his left hand. He looked miserable, standing there as if he'd been folded into quarters and mailed from Timbuktu in a shirt box. Once again, I came dangerously close to feeling sorry for him, but I managed to restrain myself just in time.

Mrs. Dorsett, a slender, sweet-faced woman, probably in her seventies, with sand-washed blue eyes, answered the door. She looked at me, then at Sonterra.

"I'm Clare Westbrook," I said quietly. "I'm

here to take a statement regarding your daughter's death. I believe we have an appointment?"

She was still staring questioningly at Sonterra. The stubble on his face *did* give him a somewhat disreputable look. "And you are?" she asked.

He waggled the badge, neatly pinned inside its leather casing. "Detective Anthony Sonterra, Scottsdale Police Department," he said. "I'm here unofficially."

Mrs. Dorsett peered at the badge, then sighed and, a little grudgingly, I thought, stepped back to admit us. "My husband is waiting on the patio," she said in a tone geared more toward civility than politeness. "If you'll just follow me, please."

Sonterra rubbed his chin with one hand as we trailed the older woman through a spacious living room filled with soft cushions and muted Southwestern colors, probably wishing he'd used one of those razors he'd bought. A studio portrait of a smiling young woman with thick brown hair and humor-filled eyes hung above the large stucco-fronted fireplace, and it seemed to me that she watched us—me, Sonterra, and her still-grieving mother—as we crossed to the patio doors.

Mr. Dorsett was seated at a table overlooking the small swimming pool, in the shade of a massive green-and-white-striped umbrella. He wore golf garb, chino shorts, a quietly expensive sports shirt, and a healthy tan. He'd lost his hair, but there was nothing wrong with his eyesight; his regard was sharp as he took us in.

Sonterra might have been wishing he'd shaved. I was definitely regretting my choice of jeans and a cotton blouse. I'd hoped to strike an unthreatening note, but if I could have traded the casual attire for one of my tight-ass conservative suits at that moment, I would have done so.

Dorsett stood, extended a strong, age-spotted arm. "Ms. Westbrook, I presume," he said. "I'm Evan Dorsett."

I nodded, shook his hand, and stiffly introduced Sonterra as a friend.

Mrs. Dorsett asked us to sit down, disappeared for a few moments, and returned with a tray containing a pitcher of ice tea and four tall, chilled glasses. Being desperately thirsty, I silently blessed the woman. After a few delicate swigs, I opened my briefcase and took out the legal pad and a couple of pens.

Sonterra scanned the backyard, with its built-in barbecue, shimmering pool, and colorful clusters of roses. "Nice place," he said.

I would have elbowed him if I could have; this was my show, after all, pitiful as it was, but in the end I was glad he was out of reach. Both Mr. and Mrs. Dorsett seemed to let out their breaths the moment he'd spoken. Somehow, with two ordinary words, he'd earned their trust. I admit I felt a stab of resentment.

"Thank you," Evan Dorsett said.

"This was our winter home, until Evan retired," Mrs. Dorsett added. "We raised our Sara Ann in Cincinnati, and I wish to God we'd all stayed there."

I laid one of my business cards on the glass tabletop, at a safe distance from the rings of condensation surrounding our glasses of tea. "I'm sure this isn't easy for you," I said, "but, as you know, I have some questions about your daughter's death. They're pretty routine."

Color pulsed on Mrs. Dorsett's fine cheekbones. She had good skin, luminous despite a number of well-earned wrinkles, and I could see that she had been a beauty in her time, like her daughter. "There was nothing 'routine' about Sara Ann's death," she said. "She went to that butcher while Evan and I were visiting my cousins in Michigan. When we got home, we found her in her bedroom, right down that hallway." She made a stabbing motion with one index finger. "She was delirious with fever and wearing these dreadful bandages. She didn't even know who we were!"

It was hard not to skirt Mrs. Dorsett's gaze, but I faced her outrage and sorrow head-on. It was the least I could do. "I am so sorry," I said.

"And yet you would defend that *fiend*?"

"Eleanor," Mr. Dorsett said gently. "Everyone is entitled to legal representation and a fair hearing. You know that."

Tears shone in Eleanor's eyes, catching the fierce Arizona sunlight. "What about Sara Ann?" she hissed. "Did *she* get a fair hearing?"

"Tell me what happened," I put in, speaking softly. I couldn't bring myself to look at Sonterra for the next few moments. I knew what I would see in his eyes if I did.

"She was nineteen," Evan said, when it became obvious that his wife was temporarily too overwrought to speak. "A sophomore at the university. Sara Ann was a beautiful girl, but she worried about her figure. A friend of hers had breast augmentation, and she wanted to do the same. Eleanor and I adamantly refused to finance such a thing. It seemed dangerous to us, and unnecessary." He paused, turning his glass of tea, heretofore untouched, round and round in its sparkling circle of moisture. "Sara Ann was stubborn and independent, and she had a hefty savings account, since she'd worked all through high school and during the summers. While we were in Michigan, she went to Netherton and had her breasts enlarged."

Mrs. Dorsett sat up straight in her chair, arms tight around her middle, looking as if she feared she would crumple into fragments if she relaxed, and never get herself back together again. My heart went out to her. "He killed her," she said.

"Eleanor," Mr. Dorsett repeated, but softly. He reached over, caught hold of her hand, and squeezed it.

"She developed an infection," Eleanor

said, staring into the distance, beyond the stucco walls of her small, lush garden. "That so-called *doctor* sent her home the *day* of the operation. She lay there, in her room, all alone in this house, in terrible pain, too sick to summon help for herself. She died two hours after we had her admitted to the hospital."

Sonterra spoke at last, very quietly. He was playing the good cop, I knew it, and setting me up as the bad one. Whatever worked, I thought, but I was nettled, all the same. It wouldn't kill him to let *me* wear the white hat once in a while.

"Was there any clear indication that Dr. Netherton had been negligent?" he asked.

I found his foot under the table and stomped on it.

"I can give you a file full of 'indications,' " Mrs. Dorsett said. "I'll get you a copy of our documentation."

She started to rise, but Evan restrained her gently by touching her arm.

"I'll go," he said tenderly. "Drink your ice tea, Eleanor."

Eleanor, Sonterra, and I sat in silence while Evan was gone, sipping away. I was going to take Sonterra's hide off in long, thin strips when I got him alone. I didn't go around grilling his murder suspects, did I?

The file was a slim volume of photocopies, neatly bound; I flipped through, scanning Sara Ann's hospital records, the autopsy report—I wondered if the Dorsetts had made themselves read it—and a whole list of people who were willing to testify that Dr. Netherton had harmed them in some way.

I willed the cheeseburger debris to stop bouncing around in the pit of my stomach.

"The man is a monster," Eleanor said. "He tried to buy us off—as if there could ever be enough money in the universe to make up for Sara Ann's death—but we threw his offer back in his face. We want to see him stopped, put into prison, where he belongs."

I scraped my upper lip with my teeth. "May I keep this?" I asked, my hand resting on the collection of grim, tidy facts describing the cruel end of a young woman's life.

"Take it," Evan said, gesturing. "We have copies. Maybe when you look those records over, you'll change your mind about representing that witch doctor."

"Sara Ann must have been your only

child," Sonterra speculated, his eyes warm with sympathy for both the Dorsetts as he rose. He'd probably drawn that conclusion, as I had, from the portrait in the living room. There were no other photographs, large or small, in evidence.

"We waited fifteen years to have her," Eleanor said. "*Fifteen years.* She was every-thing to us. And he took her away."

I wanted to lay my hand on Eleanor's shoulder as I stood beside her chair, but of course I didn't. It would have been an inva-sion of her space, and I didn't figure I had the right, anyway, sworn as I was to get Dr. Netherton off scot-free.

"I'm sorry," I said again, lamely.

Mrs. Dorsett fixed me with her blue gaze. "You should be," she said. "Representing that man."

"I hate this job," I told Sonterra, on an im-pulse I would soon regret, when he and I were out of the house and, I hoped, out of earshot.

Sonterra all but rocked back on his heels. "Then why the *hell* do you do it?" Obviously, the interview with the Dorsetts had upset him; he was simmering like a pot about to boil over; any moment, his lid would start rattling. "Jesus, Clare, it's as if you deliberately pick the cases that are guaranteed to piss off the rest of the universe and give them your best effort!"

I almost told him about the deal with Harvey, Sr., but then I decided—for the hundredth time—that it was none of his damn business. Besides, it would sound like an excuse.

"Maybe I *like* pissing off the universe!" I said, chin out. "What's the universe ever done for me?"

"Christ," Sonterra spat, wrenching open the passenger door. He was so keyed up that he didn't even complain about the complete lack of legroom. "Did you *look* at those people in there? Did you hear what they said? *Their daughter is dead.* Because of Netherton—your client."

I felt as though I were being swarmed by thousands of invisible bees, stung and stung and stung again. I swear to God, if Sonterra hadn't already been in the car, I would have driven off and left him standing in the street.

"People die after surgery, Sonterra!" I cried, grinding the key in the ignition, racing the motor. "Even elective surgery. It's not necessarily anyone's fault!"

"You can bullshit yourself all you want, Counselor," he shot back, "but I'm not buying."

"Fine!" I shouted, because if I *hadn't* shouted, I would have sobbed, and I wasn't going to give Sonterra the satisfaction of making me cry. Not in broad daylight anyway. "I didn't ask you to come down here and butt your head into my business, you know. That was *your* idea. So why don't you just get back in your fancy *sports utility vehicle* and go back to your own jurisdiction? Maybe, for instance, you could *find James Arren?*"

Sonterra muttered a four-letter word.

I was primed for a fight, but my cell phone rang before I could say anything more. I dug it out, pushed a button, and barked, "Hello!"

"Clare?" It was Emma, sounding small and uncertain, and I could have gnawed off my tongue for snapping at her.

"Hello, sweetie," I said. "How are you? Is everything okay?"

"I'm fine," she answered, but I could tell she was lying by the slight tremor in her voice. "What about you?"

"I'm okay," I said. "And cut the 'fine' stuff. You sound scared to me. Why aren't you at school?"

"I am. It's lunch hour. Kip let me bring one of his cell phones, and I have an actual *bodyguard*, waiting in the corridor and following me everywhere, like I'm Madonna or somebody. I think Kip and Loretta are scared my dad will kidnap me. Did—did you know he's missing?"

I drew a deep breath and let it out very slowly. "Yes," I said. "I know." I figured Arren was likely to come after me, not Emma, which was why I hadn't rushed back to Scottsdale, collected her, and left the country. "Honey, have you heard from him? It's really important that you tell me if you have."

"No," Emma said, flatly. "I haven't. Monica hasn't either—I called and asked her." Pause. "When are you coming home?"

"In just a couple of days, honey," I promised. "By Friday at the latest."

"I'm scared, Clare." She sounded haunted, and little wonder. What private memories were buried, maybe forever, in the depths of her subconscious mind? She must have remembered *something* from the days just before her mother's murder.

"I know, honey," I said. "I'm scared, too." I hated admitting that, especially with Sonterra listening, but I didn't want my niece to think she was hanging out there on that limb all by herself. "Everything will be okay, Emma. I promise, you. No matter what I have to do to make it happen, you and I will be okay." I slanted a look at Sonterra, expecting more reproof, and was taken aback to glimpse sadness in the lines of his face.

"You're all alone down there," Emma fretted. "What if somebody comes after you, and you get killed, like Mr. Kredd and Ms. Baylin and that—that woman?"

"I won't get killed," I said, desperate to reassure her in any way I could. "And I'm not alone. Detective Sonterra is with me." No point in adding that I'd been doing my best to chase him off.

"No way," she said, instantly cheered. "Tony is *there?*"

"Way," I answered.

"And the two of you are staying in a hotel together, right?"

Fortunately, he took the phone before I had to answer that one.

"Hey, squirt," he said. All semblance of anger was gone from his voice and his expression, though I knew he still had plenty to say to me, all of it incendiary. "You'd better not be playing hooky. I'd hate to have to run you in on a truancy charge."

They chatted while I navigated the traffic, on the way to my next appointment. I was to meet a woman named Sandy Piedmont in the upstairs restaurant at the Omni Hotel. We would talk over lunch, with Harvey, Jr., picking up the tab, but my appetite, usually so resilient, was nonexistent.

I was thinking about James Arren, though I'd managed to bar him from my thoughts for most of the morning. What rock had that son of a bitch crawled under?

"Sure," Sonterra told Emma, in answer to some question. I wanted to wring his neck for being able to calm her down so easily when I'd had to try so much harder, but at the same time, I was grateful to him. "When we get back, we'll go out to CrackerJax and play some miniature golf. In the meantime, be cool." He smiled, listened. "Do you want to talk to Clare again?" She must have said no, because his next words were, "Okay. Bye."

He pressed the *end* button and handed me the phone.

The thing rang again, instantly.

"Hello?" I said pleasantly, chagrined because of the way I'd greeted Emma.

"Kredd, here," Harvey, Jr., said. "How's it going?"

I was definitely getting a headache. I could feel a tiny knot forming, just at the base of my skull, growing. Tightening. I decided not to mention the attack on my life or Sylvie's death. Some things are better said face-to-face. As for Sonterra, well, I wasn't about to say he was hanging around, now or ever. "I just left the Dorsetts. I'm on my way to meet Ms. Piedmont at the Omni."

"How did the Dorsetts strike you?" Junior asked, in a conspiratorial tone that made my hackles rise. "Money-grubbers, right?"

"No," I said, hating myself for not telling Junior he could fire me, he could sue me for what I owed against the contract, anything, but I was *not* going to stand up in a court of law and try to convince a judge and jury that Justin Netherton deserved even the benefit of a doubt. "No, they seemed like decent, ordinary people. Heartbroken, of course. Sara Ann was their only child."

"Hmmmph," Harvey, Jr., said, as if I hadn't spoken. "Looking to tap into Netherton's malpractice insurance, I'll bet. Nick him for a couple of million. *That* would probably dry their tears."

I held my tongue. Saint Clare.

"Anyway," Junior said, with a deep sigh, "Netherton wants to meet with you tonight, over dinner."

If I hadn't been in heavy traffic, I would have bounced my head off the steering wheel a couple of times. "Really?" I said carefully. "Where?"

"His place," Junior told me casually. He gave me the address, which was unnecessary, since I had it in my briefcase. "Seven o'clock."

I glanced sideways at Sonterra, wondering how I could get rid of him. "I'll be there," I said.

Chapter Thirty-one

As Sonterra and I drove down the curving, palm-lined driveway at the Omni Hotel, my brain was going in a thousand directions at once. I was always conscious, on some level, that James Arren was Out There, maybe watching me, maybe even watching Emma, awaiting his chance to get past the bodyguard Kip had provided. Sylvie's death weighed on me in a way that neither Harvey, Sr.'s nor Janet's had, and I'd almost been killed myself only the night before. It was hard to focus, given all that, but I wasn't about to give up on what I'd come to Tucson to do—it seemed to me that the only way to untangle the snarls in my life was to work my methodical way through the tasks at hand, one at a time. I can't help it; that's the way my brain is wired.

I spotted Ms. Piedmont, the next hostile witness on an impressive list, right away. No real challenge there; she was the only person in the lobby. Tall, well-dressed, and supremely confident, she exuded class. In the looks department, well, she and Julia Roberts might have been separated at birth.

Her sea-green eyes flicked over Sonterra with frank appreciation, which amused me.

"Clare Westbrook," I said, putting out my hand. She was wearing a dove-gray suit, with a colorful silk scarf tucked into the neckline. I was painfully conscious, once again, of my jeans. I was born and raised in Tucson; maybe I was regressing a little, turning into some earlier version of myself. At this rate, I'd be wearing my old short-shorts and silk-screened boob shirt by tomorrow.

Like I could get into those shorts.

"Sandy Piedmont," said the woman I was scheduled to interview, and we shook hands.

"This is Tony Sonterra," I said. "He's a friend." I'm not sure why I felt I had to clarify that last part.

Sonterra smiled his perfect smile. "Glad to meet you," he said.

I'll just bet, I thought, beginning to feel slightly less generous where Sonterra was concerned. "Shall we get some lunch?" I said, gesturing toward the stairs leading up to the restaurant. I knew the place had a terrace, with a nice view, and I hoped they'd let me in, dressed the way I was. You can take the girl out of Nipples . . .

Tomorrow, I assured myself, I'd wear a lawyer suit.

"I'm famished," Sandy said. Her voice was musical.

"Me, too," Sonterra replied. His voice was low and sexy.

I didn't say anything. No telling how *my* voice would have sounded, since I was starting to wax a tad jealous.

Lunch was the last thing I wanted, since my stomach was still wedged behind my breastbone, an after effect of the demoralizing interview with the Dorsetts, not to mention the hair-raising events of the night before; and the subtle interaction between Sonterra and Ms. Piedmont wasn't helping.

The hostess guarding the entrance to the restaurant upstairs didn't bat an eye at my cowgirl garb, and she didn't seem to notice Ms. Piedmont, either. She had eyes only for Sonterra, he of yesterday's clothes and yesterday's beard.

"I understand you represent Justin,"

Sandy said moderately, studying me over the top of her menu, when we were seated on the terrace. A soft breeze swept through, carrying the scent of exotic flowers and ruffling the tablecloths.

"Yes," I said. Since she'd used his first name, I concluded that her relationship with Netherton had been more than merely professional.

"Justin and I were—intimate—for almost five years," she said.

I put down the breadstick I'd just taken from the basket in the middle of the table.

She arched perfect eyebrows. "Up until the surgery, that is."

My gaze wanted to go to her bosom, but I wouldn't let it. I hate it when people talk to my breasts, though of course it usually happens with men, not other women. "If you don't mind my saying so," I said, "you seem fine to me." *Funny, you don't look deformed.*

Sonterra lifted his glass in an almost imperceptible gesture of agreement, but this time, I rose above the urge to bury my heel in his instep. If he was wishing he could hook up with Sandy later, I just didn't care. Much.

Sandy laughed, and I realized that I liked her, in spite of everything. Yes, she was beautiful. Yes, Sonterra obviously thought she was hot. But that didn't mean she and I were automatic enemies, duty-bound to compete. That was not my typical approach to life and femininity, and I suspected it wasn't hers, either.

"Thanks," she said. "What Justin did to me doesn't show when I have my clothes on. In fact, the worst of it doesn't show when I have them off."

Sonterra rattled the ice cubes in his drink and wisely refrained from comment, though in a sidelong glance, I saw the wheels going around in that brain of his. They made a sound as they turned—*boink, boink, boink.*

We placed our orders—I couldn't handle anything more ambitious than salad—but Sonterra asked for prime rib, and Sandy had the trout. I knew Junior's blood pressure would rise when he saw my expense report, and that cheered me up a little. Clare, Clare, quite *contraire.*

"You seem like an intelligent woman, Clare," Sandy said conversationally, spreading a cloth napkin on her lap while we waited for the food to arrive. "Why on earth would you want to defend someone like Justin Netherton?"

I was getting tired of that question, especially since I couldn't answer it honestly. "I work for Kredd and Associates, up in Scottsdale," I said. "Dr. Netherton was originally Janet Baylin's client. She turned the case over to me before she"—I swallowed—"died."

"Ah," she said. "It seems the Kredd firm has been beset by tragedy lately. Any progress in the investigations?"

Sonterra concentrated on his prime rib. I gave him points for not slipping into a phone booth and leaping out as Super Detective, complete with cape and tights, able to solve the Kredd-Baylin case in a single bound. I wondered, too, if his new beard put Sandy off, or if she found it downright sexy, like I did. The strangest thoughts go through my mind sometimes, especially when I'm juggling problems, which is most of the time.

"Yes," I said simply, and a little lamely. "I mean, yes, there have been several deaths." I glanced at Sonterra. "As for the investigations, well, they seem to be stalled."

A muscle bunched in Sonterra's jaw, but he didn't speak.

"That's a pretty high mortality rate," Sandy observed, between delicate bites of trout. "I'd be afraid to work in that place if I were you."

Since I was there to look for weaknesses in the prosecution's case, I didn't mention the threats or attempts on my own life. Right about then, I figured I had an ice cube's chance in hell of winning the Netherton battle, and thus my freedom, but surrender wasn't an option, either. "If you would tell me a little about your surgery," I said, "I'd appreciate it." I could use the vindictive ex-girlfriend gambit at Netherton's trial, I supposed, and paint Sandy as a scorned woman out to discredit a successful, accomplished man, but I wasn't about to stoop that low. Yes, I'm a lawyer, but I have standards, whatever Sonterra might think.

"He was supposed to give me great breasts," she said calmly, but there was a charge of fury in her eyes. "Instead, he left me looking and feeling like a freak in a sideshow."

To reiterate, she looked okay to me, and I

figured she looked *more* than okay to Sonterra, which thoroughly pissed me off. "What happened?" I asked, bracing myself for the answer.

"I guess his concentration was off that day," she said, without so much as a flicker of hesitation. She shrugged, glanced away reflectively for a few moments. "I should have known better than to trust him."

I set down my fork, my backbone rigid, and I sensed that Sonterra was on the alert, too, though he didn't move or say anything. "You mean the doctor made a mistake?" It's a lawyer's job to clarify the facts, however obvious they might be.

"I *mean* he was high on something, probably coke, though I didn't realize that until later. When I woke up and saw what he'd done, I didn't stop screaming for an hour." Maybe she felt Sonterra's gaze on her; she glanced in his direction. I didn't look to see if *he* was looking, because I'd have had to tear his face off if he was. "I've had reconstructive surgery since then, but things like that don't just leave physical scars. I've got marks on my soul."

I swallowed the bile stinging the back of my throat, thinking of Sylvie. Marks? She'd had tire tracks, and my client was partially responsible. "Did you hire a lawyer? Call the police?"

"Always a last resort," Sonterra muttered, in what I would definitely describe as a snide tone.

I ignored him, except to bump my knee hard against his thigh.

Sandy sighed and, for a moment, her expressive eyes were blank, as though she were looking inward, surveying the bleak landscape of her spirit, temporarily unaware of Sonterra and me and the rest of the world. When she looked at me again, though, she was fully present in the moment. "Justin paid me off. I'm not proud of it, but that's what happened." She stopped, drew a slow, quivery breath. "Anyway, he's a famous doctor, and I'm a—well, a former call girl. I figured he had the advantage."

I didn't glance at Sonterra to get his reaction to the call-girl tidbit. I guessed I'd be treated to his opinions later.

Before anyone said anything else, though, his cell phone rang, and he answered it with a brisk "Sonterra," excused himself, and left the table. Sandy followed him with her eyes until he vanished inside the hotel.

"Nice guy," she said.

I shrugged. "He's all right," I agreed.

She sighed again. "There's nothing going on between you?"

There was plenty going on, of course, but it was all subterranean and, anyway, I felt no inclination to explain. "He's available," I said, which was generous of me, given that Sonterra could have been in a relationship, for all I knew.

Sandy gave a soft, sad little chuckle. "Not to me," she said. "I've already made too many true confessions. Most men can deal with implants, but very few can get past the call-girl thing."

I didn't comment. "You and Netherton were finished, after the surgery?"

Her eyes flashed. "Oh, yes," she said. A long, unnerving pause followed. "We were through before then, actually, but I couldn't bring myself to face facts. I wish I hadn't given him back the videotapes."

Videotapes? I thought. *Shit.* "What was on them?"

She tilted her head to one side, *so* not fooled, and countered with a question of her own. "Are you worried that I'll dig up a copy and turn it over to the prosecution, Ms. Westbrook?" she asked, without any rancor at all. I would have felt better if she'd been even a little bitchy. "There's probably no need—they seem to have an ironclad case already."

Ironclad case or not, I had to win this one. If I failed, I'd be stuck at Kredd and Associates for what seemed like the rest of my natural life. "Maybe you're angry," I said carefully. "Maybe you want me to think there were incriminating tapes because of the breakup. You were angry and hurt, and now you're out for revenge."

"Oh, I'll get back at him, all right," Sandy said. "Justin Netherton will pay in spades for what he did to me."

"If he truly injured you," I said carefully, "then you have my complete sympathy. If he didn't, I'll find a way to prove it."

She smiled, a little sadly, I thought. "I like you, Clare," she said. "Under other circumstances, we might have been friends."

"That would have been nice," I answered, and I meant it.

Sandy consulted her watch, a slim gold affair with floating diamonds in the face.

"Are we through?" she asked. "I have another appointment." She leaned in a little way and whispered, "Hollywood."

I didn't pursue the reference to Tinseltown, figuring it had no bearing on the case, and gave her my card. "We're through," I answered.

"Say good-bye to Mr. Sonterra for me," she said, standing. She regarded me solemnly for a long moment, as if sizing me up. Then she shook her head. "Justin will try to get you into bed, you know," she said. "Watch out for him."

With that little volley still smoking in the middle of the table, she turned and strolled away.

She met Sonterra in the terrace doorway, and they spoke a few words to each other before she went on her way and he came toward me. I hoped they weren't exchanging phone numbers, but no power on earth could have made me ask.

"I have to go back to Scottsdale, Clare," he said. "Now."

"What happened?" I asked, as he sat down. He was on the edge of his chair, sitting the way people do when they're itching to bolt.

The waitress brought the check in a leather folder; I read the bill, tucked Harvey, Jr.'s credit card inside, hoping it wouldn't be denied, and focused intently on Sonterra.

He didn't answer until we were alone again.

"A couple of fresh bodies just turned up in a county landfill. Eddie and I got the folder."

I let out my breath. A lot of murders go down in Maricopa County, and the sheriff's staff is limited by the usual budget constraints, so the municipal departments help out. Sonterra had a job to do, just like I did. "Sounds nasty," I said, sympathizing.

"Come with me," he said.

The waitress returned with the check; I added a tip and signed on the dotted line, stashed the company card, and stood. "I can't, Sonterra. You know that."

He glared at me.

I pretended everything was all right, which it obviously wasn't. "I'll drop you off at your car," I said. I was going to miss Sonterra. When I went back to my hotel room that night, I would be lonely for sure, and I would feel a whole lot less safe than I had with him holding me, or sleeping in the next bed.

And I would have died before telling him that.

A muscle bunched in his jawline, and the expression in his eyes was fierce. "I don't know why I'm bothering to say this," he told me gravely, "because I know you won't listen, but you're in too deep here, Clare. Some nasty people are obviously out to get you, and one of them might be James Arren."

Yes, James. James, who'd had six years to work up a good, solid hatred toward me.

I would have liked to go home—I missed Emma and Bernice, Mrs. K and Loretta, and I longed to sleep in my own bed—but I couldn't leave just because the job I had to do was a tough one, with a scary side. I was a big girl, with a niece to support and bills to pay. I lifted my chin.

"I can handle this," I said, hoping to God I was right.

Chapter Thirty-two

A heated silence lay heavy between Sonterra and me the whole way back to the hotel, and when we arrived, Sonterra didn't bother to go inside and collect his sundries from the room we'd shared. In the parking lot, I put on the brakes beside the SUV, and he got out of the rental, walked over and unlocked his rig, slipped behind the wheel, and started the engine with an unnecessary roar.

He'd been too stubborn to say good-bye, but now, staring at me through the side window, he mouthed, "Be careful."

I nodded, and he drove away, pulling out onto the highway. When he turned the corner, out of sight, I headed in the opposite direction. I still had several hours before I had to be at Netherton's place for dinner, and I meant to make the most of them.

The lot at Nipples was jam-packed, but there was no sign of the pickup with the pit bull in the back, and I chose to see that as a good omen. I parked the rental, flipped the locks, and headed for the side door, always propped open. Neon, cigarette smoke, and jukebox music spilled out into the hot, hazy afternoon light.

I pulled off my sunglasses, straightened my spine, and walked in like I owned the place.

The honky-tonk gods were with me; the bar was lined with cowboys, who were generally chivalrous, in my experience, which was extensive, considering how many drinks I'd served in that place, and though the guys at the tables watched me as I passed, there were no lewd remarks or "Hey, baby's." There was no sign of Freddie Loren, either, which was good, although I would have liked to ask him what he knew about Ellie, who was evidently a regular.

Henley Eggleman was at the pool table, just about to break.

It seemed odd for a bereaved man to be in Nipples in the middle of the afternoon the very day after his girlfriend's horrible death, but, hey, we all handle sorrow in our own way.

I approached him.

"You," he said. Well, I hadn't expected a warm reception, after all.

"Hello, Henley," I said. "Buy you a beer?"

He studied me suspiciously, like he smelled a trick, but the pull of free booze was evidently too strong to resist. "Okay," he said.

We sat in the back booth, near the hall-way leading into the rest rooms, and a gum-smacking waitress took our orders. He ordered his beer; I asked for a diet cola. Henley raised an eyebrow at my choice, but offered no comment.

"It was terrible, what happened to Sylvie," I said, and I meant it. If I could have gone back in time, I'd have taken Sylvie by the hand and dragged her out of that trailer, rented her a room at the hotel, anything. And I wouldn't have left her alone till I found out what it was she'd known about Tracy's death.

"Yeah," Henley agreed. He was either a man of few words, or dumb as a lug bolt. Tough choice.

"The police say it was arson. Do you have any idea who did it?" I asked. I widened my eyes a little, and I was very careful to keep my tone noncommittal.

"Nope," he said.

The beer arrived, along with my cola. I hoped the brew would loosen Henley's tongue.

"Might have been you," he ventured craftily, when the waitress was gone.

I didn't flinch. "But it wasn't," I said. "What reason would I have to kill Sylvie?"

"She was *real* upset after you left."

"Because of the conversation we had."

He waited for me to say what Sylvie and I had talked about, but I didn't. If she hadn't told him, I wouldn't either. "I didn't do it," he said, with a note of petulance in his voice.

"Do the cops think you did?" I'd already checked his record on the Internet, since Sylvie had mentioned that he was on probation. The charge had been petty larceny, which might mean he wasn't the violent type.

He took a couple of audible swallows from his beer, lowering the foam level to half-mast, then shrugged those meaty shoulders of his. He had an unhealthy pallor, like most guys who spend too much time in bars, swilling too many brewskies and living on nachos and chili dogs. "Who knows?" he said. "I had to answer a lot of questions, and I'm not supposed to leave town. Like I would, anyways."

I remembered the headlights coming at me the night before, the sound of the whole side of my car being bashed in, my dive for the shrubbery. "You drive a tow truck, don't you, Henley?" I asked. There'd been one parked outside Sylvie's place the night before.

"My sister's boyfriend owns a wrecking outfit. I drive for him sometimes."

It would have been so easy if Henley had been the one to come after me, so convenient, but my gut said he not only hadn't killed Sylvie, he hadn't ruined my car and tried to grind me into the wall of the hotel, either. He was a loser, and probably a louse, but when I tried to imagine him torching his girlfriend's trailer, or behind the wheel of the rig that had almost turned me into a grease spot, the pictures just wouldn't come.

"Who would have wanted to hurt her, Henley?" I asked.

"Nobody. I told the police that, and I'm telling you. Sylvie didn't have no enemies." He actually choked up, forcing me to revise my earlier opinion that Nipples was a strange place for him to hang out so soon after the tragedy. Now I realized he probably found the familiarity of that dump comforting, a home away from home. Guys like Henley don't usually come from warm, loving families.

I touched his hand, and the gesture was sincere. "I'm sorry, Henley," I said again.

"She never had it easy," he lamented. His eyes were wet, but he was trying to control his emotions; I could see that. "Poor little Sylvie. Things went against her from the first."

I didn't say anything, because I wanted him to keep talking. I tried to let him know, by my expression, that I understood, and God knows, I did. Sylvie's childhood had been much like Tracy's and mine, and it wasn't lost on me that of the three of us, I'd been the only one to make it out.

"Even before the operation, she had all kinds of trouble. Fell hard for a married guy, and he dumped on her, even though she was pregnant. Did you know that?"

Sylvie and I hadn't been especially close; we'd worked together for a while, that was all. She'd never mentioned being involved with somebody else's husband, or being pregnant, but she might have confided in

Tracy or Loretta. "No," I said quietly. "It must have been awful for her."

Henley drew in a deep breath through his nose, causing a slurpy sound in his sinuses. I took a quick sip from my cola, trying to hide my instinctive reaction, which was disgust. "It was. He did her real dirty. In fact, maybe it was him that set fire to Sylvie's place. She acted like she had something on him."

Now he'd piqued my interest. I took a notebook, similar to Arlo Browder's, from my purse, along with the fancy pen Loretta gave me when I passed the bar exam. "Like what?" I prompted, hoping I sounded casual.

The answer was another shrug. "Who knows?"

"You remember his name, Henley?"

"She wouldn't say," Henley said. "She claimed the whole thing was over and done with and I ought to let it lie. Now I wish I'd made her tell me."

"Did this guy ever visit Sylvie? Call her on the phone?"

Henley flushed, and the big vein in his neck bulged. "I wouldn't have stood for that," he said. "They was old news. She was *my* woman."

I bit the inside of my lower lip to keep myself from treating Henley to my opinion of ignorant, quasi-employed dolts who say they won't stand for things and refer to their partners as "their women." He wouldn't have had a clue what I was talking about anyway.

"You're sure?" I asked carefully. "If this guy set the fire, he might have been hanging around a while."

"Like I said," he reiterated. "I wouldn't have stood for none of that kind of thing."

"You were pretty serious about Sylvie, then?"

"I wanted to marry her. She said it would screw up her disability payments if we did, so I laid off asking her."

Getting hitched to Henley Eggleman would have screwed up a lot more than her food stamps and medical care, and Sylvie had been smart enough to know it. Maybe she'd learned her lesson the hard way, from her married lover. I wondered what had happened to the baby she'd been carrying, but I didn't ask. If Henley knew, and he probably didn't, he wouldn't tell me.

I slid my card across the table. "If you remember anything, or hear something, will you call me?"

Henley pondered the question, and I could see it was an effort. He sucked down some more beer, then sighed. "Why should I?"

Because I'm trying to find the connection between Sylvie and what happened to Tracy, I thought. "I might be able to help."

His brow puckered. "Are you a cop or a social worker or something?" he demanded. He hadn't looked at the card. "Sylvie said you was a lawyer."

"I am a lawyer," I said, "not a cop. Did you ever rough Sylvie up, Henley?"

Another flush climbed his thick neck to throb in his cheeks. "I lose my temper sometimes," he admitted grudgingly. "That ain't a crime."

"It is if you hit her." *Or burned her to death inside a trailer.*

Henley made a meaty fist of one hand and bashed it down hard on the tabletop, making his nearly empty beer and my nearly empty cola bounce slightly. Several of the before-five drinkers turned to look in our direction, though their faces showed a singular lack of interest. For all I know, they might have been hoping for a fight, just to break the monotony of a lazy afternoon at Nipples.

"I never laid a hand on a woman in my life!" Henley snarled.

He looked as if he'd like to lay one on me, without unbending his fingers first, but Gram, my mother, and the state of Arizona didn't raise me to be a fool. I sat back, calmly, and didn't throw any more fuel on the fire.

"You better just get on back to wherever you came from, lady," he said when he'd recovered some of his composure, such as it was. "This ain't a good place for you to be."

I leaned forward slightly. "Are you threatening me, Henley?" I asked.

I never got an answer, because Arlo Browder chose that moment to come strolling into the bar, through the side door. He took off his hat, scanned the room, and headed straight for our table.

"I gotta go," Henley said, rising with more grace than I would have expected, given his bulk.

I'd hoped that Detective Browder was looking for Henley, not me, but he didn't so much as break his stride when Henley bolted, ostensibly heading for the rest room. I'd worked at Nipples for three and a half years; I knew there was a back door, just to the left of the cigarette machine, opening onto the alley behind the bar.

Arlo slid into the seat Henley had warmed up for him, setting his hat aside on the bench. "Well," he said, "if it isn't Ms. Westbrook."

The waitress came back, looking put-upon. "You want somethin'?" she asked Browder.

"How old are you?" he countered.

"Twenty-two," she said. "You want to see my ID?"

"Yeah," he replied. "I do. Bring it over, along with an orange soda."

The girl walked away. I wondered if she'd be back, or if she'd slip out the same door Henley had and vanish. Nipples had a repu-tation for hiring underage waitresses; I ought to know. I'd been barely eighteen when I started there.

"Do you hang out here a lot, Arlo?" I asked.

He smiled. "Nope," he said. "I was look-ing for you."

"What made you think I'd be here?" As if I didn't know.

"Sonterra told me you might come around asking questions about your friend Sylvie."

I felt an overwhelming sadness, and tried, without success, to drown it in diet cola. Poor Sylvie. Dear God, I hoped she had died before the flames reached her. "Do you have any suspects?" I asked.

Arlo spoke quietly, even gently, and cocked a thumb in the direction of the rest rooms. "The boyfriend is a person of interest, of course. It's usually the nearest and dearest in a case like this." He leaned forward, frowning a little. His fingers were laced together on top of the table. "I hope you're not playing cop, Ms. Westbrook."

"Why would I do that?"

"Because you think we dropped the ball with your sister's case, maybe?"

Before I could answer, the waitress reappeared with the orange soda Arlo had ordered, along with an Arizona driver's license. The newer ones have a hologram on the front, which makes them hard to fake.

Arlo examined the ID, then looked up into the girl's face. "Mary Jean," he said, "this is

no place for a nice kid like you. I hear
they're hiring over at The Home Depot."

She nodded without interest, cracked her
gum, and turned away. I could have told her
a thing or two about the pitfalls of working
in a place like Nipples, but I didn't bother,
because I was positive she wouldn't listen.
At her age, I knew everything, too.

"Now that you mention it," I said, watching Arlo's throat work as he swallowed orange soda, "are you planning to reopen
Tracy's case?"

He set down the mug, nodded thought-
fully. I decided I liked Browder. "I was a
rookie when that went down," he said. "But
I remember." He shook his head. "They de-
clared her a runaway wife. If you had any
idea how many people disappear on purpose—"

It seemed like a good time to remind him
about the digital photo of Tracy, even
though I knew Sonterra had already filled
him in, so I did. I also specified that my sister had been an *ex*-wife, when she disappeared, with a child she would never have
left behind.

"Scottsdale P.D. forwarded the photo to
me a few days ago," he said, with a dis-

tracted nod. "That's the other reason I came looking for you."

"Then you really *are* reopening the case?" My spirits rose a little.

Arlo nodded. "Given what the M.E. up in Maricopa said, after looking at the picture," he told me, "I don't figure we have any choice. I'd appreciate it, Ms. Westbrook, if you could give me a rundown on what you remember about the events surrounding your sister's disappearance."

I felt a rush of bittersweet relief. At last, at last, someone in authority was ready to listen. I glanced at my watch, saw that I still had some time before I had to get ready for dinner with Netherton, though not a lot. Tracy's story was too important to rush through.

"Maybe we could do this late tomorrow afternoon?" I suggested. "I have business to attend to tonight, and a couple of depositions scheduled for the earlier part of the day."

Arlo nodded, laid a bill on the table for my cola and his orange soda, plus tip, and stood. "I'll look for you down at the station, around four o'clock."

I agreed to be there, and we went out to

the parking lot together. He waited by the rental car until I was safely inside, with the doors locked.

It just wasn't the same, that car, without Sonterra stuffed into the other seat like a pretzel.

I dialed Loretta's number on my cell phone.

"Hey," she said.

"How's Emma?"

"She's fine, Clare. When are you coming back?"

I sighed. "I'm not sure. Listen, Loretta— you knew Sylvie Wyand fairly well, didn't you? Do you remember her being involved with a married man while she worked at Nipples?"

Loretta was pensive. "I remember, but I never knew the details. She was real secretive about it."

"There was a pregnancy."

A short silence followed, while Loretta sifted through some mental files. "She had an abortion. The guy paid for it. That's about all I know."

"Will you call me if something comes back to you?"

"Sure," Loretta sounded worried. "Why does this matter, Clare?"

"I'm just curious."

"Right," Loretta said, unconvinced.

We chatted for another minute or so, then disconnected. I tried to concentrate on my driving, but my mind was going ninety miles an hour.

Back at the hotel, the room was too quiet. The beds were made, and the message light on the telephone was not blinking. I'd strolled right past the front desk without being asked to leave because of the criminal element I seemed to attract.

I should have known it was all too easy.

Chapter Thirty-three

Maybe it was morbid curiosity that made me go out of my way to drive by Sylvie's burned-out trailer en route to Netherton's mansion, and maybe it was a need to pay my respects. I felt a little guilty, too—for being alive when she was dead. My life could have turned out much the way Sylvie's had, if Gram hadn't taken up the cause of education and set some strict ground rules as soon as Tracy and I came to live with her.

My mind was a busy place as I sat at the curb in my rental car, staring at the twisted, blackened rubble that had been Sylvie Wyand's home. Crime-scene tape enclosed the place, reminding me of the yellow ribbons people put on trees and windows and doors as a hopeful welcome-home to loved ones they will most likely never see again.

I wanted to cry, looking at those wretched ruins. What dreams had died with Sylvie?

Would anyone mourn her, besides Loretta and myself, Henley, and the scary woman, Ellie Mitchell, whom I'd met the first time I went back to Nipples? I made up my mind to scan the newspaper for Sylvie's obituary and a funeral announcement. If there were services, I would do my best to attend.

I was hitting a lot of funerals these days; I'd gone to Harvey's already, and I was still planning to attend Janet's. A flashback spread across my mind's eye; once again, I saw those headlights coming at me in the hotel parking lot the night before. If I wasn't careful, I'd end up at still another ceremony of sorrow, this time as the guest of honor.

I pulled slowly away from the scene of Sylvie's death, and headed for Desert Sunset Boulevard, resigned to an interesting evening.

Netherton's place was even grander than I'd expected, taking up a chunk of hillside and boasting its own electronic gate and a long, curving driveway ending beneath a tall portico. Beside the front doors stood a life-size bronze statue of a rearing stallion with an Indian brave mounted on its back. Pricey, indeed; such pieces were usually owned by city governments, not individuals.

I took a deep breath, briefcase in hand, extended my free arm, and rang the door-bell. A complicated chorus of chimes sounded inside the house.

A middle-aged maid answered, clad in a crisp uniform, and I was ridiculously glad to see her. Sandy Piedmont's warning at lunch had gotten to me; I was relieved to know I wouldn't be alone with Netherton after all.

"Come in, Ms. Westbrook," she said. She had a Spanish accent and a warm, sincere smile, though there was a troubled expression in her eyes. "Dr. Netherton is expecting you."

I nodded, but said nothing.

She stepped back and gestured for me to enter. I stepped over the threshold into an amazing two-story foyer, with its own waterfall and a floor of multicolored stones. Exquisite twin staircases curved at either side of the large room, leading to the second floor.

"Clare!" Netherton said cheerfully, coming down the right-hand staircase at a graceful clip, beaming at me all the while, as though we were the oldest and best of friends. He took my hands in his and, before I could sidestep him, kissed me on either cheek,

European style. Maybe he was trying to impress the maid; he wasn't getting anywhere with me. "Thank you for coming."

As if I'd had a choice in the matter. I gave him a wooden smile and moved just out of reach.

The housekeeper closed the door and disappeared through the enormous archway to our right. I wanted to hurry after her, or beg her to come back, even though it bothered me a little, the way she'd looked at me when I arrived.

"Would you like a glass of wine before dinner?" Netherton asked.

"No, thanks," I said. I never drink if I'm going to be driving within the next few hours, and I had every intention of getting out of that place, lovely as it was, as soon as possible.

He pulled a face, meant to convey disappointment, I guess; maybe he thought it would come off as cute.

I hate cute.

Netherton was wearing an expensive black silk shirt that would have been great on Sonterra, tailored slacks, and Italian shoes. On the doctor, the outfit had a singles-cruise flavor; a cheap toupee and a few gold chains around his neck would have completed the look.

"Perhaps you'd like a tour?" he asked.

Oh, yeah, I thought. *I especially want to see the master suite and, of course, your etchings.* "Another time," I said. "We have a lot of work to do."

"Dinner, first," he insisted, waggling a finger at me.

"I'm not very hungry," I confessed. Okay, I lied; it wasn't the first time, and won't be the last.

He took my elbow and hustled me through a massive living room and then out onto a terrace overlooking the most incredible garden I have ever seen. There were topiaries, statues, fountains, and so many red roses that I half expected to catch a glimpse of *Alice in Wonderland's* Red Queen, with a dripping paintbrush in one hand.

A small table stood under a canopy of trees, set for two. The candlesticks were sterling, I was sure of it, and the china was as translucent as a wispy spring moon.

Netherton drew back my chair, and I sat, but I perched the briefcase on my lap, prim as an old maid on a crowded bus. He lit the candles with an all-too-practiced grace, then took the chair across from mine. If a string quartet came out of the bushes and launched into a rendition of "Some Enchanted Evening," I was out of there.

Alas, no one turned up but the maid, who told me quietly that her name was Maria. She served the salads, and then vanished again. Around the garden, fairy lights came on in stages, a slow wave of shimmer, twinkling in the trees and shrubs like a legion of fireflies. Had Sonterra been sitting across from me, I might have had my head turned. As it was, I couldn't wait to get back in my car, lock the doors, and speed away. I was trying not to be prejudiced by the things I'd heard from Sandy and the Dorsetts, but it was getting harder and harder to be objective.

This guy creeped me out.

I forced myself to take a bite of the salad and found that, surprise number one, it was delicious and, no surprise at all, I was famished. I picked up my fork and started to eat, and Netherton followed suit, looking on with approval and taking an occasional sip from his wineglass. Mine remained empty; wine would be easy to lace with something nasty and, besides, I was driving.

Maybe I was being a little paranoid. It would be forgivable, given recent events.

The next course was mushroom risotto, and I have a weakness for the stuff. I ate that, too. Occasionally, I glanced at the fairy lights, to make sure they weren't starting to blur. They remained crystal clear.

After the risotto came eggplant parmesan, also delicious, and apparently free of fast-acting poisons, since I didn't pass out or even get woozy. Dessert was lemon gelato, and I dug right in.

"You are quite lovely, Clare," Dr. Netherton said. Oh, he was a smooth one.

"Thank you," I replied coolly, "but I hope it won't be necessary to remind you that I'm here as your attorney and nothing else."

Again, that hurt-little-boy look. I refrained from rolling my eyes, but just barely.

"How is my case progressing?" he asked, suave as could be. I decided that if they ever made a movie of Dr. Netherton's life, Anthony Hopkins would have to star in it. "Did you go over that stuff I gave you?"

I dabbed at my mouth with an antique linen napkin and then sighed. "I'm afraid none of it was very helpful," I said honestly. No point in sugarcoating anything. "I've spoken with some of the prosecution witnesses and—"

Netherton's expression was thunderous. "Which ones?" he demanded.

I didn't like telling him—it felt like a betrayal of the Dorsetts and Sandy Piedmont, even of poor, dead Sylvie—but I didn't really have a choice. Technically, I worked for Netherton, whether I liked it or not. "Your ex-girlfriend, for a start. And Mr. and Mrs. Evan Dorsett."

Something flickered in his eyes and was gone. His face hardened visibly. "Sandy," he said. "That—woman is crazy."

I nodded, noncommittal.

"I'm sure she told you that ludicrous story about my being high on drugs in surgery." He studied me. "You didn't believe it, did you?"

"She seems like a rational person," I said calmly. There are times when lawyer-speak comes in handy.

His right temple began to throb, but then he got a grip. "Sandy is unbalanced," he explained regretfully.

The disturbing thing was that, to me, Sandy had seemed anything *but* unbalanced. She was either a very good liar, and that was quite possible, of course, or my instincts about people needed work. "Did you know she'd been a call girl when you met her?" I asked. I like to come out of left field once in a while, shake things up and see what happens.

Netherton sighed. His changeable eyes were kindly now, blazing with an almost saintly glow. His voice was a near croon, silky and hypnotic. "I thought I could save her," he said.

There should have been violins.

I opened my briefcase with a snap and gave Netherton a brisk rundown on the interviews I'd already conducted. I didn't mention that I had three more on tomorrow's to-do list; I suspected he might be the type to lurk somewhere nearby and eavesdrop.

Presently, Maria served coffee from a silver pot, casting one or two sidelong glances my way as she did so, and Netherton asked her to bring a file from his study. She returned momentarily with a fat manila folder.

Netherton thrust it at me. "Here," he said. I guess he'd given up on the charming-host approach.

"What's this?"

"A list of all the people who were *happy* with my services," he told me. It was getting dark and the candles and the little twinkly lights weren't bright enough to see by. "Why don't you interview some of *them*?"

I felt a little leap of hope. Maybe we *could* make a decent case. Maybe Sara Ann Dorsett's death had simply been a tragic accident—certainly those things happen—and not an incidence of criminal malpractice. Sylvie's might have been, as well, and as for Sandy, well, she *was* a former main squeeze. *Former* anythings didn't usually sing the praises of their one-time lovers, especially in a court of law.

Get real, chided a voice in my mind.

"I will," I said, in a tone that might have been mistaken for enthusiasm. "I'll start calling them tomorrow."

"Good," Netherton said. He stood up, indicating that the meal was over, then, as if that wasn't a clear enough message, snuffed out the candle flames with his fingers. For a moment, we were enclosed in darkness, and I felt a little nervous.

"I have a media room," he added, apropos of nothing, as we stepped into the softly lit living room. A jazz CD was playing somewhere, soft and smoky.

I looked at my watch. "And I have an early meeting," I said brightly.

Netherton sighed. "Clare," he said, "are you involved with someone?"

Naturally, from his viewpoint, I had to be "involved." If I wasn't, how could I possibly have resisted his suave manners, his money, his media room? Since I couldn't afford to tell him that I wasn't interested because I thought he was a sleazeball with a colossal ego, I prevaricated.

"Yes," I said, with feigned regret. "I'm sorry, but it's quite serious."

He chucked my chin, perhaps envisioning himself as Cary Grant, up there on the silver screen, nobly giving up the girl of his dreams. Fortunately, he didn't deliver a line; I might have laughed if he had.

"Thank you for dinner and a"—I hesitated only briefly, searching for a suitable adjective—"a memorable evening."

"Where are you staying?" he asked.

I had to tell him. If I didn't, Harvey, Jr., would; in fact, I was surprised he hadn't already done so. I gave him the name of my hotel.

"There's plenty of room here," he said, gesturing with both hands to take in the surrounding palace.

I shook my head.

He scowled. Netherton, I could see, was the type who was cordial only as long as he liked the answers he was getting. "Maria!" he shouted, startling me. When the maid appeared, looking mildly anxious, he snapped, "See Ms. Westbrook to her car. She's leaving."

Maria nodded, and she and I walked out of the house together. My rental was waiting a few feet from the bronze statue, and I peered inside before opening the door.

"Thank you, Maria," I said, settling myself behind the wheel. "Everything was delicious."

She stood with her backbone straight, gazing down at me with an unreadable expression. "Your name—*Westbrook*. It's not so common, right?"

I stopped in the act of inserting the key into the ignition. "I guess not."

"Your people are from Tucson?"

"I was raised here, but—"

"I used to work for a family by that name."

She frowned. "You look so much like Mrs. Westbrook—when I first saw you—"

A lump gathered in my throat. I started the car. "I've never met the Westbrooks," I said, cutting her off. I was curious as hell, I admit it, but my family history wasn't exactly the American Dream, and I couldn't see what good it would do to dredge up a lot of old stuff.

I had my hands full with *new* stuff.

"She's dead now," Maria said, in a tone of sad reminiscence. "She was a wonderful woman, always so good to me. Mr. Westbrook, too. Their son—"

I shifted the car into reverse. "I have to go," I said, and drove away. Here I'd survived dinner with Netherton, only to be ambushed by something I'd thought was gone forever, never to be resurrected.

You look so much like Mrs. Westbrook . . .

I was still trembling when I got back to my hotel, maybe half an hour later.

The message light on my phone was blinking madly, and I was almost afraid to pick up the receiver, but I made myself do it. If I gave in to fear at every turn, I reasoned, pretty soon I'd be huddled inside my condo twenty-four-seven, watching soap operas and eating ice cream out of the carton, with the curtains drawn.

I punched the appropriate button and waited with my pulse pounding in my temples. "You have three unheard messages," the robot operator informed me.

The first was from Harvey, Jr. He instructed me to call him first thing in the morning and tell him all about my meeting with Netherton. It occurred to me that Junior might have expected me to sleep with my client, even set me up for it, but I dismissed the idea as stress-related paranoia.

My second caller was Sonterra, wondering if I'd come to my senses.

Because the two previous calls were normal, the third one caught me off guard. "You don't learn, do you, bitch?" snarled an ugly voice, obviously disguised. "You just don't learn. Well, by the time you hear this, I should be hiding behind your shower curtain. Care to have a look?"

My stomach dropped, and my heart shinnied up into my throat, scrabbling for a place to hide. The room had a balcony, but I was four floors up, and taking that route was out of the question. I could pick up the phone and ask for help, but it would take too long for the police to arrive, and I didn't have a lot of confidence in hotel security, which probably consisted of one paunchy rent-a-cop in his mid-sixties. Besides, if the caller really was in the bathroom, he would hear me placing the call, kill me, and escape before the elevator made the trip down to the first floor and back up.

There was only one way out, and that was past the bathroom, through the door, and into the hallway. The assailant would have a good chance of grabbing me as I passed, and even if I eluded him that time, he had only to chase me onto the fire stairs. I wasn't about to wait for the elevator.

I considered shouting for help, but I was too scared. I wasn't even sure I could whisper, let alone scream.

Inspiration struck. The idea wasn't much, but it was all I had going for me at the moment. I fumbled in my purse, clasped the pepper spray in my hand, popped off the top, and put my thumb on the lever. Then I crept into the bathroom, so scared that I was shivering in every individual cell, and flung back the shower curtain, ready to blast the guy in the eyes.

No one was there.

I dropped the pepper spray and sank to my knees, swirling dizzily in a backwash of pure terror. I rested my forehead on the edge of the porcelain tub, letting the coolness restore me a little, and tried to collect myself. Just as I was about to lift my head, I felt the barrel of a pistol touch the nape of my neck.

It's a wonder I didn't wet my pants.

"Don't turn around," a voice said. Man? Woman? I couldn't tell. "And don't move."

"Who are you?"

"You know I'm not going to tell you that." I smelled tobacco. Beer. Body odor. Henley? No. Somehow, I just knew it wasn't him. "Shut up and listen to me, and maybe I won't hurt you."

"I'm listening," I said. I have to try for the last word, even when it might actually *be* the last word. I guess it's the lawyer in me.

The gun barrel prodded the base of my skull, hard. "I told you to shut up, didn't I?"

It took all the strength I had not to say "Yes."

"What happened to your sister, and what happened to Sylvie," the intruder went on, in a raspy whisper, stirring something beneath the surface of my waking memory, "either of those things could happen to you. You don't want that, do you?"

I shook my head, bit down hard on my lower lip. The pepper spray was on the floor, next to my right knee, and I calculated my chances of grabbing it and turning the nozzle on my captor before whoever it was could shoot me. The answer was easy: I'd have a bullet in my brain as soon as I moved a muscle.

"Then you just go back home and take care of that pretty little niece of yours, while you still have her, and let things rest down here in Tucson. You got that?"

While you still have her. Somehow, those words scared me even more than the situation I was in at the moment. I managed a nod.

"I really hate to do this."

I squeezed my eyes shut. Waited to be shot.

Pain exploded at the back of my head, there was a thundering roar in my ears, and I felt myself falling and falling, the drop much greater than the distance from my knees to the floor. I was absolutely certain that I was dead or dying, spiraling toward the heart of the universe.

I was, of course, very much alive.

I woke up sometime later, my hair and clothes sticky with blood, the floor and the side of the tub splashed crimson. A gnawing ache pulsed through my head; I groped my way to the toilet and got sick. Then, when I'd wiped my face on a handful of tissues snatched from the holder built into the side of the counter, I reached back to explore the wound with my fingers.

I hadn't been shot, I decided, with considerable relief, but I had a nasty gash on the back of my head, and the pain was relentless, pounding at me like repeated blows from a sledgehammer. Apparently, my attacker had struck me with the butt of a gun, knocking me unconscious.

A long time passed before I was able to raise myself to my feet by clutching the toilet rim and the side of the counter, but after several miserable failures, each of which made it that much harder to try again, I succeeded. The mirror presented me with another shock. I looked like something out of a teenage-slasher movie, and I almost screamed when I saw myself.

I leaned forward, peered at my eyes, trying to remember the signs of a concussion.
Something about the pupils—bigger or
smaller, or one big and one small. I gave up.

A trail of crimson marked the doorframe
and the walls and finally the spread on the
bed nearest the bathroom, the one Sonterra
had slept in, as I made my slow, agonizing
way to the telephone on the nightstand.

I nearly fainted before I could stab a
bloody finger at the O.

"Hotel operator," chimed a friendly femi-
nine voice.

I closed my eyes, one arm clutched
across my middle. "I need an ambulance," I
said. The receiver slipped out of my hand,
clattered to the floor.

"Hello?" I heard the operator calling, from
down there on the carpet somewhere. "Ms.
Westbrook? Ms. Westbrook?"

"Help me," I said. I had no idea if she
heard me.

The sweet, shrill sound of a siren reached
my ears a few minutes later. The hotel security guy came into the room and sat down
on the bed beside me.

"Are you all right, miss?" he asked.

I would have laughed, if I hadn't needed

all my energy to keep from passing out again. He was trying to help, though; I had to give him that much credit. He went into the bathroom, soaked a washcloth in cold water, and pressed it to my nape.

"I have a daughter about your age," he said.

I started to cry.

The EMTs arrived—later I heard that they'd had to push their way through a crowd of horrified guests and employees blocking the doorway—and medical things started happening. I was placed on a gurney, and an IV was started. The rest is mostly a blur, although I know I was wheeled into the elevator and through the lobby, and I remember the flashing red light on top of the ambulance.

Chapter Thirty-four

I woke up in a hospital bed, my head wrapped in bandages and hurting like hell, to find Sonterra standing there, glowering down at me. The first thing I thought of, believe it or not, was that he'd shaved.

"Are you satisfied now?" he demanded. "Or do you plan on hanging around here until you end up dead?"

"Your bedside manner leaves something to be desired, Sonterra," I said. Strangely enough, I was grateful that he was his usual grumpy self; I might have broken down completely if he'd shown any tenderness at all.

"What the hell happened this time?"

"Somebody hit me over the head," I said, though that should have been obvious to a detective. I couldn't help asking. "Do I have a concussion?"

"No," he snapped, softening ever so slightly. "Just a bad haircut and a lot of stitches. The miracle is, you don't have a skull fracture."

I felt a rush of anxiety, like I ought to go somewhere, do something. I just couldn't think where or what. "When can I get out of here?"

Sonterra remained gruff. "That's for the doctors to decide. For tonight—maybe for a while—you're going to stay right where you are."

"Arlo must have called you," I said, and my voice cracked. "That's why you're here, isn't it?"

He nodded, reached over, and poured a glass of cold water, which he held to my lips. I sipped thirstily. "He'll be here first thing in the morning," he said.

My head felt as though it had been run over by Henley's sister's boyfriend's wrecker. I rustled up a smile. "I could use some pain meds," I said. "Roughly the same dose they'd give a polar bear."

"That's why they installed this thing," Sonterra explained, showing me the small vial attached to my IV bag by a tube. "You just press on it with your thumb, like this, and it releases a shot of Demerol."

"You don't have to stay," I said.

"Well, I plan to do just that, Counselor, so get over it."

I didn't have the strength to fight back. "The Demerol isn't helping," I told him.

"It's been two seconds, Clare. Give it time."

"I think I could sleep."

"Go for it."

When I awakened, sunlight was pouring into my hospital room, and Sonterra was sound asleep in a chair next to my bed. During the night, he'd sprouted another beard; testosterone is amazing stuff.

I pressed the magic button and waited for another dose of Demerol to hit. That stuff isn't what it's cracked up to be—I was still hurting, big-time, when Sonterra woke up, half an hour later.

He went into the bathroom, ran water, and came out shaved, with his teeth brushed and his hair combed. A nurse's assistant had just cranked up my bed, and a tray of runny scrambled eggs, gray bacon, and soggy potatoes awaited me.

"Eat," Sonterra said. He probably got a kick out of bossing me around, since I was helpless and everything.

I picked up a fork and stabbed at the

eggs. "I need to call Harvey, Jr.," I said. "And my appointments will have to be rescheduled—"

Sonterra appropriated the fork, speared a chunk of egg, and jabbed it at me. I took it with the utmost reluctance. "I called Loretta, and she's going to call your boss," he said. "As of now, you don't have any appointments to worry about."

"You called Loretta? My God, Emma will be scared to death!"

"Relax. Emma doesn't know anything's happened. We figured she ought to hear the story from you, face-to-face."

I did relax a little then, but not much.

Fifteen minutes later, my doctor arrived, with a worried Arlo Browder close on his heels. Sonterra and Arlo went out; I heard them talking in the hall, though I couldn't make out the words.

"When can I get out of here?" I asked the doctor, a handsome guy who looked as if he should still be parking cars or flipping burgers for a living.

He smiled patiently and donned his stethoscope. "Maybe tomorrow," he said, avoiding my eyes, and began the examination.

Chapter Thirty-five

It soon became apparent after Arlo's return from the hospital hallway, where he'd been chatting with Sonterra, that he'd come on official business.

"What happened last night, Clare?" he asked, without preamble, taking the chair Sonterra had slept in and bringing out the requisite notebook. Sonterra hovered at the foot of my bed, somber as an Irish-Spanish angel of death, awaiting my answer.

My head was killing me but, of course, the report had to be made. I wanted whoever had clobbered me caught, preferably before they came after me again. Next time, they might actually pull the trigger. I pumped some Demerol—frankly, I still think the nursing staff was merely humoring me, that the little vial contained liquid aspirin or something equally innocuous—and launched into the story.

I told Arlo and Sonterra how I had come

back to the hotel, after dinner with Justin Netherton, and listened to my messages. I described the third one, where the caller claimed to be hiding behind my shower curtain. I said I'd gone into the bathroom with some trepidation, armed with pepper spray, and found the bathtub empty, that I'd sunk to my knees out of relief, thinking I was alone. That someone had stepped up behind me then, and pressed a gun barrel to the back of my neck.

I watched Sonterra's face as he listened, and was both gratified and alarmed by the fury I saw there. I knew, of course, that his ire was mostly directed at my attacker, but some of it was at me as well. I had a pretty good idea what he was thinking: if I'd just do as he said, I wouldn't get into these messes.

I went on to say that I'd been struck, probably with the gun butt, and truly believed I'd been shot and, finally, gave an account of my regaining consciousness, getting to the phone, being comforted by the security guard. The only thing I left out was the throwing up.

"You didn't get a look at this person?" Arlo asked. "Or recognize the voice?"

"It was distorted—nobody in particular came to mind. And, no, I didn't see anything, either." Except for my life passing before my eyes, of course.

"You must remember something," Sonterra prodded. If he was this tough on everybody he grilled, it was a wonder he ever got a straight answer out of anyone.

"There was a *feeling*," I admitted, thinking hard and getting nowhere, "that I was missing something, that something was familiar—"

"It might come back to you," Arlo said, without looking up from the notes he was scribbling. That ended the interview, apparently, for when he did lift his eyes, he was smiling. He closed the notebook and tucked it into his shirt pocket. "You're one tough lady," he said. "If you ever want a job as a cop, call me."

"Don't hold your breath," I said, with a pointed glance at Sonterra.

Arlo simply shrugged.

Sonterra's smile was slow to make the scene, and dead on arrival. As soon as I got out of the hospital, and my head healed up, I figured he was going to give me hell for not listening when he asked me—make that, *told* me—to go back to Scottsdale and stop playing private investigator.

"This," I said, holding up the IV medicine vial, "is nothing but glucose."

Sonterra sighed. "Somebody clunked you over the head, Counselor," he said, as if I needed reminding. "You take a thump like that, you're going to have pain, drugs or no drugs."

"Thanks," I replied stiffly. "That makes me feel *so* much better."

Arlo cleared his throat, a diplomat in jeans, boots, and snap-up shirt. "I'd better be on my way," he said. "I'll get back to you, Clare, after we've processed the crime scene." He slapped Sonterra on the back as he passed him, nodded to me, and went out.

"Get some rest," Sonterra told me, taking a light hold on my right foot, through the sheets, and giving it a wiggle.

"My head hurts," I said. "I'm never going to be able to sleep."

"Try closing your eyes."

I closed them, and immediately proved myself wrong. Lights out.

When I woke up, lunch was being served and Sonterra was nowhere in sight. A giant bouquet of flowers stood on my bedside table, and I managed to get the card without dislodging my IV needle.

"Get well soon," the message read. *"Best wishes, Kredd & Associates."*

Well, I thought, not exactly warm and cozy, but at least I wasn't fired. Yet.

I was doing my best to eat the grilled cheese sandwich on my tray when a nurse put her head into the room and smiled.

"Mr. Sonterra asked me to tell you that he'll be back this evening during visiting hours, so don't do anything stupid." She shrugged and smiled. "His words, not mine. In the meantime, there's a woman here to see you. I told her she ought to come back later, but she's adamant. Says her name is Maria Gomez, and that you'll remember her from your visit to Dr. Netherton's last night. Should I send her in?"

I let the droopy sandwich plop onto the tray.

"She does seem nice," the nurse added, as if that made a difference.

I merely nodded my acquiescence. Under other circumstances, I might have refused this particular visitor, but in spite of the uneasiness our last encounter had caused me,

I was mildly curious about her reasons for coming to see me. Curiosity and Demerol are a wicked mix.

A few minutes passed before she stepped into the room.

"Hello, Clare," she said, looking me over anxiously.

I nodded a greeting, and even that small effort made my head throb.

Maria was carrying a rosary in one hand and, as she approached my bed, she kissed the beads and crossed herself. This was followed by a wobbly smile.

Great, I thought uncharitably. *I'm about to be prayed for.* "How did you know I was here?" I asked, not returning her smile.

Maria zeroed in on the flowers from Harvey, Jr., and fluffed them a little with a nervous motion of her square, work-worn hands. "I wanted to talk to you about—something. When I called your hotel, first thing this morning, they said you'd been hurt, and brought here."

I waited, watching her. This was her show, not mine.

Maria dragged up a chair and sat down heavily. Her fingers moved over the rosary beads at high speed. "Last night, I told you

I thought you resembled a woman I used to work for—Mrs. Westbrook," she reminded me, gazing intently at my face now. "I just can't get over it, how much you look like her."

"And?" I prompted. I knew what she was going to say and, since I couldn't stop her, I wanted her to say it and go. Paradox, thy name is Clare.

"Mrs. Westbrook had a son named Thomas," she said carefully.

Thomas Westbrook. Up until that moment, despite the references to my resemblance to the deceased matriarch, I was hoping there had been some mistake, that these were some other Westbrooks, not mine. " 'Had?' " I echoed.

Tears brimmed in her eyes, and I softened toward her a little, knowing it hadn't been easy for her to approach me. "Thomas died in an automobile accident a couple of years ago," she said.

I felt a stab of—*something*, though I wasn't prepared to call it grief. How do you mourn someone you never knew? "I see," I said, though I didn't. Not entirely, anyway.

"I believe he was your father," she said.

My headache intensified, and the churning in my stomach threatened disaster. "Well," I said moderately, attempting in vain to blast myself with more Demerol, "he and I weren't actually acquainted." I have a gift for brevity; Thomas Westbrook had gotten my mother pregnant and abandoned us both before I was born. Mom had given me his last name, maybe as a joke, maybe just to get back at him for leaving her with an illegitimate child to raise on her own.

"Thomas was a good man," Maria said firmly. Her dark eyes flashed with conviction.

"You couldn't prove it by me," I replied, swallowing hard.

She frowned. "You're very bitter."

"Damn straight," I replied, though I felt a little guilty, swearing in the presence of rosary beads. I knew a little about my father, thanks to Mom's drunken ravings—he was a spoiled only child, born into one of the wealthiest families in Arizona. He'd never sent me so much as a birthday or Christmas card, let alone paid child support. Just how choked up was I supposed to be now, all these years later, to learn that he was dead?

Maria sighed, closed her eyes for a moment. Maybe she was praying for the salvation of my stubborn soul. "Thomas was very young when he knew your mother," she said. "You mustn't be too hard on him."

Such drama was worthy of a soap opera. I waited for the organ music, and the commercial. Fade out, roll the credits, and Clare gets on with her life.

"Okay," I said tersely. "I forgive him. Are you satisfied?"

Maria looked as though I'd stabbed her. "He was your father. Don't you care about him at all?"

"I was his daughter," I shot back. "Same question, in reverse."

"I guess it's natural that you'd feel that way," Maria conceded with another sigh, "but I had hoped—"

"Why did you come here?" I asked bluntly, tired of trying to figure it out. "If Thomas Westbrook is dead, it's not as if he and I could resolve our differences."

She gazed at me sadly. "The Westbrooks had a great deal of money," she said after a long time. "I received a generous bequest, but I know the remainder went unclaimed. You may be the only living heir."

Maybe some people would have cheered at that news, but I felt as though I'd been struck in the belly with a ramrod. My mind tripped backward in time: I remembered the foster-family Christmases, when the *real* kids got the good presents, and I got underwear and school supplies. I remembered giving an address at my high school graduation and fantasizing that somebody—anybody—from my father's family might be in the audience, feeling just a little bit proud. I'd had a tough time growing up, and Thomas Westbrook's patent disinterest in my welfare was a large part of the problem.

Despite a concerted effort, however, I couldn't work up all that much sympathy for myself. My state-appointed caretakers had been good to me, and eventually, I got to be with Tracy and Gram, though all too briefly.

"I don't want any of their money," I said.

Maria reached into the pocket of her housekeeper's uniform, pulled out a piece of paper, and laid it on the bedside table. "I wouldn't be too hasty if I were you," she said. "This is the name and number for the attorney handling the estate. Maybe you'll want to give Mr. Kass a call."

"I probably won't," I warned. I wanted to cry, but I didn't give in to the urge.

At the door, Maria paused and looked

back. After a moment's hesitation, she gave me the location of the family plot. I knew where the cemetery was, but I had no intention of going there, then or ever, so I merely gazed at the woman, waiting for her to leave.

I had important things to do, like bitching about the food and begging the nurse for better drugs.

Chapter Thirty-six

Two days later, after a lot of paperwork, a much-needed shower, and a light-fingered shampoo, I was finally released from the hospital, and Sonterra, who had been driving back and forth between Tucson and Scottsdale a lot, came to get me. Loretta had sent a few of my clothes, and I dressed hastily, eager to be gone.

While I was signing a few last-minute papers—the hotel was picking up most of the charges, through their liability coverage, which would please my HMO, I was sure—Sonterra took my growing collection of flowers and cards to his car. His bad mood held, and I wondered why he kept coming back.

When we were both in the rig, seat belts fastened, he finally deigned to speak to me. "Want anything to eat before we hit the road?"

"Yeah," I said. "A Big Mac."

He let out a raw-sounding chuckle and shook his head, and we stopped at the first pair of Golden Arches we came to, lining up behind several other cars in the drive-through lane.

Sonterra popped Chicken McNuggets while I demolished my burger and fries. Within a few minutes, we were on Highway 10, headed back toward Phoenix.

I thought about Harvey, Jr., and all the work that I'd left undone in Tucson, and some of my happiness at escaping the hospital evaporated. I'd missed Janet's funeral, and Sylvie's, too, and I'd never finished interviewing the prosecution witnesses in the Netherton case, let alone called the list of satisfied customers the doctor had given me at dinner.

I let out a long sigh.

Sonterra reached over and touched my thigh, sending a charge through me that was out of all proportion to the brief, light pass of his fingers. He sensed it, probably felt me stiffen, and grinned. "You know," he said, "you seem a little—*tense.*" It was a private joke from *The Scent of a Woman,* which we'd rented and watched together, back when we were—well—dating.

"Shut up," I said.

He laughed. "Same old Clare," he said. "I can't tell you what a relief that is. If you'd said something sweet, I'd have figured that knock on the head was more serious than we thought."

He'd started me thinking about some of his methods of easing tension—they're an art form with him—and I didn't appreciate it. "Making any progress with the Kredd case?" I asked, because I knew he wasn't. Sonterra and his partner, Eddie, had been going through files at the firm, between forays to the landfill, which was still sprouting bodies, trying to weed out the one malcontent who might have hated Harvey and Janet—and me—enough to kill.

No doubt it was an embarrassment of riches.

Sonterra ignored my question and popped a CD into the slot on his dashboard. Andrea Bocelli's voice flowed from the speakers.

Dirty pool, I thought.

"I called my insurance agent yesterday, between hits of Demerol," I said, to distract myself from the fantasies the music inspired: dancing barefoot with Sonterra, in some Tuscan vineyard, at sunset. "They're springing for a new car."

"Good news," Sonterra said, then went back to humming along with Bocelli.

I nodded. "I think I'll get something used, and bank the difference."

Sonterra nodded, watching the road. I couldn't help admiring his profile.

"A woman named Maria Gomez visited me in the hospital," I said, out of the blue. Up until then, I hadn't told anybody about that conversation, not even Loretta, who had phoned every five minutes. I was still processing what little information I had.

He turned down Bocelli. "Who?"

"Mrs. Gomez used to work for my father's family," I replied, wondering why I'd brought the subject up at all, and barely resisting a powerful urge to chew on a fingernail.

"Your father?" Sonterra looked blank, as though he'd always figured I was spawned in a petri dish or something.

"Thomas Westbrook," I heard myself say.

"Ah," Sonterra said. "What did she want?"

I wasn't about to tell him about the money, since I had no plans to claim it. He wouldn't have understood my abhorrence for the family fortune—I wasn't sure I understood that myself. And explaining seemed like too much work. "To tell me he's dead, I guess," I said, sounding lame.

"You didn't know that?"

"I didn't know squat," I said.

He flashed a grin. "I never thought I'd hear you say that."

"Life is full of surprises."

"Yeah." Sonterra stopped smiling. "So, how do you feel about that? His being gone, I mean?"

"He's been 'gone' all my life," I replied. "Why would I feel anything?"

"Because you're supposed to, that's why. When you find out somebody's dead, you're duty-bound to feel something."

"Says who?"

Sonterra rolled his eyes. "Remind me never to get on your bad side, Counselor," he said.

"Too late," I replied, and smiled sweetly.

He turned the music up again.

I fiddled with the air-conditioning. "Does it seem hot in here to you?"

He shook his head. Gave me a slightly evil grin. "You want me, that's all."

"I don't need this, Sonterra," I said.

Sonterra touched my thigh again, but this time, he lingered awhile. "Don't get me started on what you *need,* Counselor," he said.

Chapter Thirty-seven

Yes, I had a knot on the back of my head the size of a cantaloupe and, no, I didn't feel the least bit glamorous, but by the time we pulled into my driveway in Cave Creek, I'd talked myself out of all the good reasons I had for not going to bed with Sonterra.

My only hope was that Emma would be home, her presence naturally precluding any hanky-panky that might have ensued if we were left to our own devices.

Alas, there was no sign of Emma, and no Bernice, yapping a Yorkie welcome.

Darn the luck.

Sonterra carried in my stuff, and I wandered into the kitchen to get myself a glass of filtered water from the spigot in the fridge door, hoping to cool my libido a little, get a grip on my common sense. Through the window above the sink, I saw that Mrs. K was burning a red candle in her window.

I chuckled.

"What's so funny?" Sonterra asked, from behind me. I turned, and he was standing in the doorway, one shoulder braced against the framework. His Latin-brown eyes swept over me.

"Nothing," I said. The word came out as a croak, sounding for all the world like a lie. Which, of course, it was.

"Let me put you to bed."

Oh, God.

I lifted my chin. "I'm okay now, Sonterra," I said. "You can go."

He crossed the room, leaned against me, effectively pinning me to the edge of the counter. I was uncomfortable, but it wasn't because he was hurting me; on the contrary, he was causing me the most exquisite pleasure. He cupped my chin in his hand, raised my face, and kissed me.

Every muscle in my body turned to warm wax, and Sonterra held me upright by the pressure of his hips. I felt his erection, and my body went on automatic pilot, shoving my brain into the background. He chuckled at my reaction, still kissing me senseless, and then laid his hands on either side of my waist, lifting me off the floor.

Instinct—or maybe lust—prompted me to

wrap my legs around his middle and my arms around his neck. By the time he carried me up the stairs, I'd turned to liquid.

My room was shadowy and cool, with dust-mote confetti floating in the air, due to my long absence. Sonterra stood me on my feet, next to the bed, and steadied me when my knees nearly buckled. He tossed back the covers and sat me down on the edge of the mattress, tugging my top off over my head. I wasn't wearing a bra, though whether I'd forgotten, or left it off by design when I got into my clothes that morning, I honestly couldn't say.

Sonterra paused, drew in an audible breath, and knelt to take off my shoes. He laid me gently on my back to tug off my jeans, and, guess what. I was in the altogether on that end, too.

He groaned, still kneeling, and ran his hands up and down my thighs a couple of times. "Clare—?" His voice was husky, hesitant.

"Don't go," I whispered. "Please, don't go."

He kissed the inside of my right knee, then the inside of my left. I felt as though I'd been strung, like a bead, on a live wire, and

I did a little groaning myself, completely un-
related to the stitches in the back of my
head.

"Easy," he said gruffly, his right hand
making a slow, sweet, fiery circle on my
bare stomach and abdomen. "Take it slow,
baby."

"No," I pleaded, barely able to speak. "I
want fast. I *need* fast."

The motion of his hand kept getting wider
and wider, slower and slower. "I know what
you need," he told me quietly, "and I'm
going to give it to you." He started kissing
the places his hand had been caressing.

"Oh, God, Sonterra," I whimpered.

"Relax," he said. I felt his thumb and forefinger part me, in preparation for a kiss of a
whole other kind.

Right. *Relax*. I moaned again, long and
low.

Sonterra eased one of my legs over his
right shoulder, one over his left.

"Oh, God," I said again, desperate now.
My hips were already writhing, and he was
just breathing on me. Once he touched me
with his lips and tongue, I knew I'd lose my
mind.

With his free hand, Sonterra reached up

to caress my breasts, then he made a wholly sensual sound, deep in his throat, lowered his head, and took me into his mouth. I cried out in welcome, clawing at the sheets with both hands.

Sonterra is a master. He suckled hard, then barely nibbled, teasing, murmuring tender words that were meant to inflame, not soothe. He kissed the insides of my thighs, and my sweat-moistened belly, and made me beg for what I wanted. What I *needed*, because damn him, he knew. He'd always known.

When he was satisfied that I was ready, he accelerated his pace, and I braced my heels against his shoulders, sobbing in ecstasy, as he brought me up, up, and, finally, over. I rocked against him, my body spasming wildly in release after release, gasping out his name the whole time.

At last, I was spent, physically at least, and Sonterra let his head rest on my abdomen; I could feel his breath between my legs. I entwined my fingers in his hair and eased my feet down from his shoulders. Small, feather-light orgasms were still making me quiver, and my nipples were hard as drawer pulls.

"Make love to me, Sonterra," I said.

He didn't lift his head, and when he spoke, his voice was rough. "Strange," he said, "I thought I just did."

"Get naked," I told him, "and get in bed with me."

"Clare—maybe—well, with your head injury and everything—"

"I mean it, Sonterra. I need you naked, and inside me."

"I don't have—"

"In the drawer of the bedside table," I said. *Just this side of the .38.* Sonterra hadn't slept in my bed in a long time, but I believed in being prepared. I'd kept a box of condoms on hand, just in case.

He fumbled for them, extracted a packet, and chuckled. Then he kicked off his boots, peeled away his clothes, and climbed in next to me. "We shouldn't be doing this," he said. This from the guy who started the whole thing in the first place.

"Why?" I asked, sliding down far enough to lick one of his nipples.

He moaned. "Because you just got out of the hospital," he ground out. By then, I was tormenting him in other ways. Not that he needed much preparation. He felt like a steel cylinder in my hand, and I half expected his flesh to sizzle.

"Occupational therapy," I said, kissing my way down his belly.

"Clare," he ground out.

I kept moving lower, kept kissing.

He gasped when I reached my destination, and I went to work in earnest.

Chapter Thirty-eight

I woke a couple of hours later to find myself alone. The condo seemed to echo, like some vast void, without Sonterra there, and I felt his absence with an unreasonable poignancy.

I lifted my head, which had begun to hurt again, and winced, gripping the edge of the nightstand to steady myself as I sat up.

There was a note next to the phone, penned in Sonterra's strong, plain handwriting. *"There's another body at the landfill. Sorry to leave without saying good-bye, but I couldn't bring myself to wake you. S."*

Since there was nobody around to catch me at it, I held the note against my chest for a moment, as if absorbing some of Sonterra's essence from the paper. Then, deciding I was acting like a fool, I got out of bed, visited the bathroom, and pulled on a bathrobe.

It was only six-fifteen, but the sun had already gone down, and I flipped on lights as I moved through the condo. Ever since I was a little kid, when I used to meet strange men in the hallway of my mother's place *du jour* late at night, I've been uneasy in the dark.

In the kitchen, I put on the tea kettle, noting as I did so that the red candle in Mrs. K's window had burned itself out. I hoped it wasn't a metaphor.

The phone rang while I was getting a mug down from the cupboard, and I answered right away, absurdly eager for the sound of another human voice.

It was Loretta. "Hey," she said.

"Hey," I said back.

"How are you feeling?"

That would have been a tough question to answer, because I felt a lot of different things—sweet satiation from Sonterra's skillful lovemaking, loneliness, considerable pain in the noggin, and something that might have been hunger. "Okay," I allowed.

"You don't sound okay," Loretta replied. "What's going on?"

"Nothing much," I said. Loretta and I talked about everything, and the mattress session with Sonterra probably wouldn't be the exception, but I wasn't ready to articulate the experience. Hell, I was still vibrating from it.

"Think we could keep Emma and Bernice another night?"

An ache lodged in the middle of my chest, but I ignored it. The simple fact was that both girl and dog would probably be better off at Kip and Loretta's, since I was still a semi-invalid. I planned to have a cup of herbal tea, and maybe some soup, take a warm bath, and crawl back into bed.

"Sure," I said. "I'm not such good company tonight."

"Something wrong?" Loretta was nothing if not persistent.

I peered out the kitchen window, trying to see the sky. "I'm just a little moody," I said. "Is there a storm coming on? The air feels heavy."

"They're predicting a good old-fashioned duck-drowner," Loretta said. "Thunder, lightning, the whole shebang. Listen, I could come over there and pick you up—"

"Please, don't," I interrupted quickly. "I mean, I appreciate the sentiment, Loretta, but I need to get some sleep. I've got to be back on the Netherton case first thing in the morning."

"I'll spare you my opinion of the Netherton case," Loretta said. She drew an audible breath, then let it out in a whoosh. "Clare, there's been no sign of James since he skipped, not even a trace. I don't like it."

"I don't like it, either," I said honestly, "but I've got an in with the cops. One strange sound, and I'm on the phone to Sonterra. He'd be here in minutes, Loretta."

The mention of Sonterra must have cheered her up, and reassured her, too, because her voice brightened considerably. "Something's going on between the two of you, right?"

I sighed. "Don't get all excited," I warned. "It's just sex."

"Just sex," Loretta repeated, lowering her voice.

"How's Emma?" I asked, before she could get started on the other subject.

"She's a little worried about you, and nervous about James's disappearance, of course, but kids are resilient. We rented a stack of movies this afternoon when she got home from school, and we're going to make s'mores. Kip has security people posted all over the property."

I smiled. "Save me one," I said.

"A security person?"

"A s'more."

"Is Tony spending the night?" Loretta wanted to know. "I'd feel a lot better if he was."

Reason enough to lie, right there. "He might come back over later," I said, with the slightest air of coyness. I hate that kind of eyelash-batting bullshit, but sometimes it comes in handy.

"Good," Loretta said.

The tea kettle began to whistle.

"Guess I'd better go," I said.

"Call me if you need anything."

"I will, Loretta," I promised. "Thanks for keeping Emma, and for caring."

"We'll hook up tomorrow."

"Right," I said, and then we exchanged good-byes and disconnected.

For a while, things actually went according to plan. I sipped my tea, forced down a bowl of chicken noodle soup—mostly so my pain pills wouldn't wreak havoc on my stomach—ran a bubble bath, and soaked.

I was pleasantly tired when I crawled

back into my bed, which still smelled faintly of Sonterra's cologne, and I must have dropped off right away.

I'm not sure what it was that awakened me; maybe thunder, maybe some primitive instinct. I opened my eyes, holding my breath, and saw a form standing at the end of my bed.

"Sonterra?" I whispered.

Wishful thinking. I knew it wasn't him.

My eyes were gradually adjusting to the gloom; I made out shoulders, legs, a head, the face covered by a ski mask. The man who'd come to kill me was armed with a fireplace poker from my own set.

My heart turned inside out with fear, and I opened my mouth.

"Don't scream," James Arren warned.

Chapter Thirty-nine

"Where's the kid, bitch?" Arren snarled. He remained at the foot of the bed, and my eyes were riveted on the fireplace poker. He was holding the thing baseball-bat style, and even though I tried to keep my cool, I couldn't help wondering if he meant to bash my brains out within the next five minutes.

An odd rush of sick relief swept through me at the mention of Emma; thank *God* I hadn't asked Loretta to bring her home during our conversation earlier in the evening. "She's not here," I said, without any inflection at all.

He slammed the club down on the end of the bed with terrifying force, barely missing my right foot, and my fear, already palpable, rose to a shrill pitch. Maybe he wasn't going to finish me off quickly; maybe he meant to work his way up my body, one joint at a time. I shoved that idea right out of my head, in the interest of survival.

"I *know* she's not here," he spat. "I'm not stupid."

His intelligence was a debatable issue, as far as I was concerned, but the time didn't seem to be right for shining a light on his shortcomings.

"She's with friends," I said. Strange thoughts come to mind when a person is facing a painful death. I had put my pajamas on after my bath, which I now saw as a very good thing, because I'd been naked after the session with Sonterra, a whole different matter from being naked in the presence of James Arren. "What is it with you?" I asked, in what I hoped was a moderate tone. "You were on parole. You had a woman and a decent job—"

"You screwed it up. Just like before."

"*I* screwed it up? How?"

"By being your bitch self, that's how," he replied. I knew then, by his breathing and his agitated manner, that he was high on something. "You turned Tracy against me, and you got me thrown in jail. Do you know what it's like in that place? And now my own kid doesn't want anything to do with me, thanks to you."

Emma didn't want to see him? That was

news to me—the last time she and I had talked about James, on the way home from dinner and a movie with the happy couple, she'd informed me bluntly that I wouldn't be welcome on the unsupervised visit, once it was permitted by the social worker. "What happened with Emma?" I asked.

I saw a tremor move through him. "She asked me if I killed her mother. She thinks I did, and the *reason* she thinks that is because you've been pumping that bullshit into her head all this time!"

"You did kill Tracy," I said. By that point, I'd reasoned that I was as good as dead anyway, so I might as well find out what I wanted to know. "Where did you dump the body, James? Where is my sister?"

His chest heaved with rage, barely contained, certain to break loose at any moment. *"I didn't kill that whoring slut,"* he hissed.

"Then who did?"

James recovered a little of his composure, such as it was. "I'll ask the questions," he bit out. "Where is my kid?"

"I told you. With friends."

"Call them," he ordered. "Get them to bring her here, right now. Emma and me, we're getting out of here, starting over someplace else. And if you tell these 'friends' of yours anything to tip them off that I'm here, I won't wait to kill you. I'll do it right now."

My first instinct was to refuse, which only proves that going with whatever leaps immediately to mind isn't always the smartest thing to do. Gathering my wits, I nodded, reached for the phone receiver. Dialed Sonterra's cell number.

The thing rang three times, four. My heart was wedged into my sinuses, and I could barely breathe. I got his voice mail, and felt my bones turn to water.

"Susan," I said, picking a name out of thin air, my eyes locked with James Arren's as I spoke, "this is Clare. Please pick up the phone. I need you to bring Emma home, right away. There's"—I decided to push it a little, since I didn't have much to lose at that point—"there's a family emergency."

I pushed the *hang up* button and set the receiver aside.

"Nobody answered," I said, after swallowing hard.

Arren cursed. "Give me that phone," he said.

My breath seized in my lungs, though I think I managed to seem calm; he was standing over me now, yanking the phone from my hand. I knew he'd pushed the *redial* button, which meant he'd get what I did—a few rings, then a man's voice saying, "Scottsdale P.D., Homicide Division. This is Tony Sonterra. Leave a message and I'll get back to you when I can."

At the discovery of my deceit, James bellowed like a bull with its balls caught in a bear trap and flung the receiver against the wall with such force that it shattered. I squeezed my eyes shut and prayed silently, addressing an urgent request to whatever deity might be listening in.

"That was a dumb thing to do, Clare," James said, spitting out the words one by one. "Now I'm going to have to hurt you." He went to the window, which was still too close to the bed for comfort, and pushed aside the curtain to look out. A hard desert rain slashed at the glass.

I tried to scrabble off the mattress on the other side, but he grabbed me by the hair, where the stitches were, and yanked me back.

I cried out from the pain, and tears stung my eyes.

"So you called your cop friend?" he rasped, his wool-masked face close to mine. "You're going to pay for that one, you little slut."

"You'd better get out of here," I heard myself say. Adrenaline was surging through my system, and my mind was on hyperalert. Guess that's what happens when you're *this* close to dying. "Sonterra checks his messages often, and it won't take him long to figure out what's going on."

"I think you're lying," Arren said, giving my hair another yank. "Little bitch. You're so goddamned much better than the rest of us, aren't you? Well, here's a flash for you, sweetheart: You're good for just one thing and one thing only, and I'm going to have some of it before I kill you."

I didn't pretend to misunderstand. His message was all too clear. "Did you kill her, James? Did you murder Tracy?"

"What do you think?" he countered, with a leer. "And stop trying to stall. You and I are gonna get it on."

By that point, I was well beyond the merely expedient and into desperate measures. It didn't look as if the prayer was going to pan out, so I turned my head, bit his wrist, and dived for the other side of the bed while he was still cursing.

He was on me before I could reach the nightstand drawer, and the .38 inside it.

He was quiet for a moment, crushing me facedown into the mattress, his grip on my hair as painful as ever. I wasn't sure if he was thinking, or listening for sirens. And I didn't dare let my imagination stray beyond the present moment, lest I panic completely.

"I've thought about this so many times," he said, almost dreamily.

Definitely more information than I needed. I writhed beneath him and, when he merely laughed at my efforts to break free, I aimed an elbow for his ribs. I connected, and he rolled off, cursing, but he still had a hold on my left arm.

I scrabbled for the drawer again. Missed again. When I toppled over the side of the bed, James was right with me.

I screamed; he backhanded me. I was half sitting, half lying down now, with him straddling me. I brought my knee up hard between his legs, and this time, the shriek came from him.

While he was doubled over, I scrambled for the gun. He kicked the drawer shut with a hard thrust of one foot, missing my fingers by millimeters, then lunged for me. With the last measure of strength in my body, I turned, shoved the pistol barrel into his stomach and pulled the trigger.

There was a muffled report, and he stiffened. Then his eyes rounded with affronted surprise, inside the holes of the ski mask, and I felt warm blood—his blood—gush over my torso. He went limp, and I pushed him off onto the floor, leaping to my feet and still clutching the .38 in both hands.

He gave a burbling moan.

I slithered free, stumbling and crawling away, keeping my distance, too shaken to go farther or even scream again. For a few heart-stopping moments, I thought I might pass out from the pain and terror.

"Help me," he whispered from the other side of the bed.

My body was frozen, wet with blood and cold with sweat, and I was shivering, but my mind was still in overdrive. The phone rang, but I couldn't reach for it. Couldn't let go of the gun. The ringing went on and on, and finally stopped.

Arren was silent, probably dead, and I sank to my knees in the middle of the room, too weak to stand. I had just lowered the .38 when he suddenly resurrected himself, like the phoenix, towering against the far wall. Then he flung himself at me, making a sound like a rogue elephant.

He groped, grabbed hold of my ankle, and dragged me toward him.

Scuttling backward on my butt, I emptied the pistol into him. Finally, he lay utterly still. And only inches from where I sat.

I definitely heard sirens, but they seemed distant, with no particular relevance to my situation. I turned the .38 in my blood-slickened hands, knowing it was out of bullets, prepared to use it like a club if James came after me again.

Chapter Forty

I was still sitting there, poised to fight for my life, when I heard several vehicles screech to a stop outside. Mrs. K's voice came to me, remotely, and there were shouts downstairs and a lot of pounding, then a crash, followed by footsteps treading heavily on the stairs.

Two uniformed cops burst into the room, weapons drawn. I looked at them dully.

"Is he dead?" I croaked. I think I can be forgiven one stupid question, given the circumstances.

One of the officers, a woman, flipped on the overhead lights and holstered her pistol, taking in the scene.

"Jesus H. Christ," her partner murmured.

"Clare!" That was Mrs. K, crouching beside me, taking me into her arms, blood and gun and all. "Oh, Clare—are you all right, honey?"

The male officer leaned down to check

Arren's throat for a pulse, looked at his partner, shook his head.

"What went on in here?" the female cop asked quietly. I couldn't read her name tag; it was lost in a blaze of reflected light.

"I should think that would be perfectly obvious," Mrs. K said, none too patiently, her arms still around me. I allowed myself to sag against her a little. "This—this *criminal* broke in here and tried to hurt her."

"We'd like to hear the story from her," said the male cop, in a reasonable tone.

More scuffling downstairs. Footsteps on the stairs.

"Clare!" It was Sonterra, and at the sound of his voice, I started to cry. The sight of him broke down the last of my defenses.

Kneeling, Sonterra edged Mrs. K aside and pulled me close. He didn't say anything at all, but just held me, hard, rocking slightly. His clothes were damp with rain and I felt the steady thud of his heartbeat through the front of my pajamas.

Eddie Columbia was there, too. Through a pounding blur, I saw him check Arren for vital signs, the way the other cop had done. "Call the M.E.," he told one of the uniforms, "and get the Crime Scene people over here."

"What about an ambulance?" the woman asked.

"Not a bad idea," Eddie said, tossing me a sympathetic glance.

Still kneeling, Sonterra cupped his hands on either side of my face and looked into my eyes. "Clare, what happened here?"

"You got my message," I said stupidly.

"What message?" Sonterra asked.

I closed my eyes and might have fainted dead away if Sonterra hadn't supported me by grasping my shoulders and giving me a slight, restorative shake. "What message, Clare?" he repeated.

"Oh, my God," I whispered. "I called your cell phone—"

Mrs. K was somewhere on the edge of my vision, a colorful flash. "I called the police, dear," she said. "I heard somebody scream."

I said, "Thank you," and promptly collapsed against Sonterra's chest, all the light seeping from my brain.

Chapter Forty-one

When I came around again, probably less than a minute later, I was downstairs on the couch, stripped of my ruined pajamas and tightly swaddled in a blanket. My skin felt sticky, and my stomach churned as memories of the deadly encounter with James Arren rushed into my mind, filling the blessed vacuum. A paramedic was listening to my heartbeat through a stethoscope, and Mrs. K and Sonterra hovered nearby, watching intently, as though prepared to intercede if the guy made a wrong move.

"Except for an understandable case of shock," the paramedic told me, with a reassuring smile, "you seem to be all right. You might want to spend the night in the hospital, just to make sure."

I was already shaking my head. I'd just gotten out of the hospital; I had no intention of going back unless I was forced.

"You can stay with me," Mrs. K said.

Sonterra's gaze burned into me. "You're going to my place," he said, and there was a note of finality in his tone that put an end to the discussion. Smiling a little, as if that had been her intention all along, Mrs. K offered no objection.

"All right," I said. Sonterra and I had our issues, and a few hours of amazing sex hadn't changed that, but I felt a need to be close to him. It would pass, I was sure, as soon as the numbing fear subsided.

I was questioned carefully, though gently, by Eddie Columbia; there seemed to be a tacit agreement that Sonterra wouldn't be able to handle the task objectively. My bedroom was thoroughly examined by a herd of technicians, and James Arren was carried out in a body bag. I wasn't sorry he was dead—I still believed he'd killed my sister, despite his denial, and he'd damn near killed me as well—but I did dread having to tell Emma that her father was gone, and I'd been the one to pull the trigger.

Emma was essentially a child, and even though she would know, on a rational level, that I had done what I had to do, another part of her would surely mourn the imaginary father she'd been trying to will, hope, and prod into existence. She might never forgive me for putting a permanent end to the dream, especially in such a violent way.

It was after one A.M. when Sonterra hefted my suitcase, quickly packed by Mrs. K, into his SUV. I climbed into the passenger side without assistance, noting with detachment that the rain had stopped. I was wearing my bathrobe, a pair of slippers, and about a gallon of James Arren's blood.

Sonterra's house, a three-bedroom Spanish style in a small development in Scottsdale, was dark when we pulled into the garage.

He got out, came around to my side, and lifted me off the seat without waiting for permission. For once, I let myself lean on him, but even then I knew it wouldn't last. He was a cop, I was a defense attorney, and we were on very different wavelengths.

Without a word, he carried me in through the kitchen, switching on lights as he went. We mounted the steps, and he pushed open the door to the master suite, carrying me to the bathroom.

I was swamped with heated memories, having been in these rooms before, on a number of other occasions, but I didn't struggle against them. After what had happened in my own bedroom that night, recollections of having wild sex with Sonterra were a welcome respite.

He set me on my feet, reached past me to turn on the shower spigots, and started taking off his clothes. His dark eyes were grim, and burning with a fire that had nothing to do with body heat. This was not about getting for Sonterra. It was about giving. Even in my jumbled mental state, I knew that.

He helped me out of the bathrobe, and drew me with him into the shower. There, with a gentleness that brought an ache to my throat and tears to my eyes, he washed away the crimson streaks running from my shoulders to my shins. When I was clean, he dried me gently with a towel, outfitted me with one of his T-shirts, and settled me in his bed.

He got in beside me then, pulled me into his arms, and held me through the long night.

Morning found me up before Sonterra, leaning against the bathroom sink and staring at my image in the mirror. I'd killed a man the night before; now I found it amazing that I didn't look any different.

He slipped his arms around me from behind and planted a kiss on my cheek.

"You didn't make love to me," I said, mys-
tified. Sonterra wasn't the type to miss an
opportunity like that. I'd been naked, and I'd
been needy. Our earlier session, before
James's arrival, had torn down a few walls.

"An omission on my part," he said.

I turned to look up at him. "Thank you," I
said.

He pulled a face, pretending to be
stricken. "For not making love to you?"

"For bringing me here. For holding me."

He kissed my nose. "Protect and serve,"
he said. "I was just trying to live up to the
motto."

I needed him, needed the distraction, the
respite I knew I would find in his arms, in his
bed. I slipped my fingers into his hair, pulled
his head down for a kiss. He groaned as his
mouth met mine.

The kiss deepened; I felt the T-shirt rising
as he bunched the fabric in his hands on either side of my waist. When he released me,
it was only to strip me bare.

My flesh seemed to ignite under his gaze.
He cupped my right breast in one hand and
leaned down to taste the nipple.

I whimpered.

He sucked.

My knees buckled; raising his head with obvious reluctance, he caught me in his arms, lifted me off my feet, carried me to his bed. For a little while, he made me forget all the death, but when I surfaced, reality was waiting.

I had to go to Emma, and tell her what had happened before she heard it on the news or at school, and I knew it would be the hardest thing I'd gone through yet, and that included the fight to the death with James Arren the night before.

Downstairs, Sonterra whipped up a cheese omelet, divided it between us, and put a fork in my hand when I made no move to eat.

"What's the plan?" he finally asked, pouring coffee for us both.

I stared at the food, took a tentative bite, set the fork down. "Emma has to be told. That's the first order of business."

He nodded, and the set of his jaw was grim. "That's going to be tough. Want some help?"

I shook my head. "It has to come from me."

He took a swig of coffee, chewing on my answer for a few moments. "Okay," he said, taking me by surprise.

"Tony," I began, "I—I'm grateful that you brought me here last night, because I really needed to be with somebody, but—"

He'd taken hold of my hand at some point, but now he let it go. "But what?"

"I don't want—well, I don't want you to get the idea that what happened between us was—"

"Anything more than sex?" he asked, in a mildly dangerous tone.

I thought about it, and couldn't come up with a better way of putting it, though surely there must have been one. I'm never going to win any awards for tact. "Right," I said.

It was as though an invisible wall slammed down between us; I felt the crash, metal colliding with stone. The floor seemed to tremble beneath my feet, and the room was suddenly void of oxygen.

"Okay, Counselor," he said evenly, "strictly business from here on."

Half an hour earlier, I'd been in his bed, out of my mind with ecstasy. Now we were strangers again. "Good," I said, but the word came out sounding a little raw.

Sonterra pushed back his chair. "Finish up," he said briskly. "I'll drop you off at Loretta's."

I nodded, took another token nibble from the omelet, and got to my feet. I was still without a car, since my rental had been totaled in Tucson, and even though I'd received the insurance check on my Saturn, I didn't expect to have either the time or the inclination to buy another until things settled down a little.

"Thanks," I said.

He brought my suitcase downstairs, and we drove to Loretta's place in miserable silence. The traffic was mercifully light, and we made good time.

Emma came out of the front door when we pulled in, and from the look on her face, I knew she'd heard something. I hadn't called Loretta after the attack, since I'd been almost catatonic, but I suspected that either Mrs. K or Sonterra had.

Sonterra reached over and squeezed my hand before I got out of the SUV, but he didn't smile and he didn't speak. I got the suitcase out of the backseat myself, and set it down on the pavement at my feet, then watched Sonterra drive away.

Emma stared at me for a long time, as though she couldn't quite believe I was really there. Then, with a strangled sob, she flung herself into my arms.

I hugged her fiercely. "I'm so sorry, baby," I said.

She clung to me, crying harder.

Loretta came out and gently steered us both inside, leaving us alone in the living room, seated side by side on the long white leather sofa. Bernice trundled in, jumping up into Emma's lap and trying to lick away her tears.

I waited until Emma had recovered a little before taking her hand and holding it between both of my own. I wondered if my flesh felt as cold to her as hers did to me.

"How much do you know?" I asked, very softly.

"He's dead," Emma said, shoulders still heaving slightly. "My dad is dead. He broke in and you had to shoot him. Loretta told me."

I put an arm around her, and she shrank from me, just a little.

My heart sank. It looked as if the road back from this tragedy might be a very long one indeed. "I'm sorry," I said again.

"It wouldn't have happened if you'd been here, with us," Emma cried, burying her wet face in the dog's furry little back for a moment. When she looked up, her eyes were fierce. "Or if you'd been with Tony. But, no, you won't let yourself need anybody!"

I bit my lower lip. "Emma, please—"

She scooted away, putting distance between us, and not just in the physical sense. "You knew he was on the run! You knew he might come after us!"

"Emma—" I reached for her, and she sprang off the couch, still holding the dog.

Loretta came back into the room, hovering near the doorway that led into her dining room, but she didn't say anything.

"*Damn* you, Clare!" Emma screamed. "Damn you for always trying to be so tough! Look what happened because you wouldn't trust anybody!" Before I could say anything in response, she turned and fled.

Loretta walked across the room and sat on the couch, in Emma's place, taking my hand.

"It'll be okay," she said. "She's had a shock, that's all."

I gave a hoarse, humorless little laugh.

"Oh, yes. I killed her father. How's *that* for a shock?"

"James's death isn't what's frightened her so much, Clare," Loretta told me quietly. "She's upset because she nearly lost you. We all are."

I leaned forward, buried my face in my hands. "Could we stay here for a while?" I asked, without looking up. "I don't think I can even step over the threshold of that condo after what happened there. Not right now, anyway."

"Kip and I will go get some of your things later, if it's okay with the police," Loretta said. "You can stay as long as you like; you know that." She shuddered. "Oh, Clare, it must have been awful. Do you want to tell me about it?"

I was surprised to find that I did.

Slowly, haltingly, I related the story of my fatal encounter with James Arren, and Loretta listened without interruption, grasping my hand. I didn't mention spending the night at Sonterra's place, or the lovemaking, but she probably guessed what had happened.

"What are you going to do now?" she

asked, after we'd talked a lot, cried a little, and had some tea in the sunny kitchen.

I looked at her in mild surprise. "I'm going to work," I said.

"You've got to be kidding," she replied, and she didn't look or sound half as sympathetic as she had before. "After what's happened, you're just going to waltz into that law office and take up where you left off?"

"Yes," I said, baffled by her reaction. I still had the Netherton case to win, after all. If I failed in that, it would mean years of selling my soul, chunk by bleeding, quivering chunk.

"I'll be damned," Loretta said. Then she walked off and left me sitting there, and refused to say another word to me until I was ready to leave, though she did lend me a suit, panty hose, and shoes, and handed over the keys to her car. Emma was still shut up in one of the guest rooms, receiving no one except Bernice.

"Sonterra's right about you," Loretta said in the driveway as I slipped behind the wheel of the Lexus and started the engine. "You are *seriously* screwed up!"

"Take care of Emma," I said simply, and backed out.

Chapter Forty-two

Everybody at the office looked at me as though I'd acquired an extra head since the last time they we met. I ignored them, went into my office, and placed a call to Justin Netherton.

I got his voice mail and left a message, relieved that he was out. While I waited for the inevitable callback, I turned my attention to the new list he'd given me in Tucson. Thrilled consumers all, prepared to sing his praises in or out of court.

I reached for the telephone, flashing briefly and viciously on the same gesture, made the night before, in my condo, with James Arren brandishing a golf club at the end of my bed. My stomach did a slow roll, and I shifted my mind to another level, yet another trick I'd learned growing up tough.

When there's work to do, you put everything else aside, and you do it.

I dialed the number for the first name on

Dr. Netherton's fan-club roster, forced a smile into my voice when a woman answered.

"Hello," I said. "My name is Clare Westbrook, and I'm an attorney. I represent Dr. Justin Netherton. May I ask you a few questions about your association with him?"

The floodgates of adulation swung open, and Marilyn Rogers regaled me with the wonders "dear Justin" had worked on her poor, sagging breasts, her droopy backside, and her self-esteem. I took notes and refrained from comment, which wasn't easy.

The next call produced much the same results, and by the time the third conversation was over, I realized that these people were practically reading from a script.

I had my head in my hands when Harvey, Jr., surprised me by walking right into the office without knocking.

"Are you all *right?*" he asked, in a hushed voice. He looked a little scared, as though my bad luck might jump right out and attach itself to him.

"I'm doing my best to cope," I responded.

He relaxed a little, eased closer to the

desk. "You're working on the Netherton case, I presume?"

I nodded, and was about to tell him about the phone calls, when he leaned against my desk, overshadowing me in a way that made me want to push my chair back against the wall. His tone was confidential.

"I hate to ask you this," he said, "especially when I know you've been through some rather trying times lately, but, well, would you mind going back down to Tucson? Dr. Netherton is getting impatient—he's threatening to pull his retainer and hire other counsel." Harvey, Jr., fixed me with an unctuous gaze. "You know, of course, that that would mean ruin, not only for the firm, but for you."

I knew it would surely be the final straw for Kredd and Associates if Dr. Netherton yanked his retainer, but now that the idea had a little time to gel in my subconscious, I wasn't quite so clear on what that would do to me. After all, I couldn't be forced to work for a firm that no longer existed.

Fortunately, I didn't say any of the things I was thinking out loud. It just so happened that Harvey, Jr., was ready for anything.

"According to the terms of your agreement, payment in full is due and payable on the day your employment ends, no matter what the reason."

I sat up very straight in my chair and didn't break eye contact. "What can I do in Tucson that I couldn't do here?" I asked quietly.

"*Persuade* the doctor to be patient," Harvey, Jr., said.

I hoped I'd misunderstood his implications. "Harvey, my niece has just lost her father. To leave her now, when I've been gone so much lately as it is—"

Harvey, Jr., spread his hands, waxing magnanimous. "Take her with you!"

Sure, I thought. The last time I'd been to Tucson, somebody had tried to run me over with a truck, then slammed a pistol butt into the back of my head. Just the kind of atmosphere I wanted for Emma, especially in her fragile emotional state.

Harvey, Jr., leaned in. "Do whatever you have to do, Clare."

I sighed. "Don't I always?"

Chapter Forty-three

Loretta and Kip's ranch house, like their place in Scottsdale, was luxurious, though of course it was more rustic. My appointed room adjoined Emma's, each having its own well-equipped bathroom and a set of doors leading out to the large, lighted pool. A massive armoire faced my bed, beautifully painted with dreamlike scenes of mountains and valleys, rivers and lakes, and housing a wide-screen TV. Cornelia, who had kept house for Kip's mother and now worked for Loretta, had turned back the covers on both beds long before we arrived.

I was in a funky mood as I went over my schedule and got ready for an early night. I knew better, but I couldn't seem to help comparing these spacious surroundings with the trailers, low-income apartments, and tract houses I'd known as a kid. In my case at least, the contrast illustrated the difference between growing up with a father, and growing up without one.

Emma hadn't said two words to me on the drive down from Tucson, despite numerous attempts on my part to get a conversation going; Sonterra and I were on the outs; and I was feeling disjointed, mentally as well as physically.

I studied my reflection in the mirror above the dresser, and my dead paternal grandmother came to mind, the woman I knew only as "Mrs. Westbrook," which just about said it all. I wondered if she would have liked me, maybe even been a little proud of the way I'd fought my way out of a less-than-promising beginning, and suddenly it was all I could do not to drive into Tucson, find the cemetery where she and the rest of the clan were buried, and pay my respects, such as they were.

I paced a little, exhausted, body and soul, but well aware that I would not be falling asleep in the near future. I simply had too much to assimilate; my mind and emotions were running three shifts and clamoring for overtime. I'd shot James Arren, putting a permanent end to my niece's hopes of having a real family, unfounded though they were. I couldn't forget the blood, the fear, the horror; I felt cold to the very marrow of my bones. My career was a mess, and there was still somebody on my trail, sworn to kill me. I was certain James had murdered Tracy, but he'd had no reason to go after Harvey, Sr., Janet, or Denise Robbins. More than ever, I needed to keep my guard up, but the strain was getting to me, for sure.

With a sigh, I set my suitcase on the bed, opened it, and took out the suit I intended to wear in the morning. It was a hand-me-down from Loretta; I still refused to return to the condo, even to supplement my limited wardrobe. The outfit was navy blue, with square matching buttons, trimmed in gold. The skirt was slim, the jacket tailored. It was a no-nonsense, don't-screw-with-me outfit, perfect for difficult depositions and tough days in court; I would tuck my hair into a French twist, I decided, to add an extra measure of authority. I hung the suit in the closet, laid out the attendant underwear, slip, and new package of panty hose, and grabbed a nightgown. Carrying that and my trusty cell phone, I went into the guest bathroom and started water running in the tub. It was a huge thing, with jets and a sloping back to lean against. My bath promised to be a spiritual experience, roughly on a par with returning to the womb.

Not, I thought, with grim humor, that my mother's body had necessarily been such a safe place.

I was up to my chin in bubbling, scented water when the cell phone rang. I nearly dropped the thing in the tub, trying to retrieve it from the toilet lid, and the flames of the candles I'd lit earlier wavered in the resulting draft.

"Where the hell are you?" The voice was Sonterra's. "In a wind tunnel?"

I shut off the jets, totally focused, every cell on code blue. "Never mind where I am," I said. "Where are you?"

He sounded worn-out. "You don't need to know that," he said flatly. "Suffice it to say, I'm on a case."

There was a roaring sound in the background; at first I'd thought it was poor reception. Now I realized it was the ocean. I can't explain it, but I felt a little peeved, as if Sonterra had tried to one-up me, location-wise. Which, of course, was crazy, because he didn't have the faintest idea where I was. I didn't plan to clue him in, either.

"You okay?" I finally asked. "Or did you just call to hear the sound of my voice?"

He laughed, and the sound, splintery as it was, made me feel a little better. "Maybe I needed a little grief," he said. "Eddie is a smart-ass, too, but somehow, it doesn't have the same charm coming from him. How's Emma?"

"She's good," I said, stretching the truth a little. I'd almost said, *She's with me*, which would have been a strong clue that I was out of town. If he knew that much, it would be a short mental leap to the fact that I was running amok in Tucson again.

"That poor kid is entitled to some good luck," he said. "She's holding up all right, then? She must have been pretty shaken when you told her what happened with Arren."

"She was," I said quietly. "But she's tough, like me. She'll work it through." *Please, God.*

"Sometimes being tough isn't enough, Clare."

"Is there a barb tucked away in that statement somewhere?"

"Don't get your back up," he said, and I flashed on the singular comfort he'd provided in my time of need. "I was just trying to get across that it's okay to depend on other people sometimes. For Emma, and for you."

I closed my eyes, tried to reinforce my defenses a little. Sonterra was forever finding a chink and prying at the mortar. "So, how long are you going to be out of town?" I asked, almost perky.

"I'll be staying here for a few days," he said. I could almost hear the gears grinding in his brain when he paused. "Sometimes I hate this job."

"Pretty depressing, huh?"

"Yeah," he said. "Look, if you need help, will you just tell me?"

I swallowed hard. "I can handle things on my own," I said. *Come and get me*, pleaded the small and usually still voice inside me. *Hold me, keep me safe.*

A sigh from him. "You're still at Loretta's?"

I bit my lower lip. "Yes," I said. After all, I *was* at Loretta's. With any luck at all, I'd be back in Cave Creek before Sonterra got wind of the fact that I'd left town.

"You're being careful, right?" Sometimes Sonterra sounds like a broken record.

"Very careful," I said. For instance, I was watching every word I said to him.

He chuckled; the sound was low, throaty, and too ragged to be comforting. God only knew what kind of demons Sonterra was dealing with that night as a part of his job, and I probably couldn't have helped, even if I'd been right there beside him. Still, I wished I could make a difference. "That's some consolation, at least," he said. "Too bad I don't believe three-quarters of the things you say."

I flushed with indignation and some chagrin, too. I hated sidling around the truth, even if I *was* a lawyer, but there are times when a person has to stretch things a little, not just for her own sake, but that of others. Sonterra had enough to think about, without fretting over me as well.

"That was a low blow," I accused.

"Yes," he said, "but all too true."

That night, I felt the distance between us, both literal and figurative, even more keenly than before. I started to speak, but my tongue got tangled.

"I'll be back in a few days," he said when the silence lengthened.

"Be careful," I said, partly because I really

wanted him to look out for himself, and partly because he always said that to me. "And, Sonterra?"

"What?"

"I sort of miss you."

"You miss the sex."

There are some things that don't bear denying, under any circumstances. "True," I said.

Again, that chuckle, the one that came from somewhere deep in that beautifully formed chest of his. I knew then, as sure as I know there are nine planets in the solar system, that the next time we saw each other, we'd head straight for the nearest bed. "When I get back to Scottsdale," he said, confirming my unspoken thoughts, "I'm going to lay you down and make a believer out of you, so wear something sexy."

I liked driving him crazy. After all, it was one of the things I did best. "Who says I'll be wearing anything at all? Assuming we don't have a public reunion, of course."

He laughed. It was a brittle sound, with plenty of fractured places. "Don't worry, Counselor," he said. "I'll make sure there are no witnesses."

"Do that," I said.

I didn't want to let him go, but, hey, I've had therapy. Besides, the conversation was about to degenerate into phone sex.

"Sleep well, Clare," he said. That voice. It's damnably soothing, especially when it comes from nearby, like beside me in bed late at night, or from across the breakfast table.

"Take care," I replied, and I was the first to hang up.

I was still soaking, and thinking about the enigma that is my fascination with the wrong men, when it finally got through to me that the water was stone cold.

I shivered, chilled, as I reached for a towel.

Chapter Forty-four

Emma was in the kitchen when I caught up with her the next morning, sharing a batch of Cornelia's pancakes with the dog. She gave me a bleak smile and a little nod of acknowledgment when I said hello.

I laid a hand on her shoulder; she shrugged me off in a subtle move.

"Is there going to be a funeral for my dad?" Her backbone was rigid, her chin jutting a little.

I felt sick to the soul. Cornelia, stationed at the stove, caught my gaze and held it. She and I hadn't had a chance to talk in any depth, but I was certain Loretta had filled her in.

"I suppose," I said, not really knowing. The truth was, the possibility hadn't even occurred to me.

"Don't you even *care* that he's dead?" Emma demanded, her voice small, but full of bitter challenge.

"I didn't mean for it to happen," I told her, blinking back tears.

"I want to see his grave," she said, folding her arms.

"Then we'll do that."

"Not '*we*.' Just me."

I suppressed a sigh. Cornelia gave me a sympathetic, hang-in-there look, and went back to stirring pancake batter.

"Okay," I said.

Cornelia turned to look at me again, her eyes full of sympathy. "Have some break-fast, Clare."

I shook my head. "Thanks anyway." I avoided Emma's stare, though I felt it scalding my flesh, by consulting my watch. "I'd better go—I have an appointment."

Outside, I climbed into Loretta's Lexus, plugged my cell phone into the cigarette lighter to save the freshly charged battery, and consulted my memory regarding the location of the restaurant where Dr. Netherton and I were to meet. As low as my opinion of my client was, thinking about him was infinitely preferable to going over the rift between Emma and me, or any of the events preceding it.

I shifted mental and emotional gears, though not as smoothly as usual.

Netherton was standing in the restaurant parking lot when I turned in, face stormy, hands crammed into the pockets of his chinos, with what looked like a newspaper clamped under one arm. I was where I was supposed to be, and I was on time, but obviously I'd already done something wrong.

Nothing new there.

I got out of the car, bringing my briefcase along, and then fetched my laptop from the trunk.

"Good morning, Doctor," I said, hoping some of my forced good cheer would rub off on him.

It didn't. He had the newspaper clasped in one hand now, and the way he waved the thing around, I thought he was going to pop me over the head with it.

"I want to sue!" he bellowed.

I looked around the parking lot, saw families going into the restaurant, coming out. A few concerned glances were cast in our direction. "You're going to have to calm down," I said. "If you don't—"

"Have you *seen* this?" he hissed, jabbing the newspaper at me.

I shook my head, took the paper, but didn't open it. "Let's go inside. People are staring, and that isn't good for your image." I started toward the main entrance, so that he would follow, and once we were there, Netherton opened the front door for me. The place was doing a brisk business, but it wasn't packed; we asked for, and got, a rather secluded table behind the jukebox, which, fortunately, was silent.

The waitress watched us with coy interest, as though she thought we wanted to be alone so we could make eyes at each other. Evidently, she hadn't noticed either the briefcase or the laptop. I gave her a look, hoping to raise her consciousness a little, but I don't think she caught my drift.

When she'd gone, I unfolded the newspaper, and felt the bottom drop out of my stomach. The headline was a screamer, and it was news, all right. "FORMER LOVER SELLS STORY TO HOLLYWOOD," it read. Underneath were pictures of Dr. Netherton and of Sandy Piedmont, sans wig, makeup, and women's clothes, dressed as a man.

My first reaction, I admit, was pure relief. The article wasn't about my killing James Arren.

Then, belatedly, it hit me. Oops. Sandy Piedmont was a *man*.

It was all I could do not to call Sonterra right then and rub it in.

"Oh, Lord," I breathed, but I was biting the inside of my right cheek so I wouldn't smile or, worse yet, laugh out loud. Sonterra, who had flirted with Piedmont during our lunch at the Omni Hotel the week before, was going to be backpedaling like mad once I broke *this* story.

"Do something!" Netherton cried. "Get an injunction, a restraining order, anything! I don't want to end up as a movie of the week!"

Too late, I thought, perhaps a bit ungraciously. I was all sympathy when I spoke, however, since I'd had a few moments to compose myself. "Doctor, this is embarrassing for you, I know, but it shouldn't have an adverse effect on your case—"

"I'll kill that bastard!"

People at the surrounding tables turned to look, their faces reflecting alarm. I tried to reassure them with an in-charge smile.

"Dr. Netherton, please," I said. "I'll see what I can do about the movie, but frankly, our options are pretty limited. Under the law, Mr. Piedmont is perfectly free to tell his story."

"But it isn't just his story," the doctor hissed, veins bulging in his neck and forehead. "It's *mine*, too!"

I suppressed a sigh. I don't know why people never seem to anticipate scandals while they're actually creating them. Instead, they're usually blindsided when their chickens come home to roost. "Have you spoken to him?"

"I tried," came the slightly calmer reply, "but he wouldn't take my calls. He wants revenge; that's what this is about, you know. Simple revenge."

No doubt for Alexander Piedmont, it was indeed sweet, but my client appeared to be on the verge of blowing a blood vessel.

I waited for him to chill out a little, and it was a long wait.

Finally, though, his color returned to near normal and he seemed somewhat less agitated.

"Do you have something new for me?" I asked politely, when his chest had stopped heaving. I had already switched on the laptop. "I've spoken to all of the people on the list you provided, and, frankly, they sounded like they were reading from a press kit. The judge is going to notice a pattern there."

He looked sheepish. "I did give them a few—suggestions," he admitted.

Maybe it was the suit I was wearing, all business and no bullshit. A pair of those little half-glasses perched on the end of my nose would have been the perfect finishing touch, but, darn it, my vision is twenty-twenty. "Dr. Netherton, we are in a great deal of trouble, the problem with Mr. Piedmont notwithstanding," I said, since the head-on approach seemed to work best with him. "I've gone over the prosecution's disclosures a million times, looking for even one loophole, and I've found zip. Nada." I paused, watching the blunt truth sink in. "If I'm going to argue this case successfully, I will need more than a chorus of country-club wives, all singing the same song in your praise. I need something solid here."

He ran his tongue over his lips. "He's a liar," he hissed, starting to look crazy again. So much for my naïve belief that we'd moved beyond the inflammatory newspaper article.

"Doctor, there are other claimants—"

"I know, I know. The Dorsetts. It's true

that that surgery went badly—sometimes that happens. Ms. Westbrook, if they prosecuted every cardiac surgeon who has ever lost a postop patient, every psychiatrist who ever worked with an eventual suicide—"

"You have a point, Dr. Netherton," I said quietly. "People sometimes die, or suffer lasting ill-effects, following surgery. And this, of course, was *elective* surgery, which makes a difference, legally and morally. But I can assure you that losing your temper in public is not a prudent course of action."

He seemed to deflate before my eyes. "All right," he said glumly.

Just then, the waitress came, chirping and fawning and fussing like mad. Netherton ordered oatmeal with skim milk, I chose bacon and eggs, which earned me a long-suffering glance from the good doctor. Now that I was in lawyer-mode, and had a brief respite from Emma's raging grief and confusion, my appetite was back.

"Why do you want me to handle your case?" I asked, when the waitress had gone away again. "I can understand why you would hire Harvey. He was Dream Team material; he had years of experience and contacts all over the place. I've only been practicing—"

"Harvey said you were the best lawyer in the firm, after him. He wanted you to have the experience, and he planned to coach you from behind the scenes."

I took a moment to recover. Harvey, Sr., had never given me special treatment, or singled me out for any kind of praise. On the contrary, he'd barked orders and suggested I prostitute myself with certain judges. "I'm a good lawyer," I said evenly. "I have an excellent, even an exceptional, mind. But it will be a long, long time before I'm in Harvey's league." Like, never, if I live right and take vitamins.

"Surely you knew," Dr. Netherton persisted, leering a little, "that Harvey had plans for you. Big ones. He was already tired of Betsy; he told me so himself. Do you really expect me to believe you never, well, *worked overtime*?"

"There was nothing—I repeat, *nothing*—romantic going on between Harvey Krudd— Harvey *Kredd* and me." But Harvey probably *had* given Netherton and a lot of other people the impression that he'd bought more than my brain when he put me through law school. The egotistical bastard.

Netherton stared at me, like a tourist watching a geyser surge toward the sky.

What a naïve idiot I'd been, for all my street smarts. Dear God, did *Sonterra* believe I'd been sleeping my way, if not to the top, to the middle? My voice turned deceptively mild. "So you naturally thought that if I'd fooled around with Harvey, I'd fool around with you?"

Not exactly rocket science. He'd served me a romantic dinner, in a fairy-lighted garden. He'd offered me a "tour" of his mansion. Yes, I'd known Netherton wanted, even expected, sex. What I hadn't figured out, hadn't even imagined, was that Harvey Kredd, my boss, to whom I was distantly related, for God's sake, had led people to believe that I was sharing his bed. He'd shot both my personal *and* professional credibility to hell in the process.

"Harvey," I said, in a furious undertone, "you son of a bitch."

I snapped the laptop shut, reached for the handle of my briefcase.

"Where are you going?" Netherton demanded.

"Home," I said. I was going to be fired, I was going to be broke, I was going to be in debt for the rest of my natural life, maybe I was even going to be sued for breach of contract, and I didn't give a damn. All along, my intuition had been telling me not to defend this sleazeball, and I hadn't listened. Well, I was listening now. I would find a way to pay back the estate, and I would get a new job, one I could be halfway proud of doing. What I would *not* do was swallow any more crap. "Get yourself another lawyer, Doc."

His expression had gone from smug to horrified. "You can't do this," he said. "Nobody else will take the case!"

There it was. No lawyer in the entire state of Arizona was stupid enough to represent him. Besides me, of course.

"Good-bye and good luck," I said, and walked out.

At first, I didn't know what to do. I was in no condition for another confrontation, or nonconfrontation, with Emma, and I was too angry to call Harvey, Jr., or even Loretta, who would definitely applaud my decision to abandon the Netherton case. Easy for her, I thought, with a flash of resentment.

She didn't have to worry about every penny that passed through her checking account the way I did.

Once I caught my breath, I decided to call Arlo Browder and ask if he'd learned anything new about Tracy's death. I truly wanted to know, and talking to him would take my mind off the fact that I'd probably just ended my career. This time next month, I reflected, I might be back to serving cocktails.

Maybe there was an opening at the Horny Toad, back in Cave Creek.

Chapter Forty-five

Browder wasn't in, so I left a rather abrupt message on his voice mail.

I drove around in big circles for a while, fuming, and I finally ended up back in the old neighborhood, where the convenience stores were run-down and there were a lot of strip-mall storefronts for rent. I found the storage unit where I'd put what was left of Gram's things after she died, along with some of Tracy's belongings, and my own. I wasn't dressed for foraging, but I couldn't bring myself to go all the way back out to Loretta and Kip's ranch for jeans and a T-shirt, not in that state of mind. And I still wasn't ready to face Emma.

The guy managing the storage place checked my ID, looked up my file, and gave me a key to number 246. I'd been making the monthly rental payments on that place for almost eight years, unable to let go of those last, pitiful vestiges of Gram and Tracy and the person I'd once been.

I'm sure my therapist could have come up with all kinds of pertinent metaphors.

I'd reached some kind of turning point, though. There would be some changes made, and not just in the course of my career.

I drove along the aisles until I came to my unit, then got out, marched over, and turned the key in the lock. The front rolled up, like a garage door, when I pulled on the handle, and dust billowed out through the opening.

There was an old floral couch along one wall, probably home to innumerable spiders and a few mice, despite the management's claim that the place was pest free. There were cardboard boxes full of Gram's old jersey dresses—I remembered packing those, and crying, a month after her funeral. Her massive collection of paperback books—mysteries, mostly, with a sprinkling of historical romances. I smiled, gazing down at one particularly lurid seventies cover, showing a cowboy and a dance-hall girl in a clench, both of them half-naked. Gram had liked the ones with a lot of sizzle, bless her heart.

I put down the book, both comforted and disturbed to find myself in this dusty shrine to our creative rendition of a family. What did I hope to accomplish?

For the moment, I merely wanted to keep busy, so I wouldn't have to think too much. On another level, I knew it was time to clear the stuff away, once and for all, and get on with my life, a sort of storage-unit feng shui. Besides, I would need the fee I was paying for other things, like groceries, now that I was facing unemployment.

Good thing they'd outlawed debtors' prison.

I found a box marked "Clare's stuff," and tore my way into it. There were clothes inside, musty and way out of fashion, and probably too small. I rooted through the contents, found some baggy old pants that I'd worn to help Gram paint her fence, along with a flannel shirt. I shook them out, stepped behind a stack of plastic storage containers, and changed out of my suit.

My high heels gave the ensemble a unique touch, but I didn't take them off. I was even less inclined toward conformity that day than usual.

By eleven o'clock, I had the throwaway

stuff stacked on one side of the unit; I
planned to have it hauled to the dump,
since no charity in the world would have
wanted it. All that was left were a few shoe
boxes full of old pictures and letters, the
one high school yearbook Tracy had owned,
and a funny-looking doll I'd earned when I
was a kid, selling chances on a punch card
to my friends at school. I wasn't sure why
I'd saved the thing, since I hadn't really liked
her in the first place. I'd been going for a
skateboard.

I chucked the doll.

I was loading up the sad gleanings when
a voice startled me half out of my skin.

"I thought that was you."

I nearly conked my head—which was still
sore from my last visit to Tucson, not to
mention the tussle with James Arren—on
the trunk lid. Henley was standing behind
me, meaty arms folded, taking in my grubby
outfit.

"You ain't dressed much like a lawyer-
lady today," he observed.

"I ain't *feeling* much like a lawyer-lady
today," I retorted.

Naturally, he missed the irony of my bad

grammar. His expression was blank, but benign, as far as I could tell.

"What are you doing here, Henley?" I asked, when he didn't take his turn to speak. It was quite a coincidence, his turning up like that, and I don't believe in coincidences.

"Sylvie kept some stuff here, so I come to get it. I'm holding a garage sale—got to raise me some cash."

Apparently, I thought, he'd dealt with his grief and moved on. Pretty good, considering the horrific way Sylvie had died, and the fact that she hadn't been gone a week. In the next moment, though, I silently chastised myself for assuming the worst. Maybe the poor guy was trying to pay Sylvie's final expenses, or finance a small headstone.

"Well," I said, waiting for Henley to step out of my way so I could get into the car, "see you around."

He didn't move.

Something crawled down the length of my spine on teeny-tiny feet. I looked right, I looked left. Nobody in sight. The traffic out on the highway, bustling along at the usual merry roar, seemed much farther away than it actually was.

I called on bravado, my old *compadre*. "Do you want something, Henley?" I asked.

The expression on his face was odd, but since I'd mostly seen him in the dark, or in the dim light that afternoon at Nipples, I figured maybe that was normal for him. "There were some pictures of your sister in with Sylvie's stuff," he said. "She was with another guy."

I wasn't tracking all that well; half my brain was already at the ranch, working things out with Emma, or at least making a beginning. "What?"

He smiled a scary smile. "I read where you kilt Jimmy. Good for you."

I let the remark about my taking James out pass without comment. "Let me see those pictures," I said, with my usual lack of diplomacy.

He smirked, putting a matchstick between his lips and then rolling it from one side of his mouth to the other. "What'll ya give me for them?"

I held on to my temper with all my strength. "What do you want?" I countered.

Henley shrugged one shoulder. "Dunno," he said. "Fifty bucks?"

I fumbled through my purse, found my

wallet, extracted two twenties and a ten, and shoved them at him. "You'd better not be jerking me around, Henley, because if you are, I'll see that you regret it."

The smirk morphed into a pouty look. Elvis-mouth, with collagen. "Now, why would I do that?"

I was out of patience, and seriously considered going back to the trunk, grabbing the jack handle, and using it to crease Henley's hair.

"You have your fifty dollars," I said. "Give me the pictures."

Henley took his time folding the bills, tucking them into the pocket of his polo shirt. I wondered if that big dog of his was lurking somewhere nearby. "She did drugs, Clare. Didn't you know that? Spacy-Tracy, they called her. In those days, she would have done just about anything for a hit of crank. Didn't Sylvie tell you that?"

"Give me the pictures," I repeated, in his face, feeling the way I had years before, on the playground, when some other little kid made remarks about my mother.

He cocked a thumb in the direction of another storage unit. "Over here," he said.

Spacy-Tracy. She would have done just about anything for a hit . . .

Unwanted memories steamrolled into my mind, things I'd successfully blocked for a long time. Tracy, coming home late, or not at all, even when we finally had it good at Gram's. I'd covered for her, over and over again, because I loved her, damn it, and because I didn't want us to get sent away. Tracy, shoplifting, saying it was just a game, and all the girls did it. Her pallor, her thinness, her nervousness—the list was growing in my mind.

But all that had changed when she'd given birth to Emma. She'd wanted, above all things, to give her daughter a good life. I started to cry, in earnest, but I fought it every inch of the way. I wiped my eyes with the backs of my hands, not caring that I was leaving smudges of dirt and mascara on my face.

Henley went into an open storage unit and came out carrying a battered manila packet. "Here," he said, shoving it at me.

The frayed circuits of my brain finally brought forth a fizzle. "You knew Tracy?"

No answer; Henley had turned his back; he was walking away.

Chapter Forty-six

Instead of going straight back to the ranch, I stuck to my prior plan and stopped off at a service station to wash up and change back into the borrowed suit. Then, on an impulse I didn't begin to understand, I drove to the cemetery Maria Gomez had told me about, and found my father's grave. Maybe I needed to be someplace quiet, where I could think, before I looked at those pictures.

I sat on a bench within spitting distance of Thomas Westbrook's final resting place, trying to prepare myself for whatever the photos would reveal. A lump hardened in my throat, and my eyes burned, but I couldn't cry any more. I wished, briefly, for Sonterra to appear by magic, striding toward me, able to make everything all right.

Of course, he didn't show. I would have to face my personal demons on my own.

I took out the pictures, blinked a couple of times, and forced myself to focus. The first one, apparently taken with a cheap instant camera, showed Tracy talking earnestly with a man I didn't recognize. They sat across from each other at a picnic table, probably in a park or one of those rest areas along the highway. I could clearly see her wedding band, so I knew she'd still been living with James when the shots were taken.

I should have felt relief, I suppose, since I'd expected an entirely different image, something pornographic, or worse. Instead, my anxiety grew.

I flipped to the next shot, fingers trembling. Tracy and the man again, kissing across the tabletop. The interlude was passionate, and illicit, considering the wedding ring, but nothing in it justified Henley's smirk back at the storage place, or my rising sense of dread.

"Hello." The voice was cheerful, and male, and it nearly made me jump out of my skin.

I looked up to see a young man, probably in his mid-thirties, vaguely familiar, affable-looking, nondescript, a little rumpled. "Do I know you?"

He sat down on the bench beside me, though I hadn't encouraged him in any way. "We've met," he said, and smiled, but there was something in his eyes, something in his manner, that unsettled me deeply.

I was about to ask if he'd been following me and, if so, why, when my cell phone rang.

The man next to me gazed at my father's gravestone while I dug for my phone, snapped it open, and said, "Clare Westbrook."

It was Arlo Browder calling. "Hello, Clare," he said.

"Arlo," I said. "Any news?"

"We've tracked down a guy named Ben Dupree," he said. "Evidently, he and your sister were involved." He paused. "He says they were planning to get married."

I glanced uneasily at the familiar stranger, who was standing several feet away now, with his back to me and his hands wedged into the pockets of a blue windbreaker. Then, registering what Arlo had just said, I looked down at the pictures in my lap. "Ben

Dupree," I mused. That would be the guy kissing Tracy across the picnic table.

"Are you okay?" Arlo asked, maybe picking up on something in my voice. "You sound a little off."

My visitor turned, openly listening, and regarded me with a sort of sad resignation. My gaze went automatically to his right hand, knotted in his pocket. "Do you think you could send a car out here?" I said, and gave him the name of the cemetery and my approximate location. "There's this man—"

"Hold on," Arlo said. I kept an eye on my unexpected companion while I was waiting. When Browder came back on the line, he said, "Sit tight. There's a unit in the area, and they'll be with you in a couple of minutes."

"The police are coming," I said clearly, as though confirming Arlo's promise, making sure to raise my voice a little.

The man who'd apparently followed me into the cemetery paused, then turned and walked away at a fast clip. I let out my breath.

"He's leaving," I told Arlo.

"All the same," Arlo replied, "I'm staying on the line. Give me a description, Clare."

I rattled off the standard details—medium, medium, medium.

"Did you see his car?"

The parking lot I'd used was some distance away, and only one of several. I stood up, spilling the pictures onto the ground, and craned my neck, but saw nothing besides neatly trimmed grass, headstones, and statues. My polite stalker had vanished into the trees. "Sorry, no," I said, sinking back to the bench. My knees were weak, and I took a few deep breaths before bending down to retrieve the photos.

"Did he say anything important?"

"Just that we'd met," I said, racking my poor, beleaguered brain to remember where. "I know I've seen him someplace—"

"Maybe he was the one tried to run you down, and then bashed you over the head in that hotel room."

I shivered, shook my head. "No," I murmured, operating on instinct. "No—I don't think so—"

I heard the crackle of a radio, looked up, and saw two police officers striding toward me, looking purposeful.

"Your guys are here," I said, almost dizzy with relief. "Thanks, Arlo."

I spent the next half hour answering questions, and then the police escorted me to my car, waited until I'd gotten inside, locked the doors, and started the engine. When I drove off, they followed me for a while, just in case.

Maybe that was when I began to revise my attitude about cops.

At the turnoff to the ranch, I pulled over, reached for the pictures Henley had sold me, and stared at them blindly for a few moments, trying to figure out what I was supposed to see in them besides Tracy having an affair. Maybe for James that had been reason enough to kill her.

I went through them again. Tracy and the man, probably Ben Dupree, engaged in various incriminating, but not indecent, behavior. I was about to give up when I realized that one photo had stuck to the back of another. I peeled it free, scanned the scene, and sucked in my breath.

The shot had been taken at a party. There were streamers, and everybody was smiling. Tracy, James, and, beside him, his arm around her shoulders, Ellie, the woman who'd so reluctantly helped me hook up with Sylvie.

I squinted at the computer-generated banner suspended behind them.

"HAPPY BIRTHDAY, MOM."

Chapter Forty-seven

I sat there in my car, in the driveway at the ranch, for fifteen or twenty minutes, trying to collect myself a little, and pored over the party picture. It bothered me on an elemental level, in the same way the man at the cemetery had, though I couldn't have said precisely why.

Was Ellie James Arren's mother, or simply another guest at the party?

I turned on the heater, even though it was seventy-five degrees outside, and tried to think. All I knew for sure was that I ought to take Emma and head straight back to Scottsdale, where a lot of music waited to be faced, but I just wasn't ready to go eyeball-to-eyeball with all those challenges. My mind was spinning.

I glanced down at my suit, which had definitely lost its pizzazz. My hair was full of dust from the storage unit, and I could feel the French twist slipping badly.

Get your thoughts in order, Clare.

Number one priority: Emma. I would take things slowly with her, I decided. She and I would spend one more night at the ranch, but, first thing in the morning, we would be on our way home.

Home. We didn't precisely have one, since I still regarded the condo as uninhabitable, but I would worry about that later. The first order of business would be going to the office one last time and facing off with Harvey, Jr. In a weird sort of way, I was looking forward to that.

I pulled back onto the driveway and headed for the ranch house.

To my surprise, Emma came out to greet me. She didn't smile, but she wasn't glaring, either. I smiled for both of us, and touched my niece's hair.

"Some lawyer called you," she said. Her eyes were puffy, and she was a little pale.

I resisted an urge to hug her, hard. "Harvey, Jr.?" I asked.

She shook her head. "He said his name was Walter Kass. He wouldn't tell me what he wanted, or how he got this number."

I bent my knees slightly, to make eye contact with Emma. "Did he say something that worried you?"

She looked down at her feet, then up into my face. Her expression was bleak. "I thought maybe you were going to get in trouble for what happened with my dad."

I put an arm around her shoulders, knowing it was a risk. "It was self-defense, honey," I said quietly. "I'm not going to be charged."

Emma searched my eyes. "Really?"

"Really," I confirmed, braced for her reaction. Would she be relieved, or angry? I had no way of knowing.

She started to cry, and sort of sagged against me. "Oh, God," she whispered, "I thought they were going to take you away. I thought I was going to be alone—"

I dropped my briefcase and purse to hug her. "Nobody's going to take me away, baby," I said. "Nobody."

Something broke loose in Emma in that moment. She clung to me, wailing with grief. We must have made quite a spectacle, standing there in the driveway, clutching each other like a pair of shipwreck survivors caught in a riptide, but I didn't give a damn how we looked to anybody else.

We *were* survivors, Emma and I, and I would do anything, anything in the world, to keep it that way.

Chapter Forty-eight

Emma and I talked until we were both exhausted. We talked about Tracy, about my deal with Harvey, Sr., and about James. She fell asleep, finally, curled up in the middle of my bed in the ranch guest room, with Bernice snuggled beside her.

I wandered into the kitchen, planning to brew some tea, and happened to see Walter Kass's name and number scrawled on the chalkboard next to the phone. Curious, and in need of something to keep myself busy while the electric kettle came to a boil, I reached for the receiver and punched in his number.

He must have been eager to talk, because his receptionist put the call right through.

"Clare Westbrook," he said, in a tone of surprise, as if he'd begun to doubt that I actually existed.

"What do you want?" I asked. I'd long since used up my daily ration of tact.

There was a smile in his voice. "I represent the Westbrook estate," he said. "You're a hard lady to catch up with."

I drew a stool over from the breakfast bar and sat down. "I'm in the phone book," I told him.

"We had to make sure there were no other direct descendents. It took a while."

I closed my eyes. Waited. It crossed my mind that the Kredds were out in the cold, not being progeny. Tough break for them.

"The Westbrook assets were substantial ones," Kass went on. "You stand to inherit a considerable sum—before taxes and other expenses, of course."

"Of course," I said. By then, I was on autopilot.

"I'd like to meet with you and discuss the matter."

"Listen, Mr. Kass, I don't mean to be rude, but I wasn't close to my family. I'm not really interested—"

He sighed. "Ms. Westbrook, we are talking about a great deal of money."

I wanted to tell him to take my father's estate and shove it, but I was facing unem-

ployment and a mountain of debt. Emma
and I needed to make a new start, maybe
somewhere far away. A few thousand dollars would come in handy.

"Hit me with your best shot," I said
wearily.

"Twenty-seven million dollars," he said.

I gripped the edge of the counter for support. The tea kettle began to whistle a shrill
song; I yanked its plug from the wall.

"Did you say—?"

"Twenty-seven mil," he repeated.

Without a word, I laid the receiver down,
slid off the stool, and dropped to my knees
in the middle of Loretta's kitchen floor, hy-
perventilating.

"Ms. Westbrook?" Kass's voice seemed
to come from another dimension. "Are you
there?"

I got back on my feet, scrabbled for the
phone, and pressed it to my ear. "If this is a
joke," I said testily, "it's a sick one."

Kass laughed. "It's no joke," he said.
"When can you drop by my office?"

I looked at my watch. "Five minutes?" I
asked.

Chapter Forty-nine

I had to tell somebody the news. Sonterra was my first choice, but I quelled that reckless impulse quickly enough, in favor of Emma.

I hung up the telephone, after agreeing to visit Mr. Kass's office first thing the next morning, headed for the guest room, and I stopped in my tracks on the threshold, feeling as though I'd just been struck by the proverbial freight train.

My dead sister was standing beside the bed, gazing down at Emma, stroking her hair. Tracy turned her head, very slowly, and looked at me with a plea in her eyes.

I forgot about James Arren, the stranger in the cemetery, and even about the twenty-seven million. I closed my eyes, certain that I was hallucinating, and when I opened them again, Tracy's ghost was gone.

I groped for the slipper chair in the corner and collapsed onto the seat. My stomach had shinnied up into my throat, and I still couldn't catch my breath. I leaned forward, gasping, to put my head between my knees.

Emma woke up, blinking. "I dreamed my mom was here," she said, with an expansive yawn. Then she squinted at me, and grimaced. "Hey, are you okay? You look awful."

"I'm—okay," I managed.

Emma swung her legs over the side of the bed, Bernice huddled in her arms. "I don't believe you," she said simply. "I'm going to get Cornelia."

"No," I said quickly. "Please, Em, I'm all right. Really."

She crossed the room, dog in tow, and perched on the arm of the slipper chair to drape an arm around my shoulders, effectively reversing our roles.

"You're really under a lot of stress," Emma said, sounding older than her years. "Things will get better, Clare. You'll see."

"Emma, I need to tell you—"

"Just get into bed," she said gently. "I'll bring you some bottled water—or would you rather have tea?"

I almost clutched at her hand, asked her

not to leave. Surely I'd imagined Tracy's presence. Maybe, I thought, I'd imagined Walter Kass's call, too, and the Westbrook millions. "Water, please," I said quietly. "And some aspirin, if you can find any." What I really wanted was a double shot of Jack Daniel's, but I didn't figure it would be right to send a kid for liquor.

Emma patted my back and, after a moment of worried hesitation, left the room.

I sat there trembling for a few seconds, wondering if I was finally cracking under the strain, then made a trip to the bathroom.

Emma had been and gone when I got back. She'd left the water on the bedside stand, on a coaster, and two aspirin tablets lay next to it.

I hesitated in the bathroom doorway, wondering if Tracy was about to reappear. The heebie-jeebies had definitely taken hold and, for a heartbeat or two, I couldn't make myself go near the bed. When I finally managed to shame myself into moving, I practically dived for the aspirin and water.

Then I began to feel silly. Of course I hadn't really seen a ghost. I was tired, I was stressed-out, and I'd recently suffered a head injury, along with other traumas. The vision of Tracy had been a waking dream, an aberration, a little communiqué from my subconscious mind.

What message was I trying to send myself?

Chapter Fifty

I took the aspirin, gulped down half the water, and crawled into bed.

I slept soundly that night, maybe because I was worn to a frazzle. Inheriting a fortune can take a lot out of a person.

In the morning, I made the bed quickly, put on jeans and a short-sleeved cotton blouse, and dashed into the bathroom. My hair was wild; I tamed it with a brush and water and applied a little makeup.

When I stepped into the kitchen, Emma and Cornelia were there, with Bernice, watching the early news on TV.

Emma favored me with a brilliant smile, and I realized that helping me, even a little, had given her a chance to be the strong one, for once. My opening up to her had been good for both of us. Maybe, I reflected, there *was* such a thing as being too independent.

Though I had one eye on the clock, because of my appointment with Walter Kass, I decided to borrow Kip and Loretta's computer and check my e-mail while breakfast was cooking. Cornelia believed in hearty, ranch-style meals, so we were having bacon and pancakes and eggs, along with hot, fresh coffee and fresh-squeezed orange juice. I was ravenous, and except for a slight headache and a sense of disorientation, I felt semi-okay.

I went into the office, which was just off the kitchen, a cup of coffee in one hand, sat down at Loretta's desk—Kip's was across the room—and logged on.

The flag was out on the little cyber mailbox, and I drew a deep breath. My cell phone had remained blessedly silent since the night before; a small miracle, considering that Justin Netherton must surely have called Harvey, Jr., by now, screaming for his money. Junior, in turn, would be out for my blood.

The hell with Harvey, Jr. I was rich; I could simply hand him a check and tell him what he could do with it.

Restored by that satisfying image, I focused on the mail list.

There were the usual ads, some disguised as e-mails from friends, others unashamedly commercial, all of which I deleted without opening. Presently I came to one sent from my computer at home. A little chill moved through my system, vein by vein.

I opened the e-mail. *"Clare, Clare,"* it read, *"don't you know it is an evil thing to defend the wicked in their sin? I will come for you soon."*

Shaking, I rechecked the sender's address, sure I must have been mistaken, but it was mine, all right. For one crazy moment, I wondered if I had a split personality, and one side was trying to mess with the other.

I laid a hand to my throat. Was this a joke, a cruel and stupid prank on the part of someone at the office, for instance? I didn't think so. There was a wistful note to the words, as if the sender regretted having to act, but was compelled by some greater force.

Like madness.

I stood up, sat down again. Reached for my cell phone, withdrew my hand before my fingers could close around it.

Whom could I call? Sonterra? He was still out of town, as far as I knew, on his mysterious case. Arlo Browder? I wasn't sure I could explain in any coherent way, not without taking some time to process this latest attack on my sanity.

I picked up my mug and took a few sips of strong coffee, in an effort to steady my nerves, swallowing as I read and reread those simple but alarming words. In time, I was able to save the thing to my files and move on to the next e-mail.

It was from Emma. "Can I get my nose pierced?" she'd written.

"NO," I typed, and hit *send,* though not before I'd missed the appropriate key twice.

I moved on, taking slow, deep breaths. *Concentrate on the normal stuff, Clare. One foot in front of the other.*

The next one came from Loretta. She was on an impromptu business trip with Kip and would be returning soon. Emma and I were to let ourselves into the Scottsdale house when we got back and make ourselves at home.

I almost didn't open the last e-mail, which had popped up while I was typing in my rather jumbled reply to Loretta. I wanted to think, square things away in my head, make some sense of it all. *Then* I would call Arlo.

I clicked on the final subject line, which read, *"Roses are red, violets are blue . . ."*

The message box was empty, except for the link, underlined in blue. *"Tracy is dead, and so are you."*

James Arren had killed Tracy, I was sure of it. But he was gone for good, thanks to me. So who had sent this monstrosity?

Two death threats in one morning. It had to be a record.

My coffee boiled up into the back of my throat. I should have shut down the computer, then and there, and refused to go any further until I was in Arlo Browder's office at the police station, but I couldn't even bring myself to rise out of the chair. I moved the cursor to the link and clicked. From the kitchen came the sounds of cooking, Bernice's yapping bark, and Emma's and Cornelia's laughter.

The cyber-connection was made, and my own face filled the computer screen. There were rotting leaves behind my head, causing the shot to resemble the earlier one of Tracy, and my skin was a bluish gray color. What really got to me, though, was my eyes, wide open and totally vacant. There were no irises, no pupils.

I sat there for a long time, stunned, staring at my own death mask. Gradually, it dawned on me that someone had doctored my college ID photo, taken when I started at the university, scanned it into a computer, and worked their ugly magic, using one of the popular photographic programs.

I suppose a little wishful thinking was inevitable, the human mind being what it is. As soon as the shock began to subside a little, I started thinking that the M.E. must have been wrong. Tracy was alive; her picture had been faked, as mine had. Of course. *Tracy was alive somewhere; I had only to find her.*

I fumbled for my cell phone, dialed most of Sonterra's number, and then hung up. "Get a grip, Clare," I muttered to myself, following that with a series of deep breaths. "She's dead. Damn it, *she's dead.*"

I was still engaged in the struggle between common sense and wild speculation when a little trill sounded from the computer, and an instant message appeared. The screen name was Digger, with a series of numbers following.

"Emma, little sweet girl, is that you?"

"Little sweet girl?" This was no kid, I was sure of it.

I typed slowly and carefully; answering too fast might have blown my cover. *"Yes, it's me. How are you, Digger?"* (*Who are you, and where are you, you sick bastard, and what are you doing, contacting my thirteen-year-old niece?*)

"I'm okay. Glad to be home from boarding school."

"That must be good," I wrote, playing along.

"We need to get together, just you and me. Maybe we could meet someplace private, this weekend."

"Maybe. Do you want to meet my aunt?" (Translation: *She wants to meet you, sucker, and cut off your balls with a pair of dull pruning shears.*)

"Baby, you know I can't meet Clare yet. I want this to be personal, just us."

I drew a deep breath, let it out slowly. *Yeah,* I thought. *It'll be "personal," all right. Just you, me, and about two hundred cops.*

"OK," I typed. *"I'd better go now. She wants me to do my homework."*

"I'll be in touch."

I didn't answer; I was too shaken to type.

I had a wild urge to storm out into the kitchen and confront Emma, then and there, demanding to know who the hell Digger was and raving that I'd warned her about talking to strangers on the Internet, but it wouldn't have been a smart move to act without thinking the matter through first. Things were good between my niece and me, or I'd thought they were. I wanted to keep it that way.

If I came on too strong, she might simply go underground and converse with this pervert some other way. Or, God forbid, she might actually agree to meet him, without my knowing.

I realized that I'd broken out in a cold sweat.

I logged off. Happy noises were still coming from the kitchen. I remained sitting right where I was, feeling more alone than I ever had. There was a strange, echoing buzz in my ears.

"Clare!" Emma called. "Breakfast is ready!"

"Be right there," I heard myself say. I sounded so normal.

But at least five minutes must have gone by, without my moving. The ring of my cell phone broke the spell. I snatched it up and barked, "Hello?"

"Hello, Clare. Did you like your picture? You really do look like your sister." I felt sure this was the same voice I'd heard the night of my assault, when the caller had claimed to be hiding in the hotel bathtub.

Tracy and I had never resembled each other, but that was beside the point, and both the caller and I knew it. He—or she—was telling me I was going to die.

"Who the hell are you?" I demanded.

A creepy chuckle sounded in my ear. "Wouldn't you like to know?"

"What do you want?"

"That's easy. I want to kill you."

"Why?"

"Because you would look so pretty dead."

"You killed Tracy, didn't you? It wasn't James at all; it was you!"

No hesitation, no note of remorse. "Yes. And no. James was definitely involved."

"In God's name, *why?* Why did you have to hurt her?"

"Because she was an interfering bitch. Like you."

"Who is this?"

Silence, except for breathing.

I was standing now, and gripping the phone so hard my hand hurt. "They'll find you, whoever you are," I said. "They'll find you and lock you up, once and for all."

"You can dream," came the crooned reply. And then there was a click, and the line went dead.

I immediately checked the caller ID panel, but I knew before I looked what I would find. "UNKNOWN NUMBER, UNKNOWN NAME."

Back to square one.

Hell, at this rate, I wouldn't live to collect that twenty-seven million, let alone spend it.

Chapter Fifty-one

Walter Kass's office was modest in size, but tastefully furnished. He was middle-aged, with kindly eyes, thinning hair, and a few pouches and wrinkles. "Sit down," he said with a smile, gesturing toward one of the two leather chairs facing his desk.

I was glad to take a load off. I'd had more than a few surprises lately, and my knees felt like they'd never be quite solid again.

When I was settled, Kass reached for a plump file sitting atop the credenza in back of his desk, laid it on the blotter, and met my gaze straight on. "Well, Ms. Westbrook," he said, "it is indeed a pleasure to make your acquaintance."

I merely nodded. Frankly, I didn't trust myself to speak clearly, and my eyes felt as if they'd grown to twice their normal size.

He seemed amused. "Any questions?"

I cleared my throat, scanned the room, half expecting someone to jump out of a hiding place and yell *Gotcha*! "Is this for real?"

A chuckle from him. "Oh, yes, it's the genuine article," he said. "You are a very rich woman, Ms. Westbrook."

"Clare," I said, croaking a little. "If you're about to make me rich, feel free to call me by my first name."

He smiled, opened the file. "Clare, then. If you'll sign these papers, you should have your money within a few weeks."

I swallowed, took the pen he handed me, set it down again. I might have been in shock, but I was still a lawyer. I wasn't signing anything without reading it first.

Wordlessly, since he was a lawyer, too, Kass handed me the folder.

I read what appeared to be my grandfather's last will and testament. His fortune was to pass to his wife, upon his death, which it had, and then to their son, upon hers. My father, Thomas Westbrook, had inherited a thriving investment business, and apparently, he hadn't squandered a cent.

I found myself focusing on their names, my grandparents', that is, hungry for anything that would shed a glimmer of light on my origins. My grandfather was George, my grandmother, Lorraine. I stored those tidbits in a private corner of my heart and read on.

Maria Gomez had inherited a nice nest egg upon my father's passing, enough to make me wonder, albeit briefly, why she still held down the job at Netherton's place, but there were no other bequests mentioned. The estate was to go to any remaining Westbrook, as long as he or she was a direct descendent; failing that, a variety of charities would benefit.

I was the sole heir, as it happened, and slated to receive nearly twenty-eight million dollars, before estate taxes and Mr. Kass's fees, of course.

The room was suddenly a vacuum, void of oxygen.

Wordlessly, Mr. Kass got up and left the room, returning momentarily with a glass of water. Maybe he dealt with people like me every day, though that seemed unlikely.

"Sign the affidavits, and it's yours," he said, rather gently, while I sipped.

I signed, my hand trembling as I did so.

"There's an advance clause," Kass told me, when I started, shakily, to rise from the chair. Rich or not, I had other things to do, like call Arlo Browder about that morning's ration of death threats and touch base with Sonterra.

I stared at him, confused.

He produced a leather-bound checkbook from his middle desk drawer, flipped it open, and wrote a check. Then he signed it with a flourish, tore it out, and extended it to me.

I took it, after a moment's hesitation.

When I saw the amount, I had to sit down again. Roughly five years' salary.

I sat up a little straighter and smiled. *Screw you, Harvey, Jr.*

Chapter Fifty-two

When I got back to the ranch, Cornelia informed me that her husband, Sam, had taken Emma out for a horseback ride. She was off to do some grocery shopping; did I want to go along?

Everything was catching up to me, and I felt funky, so I demurred, and when she was gone, I placed my call to Arlo. I got his voice mail, which annoyed me a little, and briefly related the story of the two e-mails, apparently sent by different people, both predicting my imminent death and, lastly, the anonymous call I'd received at home, following the same dismal theme.

I was getting more popular every day.

After that, I tried Sonterra's number, though I didn't know what I planned to say. I left a bumbling message. "Hi, it's me, Clare. Guess you're busy. Bye."

I was downright restless by then, so I turned on the TV on the kitchen counter, using the remote to flip from one channel to the next. I finally landed on the noon news, which proved to be the same old conglomeration of murder, mayhem, scandal, and shame.

No wonder so many people are on Prozac, I thought. A steady diet of global reality will do that. One more indication that denial has its place in the cause for better mental health.

I was about to cruise the movie channels when a familiar face appeared on the screen, nearly causing me to jump out of my skin. Justin Netherton.

I ratcheted the sound up a few notches.

"A local doctor was found dead at his home today, just before dawn, by his long-time housekeeper," the newscaster said, without a flicker of expression anywhere. "Police have not made a statement regarding cause of death," he went on, "but Dr. Netherton had been weathering a storm of accusations recently, and sources say he was despondent. Let's go to Ted Halloway, live at the scene. Ted?"

The reporter stood in front of Dr. Netherton's house, every window blazing with light behind him, even though it was broad daylight. An ambulance was parked near the open front door, and various official cars flanked it. I watched, dazed, as Arlo strode out of the house, looking grim and a little rumpled.

"Here's Lieutenant Arlo Browder, with the Tucson Police Department," the on-camera newsman said, with the same exuberance he might have used to emcee the Miss America Pageant. "Do you have a statement for us, Lieutenant?"

It was clear that Arlo had a statement for them, all right, but it wasn't one he could make on television without getting called on the carpet by the brass before the day was out. He smoothed out his expression quickly, and went right on walking, forcing his interrogator to double-step alongside to keep up.

"There has been a homicide," Arlo said evenly. "Let me remind you that that simply means a death, not necessarily a murder. Dr. Netherton apparently drowned in his swimming pool, and we are conducting an investigation. When we know something definite, we will share that information with the public."

I was literally unable to move. Netherton

had been upset about the upcoming movie of the week, an exposé of his private life, among other things. Had he ended his own life?

Arlo shouldered his way through the crowd of reporters and curious onlookers, most likely heading for his car, and the rest of us watched with familiar, helpless horror as a body bag was carried out of the house, placed on a stretcher, and loaded into the back of the ambulance. Perhaps most telling of all, the flashing lights on top of the vehicle were switched off before it pulled away.

No need to hurry. There would be no reviving Dr. Netherton.

I turned off the television set, sickened, and even more shaken than I had been before. Even being lousy rich didn't console me all that much.

I was pacing again when the kitchen phone rang. I pounced on it, since I'd given Arlo the number at the ranch as well as the one for my cell, and felt a distinct jolt when I saw the name *H. Kredd* in the caller-ID panel.

"What the *hell* happened down there?" Junior demanded.

I sank into one of the chairs at the kitchen table. Where to start?

"What do you mean?" I asked. Confusion can be a good stall tactic, whether it is genuine or not.

"*First* you insulted a valuable client," Junior raged, in a spitty-sounding burst of words. "*Then* you had the *gall* to walk *out* on the man, in a *public place*—"

I was rocking back and forth slightly on the chair seat, and when I realized it, I made myself stop. I said nothing.

"And *now* I learn that the poor man is dead!" Harvey, Jr., finished.

"I had nothing to do with that," I said, digging in for a fight.

"There was a message waiting for me when I reached the office this morning," Junior seethed. "It was from Dr. Netherton's accountant. Apparently, the doctor's last official act was to withdraw his retainer, and I don't have to tell you what that will mean to this firm. You've got some fancy explaining to do, Counselor."

I was still silent, mainly because I knew anything I said just then would be inflammatory and probably make matters worse. Besides, when I told Harvey, Jr., to stick his officious attitude where the sun didn't shine, I wanted to be looking him in the face.

"Exactly when do you plan to grace us with your presence?" Junior demanded. His blood pressure must have been higher than the national debt.

"I'm driving back today," I said moderately. "There's a possibility, of course, that the police will want to question me before I leave." I considered the scene at the restaurant the morning before, when I had told Dr. Netherton to get another lawyer. Had he gone right home and drowned after that, or had it happened later in the day? I hoped it was later—I had a good alibi for the evening, since I'd been at the ranch, and both Cornelia and Sam would vouch for me. All the same, if the cause of death did turn out to be a willful act of violence on the part of another person, I would probably be on the list of possible suspects.

There was a blistering silence on Junior's end of the line. Then he barked, "My father would have been very disappointed in your recent performance, Ms. Westbrook!" and slammed the phone down so hard that I winced.

My sinuses closed, and I beat a hasty retreat for the guest quarters, where I promptly fell into a comatose state. I dreamed I was lost in an underground cavern, trying to follow the sound of ringing bells back to safety.

I woke up surprised to find myself lying on the bed, feeling crummier than ever and fully clothed except for my shoes. Cornelia, upon her return from the supermarket, came looking for me.

"Clare, you look *horrible.* What's wrong?"

"I need my cell phone," I managed to say. "Please."

Looking alarmed, Cornelia fetched it from the kitchen. When she handed it to me, I sat up, fell back on my pillows, and tried to focus my eyes as I thumbed my way through the list of message numbers. *Arlo Browder. Arlo Browder. Arlo Browder. Tony Sonterra. Mrs. K.*

I called the last number back first, sitting up with another groan, then falling back down again. My head was pounding and I was nauseated—either the lump on my noggin was acting up, which seemed unlikely, or I'd been slammed by one of those twenty-four-hour bugs. Just my luck. Inherit a fortune, come down with the plague.

"Mrs. K?" I said thickly, when she picked up. "It's Clare. Did you call earlier?"

She sounded worried. "Yes," she said. "I had a brilliant idea. You and I should trade condos. That way, you won't have to go back to your place until you feel ready." Pause. "There was a man here, Clare, knocking on your apartment door. He said he was—he said he was looking for Emma."

"What?"

"That's all he said. He didn't give his name. I saw a woman—at least, I *think* it was a woman, waiting for him in a silver car, but I couldn't make out the license number. They drove away too fast."

I could barely speak. "When did this happen?"

"Early this afternoon. I called you immediately, dear, but I got your voice mail."

"I'll be back as soon as I can. If you see these people again, call the police."

"I will, dear," Mrs. K said. "I should have done it before, but—well, the man seemed so *polite*—"

Polite. "Can you describe him?"

"He reminded me of a biker, or somebody like that. I've never seen him before."

Henley? "A big guy, with a pouty lip?"

She sounded patently uncertain. "I guess—"

"I might ask you to repeat the details when I get home."

"Of course, dear," Mrs. K said. "I'll see you tonight, then? I'm getting my condo ready for you and Emma."

"Thank you," I said, touched. "You're very kind." I felt dizzy; the cold, or whatever it was, was getting worse with every passing moment. "I'm not sure if I'll make it back tonight or not, but I plan to try."

"Don't overdo, dear," Mrs. K cautioned.

After we said good-bye, I listened to Arlo's messages next, starting with the first, and each was terser than the last.

Number one, serious but calm. "Clare, call me at five-five-five eight-nine-oh-seven," he said.

Number two, more serious, less calm. "Clare? This is important. Get back to me, please." He gave the number again.

Number three, downright testy. "Clare, you are scaring me. Where the hell are you?"

I dialed his number.

"Browder," he snapped. I'd heard Sonterra use that tone, on the few occasions when I called him at work. It meant he had his back to the wall and was fighting for his life with both hands and both feet.

"It's Clare," I said testily. "And I *did* call you. If you ever checked your office messages, you'd know that."

No mention of his own culpability. Just like a man. "Are you all right? Where are you?"

Cornelia, bless her heart, had left the room, only to return with one of those digital thermometers, still in the box.

"I'm fine," I said, to her as well as Arlo Browder. "I'm at the Matthews ranch, just outside Tucson."

Cornelia smiled, opened the box, took out the thermometer, and stood ready to stick it under my tongue.

"I don't believe you. You sound strange."

"I might have the flu," I said. I opened my mouth for the thing, since I knew Loretta's henchwoman wasn't going to give up until she got a reading. "Where's Emma?" I asked.

"In the living room," Cornelia said.

"Who's Emma?" Arlo wanted to know.

"My niece," I said.

That was apparently enough chitchat for Browder. "Justin Netherton was your client, wasn't he?"

I talked around the thermometer, which garbled my words a little. "Yeth," I said. "Buth I dudn't kill hum."

"You *are* sick," Arlo allowed, softening a little. "And nobody said you killed him. There's still a possibility that this is an accidental death."

"I dowth it."

He sighed. "Me, too. Officially, though, we're not ready to say it was murder."

The thermometer beeped, and Cornelia pulled it out of my mouth, frowning at the reading.

"One-oh-one," she mouthed, and hurried out. I hoped she wasn't about to summon an ambulance or something.

I lay back against the pillows, feeling a whole lot worse now that I knew I was running a fever. "What exactly happened to Netherton? I mean, the news said he'd drowned—"

"Somebody cracked him in the head and dumped him into the pool," Arlo said. "Jesus, I've never seen so much blood. The water was streaked with it." So much for the suicide theory.

"Which means he was alive when he went in, right?"

"Probably," Arlo allowed.

"What time did it happen?"

"Sometime between six and ten last night, according to the M.E.'s best estimate. The housekeeper arrived early, and when she saw the patio lights were on, she figured the doctor must be out there having breakfast, and went to see if he needed anything. That's when she found him and called us."

"Poor Maria," I said.

Arlo jumped right on that statement. "You know her?"

"Not really," I replied. "I've met her a couple of times. Turns out she used to work for the Westbrook family." No need to mention the twenty-seven million, or the fat advance check burning a hole in my purse.

"Hmmm," Arlo said. "What was your impression of her?"

"She seemed like a nice person. I can't see her clunking the doctor on the head and pushing him into the pool, Arlo."

"Yeah," he agreed, sounding weary. "That

was our take on it, too. Which leaves us with the lover—the one who's been raising hell in the newspapers lately. We brought him in for questioning this morning, but he hasn't been charged."

I waited for him to say I ought to stop by the police station for a little game of truth or consequences, but he didn't. Maybe he was afraid of catching whatever it was I had. "I only interviewed Sandy briefly, don't think she would have done a thing like that," I said.

"Stranger things have happened," he said.

I drew a deep breath then and told Arlo about the most recent threats and the picture of me as a corpse. I also related what Mrs. K had told me about the man showing up at the condo, asking about Emma, though I didn't expect anything on that score. After all, Cave Creek wasn't his beat.

"Jesus," he breathed. "Send me the picture, will you? The e-mails, too." He gave me an e-mail address, which I hoped I would remember once we got off the phone. My head was stuffed with cotton batting. "Have you told Tony Sonterra about this yo-yo your neighbor talked to?"

"Not yet," I said. "He left a message earlier, but I haven't gotten to it yet."

"You heading back home today?"

"I was planning to," I said. "Unless I'm being detained for questioning. Your messages did sound a little urgent." *And unless this flu bug kills me first.*

"I knew you were associated with Netherton," Arlo said. "I wanted to make sure you hadn't been caught in the cross fire, so to speak." He paused, sighed. "I don't figure you had anything to do with his death, which isn't to say I won't be calling you with the occasional pop quiz. I also wanted to let you know that we're still working on Tracy's case. This Ben Dupree character is a regular Chatty Cathy. I'll keep you posted."

"Thanks, Arlo," I said. At some point, I wanted to meet Dupree myself. I had questions of my own.

"You sound too sick to drive. Maybe you'd better hang around Tucson for a few days."

"Is that an official order?"

Hail the return of Cornelia, bearing a tray and looking determined. In the short time she'd been gone, she'd nuked a bowl of chicken soup. I was touched by her solicitude—I just wasn't hungry.

"No, but check your cell phone messages a little more often, will you?"

"If you'll check yours," I countered.

He laughed, we said good-bye, and I rang off.

"I can't eat this," I said.

"Try," Cornelia urged, hovering beside the bed. "It's still the best remedy there is for colds and flu."

I took a spoonful, tasted it. The stuff was delicious, and my stomach rumbled for more. "Okay," I said. "You win. It's wonderful, and I'll eat it."

She nodded and left the room.

I ate with one hand and dialed Sonterra's cell number with the other.

"Sonterra," he said. He sounded like his old, testy self. For some odd reason, I found that reassuring.

"Clare," I replied, my lilting tones making a sweet contrast to his snarl.

"You're in Tucson!" he accused. He sounded mad enough to turn me to the wall and frisk me; just my luck to be *way* out of reach.

"Last time I checked the books," I said mildly, "there were no statutes forbidding me to leave Maricopa County."

He began again, making a real effort, this time, to moderate his tone. "Don't be a smart-ass," he said. "The s.o.b. who offed Harvey Kredd and the others is still out there, remember."

I told him about the man Mrs. K had seen, which did nothing for his disposition. After that, I could hardly bring myself to bring him up to speed regarding the new e-mail messages and photo, the instant messaging, or the you-have-to-die phone call, not to mention Dr. Netherton's untimely death, but I bit the bullet and did it.

"You waited until now to tell me this stuff?" he growled.

"You were too far away to help, and you were busy."

He was quiet, absorbing what I'd said, but the stillness had a dangerous quality. "When are you coming back?" he asked.

"Soon."

"I'll find out who the visitor was," he vowed grimly. Another period of incendiary assimilation followed. Then, "What the hell are you doing in Tucson, anyway?" We were back to that, were we? I was almost relieved; it seemed so normal.

"I came on business," I said. I thought of Justin Netherton, floating in his swimming pool. I figured he'd been done in by an angry patient, perhaps, or one of their family members. There was even the possibility that it was a simple burglary, turned nasty, though I doubted that. "I left you a message earlier—didn't you get it?"

"Sure I did. So I called your office, thinking you'd be there. Let's see, why was that? Oh, yes—because you *said* that was where you'd be, the last time we talked, and I had no reason to think you'd left town. The receptionist—Heather somebody—told me you were in Tucson."

"I know I said—"

"I hate being lied to, Clare. I *really* hate it."

I sighed. I wasn't ready to apologize. "Let's not get into that right now," I said.

"Okay," he agreed grimly. "But you and I are going to have to talk ground rules pretty soon."

I agreed. I had some ground rules of my own.

"You must have a lot to do," I said, hoping he'd reciprocate because of all I'd told him, and fill me in on the case he'd been working on out of town.

"Yeah," was all he gave up. "See you tonight?"

"If I can travel and unless I'm contagious, yes. I won't be at Loretta's, though. Mrs. K is swapping condos with Emma and me."

"What do you mean, 'unless you're contagious'?"

"I'm coming down with something."

"Maybe it's an attack of conscience," he said, and there was still an edge to his tone. "Next thing you know, you'll be telling Kredd and Associates where to get off and using that slick brain of yours to defend *innocent* people."

I could have told him I was history at the firm, for about twenty-seven million reasons, but just then, I didn't feel like giving him the satisfaction. Let him read it in the paper. "Here's a refresher for you, Sonterra," I retorted. "*Everybody* is innocent until proven guilty."

"Oh, yeah," he said. "I keep forgetting."

I found myself smiling, even though I'd

been irked as hell, just a moment before.
"Good-bye, Sonterra," I said.

"Can I still call you later?"

"Sure," I told him. "I might not answer the
phone, though."

I hung up first. Point of pride.

Chapter Fifty-three

"You can't drive with a fever of a hundred and one," Cornelia said half an hour later, when Emma looked in to make sure I was alive and then vanished again. I'd just finished a fast shower and a half-assed makeup job, and I was almost ready to hit the road. During the drive home, I would tell my niece about the money.

"I feel perfectly all right," I said. Except, of course, for the throbbing headache, the dizziness, the upset stomach, and those pesky little flashes of light at the corners of my eyes.

"Nonsense. You should see a doctor."

"Have you ever heard the term 'HMO'?" I countered. "Six hours in the waiting area, five minutes in the examining room. 'You have the flu, Ms. Westbrook. We recommend that you go home, take two aspirin, and get into bed.'"

Cornelia looked exasperated, but she

was smiling a little, and shaking her head. "Stubborn," she said.

"I've got a corner on that," I replied. Emma, hovering in the doorway, rolled her eyes.

"Does this mean I have to go back to school?" she asked.

"Absolutely," I replied, though I wasn't so sure. I wanted to make sure she was safe before I let her out of my sight again.

Emma stuck out her chin. "What if Bernice and I catch what you have?"

"You have a gift for inspiring guilt," I told her.

Cornelia stood beside Emma, arms folded. "The child is right," she said staunchly.

"Hell," I said. "Harvey, Jr., is up there waiting to fire me, and you two want me to miss it?" If I'd been looking forward to that confrontation before, I was *really* ready for it now that it didn't mean Emma and I would be moving into a homeless shelter.

An expressive glance passed between Cornelia and Emma.

"I'm calling Tony," Emma said.

"Don't you *dare*," I said, shaking a finger at her.

Cornelia sighed. "I'll get one of the ranch hands to drive you up there," she said. "He can catch the bus back to Tucson."

So it was settled, finally.

The ranch-hand turned chauffeur didn't say much during the drive to Phoenix, but he was a competent driver. The trip seemed twice as long as usual, and I felt pretty woozy a couple of times, but we dropped our escort off at the bus station in Phoenix, after giving him the money for fare, and I took over the wheel. We made it back to Cave Creek by mid-afternoon. Emma and I were both frazzled; only Bernice remained totally Zen.

Mrs. K had her condo ready for our occupation, and I blessed her as I carried our bags and the boxes of stuff from the storage unit into her place.

"Get some rest," Mrs. K told me, taking the last carton from my arms. "I'll bring over some of your things later."

I felt as though somebody had taken a hacksaw to the inside of my throat. "Thanks," I said. The layout of Mrs. K's place was the exact opposite of ours, the same floor plan in reverse, and I was a little disoriented at first. Emma finally took my arm and showed me the way to the master bedroom.

I took a quick, cool shower in Mrs. K's bathroom, slathered my chest with something vaporous from the medicine cabinet, pulled on some ancient sweats—fetched by Emma—and tumbled into bed. I was asleep almost before my head hit the pillow, and when I woke up, Emma and Bernice were peering at me.

"No need for the mirror test," Emma told the dog. "She lives."

I pulled the sheet up over my mouth and nose. "Don't get too close," I said, through the weave.

"It's a little late for that, don't you think?" Emma asked, and I caught a brief glimpse of the woman she would one day be—a smart-mouthed broad, just like her aunt.

Using the back of one hand, she tested my forehead for fever, and my heart turned over. I loved that kid.

"You're still pretty hot," she said. "Want some juice or something? You're supposed to drink a lot of liquids when you're sick."

I wondered if white wine counted, and decided it was probably a medical gray area. "Cranberry, if there is any," I said, still talking through the sheet.

She and Bernice rushed off to the kitchen.

I heard cupboard doors opening and closing, ice cubes rattling into a glass, more cupboard doors. The doorbell rang just as Emma was thudding up the stairs.

"Crap," I heard her mutter. Guess it could have been worse.

"Don't answer that!" I croaked.

Emma came in, set the glass on the nightstand.

The doorbell rang again, and it was clear that Emma didn't intend to ignore it.

"Look and see who's there before you open the door," I commanded, holding on to an illusion of power. Emma dashed back downstairs, Bernice yapping at her heels.

Another ring, politely insistent. Not Sonterra, then.

"It's only Mrs. K!" Emma yelled up the stairs.

I relaxed a little and sipped my juice. I could hear Emma and our neighbor talking earnestly.

A few moments later, Mrs. K swept in,

looking very mystical in her multicolored caftan and smelling of patchouli.

"Great Zeus," she said, "you look even worse than you did earlier!"

With all this encouragement, how could I help having a speedy recovery?

She shook her head in busy dismay. Mrs. K wore a Dear Abby–style coiffure, with lots of spray. If she ever tried to board an airplane, security would surely ban her, pending a shampoo, declaring that side-sweep of hers a lethal weapon. "I wonder if it's karma," she mused.

"I hope not," I replied. A simple case of flu is one thing, and penance for screwups in past lifetimes is another. Frankly, I had all I could handle keeping *this* one going.

She crossed to me, frowning, and waved her hands up and down, a foot or so above my nearly prostrate body. I knew she was checking my energy field, and finding it wanting.

"Oh, *dear*," she said. "This calls for chants and smudging."

Chants I knew about. "What's smudging?"

I soon found out. Mrs. K didn't bother to answer; she just went downstairs, then came back quickly with a bowl of coarse salt, a plastic fire-lighter, and a bundle of dried grasses or twigs. The thing resembled a small torch, the kind Zulu jungle runners might carry in an old movie.

"White sage," she said, with a grave air. "This will clear the room—and your aura, of course—of negative influences."

"Speaking of negative influences," I said, as she concentrated on lighting the thatch of weeds in her hand. "If Tony Sonterra stops by, I'm not receiving."

Mrs. K gave me a look of injured reproof. "Such a nice man, too," she said. "And hot." The weeds finally caught, but instead of flaming, as I'd feared, they smoldered, releasing a smell I hadn't come across since college. I waved a hand in front of my face. "Lie still," she counseled, turning to the subject at hand, which was, unfortunately, me. "All your meridians are reversed."

Emma and Bernice appeared in the doorway, probably drawn by the smell of Mrs. K's purification ceremony.

"Emma," I said, a little weakly, "there are some boxes downstairs in the entryway, the ones we brought in from the car. Will you bring up the small one with your mom's name written on the side?"

She nodded, disappeared, and returned quickly, carrying a dusty, half-collapsed carton that had once contained a pair of cowboy boots. "Size 11," according to the yellowed sticker curling on the side. Too big for my sister's small feet.

I plumped the pillows, sat up straight, and carefully removed the lid.

There were a few notes from high school—just kids' stuff mostly—about skipping study hall to grab a smoke, who went out with whom last Friday, which male teachers were "fine" and which were geeks, things like that. I found a journal, too, one of those cheap ones they sell in office supply stores, and opened it eagerly. Tracy's handwriting was small and scratchy—she'd had that kind of life, I thought sadly, always cramped by circumstances with a great many rough edges. As far as I could tell, though I was pretty rummy, there was nothing there that would help with her case. I resolved to look again, later.

Meanwhile, Mrs. K continued the ceremony. After much mojo, she wrapped it up and took her leave, promising to stop in later and fix supper for Emma and me.

I rested on the pillows, still holding the box on my lap, and closed my eyes. As soon as I was sure Mrs. K wasn't going to double back, I intended to get up and open a window. Instead, I went to sleep.

When I woke up, Sonterra was sitting on the edge of my bed, looking wan but otherwise excellent. He'd had a shower recently, and his dark hair was still damp.

"Hey," he said, eyes twinkling, "what have you been smoking in here, Counselor?"

Chapter Fifty-four

Sonterra gathered the contents of the shoe box, put them inside, and set the whole works on the nightstand. Then he stretched out on the bed beside me, with the two extra pillows propped behind him. He was wearing jeans and a navy blue T-shirt, but he'd already kicked off his boots.

I was glad he was there but, for some reason, I couldn't bring myself to say so. "I told you I might be contagious," I said.

"Probably just a twenty-four-hour bug," he replied. "There's a lot of that going around."

It turned out he was right, but at the time, I was a little miffed. Maybe it *was* just a virus, but at the moment, it felt more like the Black Death. Trust a man to minimize a woman's suffering. When *Sonterra* gets a minor cold, he expects an immediate investigation by the Centers for Disease Control.

"Don't blame me if you get sick," I said, with a sniff.

"Oh, that's way down the list," he said. "Of things I'd blame you for, I mean."

"Don't start," I warned, though I knew it would prove a futile request, in the long run anyway.

He sighed. "I wasn't going to 'start,'" he told me. "Right now, I'm just here to lend moral support, and maybe get some in return."

I laid my head on his shoulder. I'm not made of steel, though it sometimes seems that way.

"Emma's in the house, you know," I reminded him, just in case he was in the mood to ravish me mercilessly. If she'd had a driver's license, I might have sent her on an errand.

He chuckled. "Yeah," he replied, "I know. She let me in. Relax, Clare. We're just lying here, fully clothed, doing nothing at all to scar her psyche." He lowered his voice. "Besides, she's thirteen. She *knows* we've had sex. Kids are sophisticated these days."

I sighed. He was probably right; Emma

didn't miss much. "She's growing up too fast."

"They all do," he said. I drifted off to sleep again after that, and when I woke up, he was gone. I switched on the bedside lamp, and found a note propped against the face of the alarm clock. *"You're not off the hook, Counselor,"* Sonterra had written. *"Do NOT go back to Tucson without checking with me first. The word from Arlo is that things are heating up down there, big-time, and I'm not talking about the weather."* He'd signed with a large, definite S.

The first thing I realized, after reading that note, was that Sonterra's macho attitude pissed me off. The second was, my twenty-four-hour bug had checked out early. I felt electrified, in a scary sort of way, as though I'd just been dosed with enough adrenaline to excite a fossilized fish.

Maybe, I concluded, it was Mrs. K's energy therapy. Scoffers beware—I've had enough experience with her methods to know she's got *something* going for her. It's just that her aim is a little off sometimes.

I tossed Sonterra's note, reclaimed Tracy's box of mementos, a sad collection if I'd ever seen one, and took myself downstairs to the office. There, I flipped on the desk lamp and settled down to examine every scrap my sister had left behind. I was so sure I would find something—only a matter of time, I told myself.

She'd written a notebook full of dark, melodramatic poems while she was in high school, and I read them, one by one. I'd had no idea, even with all the surface problems to serve as red flags, that my sister was such a lost soul. Of course, I was a kid then myself, grappling with monsters of my own.

After midnight, I set the box aside, needing a break, and went into the kitchen to brew a cup of tea. By the time I got back and settled in, Bernice had padded downstairs to join me, curling up at my feet, looking more like a rag mop than a dog. I smiled, comforted by her presence, even though she couldn't have protected me from anything bigger than a spider.

I sipped my tea and turned to my trusty laptop, since my desktop computer was still in the other condo, logging on to the Internet more out of compulsion than desire. I was understandably nervous about what might be awaiting me there, but this was certainly no time to bury my head in the sand.

There were no new e-mails, to my relief, but when I checked my favorite news site, I found out why Sonterra had said things were "heating up" in Tucson. Sandy Piedmont had been cleared of all suspicion, but Justin Netherton's death had definitely been classified as a murder.

I called Sonterra, because I was still irritated enough not to care if he got his rest.

"What?" he greeted me, thick-tongued. No hello, no nothing.

I felt a clenching sensation, down deep. I didn't explore its meaning.

"Did I mention that Sandy Piedmont is a man?" I said. I figured he already knew, but I enjoyed saying it. "You remember—the person you were ogling during lunch at the Omni?"

"Clare?" Sonterra rumbled, clearly annoyed. "Are you out of your head with fever or something? Do you *know* what time it is?"

I ignored all of that. "Well," I demanded cheerfully, "what do you think?"

"I think you're nuts," he said.

"He turned you on," I said.

That brought him wide awake. "He did not!" he shot back.

I decided not to push the matter—yet. "He did look great as a woman, though," I said. "Frankly, I'm kind of disappointed. Your note said Tucson was heating up. Justin Netherton was officially iced. That's old news, Sonterra."

Sonterra was still cranky. "This is about that Dupree character they rounded up," he said. "According to Arlo, the dude has been in hiding since your sister's murder. Turns out Arren put the hurt on him, big-time, with help from some of his buddies, after he found out Tracy planned to take Emma and run away with the boyfriend."

"Oh, my God," I whispered. "When was this?"

"A week or two before Tracy disappeared, according to Lover Boy."

"And Dupree just left her to face James on her own," I said, a gorge of bitterness burning in my throat.

"He was in traction in some Mexican hospital," Sonterra said.

"Why didn't you tell me any of this?"

"Counselor, you were toes-up last time I saw you."

"That bastard," I said, meaning James, meaning Dupree and my father and both Harvey's, and maybe all men in general.

I started to cry.

"I'm coming over there," Sonterra announced. I could see him throwing back the covers, sitting up. Since Sonterra sleeps in the nude, this little vision bordered on an X rating.

"Don't you dare," I snuffled.

He didn't say another word; he just slammed down the receiver, hard enough to make me jump. I hung up, heard a familiar sound from the computer, and turned to see an instant message from dear old Digger. Maybe it was the late hour, but it took me a couple of moments to realize he wasn't addressing Emma. He knew he was talking to me.

Chapter Fifty-five

"Isn't Emma lovely?" The instant message began. *"I can hardly wait until she and I can be together for good. That will right a lot of wrongs."*

"Who are you?" I typed, hammering at the keys.

"Wouldn't you like to know?"

My fingers flew. *"You're damn right I would. This is all very cute, you know, even coy, but not very original."*

"She's all I have left now. Everything and everyone else is gone."

"Tell me who you are, you damned coward. My guess is, you're the man who came to the condo and spoke to my neighbor, looking for Emma."

"I don't know what you're talking about." The bloody liar.

"Leave Emma alone," I wrote back furiously. *"She's not going to be corresponding with you anymore."*

"She's got as much of my blood in her veins as she has of yours, maybe more."

"I don't believe you. Prove it. Start by telling me your name."

"Nice try, Clare. Do you think I'm stupid?"

"Probably. Most crooks are."

"Emma needs her family."

"I'm her family," I shot back.

"Not for long." With that chilling adieu, Digger was gone.

Digger. Even the name gave me the chills. I printed a transcript of the conversation and stashed it in my purse.

Headlights flashed in the driveway just as I was crossing the living room to put my empty teacup in the dishwasher. I watched through one of the windows on either side of the front door as Sonterra got out of his SUV and stormed up the walk. He was agitated, all right; he started toward the old place, then turned on his heel and righted his course.

I knew I'd have to let him in. He'd wake up everybody in the complex if I didn't, pounding on my door.

"What are you doing here?" I hissed, stepping back as he blew over the threshold like an ill wind.

"I came here to protect you, damn it!"

"I don't need your protection." I shut the door with maybe a little more force than was strictly necessary.

"Oh, right. You have the survival instincts of a snail!"

"Stop yelling!"

His nose was within a fraction of an inch of mine. "Is this better?" he snarled, in a dangerous undertone.

Emma appeared at the top of the stairs. "Sheesh," she said. "Could you two keep it down? Bernice and I are trying to sleep up here!"

Sonterra chuckled. He nearly choked on it, though. "Everything's cool," he told her.

Sure, I thought.

"Sorry, Em," I said aloud, as lightly as I could. "Go back to bed."

Her door closed a few moments later.

"I thought you were sick," Sonterra accused, whispering now.

"I got over it," I snapped back. Before I could formulate the words to tell him of Digger's latest instant-message exchange, his attitude reared its ugly head.

He shoved a hand through his hair. "This is going to be a miserable night," he said.

He was right about that much. He watched TV downstairs, with the volume turned low, while I lay upstairs, staring at the ceiling, wondering about my taste in men, and hoping that my damn stubborn pride wouldn't finally get the best of me.

Chapter Fifty-six

At six A.M., Emma poked her head in my door to say Tony was taking her out to breakfast, then to school. Filling him in on Digger would have to wait until he'd dropped Emma off at school.

I showered, dressed conservatively, got into my borrowed car—the insurance check for the Saturn was still languishing in my purse, as was the advance on my inheritance—and headed resolutely for the office.

Heather greeted me with a sympathetic smile—no doubt she figured I was about to get the ax—and I didn't enlighten her concerning my new status as a woman of independent means.

"You're supposed to wait in the conference room," Heather told me, avoiding my eyes.

I lifted my chin, straightened the strap of my shoulder bag, and marched along the hallway, loaded for bear. Junior took his sweet time joining me, but that was okay. I could wait. I took the check Walter Kass had given me out and passed the time counting zeroes.

I was *free*, I marveled. I could do whatever I wanted with the rest of my life; hopefully, it would be a long one, though the chances of that seemed less than spectacular at the moment.

I decided I was through waiting. Just as I got to my feet, prepared to storm the boss's office and tell him what I thought, Junior deigned to join me in the conference room.

"I'm out of here," I said, without preamble.

Junior looked miffed. Obviously, I'd robbed him of some of the pleasure of sending me packing. "May I remind you that you owe this firm a great deal of money?"

"Write it up," I told him. "You'll have a cashier's check by the end of the day."

He should have been happy; after all, the family business was on its last gasp, and an influx of cash would surely be welcome. Instead, he paled. "Clare," he said, in a faintly condescending tone, but with a note of entreaty. "Let's not be hasty—"

"What the *hell* are you talking about?" I

demanded. I was in no mood to play games. He'd called me on the carpet, making it plain he meant to fire me, and now he was urging me not to be *hasty*?

Harvey, Jr., cleared his throat. "My father," he said, "was not always the most forthcoming of men."

I almost laughed at that one, but Harvey, Jr.'s grayish pallor stopped me. "No," I agreed, one hand on the doorknob, waiting.

"The contract was a fake," Junior said, flopping into the leather chair behind his father's desk.

"What?" I let go of the doorknob.

My erstwhile boss looked away, looked back. I crossed the room and sat down on the edge of a chair, facing him. Waiting.

"The money my father gave you came from the Westbrooks," Junior said. "Dad just sort of—well—*laundered* it for them, funneling it through the company—"

"And let me believe I owed him seven years of my life."

"That was only supposed to be temporary. Thomas Westbrook was afraid you wouldn't accept help if he offered it directly, so he turned to us. I guess Dad got carried away with the whole thing." He sighed.

"Dad got carried away with a *lot* of things, it seems." This last, I supposed, was a reference to the fact that, although Harvey, Sr., must have made millions during his working life, he'd left his company and his family virtually bankrupt. None of my concern, I decided.

I leaned forward. I felt strangely calm; in fact, I wasn't even all that surprised. Harvey, Sr., had been the master of dirty tricks. "What about you, Junior? What's your excuse? You knew all this, obviously, and you didn't bother to tell me."

"I *didn't* know," he protested, and I half-believed him, he looked so earnest. "Not until your attorney, Walter Kass, called this morning, that is."

I got to my feet. "Good-bye, Harvey," I said, "and good luck. You're going to need it, from the looks of things."

"Clare, if you would simply invest—"

Invest, hell. I'd just *invested* several years of my life. I walked out, slamming the door behind me, and Harvey, Jr., had the good sense not to tag along, trying to make his case. I strode into my old office, for the first time since Janet's murder, and began collecting personal items in a cardboard carton I'd snagged from the copy room on the way.

I took my time packing and tying up loose ends with clients—only Heather had the guts to come and say good-bye—and was the last to leave the office that afternoon, even though it was still only about three o'clock. Junior had reportedly closed the place down early, claiming it was because the walk-in trade was unusually light and he and a couple of the other staffers were coming down with the flu.

Like Sonterra said, it was going around, but I was pretty sure the bug couldn't be blamed for Junior's bad mood.

Chapter Fifty-seven

I'd left Loretta's Lexus in the basement parking area, instead of the outside lot, and I took the elevator down.

Some people say they know when they're being watched, but it came as a complete surprise to me. The man from the cemetery stepped out from behind one of the pillars, smiling almost apologetically.

"I hope I didn't scare you," he said. In view of coming events, that was a very strange thing to say. And it was too late, because just then, it all fell into place, albeit too late, and I felt a quiver of primitive fear.

" 'Three for three,' " I said, musing. "You're Danny Murdock." I had the presence of mind to reach into my purse and get hold of the pepper spray, but he was faster. He drew a .45 caliber pistol from the pocket of his jacket—the same one, no doubt, that he'd planned to shoot me with in Tucson, next to my father's grave.

"I was waiting for you to remember," he said, with a diffident smile.

"It was all about revenge," I said. "You lost your wife and your two children when Ned Lench crashed into them, and you wanted three lives in return."

"I didn't plan it that way in the beginning," he told me mildly, almost with regret. "I just wanted to punish you and Harvey Kredd for setting Lench free. If you hadn't fought so hard for him, my family would still be alive."

"What about Janet Baylin?"

"I thought she was you. She was driving a car like yours, and she was in your office."

"And Denise Robbins?"

"Another bungled attempt," he said. "I don't think I'm cut out for this kind of thing."

I was fixated on the .45, watching the barrel waggle back and forth as he talked. "Put the pistol away, Danny," I said reasonably. "There's been enough killing."

He shook his head, looking sad. "No," he replied. "I've come this far. If I let you walk away now, I'll go to prison for sure."

I felt remarkably calm, suddenly, as if I were standing outside myself somehow, watching the scene unfold. The New Clare was definitely in charge. Too bad she had a lifespan of approximately ten seconds. "I can help you, Danny," I said. "I know you don't believe that, but it's the truth. You belong in a hospital, not a prison."

His expression was strangely dreamy. I knew he believed that shooting me was going to give him peace, drive out his demons once and for all, and frankly I didn't have much hope of convincing him otherwise. " 'Clare, Clare,' " he said, quoting one of the e-mail messages he'd sent, " 'don't you know it is an evil thing to defend the wicked—?' "

I was struck by a flash of insight. "Dr. Netherton?"

He nodded. "I was afraid you were going to get him off. Let him get away with hurting all those people. I had to put a stop to it."

In the space of an instant, Danny's face contorted with grief, with fury, with a dozen other emotions, harder to define, and he shook his head violently. "My family was destroyed, Clare, my wife, my children, all of them *gone*. My son's head was crushed, my wife's spine completely severed on impact. Practically every bone in little Abigail's body was broken. Do you know how long it took them to die?"

I held his gaze. "I'm sorry, Danny," I said. And I meant it.

"You're 'sorry'?" he retorted, his face suffused with color, his hand tightening on the .45. "Too little, too late!"

"Taking the law into your own hands and killing people won't bring back your family, Mr. Murdock. Harvey and Ms. Baylin and I were doing our jobs, that's all."

He seemed about to choke on his rage. "Your *jobs*? You were as bad as he was, all of you, unleashing somebody like that on society. How could you?"

This was no time for the innocent-until-proven-guilty spiel. Lawyer Woman was fresh out of answers.

Just when I thought all was lost—let's face it, a .45 in your face pretty much sums things up—I heard the squeal of tires on pavement, and so did Danny, distracted as he was. He whirled, squeezing the trigger as he did so, and making a huge, blossom-shaped hole in the trunk of Loretta and Kip's car. I yanked the pepper spray out of my purse and dodged behind a pillar, just as a big Buick, circa 1985, came roaring toward us, with Mrs. K at the wheel.

Chapter Fifty-eight

Mrs. K thumped Danny with the bumper, and he went sprawling, the gun skittering across the oil-stained concrete floor of the garage. I grabbed it and pointed it at Murdock, who was moaning and bleeding. He would live, but it didn't look as if he was going anywhere for a while. In fact, traction was a distinct possibility. He was in line for some major antipsychotic drugs, too, I figured.

Mrs. K leaped out of the car. "Clare!" she shouted, pale behind her makeup. *"Are you all right?"*

I wanted to faint, but, yes, I was all right. I nodded, then groped for my cell phone, dialed 911, gave the details to the dispatcher, and kept the gun on Murdock while the woman on the other end of the line promised to send a squad car and an ambulance.

With trembling fingers, I called Sonterra

next. This was his case, after all, his and Eddie Columbia's. He deserved to be notified. Besides, I needed to see him.

It was probably fate that I got his voice mail. I blurted out what had happened and hung up.

"How did you know I was in trouble?" I asked Mrs. K, now that all the official bases had been covered.

"I didn't," she said, and when our eyes met, I knew she had bad news. "Oh, I was afraid of this. You don't know, do you?"

I leaned against the pillar, my knees like water. I heard sirens in the distance. "What?" I asked. "I don't know *what*?"

"The school tried to call you at work, but they got the answering service, so they contacted me. Emma was feeling sick—she probably caught what you had—and she wanted to come home. I went to get her, of course, but when I arrived, she was already gone. One of her friends told me she'd been picked up by a woman in a silver car."

If Mrs. K hadn't steadied me, I would have collapsed. "No," I whispered. *"No."*

A Scottsdale police car sped into the garage and came to a rubber-shrieking stop. Two uniformed officers jumped out and ran toward us, their guns trained on Mrs. K and me. An ambulance whipped in behind them.

"Drop the gun, ma'am!" one fresh-faced young officer commanded. "Right now."

I extended it to him butt first, nodding to Danny Murdock, still bleeding on the floor. "This man just tried to kill me. He also admitted to murdering Harvey Kredd, Janet Baylin, and Denise Robbins, as well as Justin Netherton." For such an ordinary-looking man, Murdock had cut a wide swath.

The EMTs moved in, doing their work with quick, merciful skill. Murdock was in a lot of pain, and even though he'd almost killed me, even though he *had* killed four other people, I felt profoundly sorry for him. He'd lost his wife and children in a needless, brutal tragedy, and his mind had slipped its moorings. It wasn't too hard to imagine how that could happen.

It was then, of all times, that I really *got* that there were clients I could defend in good conscience, even knowing they were guilty. If Danny Murdock would let me take his case, I would fight hard for him.

"I've got to go," I said, to everyone in

general, as soon as they'd moved Murdock from behind my car. Emma's name was pounding in my chest, over and over, like a second heartbeat.

I had to find her, and fast. If I didn't, I would probably never see her again.

Chapter Fifty-nine

"We'll need a statement," the older officer insisted.

"I'm the one who ran the man down," Mrs. K argued, waving her arms. She looked like a South American bird in her tropical-print caftan. "I saw that he was about to shoot Miss Westbrook here and I smashed into him with my car."

The cop wasn't giving an inch. He nodded, acknowledging Mrs. K. "We want to hear everything you have to say, ma'am," he assured her. "But we'll still need that statement from Ms. Westbrook."

"This is an emergency," I cried, wondering how long I'd get in the slammer if I pepper-sprayed the cop and made a run for it. Too long, I decided. "My niece—I think my niece has been kidnapped."

Just then, Sonterra rolled in, at the wheel of his SUV. He leaped out, leaving the motor running and the door hanging open, took one look at me, and grabbed me by the upper arms.

"What the hell—? *Are you all right?*"

"Emma," I gasped. "A woman in a silver car took Emma! It's Digger—I know it's Digger."

Sonterra showed his badge to the other cops, then wrapped an arm around my waist and hustled me toward his car. "I'll see that you get a copy of Ms. Westbrook's statement," he called over his shoulder, and then we were inside the rig, backing out.

"Who the frick is Digger?" he demanded, leaving some of his tires on the pavement.

I was really out there on the edge by then, shaking so violently that my teeth chattered. Tears rose in my eyes, and overflowed, and Sonterra leaned across to open the glove compartment and pulled out his trusty packet of tissues, thrusting them at me as he turned off Scottsdale Road onto Frank Lloyd Wright Boulevard. I knew he was headed for the freeway.

I mopped my face and blew my nose, hard.

Traffic was thick on the 101 South; Sonterra produced a cop light from under his seat, reached out the window, and stuck the thing on the roof. People got out of the way after he switched it on.

"Talk to me, Counselor," he said. His knuckles were tight on the wheel.

I explained, haltingly, that Emma had been engaged in an ongoing Internet correspondence, unbeknownst to me, until very recently, with someone using the screen name Digger. I gave him a condensed version of my own exchange with Digger, and even though he'd already heard the story, I told him about Mrs. K's meeting with the man looking for Emma, accompanied, according to my eccentric but trustworthy neighbor, by "a woman driving a silver car." The person who had snatched Emma after school had been at the wheel of a vehicle with the same broad description.

"Do you have any idea who these people are?"

"Only a hunch," I said.

"Which is?"

"Digger was involved in Tracy's murder, along with James. It's somebody in Tucson."

"I knew it," he said, which explained, if not *how* he knew, why he'd been heading south, toward the turnoff for Highway 60 East, and Tucson. He reached for his cell phone, which was plugged into the cigarette lighter, and called his partner, Eddie, to make sure he'd heard about the bust going down at the offices of Kredd and Associates. When he'd taken care of that, he called Lieutenant Arlo Browder on a direct line.

He got through immediately, and brought Arlo up to speed on the latest developments, including the woman in the silver car.

Arlo was on Sonterra's speaker phone. "That ties into something we ran across investigating the Wyand murder," the lieutenant said. "Let me do some checking and get back to you."

We were well past Gila Bend, and rolling, by the time Arlo called.

"There's a silver Corolla registered to a woman named Ellie Mitchell," Arlo said. "Want us to pick her up?"

I thought of the picture Henley had given me, the one showing James Arren with his arm around Ellie Mitchell. "HAPPY BIRTHDAY, MOM."

"Yes!" I cried.

"You got it," Arlo replied.

"Arlo, there's somebody with her, and they've got Emma! I'm sure of it!"

"Take it easy, Clare," he said. "We'll round them up."

"She was James Arren's mother," I added. Which made her Emma's grandmother. A light came on in my stress-addled brain.

Sonterra cursed.

I couldn't get the woman out of my mind. Ellie, I knew now, had been the one who'd sent the death pictures of Tracy and me, the one who'd tried to run me over in the hotel parking lot and smashed my car into scrap iron. And she, smelling of cigarette smoke and stale beer, the faint echoes of which had teased my memory but remained elusive while she was holding a gun to the back of my head in that hotel bathroom, had been the one to knock me out. Maybe she'd even set fire to Sylvie's trailer, though that seemed like a stretch. I'd had the distinct impression, during our encounter at Nipples, that she'd been protective of Sylvie.

"Ellie Mitchell," I gasped. "She's Digger! She's the one Emma has been corresponding with."

"We'll find her, Clare," Arlo promised.

"Hurry," I pleaded. "The woman is insane. God knows *what* is going on in her mind right now." I have never been so scared as I was then, not even when I was looking down the barrel of Danny Murdock's .45, knowing full well that he intended to put a bullet between my eyes.

Sonterra was driving at a hundred plus now; an Arizona state patrol officer flashed his headlights in acknowledgment as we passed.

We were about twenty minutes outside of Tucson, and I was on the verge of hysterics, when Arlo called again. I knew by the sound of his voice that things were not going according to plan.

"We found them," he said.

"Where?" I demanded.

"They're holed up in a camping area, in the foothills. The girl is there, and the woman. No sign of the male accomplice, but he might be around somewhere."

Sonterra took over. "Have you been in direct contact yet?"

"Can't get close," Arlo said. "The woman's armed with a shotgun, and we don't want to risk injury to the child."

I put a hand over my mouth.

"Give me directions," Sonterra snapped.

Chapter Sixty

Arlo reeled off a series of streets and country roads. I rolled down the window after the exchange had ended, gulping air. I didn't need anybody to tell me Ellie and Emma were in the very spot where Tracy had been murdered; my every instinct screamed that it was true.

Once we reached the knot of police cars and ambulances parked on the unpaved Park Service road, above a creek, I was out of the rig and running—quite an undertaking in high heels and a slim-skirted suit—before Sonterra even got the car stopped. He caught up to me before I could start down the bank, though, wrapping both arms around me from behind and hoisting me off my feet. I struggled and kicked so hard that we both nearly went down, but it was no use; his grasp was like steel.

"I have to go down there," I said, breathless, when Sonterra made a tentative move to release his hold, testing to see if I'd bolt. Which I would have, in a heartbeat.

"No," he said, breathing hard. "I'll do it."

"She'll shoot you, and maybe Emma, too," I argued. "It's me she wants—she knew I'd come."

Arlo separated himself from the others and came toward us. "It's true," he told Sonterra. "Emma just called us on a cell phone. She said Mrs. Mitchell will trade her for Clare."

"I'm coming!" I called down to Emma and her captor.

Sonterra's right temple pulsed visibly. He grasped my wrist. "Don't be stupid!"

I wrenched free and gave him two hands to the chest, hard. "Get out of my way!"

Arlo, having a cooler head than either of us, produced a .45, and wedged himself between Sonterra and me. "You're sure you want to do this?" he asked me quietly.

"I don't have a choice, do I?" I asked, frantic to reach Emma.

He helped me into the vest, showed me the pistol. "You know how to use a weapon?"

I guess he'd forgotten that I was the one who blew James Arren to kingdom come.

"Yes," I said. You don't grow up the way I did, and work in a seedy bar, without learning to handle a gun. I flipped the safety off, avoiding Sonterra's eyes, which were probably shooting fire, while Arlo gave me a hasty briefing, and then I started down the hill.

Ellie had made camp beside the creek, and Emma was huddled beside the campfire, looking small and wretched. When she saw me, hope and terrible fear mingled in her pale little face, and she jumped up from the wooden stump where she'd been sitting and threw herself into my arms. Ellie stood nearby, shotgun in hand, but not aimed at us.

"She can go," the older woman said, with sad resignation.

I fairly thrust Emma toward the hill behind me. "Run," I whispered.

She hesitated, and I saw the best part of Tracy in her eyes as she stared at me, and the best part of myself, too. "I can't leave you. I *won't*."

"Go," I hissed. "I mean it, Emma. Get out of here *now*."

Reluctantly, she went. I kept my eye on

Ellie, ready to shoot her where she stood if she sighted in on Emma, but she didn't.

I walked toward her.

"Drop the gun," Ellie said. Looking into her eyes, I saw deep sorrow, but no fear.

"Who killed Tracy?" I asked, stopping in my tracks but ignoring her quiet order. Maybe I was in shock or something; now that Emma was safe with Sonterra and Arlo Browder, up on the road, I wasn't so scared anymore. That familiar, deadly calm was settling over me.

"Jimmy did," Ellie said. "He was drunk and high, full of talk. He tricked her into meeting him, right here. Said if he couldn't have her, that Dupree fellow wouldn't, either."

Impressions, most of them grim, were rushing into my mind. It was almost as if I were tapping into images Tracy must have seen before she died. As if I were sorting through her memories, rather than my own.

"*You* were here, too, weren't you, Ellie?"

She raised the gun slightly. I felt cold, the way Tracy must have felt, lying here, bleeding and dying. "Not when it happened. Jimmy came to me afterwards. He was so scared. I came out here and helped him bury the little slut. And I took the pictures."

"Why? Why did you hate her so much?"

Ellie looked surprised by the question. "Because she hurt my boy."

"But, *murder*—?"

Her eyes were moist, but I doubted she was aware of the tears. "Jimmy had it tough, coming up. His father left when he was little. It meant everything to him to have a family—everything to me—and she was going to take it all away."

Panic threatened. Emma was safe, I reminded myself. Nothing else mattered at the moment.

"Why did you try to kill me?" I asked.

"I only wanted to scare you away, at first, so you wouldn't dredge all this up again and get my Jimmy sent to jail, like you did before. I came after you with my truck, but I wouldn't have hit you." She paused to shake her head. "You didn't scare worth a damn, anymore than that tramp sister of yours did. So I had to come back and give you a thump over the head."

"What about the e-mails?"

"Jimmy learned all about computers when he was inside," she said, with a little smile, proud of her baby boy. "He showed me how to send pictures over the Internet. I went up to Chandler and used a computer in one of the libraries there." She nodded toward the hilltop, where Emma had vanished. "I would have made a good home for her; we would have been a little family. But you had to go and kill him. It wasn't enough you took six years of his life."

I took a breath. "Now what?"

"Now I ain't got nothin' more to lose. So I'm going to shoot you dead, just the way you shot Jimmy."

I swallowed, turning numb. I was conscious of Sonterra, somewhere nearby, approaching, willing me to stay focused. "You killed Sylvie, didn't you?" Even when faced with the business end of a shotgun, I couldn't keep my mouth shut.

Ellie nodded, and for the first time I thought I saw a genuine flicker of remorse pass over her face.

I was definitely stalling, but I wanted answers, too. "Why? I thought you and Sylvie were friends."

"She and Jimmy, they fooled around some, while he was still with Tracy—no more than she deserved, cheatin' on him

like she did. He said he'd told Sylvie some
stuff he shouldn't have, while he was
drinkin', and when you went to her place
that night, I reckoned it would only be a
matter of time before she started runnin' off
at the mouth." She tapped a piece of leafy
ground with the butt of the shotgun. "She's
right here, your Tracy. She was the ruin of
Jimmy—he just wasn't right in the head,
without her and the baby." She stopped,
scrambling for emotional control. Her face
was etched deep with the kind of despair
that starts in early childhood and dogs a
person to the grave. "I loved Sylvie; she was
like a daughter to me, right from the first. I
didn't want to hurt her, but I couldn't let her
or anybody else send my Jimmy to the electric chair, no matter what he done."

There was no breeze, but I felt a chill all
the same. Tracy's picture filled my mind; her
dead face, the leaves and stones. She'd
died right here, where we were standing,
and I felt her presence strongly, as if I might
turn my head and see her standing nearby,
urging me to keep my cool.

I wanted to drop to my knees, lay my
hands, my face, my whole body, to the earth
that covered Tracy's remains, and weep for

her, but I knew she wouldn't want that. She was free, now that the truth had come out. I sensed that clinging would only hold her back, and it was time she went on to whatever comes next.

"Put the shotgun down, Ellie," I said quietly. "Let this be over, right now."

"Oh, it's over, all right," she said. "For all of us. Me and Jimmy and you."

Almost gracefully, she aimed the shotgun at me.

My throat seized up, and I couldn't speak. It was partly fear, and partly sorrow.

Ellie would have pulled the trigger for sure if Sonterra hadn't sprung out of the brush behind her, breaking her hold on the gun and sending them both rolling into the creek.

She put up a one hell of a fight, rolling and swinging her fists, but Sonterra finally got her into handcuffs and hauled her up onto the bank. Cops streamed down over the hillside, Arlo in the forefront, and Ellie Mitchell was placed under arrest and advised of her rights.

Emma came back down the hill at a dead run, breaking free of the policewoman who would have restrained her, and watched, her eyes round, as her grandmother was led away. She screamed my name.

I held my arms out to my niece, and she allowed me to hold her close. "Shhh, baby," I told her, rocking her a little as she sobbed. "It's over now. It's all over."

Sonterra stood dripping wet on the creek bank, watching us as though he expected either me or Emma to shatter into a thousand pieces. He walked over slowly, and placed a gentle hand on Emma's back, but his gaze was fixed on my face. "You okay, Counselor?" he said.

I was shaken, but I felt strong, stronger than I had in a long, long time.

"It was Arren who killed Tracy," I said, making no effort to hide the truth from Emma. She had a right to know what had happened to her mother. "Just like I always believed. Ellie wanted to cover up for him; she even came out here and buried the body." I looked down at the damp ground.

Sonterra put his arm around Emma and started up the hill while I lingered to spend a few moments saying a final good-bye to my sister.

Presently, he came back for me. "Let's get out of here," he said gently.

I was bristly with grief. I didn't want gentle.

"Arlo needs a statement," he told me, nodding toward the crowd at the top of the hill. "Are you up to that?"

"Do I have a choice? They've got the guns and badges."

A muscle tightened in Sonterra's jaw. "You're going to have to get over this thing you have about cops," he said. Then he had the nerve to turn his back on me and walk off, heading uphill and never looking back.

I followed him at an angry clip, picking my way gingerly between rocks and rabbit holes. Not an easy climb in heels.

"What thing?" I demanded.

No answer. Sonterra just kept climbing.

"Damn you, Sonterra, *what thing*?"

Chapter Sixty-one

A week after the confrontation with Ellie, Sonterra and I met for dinner at the Satisfied Frog, sister restaurant to the Horny Toad. He was holding down a table for two when I walked in, the peanut shells on the floor crunching beneath my favorite shoes.

He stood, admired my white linen pantsuit with a sweep of his dark eyes.

"Unemployment looks good on you," he said, drawing back my chair.

I sat down, waited until he was seated across from me. "I'm not very good at being either idle *or* rich," I confided. "I rented a storefront in South Phoenix today, and I'm opening my own practice."

Sonterra signaled the waitress, ordered a beer for himself and ice tea for me. "That doesn't surprise me," he said. "Just who will you be defending, if you don't mind my asking?"

"I'm only accepting clients I really believe

are innocent," I said. "That ought to make you happy, Sonterra. Of course, I did offer to represent Danny Murdock."

Sonterra's eyebrows rose a notch. "The man who did his level best to kill you?"

"He wasn't in his right mind," I replied.

He shook his head. "Whatever," he said. The waitress brought our drinks, and we ordered food—steak for Sonterra, fried chicken for me. I was in the mood to splurge.

"So what about us?" he asked, after we'd made small talk through the meal.

"What about us?"

"Are we on or off?"

I considered. "A little of each, I guess," I said.

He grinned. I have no defenses against that grin. "This feels like an 'on' night to me," he said. "Let's go to my place for some good old-fashioned monkey sex."

"Fine," I agreed, sounding a lot cooler than I felt.

Outside in the parking lot, Sonterra took in the one significant purchase I'd made since coming into the Westbrook millions, a brand-new Escalade, with all the bells and whistles.

"Bigger and better than yours," I pointed out, nodding toward his flashy rig, parked nearby.

He inspected the vanity license plate I'd jumped through burning hoops to get; maybe he was looking for an excuse to write me up for a traffic violation or something: MJRBCH.

Sonterra gave me a baffled look.

"Figure it out for yourself," I said.